Lost

INTERTWINED SOULS
BOOK ONE

M. E. GREENFIELD

CHAPTER 1

A Special Guest

Wyatt stared up at the same stone ceiling that greeted him every morning. He let out a sigh and stretched his sky-blue tail. The last thing he wanted to do was get up and go through the same mundane routine that was his life. Today would most likely be no different.

He closed his bright blue eyes and imagined what it would be like to live on his own and be free to explore the Seven Seas. But having an overprotective father made that difficult, especially when that same overprotective father was the King of Aquana.

Wyatt had tried to venture off on numerous occasions, but each time one of the guards would find him and bring him back. It was to the point now that even in the palace, the guards kept a keen eye on him.

His siblings didn't have that problem. Varian, the eldest at twenty-seven, never disobeyed orders. With being next in line for the thrown and Captain of the Guard, all the attention was on him. Sarah, the middle child, was three years older than Wyatt. Father doted on her and was just as protective. Besides Varian doing his duties as Captain of the Guard and Sarah leaving the castle to see her friend Lyra, who was also Varian's girlfriend, neither made any attempt to leave the kingdom.

Wyatt, however, had always been the rebellious one out of the three. He wasn't like his siblings. He couldn't be content in the confines of Aquana.

He rolled to the side, pushed himself onto his elbow, and pulled out a book from a large bookshelf. It was amazing what one could find at the bottom of the ocean. Luckily he knew a merman who was able to preserve most of them using a combination of things Wyatt didn't understand, nor cared to. He was just happy that Varian had convinced their father that Wyatt was learning to read for diplomatic purposes. Most mers didn't have that luxury. Varian had taught both Wyatt and Sarah how to read and write many years ago. Something their mother had passed down to him before her untimely passing.

Wyatt opened the book and studied the pages. He did this every day. Soon he would have to see if any new books had come in. He didn't care what they were. Mystery, romance, history, education. He would read anything. His greatest find was a set of what the land-dwellers called encyclopedias.

The surface world had fascinated him for some time, but he wouldn't let his father, or anyone else for that matter, know.

Wyatt's tail stiffened from a fluctuation in the current. Someone was outside his room.

"Prince Wyatt," a mermaid called from the other side of the seaweed curtain that acted as a door. It provided little privacy, another reason he wanted to leave. "It's time for you to get ready."

He pushed out of his bed made from woven seagrass and let out a heavy sigh. "Another fun-filled day," he muttered to himself as he returned the book.

Wyatt wanted to protest that he could in fact take care of himself, but before he could say anything, the mermaid-in-waiting entered and motioned toward a boulder that acted as a seat. Her yellow-and-green tail swayed as she waited for him. She was older and had been assigned to him since he was a boy. He would never refer to her as a mother figure, though. There was nothing motherly about her.

He reluctantly sat on the stone in front of an old mirror salvaged from a shipwreck centuries ago that leaned against the wall. He was a mix of his father's and mother's best features, blended to make a handsome merman. His youthful light brown hair had darkened so his light blue highlights were more noticeable. His eyes diverted from his reflection in the cracked mirror.

The mermaid gathered Wyatt's hair. It was shorter than most mermen his age, touching his shoulders. If he could, he would cut it even shorter. However, that would probably make him more of an outcast among his kind.

A sigh of disappointment came. "I don't know why you insist on cutting it so short," she stated as she grabbed a silver comb.

He wanted to argue with her. He wanted to tell her he was fully capable of making his own decisions on how he acted and appeared, but there was no point. Just like there was no point in arguing about his meals.

After he was ready for the day, he lazily swam to the dining hall. Rita, who prepared the food, had placed his breakfast down at the far end of the long table.

Was this going to be his life forever? Eating this sad kelp and fish egg salad for breakfast every damn day? Or kelp and crabmeat for lunch? Even dinner was the same thing. Although, sometimes Rita would surprise him by adding in shredded seaweed, which wasn't a pleasant surprise by any means.

His mind drew up images of hamburgers and sandwiches from one of the cookbooks in his bookshelf. He wondered what they tasted like. *Better than this.*

Poseidon, he wished he had some direction. If only his mother were alive. Maybe she would understand his longing for more. Or maybe not. She died when he was only a few years old. No one talked about it, but she was killed by a land-dweller. He wanted to talk to Sarah about it, but he didn't want to dredge up any ill feelings with her since she had witnessed it.

Their father tried to burrow how evil land-dwellers were into their minds because of that, but Wyatt didn't believe it. They couldn't be all bad, especially from what he had read.

He moved his food about, hoping he could slow down time, but before he knew it, he was summoned to the study for his daily teachings.

Wyatt folded his arms across his bare chest and leaned against the cool stone wall. He didn't want to be here. He didn't understand why he had to be educated on how to rule a kingdom. Varian was the next in line to be King of Aquana, not him. And why now? He was well over the age to learn everything there was to being a king. He was twenty-two for Poseidon's sake, not ten.

Even though their father was nowhere near the age to pass the crown, it felt as if these lessons were being rushed. Was he missing something swimming right in front of him? He wondered if Varian was having second thoughts about his birthright. No. His brother had been learning and training for this his whole life.

"Prince Wyatt . . ." A voice echoed but didn't register. "Prince Wyatt!"

Nearly falling off the large sea sponge seat, Wyatt caught himself on a shelf to his right that housed historic texts about their underwater world. A few scrolls shifted, and he noticed something tucked behind them.

A crimson tail swayed next to him. He snapped his head up to see his teacher, an older merman, floating in front of him. The mer's white hair with streaks of red billowed around him, and his beard hung above his naval.

Wyatt quickly straightened himself. "Huh?"

"I asked you, what role does a king play in his kingdom?" the mer restated his question.

It should have been an easy answer, but the scholar had droned on about politics and whatnot for so long that Wyatt had tuned him out before he started the lesson. These pointless teachings had been going on every day for a month now. His father had yet to give him a reason why this was necessary except to keep Wyatt busy.

"He is bound to the people," his instructor said, agitated. "He leads them and keeps the peace. He—"

Wyatt scoffed. "There hasn't been violence throughout the sea since the treaty was signed thirty years ago. There's no peace to keep. It's already kept."

His instructor looked dumbfounded.

"Contrary to your belief, I *do* pay attention sometimes," Wyatt informed.

"You are partially correct. However, there was an incident when—"

"One incident. Fine. Are we done here?" The navy-blue edges of Wyatt's fluke dug into the sand, ready to push him upright.

However, the elder merman kicked his tail, returning to his lesson. "If you'd direct your attention to our next lesson . . ."

Wyatt rubbed his hands over his face. "I'd rather be stabbed by a swordfish," he muttered.

"What was that?"

"I can't wait!" he replied, exaggerating his enthusiasm.

The scholar turned away from Wyatt and continued on with the lesson.

As much as Wyatt tried to pay attention, his eyes darted back to what was behind the rolled-up scrolls. When his teacher wasn't looking, he reached over and pulled it out. It was a leather-bound book. It looked like nothing else he had ever seen in the study. The front cover was embossed with a mermaid and a thin string wrapped around it. He carefully unwound it and flipped through the handwritten pages. It seemed to be a journal of some sort. He stopped at one of the entries.

Soul mates were something I had read in old mer-folklore. Something that didn't seem tangible, but that ended today. My best friend confessed in a love that is like no other. She found her soul mate and the

connection they have is like nothing I've ever seen.
Poseidon, to have a love like that . . .

Wyatt let out a gasp and quickly hid the book under his tail as his teacher spun around.

The mer raised an eyebrow. "I think we've done enough for today."

Wyatt silently thanked Poseidon and swam out the door without another word, clutching the journal to his chest. He was so eager to leave that when he rounded the corner, he collided with someone.

"Do you mind?" a shrill voice exclaimed.

"I am so sorry," he said, righting himself.

Floating in front of him was the embodiment of beauty. Her long red hair was tied in an intricate braid and swayed slightly in the water. The scales covering her breasts and tail were a dark copper. They reminded Wyatt of a coin the same color he had found from the surface world.

She placed her hands on her hips and looked him over. "Maybe next time don't be in such a rush." She moved her hand to the top of her head. Her eyes darted around in panic until she quickly snatched something off the floor and hid it behind her back.

"Maybe you shouldn't be lurking in hallways," he retorted. "Who are you? I've never seen you around the palace." He moved closer and twisted his head in an attempt to see what she was hiding.

"No one you need to be concerned about." She flicked her fluke, creating distance between them.

"What are you hiding?" Wyatt questioned.

"I could ask the same thing," she said, narrowing her eyes on his hand that was wrapped around the leather journal.

He ignored her comment. "If you're an uninvited guest, then I'm sure the king would say otherwise."

"I'll be gone soon enough. I hope," she added under her breath before swimming off.

He could almost hear his brother's voice scolding him for not chasing after her. But he already knew she wasn't the one. His soul mate. A silly tale as his father stated. When they were younger, Varian used to repeat the stories that their mother had read to them. For some reason, Wyatt had always latched on to that particular one. It frustrated their father more than anything that his youngest son's dates would end before they started. Mermen his age were already married and having kids.

Reading that entry renewed Wyatt's interest. Maybe the journal was the proof he needed.

Wyatt returned to his bedchamber and was about to open the mysterious diary when a baritone voice startled him from behind the curtain.

"Prince Wyatt, you've been summoned to the throne room."

"For what?" he asked, quickly shoving the journal under the seagrass of his bed.

The guard didn't reply, but when Wyatt pushed the curtain aside, he could tell by the mer's expression that it wasn't going to be a pleasant meeting with his father. Granted, they never were.

Wyatt followed the guard to the throne room's antechamber. When they arrived, he thanked the guard before the mer disappeared.

He paused at the archway, taking stock of the once-mighty mer seated across the room. His father sat on a golden throne, looking older than his age should indicate. His long, flowing, dark brown hair was streaked with navy-blue highlights that matched his tail. A few strands of gray showed his age, and his constant five o'clock shadow had grown into more of a half-hearted beard. The crow's feet and the bags under his eyes belied the fact that he slept so little. The stress of governing his kingdom alone had taken its toll.

A navy-and-yellow crown made from coral sat high on top of his father's head. Auger shells were attached, pointing upward.

Wyatt had a shorter crown, but to his father's dismay, he only wore it for special occasions.

To Wyatt's surprise, another merman he had never seen before floated in front of his father. Usually no one outside the kingdom came to court. This mer was a rather imposing figure. His hair was a deep orange that matched his tail, and his thick barrel chest sloped out into a sizable paunch that drooped below his midriff.

His father caught sight of Wyatt and motioned for him to enter.

Wyatt swam up to him. The ceiling was bright with different shades of iridescent gems. Small fish swam in and out of the pale coral walls, while any other creature knew to stay away from the throne room.

"Wyatt." Taron smiled as he greeted his son. "We have a special guest. This is King Einan of Atalana."

Wyatt bowed his head, gazing up. "Greetings, Your Majesty. I bid you welcome to Aquana."

The prince's jaw tensed as he straightened. He hardly spoke with such decorum, and when he did, it made him cringe. His fluke brushed against the ghost-white sand, causing the grains to billow under him.

King Einan looked him up and down before his deep baritone voice rang through the chamber. "Exquisite! He would be a perfect match for my daughter. The boy certainly has manners. It's sad to see such a shortage of propriety in the merworld these days. Isn't that right, Taron?"

"Quite," Taron replied tersely.

What is my father up to? Wyatt wondered nervously.

"Of course this is all a mere formality. In three weeks' time, you and my Carmea will be wed, uniting our kingdoms as it should be," King Einan said.

"Wait. What?" Wyatt blurted out in surprise. Both kings frowned in disapproval. "Forgive me, Your Majesty, I was not aware of this . . . joyous occasion," he said with gritted teeth. He turned to Taron. "Father, may I have a word in private?"

"My apologies, King Einan. I need a moment alone with my son."

"Of course. I wish I could stay longer, but I do have pressing matters that require my attention. I'll go fetch my daughter while I let you discuss." King Einan said.

"Please give the queen our regards," Taron said with a nod of his head.

The king responded in kind and began to pass Wyatt before stopping short and placing a hand on his shoulder. "I have big plans for you," he whispered and smiled before leaving.

Taron lifted from his seat. "Wyatt, I've told you time and time again that you are to stay within the boundaries of this kingdom, and time and time again, you have disobeyed me. I understand you want to explore. You're so much like your mother . . ." He cleared his throat and placed his hand on Wyatt's shoulder. "That is why I'm doing this."

Wyatt pulled away, staring at his father in confusion. "By marrying me off? That's how you think you'll solve my longing to go out on my own?"

"I thought you would be overjoyed. You'll get your freedom, a beautiful bride, and a kingdom to rule as your own. What more do you want?"

Wyatt's words were rushed. "I don't want to rule a kingdom, that's Varian's job. And she might be beautiful, but I doubt she wants to be with *me*. I need to find my—"

Taron's hands flew up in frustration. "Soul mate? You're still on that? You need to get this ridiculous notion of finding true love out of your head. Soul mates are only mer-folklore."

Wyatt opened his mouth to protest. He wanted to swim to his room, grab the journal he had found, and wave it in front of his father as proof, but he thought better. That journal was hidden for a reason. He needed to be careful.

"Maybe you're right." He shrugged, biting back his bitterness. "But I at least want to find my own bride. Someone I truly love, like you and Mom. You loved once, remember?"

"Please, don't speak of her," Taron said with pain in his voice.

Wyatt scoffed. "Because when someone dies, we just write them off and forget about them."

"Wyatt, please—"

"At least you let her explore the ocean."

"And look where that got her!" Taron yelled. "Killed by land-dwellers!"

"At least land-dwellers are free to love whoever they want and aren't forced into marriage!"

At that moment, an awkward cough echoed from behind them. Wyatt turned around to see the same mermaid he had collided with in the hallway looking back at him with a glimmer of awe.

"Is everything all right, Your Majesty?" She dipped her head shyly, showing off a crown made from the finest shells.

"Forgive me, Princess Carmea." Taron bowed slightly.

Great.

He glanced at his son, who remained silent. With a sigh, Taron added, "My apologies for my son as well. He had a long week, and I did spring this on him."

"I see," she replied.

"But rest assured, Prince Wyatt is looking forward to being united with you," Taron said.

"Father . . ." Wyatt said through gritted teeth.

She avoided eye contact. "I as well."

"I truly appreciate you and King Einan coming all this way," Taron said.

"Thank you, Your Majesty." Princess Carmea bowed her head and exited the throne room.

Taron turned to Wyatt. "Now, as I was saying . . ."

Before his father could finish, Wyatt spun around and furiously kicked his tail, leaving a wake of bubbles in his path.

CHAPTER 2
The Unexpected

Liz Brander bolted upright with wide eyes. She expected to be surrounded by the murky seawater she had been falling into only moments before. Instead, she was safe in the soft pink glow of her bedroom. Light bled through the top and sides of the roller shades that covered her two windows.

Just a nightmare.

They had been persistent for the past week and always began the same. She would get out of bed and feel the wet hard flooring instead of plush carpet beneath her feet. It was too dark to discern, but she could tell she was on some kind of boat. Storm clouds loomed above and lightning lit up the sky as heavy rain pelted her light skin.

She would grip the slick railing, trying to keep her balance from the rocking, and shuffle forward. Pushing her wet, shoulder-length, dirty blonde hair from her face, she'd try to get a better look through the darkness. She would smell salt and fish in the air. Then her ears would be assaulted with screams and other voices. Yet the storm made it difficult to hear what they were saying.

This time was different. A crack of thunder had startled her, causing her to stumble backward and over the railing. When she opened her mouth to scream, nothing came out. Before she reached the dark waters, she awoke.

Liz groaned and rubbed the sleep from her eyes. She heard a faint humming and shivered at the breeze. Her ceiling fan had been switched to the highest setting. Something her mother always did to get her up when she slept too long.

She begrudgingly rolled out of bed and turned the fan off before crawling back under the warm blankets.

Footsteps padded down the hallway toward her room. "It's nearly eleven, Liz. You need to get up," her mother nagged.

She pulled the blankets up over her head and groaned once more. If she waited any longer, her mother was bound to flip the lights on and roll the blinds up, letting the late-morning sunlight blind her. Instead, the approaching noise of the vacuum provided her the incentive to get up.

Liz sighed. There was no way she was going back to sleep now. She pushed herself to get up and slogged to the kitchen, where she poured a bowl of cereal and sat at the table, mindlessly flipping through channels on the TV.

After a while, the vacuum stopped and her mother bounded into the kitchen. "You need to get dressed," she said, tucking a strand of her strawberry blonde hair behind her ear.

"Why? I told Grandpa I would be there at noon."

"Your father had a good idea last night," her mother plodded on, "about applying at the library. You haven't tried there yet. Have you?"

"I'm sure Nicki would tell me if they had a position open."

"You never know. Stop by there before going to your grandparents' house," her mother suggested before returning back to her weekly cleaning.

Liz sighed at the thought of applying for another job. This would be the sixth one this week. She hadn't received any calls from the dozen or so other places she had applied to either. Even if she did get a callback, she honestly had no desire to work. Her motivation to do almost anything had practically vanished after she dropped out of college.

Throughout high school, the guidance counselor and every other teacher had drilled into every student's head that their next step was to pick a major and go to college. For Liz, that hadn't quite panned out the way her parents hoped. With no direction on what to do with her life, she had rushed into a major that was more intense than she thought. Despite her parents' pleas for her to keep trying, Liz decided to give up two years later from failing grades. The look on their faces had been heart-wrenching. That was a month ago.

After finishing breakfast, Liz got ready for the day and threw on a pair of jeans and a T-shirt.

As she slipped on her tennis shoes, her mom poked her head around the corner. "You're not going like that, are you? It doesn't look very professional."

Liz grabbed a messenger bag that held her laptop and internally rolled her eyes. "It's not an interview, Mom. I'm just getting an application."

Liz couldn't blame her, though. She was nearly twenty-one years old and going nowhere. When things became difficult, she couldn't help but run in the other direction. That was especially true when her grandfather was diagnosed with stage three melanoma shortly after she began classes. It had taken its toll on the whole family, especially Liz. She and her grandfather had such a strong bond that the thought of something happening to him made her distance herself from him. If she didn't see him, she didn't have to deal with her emotions. Thankfully, after his course of treatments, he was now in remission. Yet the guilt she felt for not visiting him when he needed her the most was still there.

Liz fished her car keys from her purse and unlocked her old yellow Chevy Cavalier. With a sigh she made the short drive to the library.

Inside the brick building, the only noises you could hear were the tapping of fingers on keyboards from the computer section and the muffled laughter and applause of children in another room as their reading program ended. She approached the front desk, waiting for the two people in front of her to check out. A familiar singsong voice drifted around the corner as children piled out of the activity room. A woman around Liz's age bent down to hug a little boy before he ran off to his mother.

"I'll see you next week, Michael," she said, pushing a lock of her short blonde hair behind her right ear. At a glance, she and Liz could have been mistaken for sisters.

Liz stepped out of line. It was going to be a while anyway since the old woman in front of her was having difficulty finding her library card inside her enormous brown leather purse.

"Hey, Nicki!" Liz smiled in relief at seeing her old college friend. They'd met in the computer lab that first fall semester and quickly became friends. She was probably the only friend Liz had at the moment she could truly depend on.

Nicki whispered, "Old Mrs. Miller having trouble finding her library card again?"

"Apparently," Liz replied with an eye roll. "I'm glad you came out, saves me some trouble."

"Oh? What kind of trouble?" Nicki inquired.

Liz sighed. "A job."

"You know if a job were to open here, you'd be the first person I'd call," Nicki said reassuringly.

"I've tried telling my parents that, but you know how they are. I had some time to kill anyway before I head to my grandparents' house."

"Well, your application is right here." Nicki pointed back at herself. "I wish I could do more."

"I appreciate it, I really do. I'll just tell them I filled one out."

Nicki studied Liz's face in concern. "You look tired. Maybe you should give it a rest for a few weeks and enjoy yourself."

"That's just it. I want to, but it seems every time I turn around, there's another application. It's either one my dad picked up on his way home from work or one my mom printed out. I know they're just trying to help, but it is becoming extremely frustrating filling them out and never getting a call back."

"The job market is hard right now." Nicki paused in thought. "You know, I have some vacation time coming up soon. Maybe we can rent a cabin at the lake or something."

Liz shrugged. "Yeah, maybe." The lake was the last place she would consider as a getaway. Though as it stood, anywhere away from home seemed like a vacation.

"I hate to do this," Nicki said apologetically, "but my next group is coming in fifteen minutes. I have to set up the room."

"What's the theme for today's story time?"

Nicki beamed. "The beach!"

"Now that is a place I'd love to go on vacation!" Liz echoed her excitement. "I'll catch up with you later."

"Bye, friend," Nicki said as she turned toward the children's section.

Liz made her way out the library's doors and back to her car. Driving back, she passed her navy ranch home with white shutters. Her grandparents' house was just a mile down the road, making it convenient to visit them. She passed a park on her left and after a few houses, she turned onto a gravel driveway.

A small white ranch home stood among the cookie-cutter two-story homes. Green shutters accented the windows, and a large maple tree sat to the right of the porch. A line of tulips were beginning to bloom along the pathway from the drive to the house.

Liz stepped out of her vehicle and was greeted by a cool spring breeze. She smoothed out the top of her hair, tucked a few strands of it back behind her ear, and bounded up the porch steps.

As soon as she entered through the dark green door, Liz was assaulted with the sweet smell of chocolate chip cookies her grandmother had obviously made. She slipped her shoes off next to the front door and walked into the living room. An old tube television sat on an oak stand on the far wall with a plush brown couch in front of it. The décor was homey, and she always felt welcomed.

Her grandmother, an elderly woman with short, curly strawberry blonde hair that was beginning to fade to white, was stooped over a card table, working on a half-finished puzzle. Her grandmother looked up and beamed at Liz.

"Liz! I can't believe you made the *long* trip here," her grandmother teased. She placed a puzzle piece down and embraced her granddaughter in a warm hug. "Grandpa's in the kitchen making tea."

Liz entered the kitchen to find a small plate of cookies already on the table. The tea kettle whistled, and her grandfather turned off the burner. His hair, which had been black before his treatments, was now all white. Liz was sure he was just happy to have his hair grow back. Though he was in remission, he still seemed thin and frail.

"Hi, Grandpa," she greeted, hugging him gingerly from behind. He was just an inch taller than she was.

He turned around and kissed her forehead like he always did. "Why are you hugging me like a porcelain cat? I'm not going to break." He wrapped his weather-worn arms around Liz in a great big bear hug.

She didn't realize how much she missed his hugs.

After releasing his hold, he gestured for her to sit, then prepared their drinks. Sitting at the worn oak table, Liz pulled out her laptop, while her grandmother finished placing the rest of the cookies into a container. She always packed a smaller one for Liz to take home.

Her grandfather turned around with two mugs of tea in his hands and sat next to her. His smile was warm and inviting. "Any luck on the job hunt?" He pushed his thick black glasses up the bridge of his nose.

Liz frowned. "No."

"You'll find something. You're destined for great things." He folded his arms across the table.

"You always say that." She scoffed, then opened her computer.

"If your grandpa says it, it must be true," her grandmother stated from behind them. She secured the lid and placed the container next to Liz's computer before returning to her puzzle in the living room.

"Not sure flipping burgers somewhere is considered a *great thing* to most people." Liz grabbed a cookie and took a bite. It was still warm and gooey, just the way she liked it.

"Well, you are. You're more special than you know," he said, squeezing her hand.

"I dunno about that." Liz pulled at the string of her tea bag, making the water turn a dark brown. She had heard that line from her grandfather ever since she was little. She used to believe him, but now she knew he just told her that to build up her confidence. She wasn't anything special. She was just an ordinary girl from Ohio. "Why did you want me to bring my laptop?"

"I think it's time we take that trip we've been trying to plan," he answered.

Her eyes widened, and a smile crept across her face. "Really?"

They had planned to go to Anna Maria Island, Florida two years ago, just the two of them. They even had their flight booked, but then he had received the unfortunate diagnosis. He had been insistent on making the trip despite his health and the protests of his family. Liz, however, had withdrawn from him quickly, seeing the man she knew deteriorate shortly after the first treatment, and their plans had been canceled.

Liz shook the guilty thought from her head. "I'm not sure if Mom and Dad would be too happy about me going. They've been pretty adamant I find a job."

Her grandfather waved his hand, then grabbed the small sugar container in front of them and poured a spoonful into his tea. "Don't worry about them."

"And what about you?" She couldn't help but be concerned. "You've only been in remission for less than a year."

"I feel great, and I think a vacation is long overdue for the both of us," he replied, pushing the sugar to her. "Besides, this trip is important."

"Why is that?" She removed her teabag and dumped two spoonfuls of sugar into her tea before stirring it around.

He placed his hands under his chin, and his eyes were downcast for a moment. He blew out a breath, rippling the tea, then met her blue-gray eyes and smiled. "Because I get to go to Florida with my favorite granddaughter!"

Liz gave him an incredulous look. "I'm your only granddaughter. Are you sure there's nothing else?"

"You'll just have to wait and see," he said with a wink. "We'll spend a week down there just like we had planned." He fished a folded-up piece of paper from his navy-blue pants and placed it on the table. He motioned for Liz to take it.

She unfolded it. "You kept it?" she asked, surprised.

Liz scanned down the handwritten list. She remembered sitting in this same chair two years ago, watching him write all the places and things they wanted to do on the island. Split a giant cinnamon roll for breakfast at this restaurant toward Bean Point, walk down the AMI City Pier, go shopping, get ice cream, ride the trolley, play mini golf, watch the sunset. There was one thing he wanted to do that surprised her.

"You still want to do this one?" she questioned, pointing to the seventh item that was listed. "Parasailing? You do realize you're nearing eighty, right?" She wouldn't admit it, but the thought of soaring that high scared her.

"Are you saying I'm too old to have a little fun?" There was a slight twinkle in his eye, but it quickly went away as he grimaced.

"Are you ok?" Liz asked.

"Just a little bit of indigestion."

"I told you not to eat so many cookies!" her grandmother scolded from the other room.

"Someone had to taste test them for Liz," he playfully argued. He pushed a plate of cookies toward Liz and grabbed one for himself. "Let's start looking for a house to rent."

Liz scrolled through the different rentals along the island. Most were booked up for the dates they picked, two weeks from now.

"Maybe we should look farther out where more are available?" she suggested.

Her grandfather shook his head, dabbing sweat from his brow. "No. I can't put this off anymore. You need to—" His voice caught, and he took a deep breath in and exhaled it slowly. "It's the perfect time of year to go there."

She kept her eyes on him until he motioned for her to continue.

For the next half hour, they searched rentals. Her grandfather was insistent they stay right along the beach. She had never been to Florida, let alone any beach, unless you count the one along Lake Erie.

Her grandfather finally settled on a two-bedroom condo along Coquina Beach. It was perfect, and the price was unbelievable. He gave her his credit card, and she booked the rental, as well as the airline tickets.

Liz practically bounced in her seat. "All right, now we just need to book a car rental."

Taking his glasses off, her grandfather rubbed his eyes. "Maybe we should do that tomorrow," he said, sliding his chair out and rubbing his chest.

"Are you feeling all right, Grandpa?"

"I'm just a bit tired."

Liz closed the laptop, satisfied with what they had accomplished and excited for their upcoming trip. She began to place it back in the messenger bag as her grandfather stood from his seat. Her eyes were only off him for a second, but it was a second too long. The sound of the wooden chair scraping across the floor caused her to look over her shoulder. At that moment, her heart shattered like the mug in her grandfather's hand, breaking into a million pieces.

She didn't even realize she had moved until she felt the pain in her knees from dropping to the ground. The man she had always looked up to was crumpled on the floor, clutching his chest.

This wasn't happening. It wasn't. Liz refused to believe it. Her eyes darted to the door. She wanted to run. If she ran, then this wouldn't be real. Right?

Her grandmother's voice crying into the phone barely registered in Liz's ears.

"Liz," his voice rasped. His pleading eyes looked up at her.

"It's going to be ok. Help is on the way," she tried assuring him. She looked back over at her grandmother, who was frantic on the phone. Liz didn't dare look at him. In the back of her mind, she didn't want that image to be seared into her memory.

His hand gripped hers tightly, causing her to reluctantly turn back to him. "I'm sorry," he said. His face twisted in pain. "I-I'm sorry I can't go with you."

"We can push it back a few weeks when you're better." She wasn't sure if she was trying to convince him or herself, but it wasn't working.

"You go," he insisted, placing the crumpled paper with the list of places into her hand.

"I'm not going without you!"

"Your parents . . . They're . . . Don't blame them. It's not their fault."

"You need to save your energy. The paramedics are on their way," Liz choked out.

Now both of his hands were holding hers. Tears were forming not only in his eyes but hers as well.

"I kept this secret from you for far too long."

"Secret?"

"You are more special . . . than you know," he said between gasping breaths. "Remember that."

"Grandpa?" Tears fell down her cheeks. "Grandpa, stay with me!" she shouted, gently shaking him. "I can't lose you!"

"I'll be with you . . . in here." He weakly pointed to her heart before his hands fell to the ground.

Liz didn't even hear the door open or the man behind her instructing her to move aside. When she stayed frozen in place, someone lifted her to her feet. Soon she was sitting on the footstool in the living room in front of the kitchen doorway, watching the paramedics perform CPR.

But it was too late. He was gone.

CHAPTER 3

Drifting

After leaving the throne room in a huff, Wyatt returned to his chamber. Either his father thought giving him some space would help the situation or he was too furious to follow him. The latter was more likely. He didn't mind, though. It gave him more time to read the mysterious journal he had found.

Wyatt lay on his stomach and fished it from under his bed. He opened it and flipped through the worn pages.

> During my travels, I learned that if a mer's tail is dried, it will transform into legs! I have always been interested in the surface world, even though going on land is highly forbidden in most kingdoms. Of course, I had to see for myself if this magic worked. I will not lie and say I wasn't scared, but I decided I wouldn't let my fear get in the way of something new and exciting. To my surprise, I was able to change. It was horribly unpleasant but worth the pain. I was extra cautious, transforming at night.
>
> During my time on land, I befriended a woman

whom I will only refer to as D to protect her identity. Since my parents' deaths, I haven't belonged anywhere and D has welcomed me with open arms, even offering a place to stay. She owns what is called a restaurant near the waters of Anna Maria Island. She gave me a job to help me make something the land-dwellers call "money" that they use to trade for food and other necessities. We have become very close and I consider her a wonderful friend. I feel as though I can tell her who I really am, however, there's always a risk if she does not accept me.

Wyatt's eyes widened at the new information. He tried to shake his head of the thought, but he couldn't help the smile that crept on his face. Stepping on dry land, with legs, feeling the heat of the sun, eating something besides kale and fish. He flipped to another entry.

While taking a swim in the late-night hours, I happened upon a sea siren ensnared in an old fishing net. She was so thankful that I rescued her. I noticed she had items from land. She admitted she travels to land frequently. We breached the surface, and to my amazement, she transformed right there, in the water!

She told me about these enchanted necklaces the sea sirens possessed and created to help them go on land. In ancient times, they used them to transform to lure humans into the water, but times changed and they now use them for the betterment of our species. Learning about humans, helping the mers, and even looking out for threats in case the humans become suspicious of the mer-world. She always referred to them as humans, which caught me off guard. She had an extra necklace in case of emergencies and gave it to me as a thank-you for saving her life. She also invited me to visit her colony and said I will always have a place there.

Wyatt's tail twitched with excitement. He had to calm down before he propelled himself into the wall. For all he knew, the person who wrote about their travels was long gone. *Yeah, walking with the humans*, he thought as he flipped farther into the journal.

Taron surfaced with me today.

Wyatt's mouth gaped in disbelief as he quickly sat up at attention. His father, the King of Aquana, who was certain that land-dwellers caused nothing but harm and death, had walked among them. He took a moment to let the words sink in before reading on.

He was doubtful at first about having legs but I persuaded him to come up at least once. I'm not sure who was more nervous. His father is the king, after all, and if he knew his son went on land, well, we would both be banished to the trenches of the deep. He had such a good time that he decided to come back tomorrow. I just hope I can open Taron's eyes to this wonderful world so that when he becomes king he will be more lenient on the mers that want to explore the surface world.

His father went to the surface . . . and liked it? Who wrote this? Wyatt's shoulders slouched. He was saddened that whoever wrote this had failed at convincing his father that the surface world wasn't as bad as he thought. He skimmed a few entries about his father meeting this mysterious land-dweller named D and continued to an entry sometime later.

My heart is bursting! Today, Taron and I watched the sunset on the beach. He told me he had researched some of the human traditions. He got down on one knee, asked me to be his bride, and presented me with a beau– tiful pearl ring. Of course, I said YES! I am so excited to share our journey, uniting the sea and land. While Taron and I are not soul mates like my best friend, Mara, and her husband, Mercer, we are pretty close to it!

Wyatt's breath caught, and his body went numb. *Mom wrote this?* His chest tightened with emotion. He wasn't sure if he should laugh, cry, or throw something. He couldn't believe he was in possession of something tangible that his mother once held. The only thing of hers that he knew of was a brush that their father gave to Sarah. Everything else was gone. Yet this had been hidden away. Their father had to have known it was in the study. Wyatt wondered what he would say if he brought all this up.

Why had he never heard of Mercer and Mara? Where were they now?

Wyatt didn't realize his grip had loosened until he saw the journal floating past him. He pulled it back into his chest, hugging it for a moment. He closed his eyes tight, thinking of how his mother's dream of letting mers explore the surface world would never happen. He couldn't feel tears underwater like he had read in some stories, but he could feel the stinging behind his eyes.

After composing himself, he skimmed through the journal, looking for more clues about the surface world.

"What's that?" a baritone voice asked, startling Wyatt.

He turned to see Varian leaning against the doorway, slowly swishing his deep blue tail with hints of onyx at the fluke's edge. His arms folded across his broad chest, causing his biceps to bulge. Training as Captain of the Guard had clearly paid off.

"Nothing," Wyatt quickly replied.

"You adding to your collection?" Varian pushed from the doorway and entered the bedroom. His long brown hair streaked with navy, tied back and secured with a remnant of discarded fishing line, trailed behind him.

Wyatt placed the journal on his bookshelf. "Something like that."

"You know, you don't make it easy on him." Varian pulled at his wild beard, scanning the titles of each book. Even though he wasn't much of a reader these days, he was still always interested in Wyatt's latest finds.

"Yeah, and he does? Pushing marriage on me? Is he serious? I'm not agreeing to this," Wyatt shot back. Pressuring him to date was one thing, but forcing him to marry someone he didn't even know or like for the rest of his life was unfathomable.

"I never said you had to." Varian turned around and placed his hand on Wyatt's shoulder. "You just have to tell Father you're staying in the kingdom and will find a bride on your own. That's all he wants." He paused, then added in one long breath, "And for you not to go exploring and possibly get yourself killed in the process."

With a sigh, Wyatt brushed Varian's hand from his shoulder and swam toward the window. "I know practically every mermaid in this kingdom, and none of them can be my bride."

"What about the gorgeous redhead in the hallway I saw?" Varian asked.

Wyatt shook his head. "You mean the princess I'm arranged to marry? No thanks. I'd rather find someone on my own terms. I know I have a soul mate out there." He stared longingly past the small kingdom of buildings made from coral, stone caverns, and pieces from salvaged shipwrecks.

"There you go again, focusing on finding this elusive soul mate that does *not* exist. You gotta snap out of this. Learn to love someone else."

Wyatt's jaw tensed as he turned to Varian. "They do exist. It's in Mom's journal!" he blurted out.

Varian narrowed his hazel eyes. "Mom's journal?"

Wyatt reluctantly pulled out the journal and held it up. "I found it in the study. Please don't tell Father. I don't know what he'd do if he knew I had it."

Varian floated to Wyatt and studied the embossed mermaid on the front cover. "I won't," he promised, grazing his fingers along the edges. Wyatt let him hold it. "I'd be interested to read it one day . . . after you're done." He returned it to Wyatt.

"One of the entries talks about her friend Mara. Apparently she found her soul mate." Wyatt tucked the journal behind a few books at the bottom of the bookshelf. "Mom had hoped to find a love like that."

"She did, with Father," Varian interjected, staring out the window.

Wyatt turned back around and sighed. "I know, but it wasn't the same. They had their moments. It's in the journal."

"Words on paper," Varian argued. "We're living proof they loved each other. I know you can find love, too."

"Maybe you're right." Wyatt pushed up with his fluke and swam to the window. "Look, I'm sorry for my frustration. I'm tired and maybe a little jealous of what you and Lyra have. At least you found someone before Father tried to force you into marriage."

Varian leaned against the wall of the window and laughed. "You have no idea how many times a day he asks me if I'm going to propose to Lyra. I love her, but just like Mom and Dad, we have our disagreements. Sometimes you just have to work at love." He paused for a moment. "He's just worried about you."

"He has a weird way of showing it."

Varian shrugged, not arguing that fact. He moved from the wall and toward the seaweed curtain. "Do me a favor and think about Father's proposal. You could have a kingdom of your own to rule one day."

"We both know I'm no ruler. You clearly got those genes," Wyatt sassed his older brother.

"And don't you forget it." Varian smirked. "Sleep well, runt," he said before leaving Wyatt with his thoughts.

Wyatt floated down onto his woven seagrass bed and returned to reading his mother's entries. He skipped forward to after their wedding, eager to know why his mother had stopped going up to the surface.

It has been a year now since Taron's coronation. For the past few months, he has been insistent that as his queen my place is here in Aquana. It saddens me that I can no longer explore like I once did, but Taron is right. My place is here with him, our son Varian, and our people. I'm going on land one last time to give my necklace to D for her to destroy. This will prevent the temptation to go back. I will try to visit her by the docks every so often.

Wyatt's jaw tensed as he flipped the page.

I said my goodbyes to D. As I was returning to the water, I was spotted by a fisherman. It was almost as if he was waiting for me. It's my fault. I let my guard down and didn't check the area before changing. He sped toward me in his boat, The Fortuna, and tried to capture me with a net. It was terribly frightening. Thankfully, Mara came to my rescue and cut me free but not without the man getting a good glimpse of us first. So much for ever visiting D by the docks. I wish there was a way to let her know. However, I can't risk being seen again, and I can't put my family or the kingdom at risk. I will miss her dearly. I had hoped my children could one day meet her. Perhaps one day, when it's safer.

Wyatt's heart broke for his mother. She'd wanted her children to go to the surface, and they'd never gotten the chance. He closed the journal at the sound of his father's throat clearing outside the curtain.

"Come in," Wyatt stammered as he hurriedly hid the journal under his bed and curled his tail to block any suspicion.

Taron entered the room with a stern look on his face. "That was very undignified what you did earlier."

"You caught me completely off guard," Wyatt replied. "You never discussed it with me."

Taron's expression softened. "And for that, I apologize. I misjudged the situation." He clasped his hands behind his back. "I'm not going to be around forever, Wyatt. I want to ensure your future, as well as, the future of this kingdom is safe and secure."

"It is, Father. I can take care of myself. As for the kingdom, you've positioned Varian to be a great leader. That's not my path."

He dug his hand into the sand, letting the grains move between his fingers.

"You sound so much like your mother," Taron wearily admitted.

Wyatt's brow rose. Would his father shed some light on how his mother had loved the surface world? "How do you mean?"

"Nothing, forget about it." Taron brushed aside the painful memories.

"No, I want to know. You never talk about her. It's like she meant nothing to you." The words flew from Wyatt's mouth before he could stop them.

"She was rebellious and impulsive like you," Taron snapped.

Wyatt internally winced.

"I have tried everything to keep all of you safe, and you're the only one that does not want to listen." Straightening his back, he folded his arms and stated. "As I see it, this is the only solution. You will marry Princess Carmea."

Wyatt leaped from his bed. "What? Father, you know I don't want this!"

"You have no choice," Taron said with a stern voice.

"But—"

"My decision is final! You will begin the journey to Atalana tomorrow to announce your engagement. You will be escorted by two of the royal guards. I expect you to be on your best behavior. This is no longer up for discussion. If you won't listen to your father, then you will obey your king," Taron demanded before swiftly turning around and exiting.

Wyatt clenched his fists tightly as his blood boiled. He turned and struck the wall with such force he put a hole in it. There was a small shriek from the other side of the wall. Bright blue eyes with flecks of gold peered through the opening.

"I take it he didn't call off the wedding?" Sarah quipped.

The wedding. Wyatt's throat tightened at the thought. He couldn't go through with it. He needed to escape. *And then what? Even if you could escape without the guards chasing after you, you've never been on your own. You have always had everything done for you. You can't even hunt. Just be a good little prince and marry the princess.*

"For the love of Poseidon, can everyone just leave me alone?" Wyatt yelled at not just his sister but at his subconscious.

He returned to his bed. However, he wasn't left to himself for long.

A few seconds later, Sarah swam into the room and sat next to Wyatt, putting her arm around him. "You'll never get rid of me, little brother," she said sweetly, tilting her head down to look into his eyes. Her long light brown hair with streaks of blue floated around her

"I suppose you're going to try to convince me that this arranged marriage thing is a good idea?"

Sarah sighed. "No offense, but I don't see you running a kingdom."

Wyatt gave a slight smile, playfully pushing into her shoulder. "Gee, thanks, sis."

"You know what I mean. You always did your own thing. Kind of like Mom."

Wyatt bent his tail and hugged it to his chest. "You have no idea."

Sarah gave him a quizzical look.

"I found something of hers in the study," he admitted. Pulling out the journal, he handed it to her, knowing full well she wouldn't tell Father.

Skimming the handwritten pages, her eyes widened in awe. "She wrote this?"

Wyatt nodded. "I haven't read it all, but let's just say I envy her for how much she was able to do. She explored more than we knew."

Sarah paused and looked up. "Does Father know you have this?"

Wyatt gave a half-hearted chuckle. "What do you think?"

"Here." She returned the book without looking him in the

eyes. "I'm not ready to read it yet. It's taken me a long time to cope with what happened to her." Her voice began to quiver. "I still have occasional nightmares."

Wyatt took his sister's hand. He couldn't imagine what she had gone through at that age. To see their mother murdered right before her eyes had to be traumatizing. "I'm sorry."

"You're lucky you were just a guppy. I still remember everything."

"You shouldn't blame yourself," Wyatt told her.

She pulled her hand away. "But I do. If I had just stayed put, she might still be with us today." Her shoulders slumped. "So I don't blame Dad for his rules after Mom's death. Nothing good can come from land-dwellers."

"Surely they can't all be that bad. Mom didn't believe they were."

Opening it to the entry he had read earlier, Wyatt handed it to Sarah. "She knew this land-dweller named D who seems different from everything Father has told us."

Sarah looked over the entry from her mother's hand. Her eyes lit up with every word she read. Wyatt thought maybe their mother's words would help his sister realize that not all land-dwellers were killers.

She slammed the journal shut and shoved it back into Wyatt's hands. "Well, either way, we can never go up there," she said abruptly. "So what is your grand plan to stop your wedding?"

Wyatt frowned at her quick change of subject. "I'm not sure . . ." he said, still wondering if he should stay or not. "Father is adamant on this union. He's sending me to the Kingdom of Atalana to announce the engagement. I know it's my duty as a prince to—"

"Wyatt." Sarah looked into his eyes. "What do *you* want to do?"

His fingers grazed along the embossed border of the journal cover. What he wanted to do was get away from everything: being a prince, his father, the kingdom. *The ocean.* Even if he was able to leave the kingdom, his father would have guards searching the Seven Seas. He'd constantly be on the run.

Wyatt pondered an idea in his head. Not only would his father never approve of it but it was also dangerous. However, he would be able to escape the kingdom and his arranged marriage.

He pursed his lips in thought. They'd never find him on land.

He couldn't, could he?

He had been learning about the surface world for as long as he had been reading books. He knew enough to be on his own. Plus, his mother's words were practically telling him what he should do.

I want to go on land. The words were right there on his tongue, but he couldn't say them. He knew he could trust Sarah, but he couldn't risk it.

"I know you, little brother," she whispered. "You'd never get married just because Father tells you. You don't give up that easily."

The wheels in his mind were already turning. He couldn't flee now, but he could tomorrow.

Sarah gave a knowing smile. "I know you're planning something in that rebellious mind of yours that's going to get you in trouble."

Wyatt slowly raised his head and narrowed his eyes at her. "I hate that you know me so well." He pushed up and poked his head into the hall to make sure they were truly alone. "Tomorrow when I'm being escorted to Atalana by two of the royal guards . . ." He paused for a moment, almost second-guessing himself. "I'm going to ditch them and disappear."

"Disappear?"

He could see the hurt in Sarah's eyes. "I'm sorry, but I can't stay here anymore and live my life like this."

"I understand your frustration, but I wish you would reconsider. Being forced to marry isn't something I agree with. However, disappearing will only lead to more heartache. There has to be something else we can do to persuade Dad to change his mind."

"I wish there was, but I'm out of time."

Sarah sighed in defeat. "I understand. I will always support you." Her fingers fidgeted nervously. "Are you going to tell Varian?"

Wyatt shook his head. "I love him, but he's too loyal to Father and the kingdom. As soon as I tell him, he's bound to tell Father. Or drag me to Atalana himself. I'm not sure if I could outsmart him."

Her brow furrowed. "Where will you go?"

"I'm not sure yet," Wyatt lied. He took her hands. "Please, Sarah, you need to keep this a secret. I need to live my life."

She squeezed his hands. "I will keep your secret."

"Thank you. I knew I could trust you," he replied, hugging her.

She swallowed hard. "I don't want to lose you," she choked.

He released her and stared into her glowing blue eyes. "You'll never lose me. I promise you will see me again."

She nodded.

A muffled voice sounded down the hall.

"I should go," she said. "You'll need all the strength you can get for tomorrow." She pushed up and floated to the doorway.

Wyatt stopped her just as she was about to leave and hugged her again. "I love you, Sarah."

Sarah gave a weary smile and exited the room before peering over her shoulder. "Sleep well, Wyatt. May Poseidon be with you." She bowed.

He watched her light blue tail with specks of gold sway up and down until she disappeared around the corner. He pushed his head against the wall, wondering if that would be the last time he saw his sister.

CHAPTER 4

Surfacing

The next morning Wyatt was mentally and physically exhausted after spending most of the night tossing and turning, wondering if he was making the right decision. If he did this, there was no turning back.

He sat at the rather long table in the dining hall, alone with his thoughts. The same breakfast dish he had been served nearly all his life, imported kelp and shrimp, sat uneaten in front of him. His stomach was in so many knots that food didn't appeal to him. However, he forced himself to eat so he had strength for later. Wyatt grimaced as he gulped down his breakfast.

"Everything ok, Your Majesty?" the server asked.

"Yes, it's fine. I just haven't felt that well," Wyatt said. In all honesty, it just tasted like prison food compared to what he was hoping to experience on the surface after reading more of his mother's journal.

"Oh, it's probably nervous butterflies for the princess! She is very pretty. You're very lucky to have a bride like her." She clasped her hands with elation.

"Uh . . . sure. I'm overjoyed." Wyatt sighed, looking at his sad breakfast.

Just then, Taron entered the large dining hall. His head was buried in what Wyatt assumed were important documents. "I hope your mood has changed from last night about the wedding," he addressed Wyatt without glancing up.

Wyatt took a deep breath and continued to poke at the unappealing meal. "Yes, Father, I decided that you're right. This is the best thing for me, and I'm ready to take that next step in my life and marry the princess."

"I don't want to hear—" Taron's head darted up, and he froze in place after passing Wyatt. He turned around. "Wait . . . You're agreeing with me?" Taron questioned, completely shocked.

Wyatt turned his attention away from his meal and gently placed his fork down. "As hard as it is to believe, I *can* actually change." These next words would be difficult to swallow, even for his father. "I'm choosing to marry Princess Carmea. To do otherwise would be selfish and unfair to you." He stared into his father's hazel eyes. Despite blatantly lying to him, Wyatt was intent on conveying his next words with the utmost honesty. "You won't have to worry about me anymore."

"I will always worry about you." Taron paused and sized up the man who sat before him. "I'm very proud of you."

Wyatt had to keep himself from shamefully wincing. It never seemed like he made his father proud, and the one time he did, it was a lie.

"I wish I could accompany you to Atalana," Taron said.

"I know, but it's probably better." Wyatt looked back to his breakfast and whispered to himself, "A lot better."

"Be well, my son," Taron said with a satisfied grin before leaving.

Wyatt felt even guiltier. His father hadn't expressed that much emotion since before his mother's untimely death. Pushing his breakfast away, he retreated to his room for the journey's final preparations. He removed a heartfelt letter that he wrote to Sarah the night before and glanced over it one more time for good measure.

Dearest Sarah,

If you're reading this, I hope my plan to leave the kingdom worked. I did not make this decision with haste. You and Varian mean the world to me, but I am completely unhappy in this bubble we call Aquana. I need to get away from here and be my own mer. I left Mother's journal in hopes that maybe one day I'll see you again. You always said I took after her. I hope in more ways than one.

Love,
Wyatt

Swallowing his emotions, he folded it back up and stashed it in the journal. He snuck into her room and placed it under her bed. Returning to his room, he examined the week's worth of stubble in the mirror and decided to shave. Retrieving his shark bone razor, he began the arduous process of trimming the hair clean from his face, something his father frowned upon.

After one last long sentimental look around his room, he turned and left. With a heavy heart, he proceeded to the front of the castle where the two guards were waiting for him.

"Wait," a voice called out.

Wyatt looked behind him to see Varian kicking his navy-blue tail furiously. "You didn't think I would let you leave without a goodbye, did you?"

"Would you believe me if I said I was afraid you'd stop me?" Wyatt asked with a smirk.

Varian laughed, but he soon turned serious. "You're ok with this?"

"Oh, so you *are* trying to get me to back down," Wyatt suggested with a raised brow.

"I know you," Varian said, searching Wyatt's eyes. "You don't give in that easily."

"While you may be right, I'm tired of constantly fighting against Father." Wyatt looked forward to the two awaiting guards. "I should go. Before I change my mind."

Varian placed his hand on Wyatt's shoulder. "Be careful on your travels, little brother. Poseidon protect you." He embraced Wyatt and added, "I'll see you at the wedding. Don't do anything foolish."

"Thank you, Varian. Poseidon protect you." Wyatt kicked his fluke, swimming away from his brother for what felt like the last time.

As he swam outside the castle gates, he couldn't help but glance back. There, on the second-floor balcony, floated Sarah. She peered down at Wyatt with sad eyes. She mouthed "Good luck". He gave her a slight nod, then approached the guards. They wore silver armor that sat across their shoulders and covered their upper chest and back. Even though gold was the better material to wear in the kingdom, silver wasn't as noticeable to humans when traveling outside the barrier.

Without another word, the three of them began their long journey to Atalana.

Since the Kingdom of Atalana was about a three-day swim, Wyatt decided to make his move halfway there to put enough distance between the kingdoms. That way, the guards couldn't get to either one too quickly. Along the way, he made conversation with them to lighten the mood and earn their trust. At the beginning, he did try to see if they would let him go alone, but understandably, they had orders from his father to stay with him at all times.

He didn't blame anyone. This wasn't his first escape attempt. It wasn't that Aquana was an awful place; it was quite the opposite. Yet, for Wyatt, it felt like an ever shrinking bubble. He saw the same things and the same mers day after day. It was the same constant routine. Everyone seemed content with their lives except him. All he wanted was to venture off and see other oceans, other kingdoms, other mers—and find his soul mate.

His father, however, didn't see the problem of keeping his people contained, or as he would say, protected. They were safe, yes, but there was hardly any trade, and Taron didn't leave his castle. Even Wyatt could see it was hurting their kingdom.

Midway through the second day, Wyatt raised a question to the guards. "Do you mind if we take a quick break? I'm getting a little tired from all this swimming."

Both guards raised a questioning brow.

"This is the most I've swum considering my father never lets me out of his sight," Wyatt explained. "Although it is building up my stamina."

"Yeah," Roka replied. "I could use a bite to eat anyway." His dark blonde hair with green highlights swayed with the current. "I'll search for food. Cain, you stand guard."

Wyatt waited until Roka's emerald-green tail disappeared into a kelp forest. The gills just below his ears opened and closed rapidly, while his heart drummed against his chest. He pushed any thoughts of continuing his journey to Atalana out of his mind. He had to follow his heart.

Realizing this was the point of no return, he steeled his resolve. "Look, you seem like a great mer. Don't take this personally, ok?"

"What do you mean?" Cain asked, turning just at the same moment Wyatt's fist swung, knocking the guard out cold. He wasn't a polished fighter by any means, but that didn't mean he never paid attention to Varian's defense lessons. Since their father wouldn't let Wyatt become a guard, Varian had taught him everything he knew. In that moment, it paid off.

Leaving Cain out in the open as a diversion, Wyatt hid among the tall stalks of seagrass, waiting to spring his trap on the other guard. Time seemed to stand still as he waited. Finally, Roka returned with a fist full of oysters. His eyes went wide when he caught sight of Cain lying on the seabed.

Roka released the food and immediately grabbed his weapon, a sophisticated steel retractable spear that was housed in the belt made from a whale pelt. He thrust his arm out, and the spear extended. The sharp tip gleamed, causing Wyatt to swallow hard. There was no way he could fight him without a weapon of his own, and even if he did have one, he didn't have the skill to defeat Roka. He needed to outsmart him first.

"Thank Poseidon you're back!" Wyatt exclaimed, rushing out of his hiding spot.

Roka whipped the weapon at his throat.

Wyatt put his hands up. "Whoa! Easy."

"What happened here?"

"Some sharks were fighting, and Cain got caught in the middle. One of them must have knocked him unconscious. I went to find you," Wyatt explained.

Roka collapsed his weapon and was about to return it to its holster when he paused. "I didn't see any—"

Seeing his opening, Wyatt thrust his shoulder into Roka's ribs, pinning him against a rocky outcropping. The weapon floated out of the guard's hand as he pushed back and landed a blow across Wyatt's spine. Roka's tail flicked up, catching Wyatt across the abdomen. Momentarily out of breath, Wyatt retreated, and Roka pressed the advantage. The seafloor tussle kicked up sand and shells, muddying the water. Roka lunged through the murky mess and attempted a shoulder block, but Wyatt was able to counter. Using Roka's momentum against him, Wyatt rolled over the blow and positioned himself above and behind Roka. Wyatt propelled himself downward with all the power in his tail, grasped Roka by the torso, and drove him into the ocean floor.

"Don't do this, Wyatt," Roka warned.

"Tell my father I still love him," Wyatt said as he knocked Roka unconscious with a blow to the back of the head with a nearby rock.

Wyatt paused for a minute to catch his breath, but he knew he couldn't stay there any longer in case either of them woke up. He quickly searched Cain's satchel for the map they had been using on their journey.

Wyatt studied the map that had been given to the guards since they rarely left the kingdom. "Let's see, the Kingdom of Atalana is southeast of Florida, and Aquana is due west."

If his mother's journal was correct, he should find Anna Maria Island to the northeast. He proceeded to rip up the map to confuse the guards, giving him more time.

Wyatt swam until he ran out of energy. He had never been this close to the surface before. Beams of sunlight pierced through the waters, and his eyes adjusted. Deciding to rest at the bottom of the sandy floor, he hid in an opening of a reef. He closed his eyes for a moment until a low humming drew his attention.

He sat up and frantically scanned the waters for danger. Nothing. He listened again. The humming quickly grew in intensity before it began to diminish. He decided to investigate and began his ascent. Soon, splashes of sunlight refracted through the waves mere meters above him and rippled across his body. His eyes adjusted to the sunlight as he neared the surface. It felt like his heart would soon explode with each kick of his tail.

He paused within arm's reach of the water's edge, and a terrifying thought crept into the back of his mind. Was this a bad idea? His mind flooded with countless images of his father scolding him for wandering off or exploring too far beyond the walls of Aquana. His doubts slowly consumed him. *How will I even be able to survive?*

On the verge of despair, he forced himself into a calming technique he had read about in his mother's journal. *Take two deep breaths and think one happy thought,* it read. He closed his eyes and inhaled, conjuring up an image of what he thought his mother looked like. Since he had been just a babe when she died, he would constantly ask Varian or Sarah to describe their mother. He pictured her light brown hair flowing around her. She brushed a strand of a blue hair highlight from her eyes and laughed softly. As he took another breath in, she gave him a warm smile.

An overwhelming sense of calm washed over him as if his mother was right there with him. He flicked his tail and slowly breached the surface, only letting the top of his head and eyes be seen. His wet hair clung to his face, covering his light blue eyes. He peeked through the tendrils at the breathtaking world around him. The vast expanse of blue sky above was dotted with clouds and a blinding sun that caused him to squint. He calmed himself with one more deep breath, unsure if he would be able to breathe like a land-dweller.

Here goes nothing.

He propelled himself higher, lifting his head and shoulders above the water. He breathed slowly, deliberately. The sea air felt like sand in his throat. He sputtered and gasped for the water his body was so used to breathing. His subconscious told him to dive back, but he thought about how his mother hadn't let her fear get the best of her. *I can do this.*

He focused his lungs to fill with as much air as possible. The anguish subsided until he was able to breathe normally without his throat feeling like it was on fire. He heard the humming again, but it sounded different. It sounded like it was behind him and not above him. He turned as a white blur raced past him a little too close for comfort.

"You ok?" a voice called out to his left.

Wyatt turned to see a man sitting on a board, bobbing up and down in the water. Wyatt remembered reading about surfing; a land-dweller sport where they tried to balance on a flat piece of wood on top of the waves. It seemed difficult, yet fun.

Wyatt panicked as the surfer paddled toward him. He quickly fixed his hair to cover the gills behind his ears.

"Are you ok?" the surfer repeated, sitting up. He was built like Wyatt, but his skin was tanned from being out in the sun. He ran his hair through his short, wavy sandy blonde hair, tousling it about. "I don't usually see swimmers out this far."

Wyatt just looked at him, confused and afraid to speak.

"Those guys are assholes for not seeing you." The surfer blinked a few times and his eyes squinted from the blinding sun.

"I—" Wyatt started to speak, but the sound seized in his throat and he began to cough.

"Swallow some seawater, huh?"

Wyatt cleared his throat and finally spoke. "Yeah, I took a lot in by surprise."

The surfer looked around. "Did you mean to swim this far out or were you pulled out from the current?"

Wyatt's tail swayed to keep his head above water. He was thankful the water wasn't clear like it was closer to the shore. "I like swimming long distances." He hoped that answer would suffice.

The surfer shrugged, rising and falling with the waves. "I've never seen you around here. You new?"

"Yeah, I just got here." Wyatt's heart started racing. Why wouldn't this land-dweller leave him alone?

"Cool! Well, I'm Liam. Nice to meet you." He paused for a few seconds, waiting for Wyatt's reply. "Um . . . you gotta name?"

"Wyatt."

"Well, Wyatt, maybe I'll see you around," Liam said as he started to paddle away. He stopped and peered back. "Oh, one more thing. I'd probably swim a little closer to shore to avoid those jet-skiing jerks."

Wyatt waited until Liam was out of sight before slipping back into the water. Daytime certainly wasn't the time to explore. People would clearly notice a merman washed up on the beach. He swam farther out so no one would see him and decided to hide until nightfall. He found a low area where he could hide and rest. He leaned against a rock, and soon his eyes became heavy. It wasn't long before they closed and he slept off the exhaustion from swimming.

"Ow!" Wyatt exclaimed, jolting awake from a sharp pain in his left fluke after a long slumber. He looked down to see a curious ghost crab lifting the navy-blue edge of his fluke and scurrying under. "That's no place to hide, little one."

When he looked up, there wasn't as much light shining through the water. It must be nightfall. He lifted himself from the sandy bottom and slowly swam closer to the shore. The moon peeked out from behind the clouds, illuminating the nearby beach. He considered dragging himself onto the dry sand. Even though it was nighttime and the shore was deserted, it would still be risky to strand himself. Not to mention, when he changed, he would need clothes. He ducked back under and swam around the island until he was in the bay. There had to be something he could use to cover up.

He spied a nearby marina that housed a great number of boats. Perfect. He dove back into the water, quickly revealing his tail.

Swimming under several of the boat's keels, he marveled at the size of them. They all had bizarre names. He picked one that had two towels draped over the side. It was called *Just the Tip*. Whatever that meant.

Revealing the top of his head and eyes, he floated under the dock. Something creaked above him. He pushed up against one of the pillars.

"Did you hear something?" a deep, gravelly voice asked from above.

A thud startled Wyatt as another man exited a boat.

"Just your beating heart," another man replied with a chuckle.

"I don't like being out here at night."

"Why? Afraid a mermaid's gonna get you?" The second man burst into a fit of laughter. Wyatt's breath caught.

"Come on, the boss is waiting in the truck. We need to load this stuff up. The rest of the guys are already at the warehouse."

"I still don't understand why the hell we need these chains. What is this job anyway?"

"As long as I get paid, I don't care."

Heavy footsteps faded as the two men left the dock. Wyatt let out a sigh, bringing bubbles to the surface, and relaxed his body. He decided to wait longer until he felt it was safe.

When enough time had passed he glanced up and wondered if he was still making the right decision. He squeezed his eyes shut with frustration. He could do this.

He breached the surface and took a gasp of ocean air. He coughed up seawater from his lungs, and his chest tightened in discomfort. It was difficult but much easier to adjust to breathing the second time around. He grasped the chain attached to the boat's anchor and pulled himself up. Being a merman certainly had its advantages in the water, but being one out of the water was a lot more challenging. Mers' tails were their strong suit, not their arms.

"Just a little bit farther," he said, gritting his teeth. His heavy tail dangled below him.

His grip slipped from the chain, but he caught himself, gouging his right palm in the process. Wyatt winced as blood slowly trickled down his arm. He had been so sheltered in the palace that he never experienced real physical pain. Wyatt knew if he put his hand into the salt water he would heal in an instant. He didn't want that, though. He wanted to feel like a land-dweller, to feel the pain. He couldn't have been happier.

Finally reaching the railings of the boat, he hoisted himself onto the deck, catching his breath while looking down at his bloodied hand. As much as he wanted the wound to stay, he couldn't leave any evidence of his presence on the deck of the boat. He wrung the water from his hair, letting it cascade onto his wound. It instantly began to scab over, and soon had completely disappeared.

He reached for the towel hanging on the nearby railing and frantically dried off his tail. He hoped and prayed his mother's stories were true, that he would become a land-dweller when dry. He finished drying his tail with the towel, set it aside, and waited for something, anything to happen. Waves lapped across the boat's hull, gently rocking it. Staring up at the clouded night sky, he marveled over the tiny stars. He had only read about them in books, but seeing them with his own eyes was more than he imagined.

He was about to give up and dive back in, taking it as a sign to return to his father's kingdom, when searing pain emanating near his abdomen burned down the center of his tail. The pain of his tail bones cracking and separating was unbearable. He grabbed the towel, shoved it in his mouth, and bit down hard to refrain from screaming in agony.

The tail finally split, and his scales dissolved into flesh. His fluke shrank, slowly turning into toes and eventually feet. He tightly closed his eyes and breathed shallow breaths as he rolled to his side, still gripping the towel between his teeth. By now he had surely torn a hole in it.

Slowly the pain subsided. His new legs tingled as small hairs grew on them. He lay there for a moment to catch his breath before sitting up. Removing the towel from his mouth, he stared in awe at his lower torso. He slowly raised his right leg and bent the knee back and forth, then lowered it, repeating the movement with his left leg.

"Wow," he whispered in amazement as the clouds parted, allowing him to see his legs in more detail with the moonlight.

He looked down at what else had formed. Well, that was certainly different. He recognized it from old books that had been lost to the sea centuries ago. Wyatt wasn't exactly crazy about it, but that was how a male land-dweller's body looked.

He slowly stood up, gripping the boat's railing and glanced down one more time. *I can't walk around like this.* He grabbed the towel and wrapped it around his waist.

His legs felt weak and shook as he held the railing with one hand and the towel with the other. He took his first steps. They weren't graceful by any means, but it got him to a nearby seat.

Wyatt glanced around the boat. There was nothing he could wear except the beach towel until he found clothes.

He stood up once more and started walking, shaky at first, but the more he moved, the easier it was. Wyatt left the boat and continued on the dimly lit dock. He peered into each of the three boats he passed to see if there were any clothes for him to wear. Finally, at the fourth boat, there were a few articles of clothing strewn about the deck. He held up the first thing he grabbed, recognizing it from the books he'd read. It was a slinky red dress.

I don't think this is my style. He chuckled to himself.

Throwing it down, he snatched a black T-shirt and jeans. Muffled voices from inside the cabin alerted him to leave before he could determine if they were a sufficient fit. In a panic, he jumped back onto the pier and hid in a boat a few slips farther down.

Once he was sure the coast was clear, he dressed. The pants barely fit, ending above his ankles, and the shirt was tight against his well-defined chest, showing part of his abs. It would have to do for the time being.

Wyatt left the boat and continued until the dock ended and something soft and green rose from the earth. He cautiously placed his right foot onto the hard ground, touching grass for the first time. His eyes welled up with emotion. He actually did it. He was on land.

Would his mother be proud if she was still alive? Would his father cast him out if he knew where he was? He pushed his thoughts aside and distanced himself from the docks. The short strip of grass turned into a hard surface that did nothing but cause pain on the soft pads of his feet. He knew the beach would be ahead since the island was so small.

He marveled at the darkened buildings along the way. When he heard the sound of the distant shore, his legs moved faster, gaining speed with each step. Sharp stones dug into his feet. No wonder land-dwellers wore shoes.

When cool sand welcomed him, he slowed his pace. In the

distance, waves were crashing, but he couldn't see them. The beach was pitch black, unlike the dock and streets. The only light was the glow of the moon behind the clouds. It was never fully dark underwater unless you swam to the trenches. Panic rose as he tried to maneuver in the darkness. It was scary but wonderful at the same time. He sat on the beach, close enough to catch wisps of the ocean's aromatic comfort. He buried his feet into the sand, wiggling his toes about. He definitely needed to find shoes tomorrow.

Leaning back, he peered up at the bright moon, as the clouds had cleared. He couldn't help but feel conflicted. He felt the closest to his mother he had ever felt before, yet the furthest from the rest of his family. He leaned his back onto a small sand dune behind him and closed his eyes, wondering what tomorrow would bring.

CHAPTER 5

Secret

Liz welcomed the deafening silence as she and her family drove back home. If she had to hear one more "I'm sorry for your loss," she would have walked out of the funeral home. No, she would have ran out. She was surprised she hadn't, but then again, her mind had left days ago. At this point, she was just going through the motions.

Even though she had seen his body lying in a casket just moments ago, she didn't want to believe her grandfather was gone. No matter how much her parents insisted, Liz couldn't make herself go up to his coffin to say her final goodbyes. It was bad enough that every time she closed her eyes, she saw him collapsing to the ground. She certainly didn't want her last images of him to be his lifeless body.

God, what was wrong with her?

There was a quiet sniffle next to her. Her grandmother looked so tired and frail. Liz's fingers twitched. She wanted to comfort her, to tell her she was here, but honestly, she wasn't. In her mind, she was still sitting at her grandparents' kitchen table, planning their trip with her grandfather while they sipped tea and ate chocolate chip cookies.

We can push it back a few weeks when you're better.

Trying to will the tears back, Liz squeezed her eyes shut. She hated this. She didn't want to deal with the fact that he was gone.

"What do you think he would like?" she remembered her mother asking anyone who was listening. They were in the basement of the funeral parlor picking out caskets.

Liz had thought he wouldn't want to be buried in some fancy casket. Who would see it anyway? The worms? *Just dig a hole and throw me in*, he'd always joke. *I don't want anything fancy.* Although, he probably wouldn't want to be buried in the ugly green one that was on display in the corner either.

"Liz?" Her mother's voice caused Liz to come back to the present.

"Huh?"

"Are you coming inside?"

Liz blinked. She looked around to find herself alone in her parents' red SUV that was now parked in her grandparents' driveway. "Yeah, I'm coming."

Her mother closed the passenger door. After a brief moment, Liz exited and followed her inside the house. Memories flashed before her. Good ones, like staying the night when she was little. Cuddling up on the couch with her grandfather and eating popcorn while they watched a movie. Putting the final piece to a puzzle the three of them had worked on.

She padded through the living room and stopped short of the kitchen. She stared at the linoleum floor. Memories of him on the ground, clutching his chest, were taking over. The paramedics performing CPR, her grandmother crying in the doorway as she clutched the phone. It was almost too much to handle.

She closed her eyes and took a deep breath, waiting for the tightening in her chest to go away. A hand touched her shoulder.

"I know, honey," her grandmother whispered. She rubbed Liz's back, comforting her. "I know."

Liz pulled away. "I'm fine, Grandma."

"You were always a horrible liar. Just like your grandpa," she said with a smile before leaving her alone to talk to Liz's parents in the kitchen.

I kept this secret from you for far too long. What had he meant by that?

Liz turned and walked over to the unfinished puzzle still lying on the card table as she mulled over the words. There were only a handful of missing pieces that needed to be placed. One of which was where the waves washed over the sandy shore. She studied each of the segments, trying to find which one fit, but none of them matched.

She searched the area, looking for the missing piece. Her grandmother was always losing a piece or two.

Liz knelt and moved her hand under a shelf that held her grandparents' photo albums. Nothing. Maybe it had fallen between them. She pulled them out and piled them next to her until the top album slid to the carpet and opened up. The first photo she saw was taken at the beach house in Florida where her grandparents used to live. After she was born, they decided to move to Ohio to be closer to Liz and her parents. She imagined that, if they hadn't moved, she would have been flying to Florida every summer.

Derailed from her search for the missing puzzle piece, Liz curled her legs under her, and picked up the album. The first picture she saw was of her being held by her grandmother who was standing next to her grandfather. Liz looked a few months old. Curiosity clawed the back of her mind, and she flipped back a page to find scenic pictures of the beach. On the page before was a family photo of her grandparents and parents, but Liz wasn't there. Perhaps she'd been sleeping when the picture was taken. She turned another page, but they were photos of her parents up in Ohio. Her mother always made doubles and gave them to her grandmother. But Liz wasn't in those either.

Liz's brow knitted together, and she pulled out a picture to look at the date. It was of her parents. They were hand in hand at a wedding of some sort, but according to the date on the photo, it was taken mere weeks before Liz was born. She focused hard on the image. Something was missing. Her mother's stomach was completely flat.

She wondered if her mother or grandmother hadn't written the wrong date on the back, but Liz knew that wasn't the case. They were both meticulous, so the chances of it being incorrect were slim to none. She turned back another page, discovering more photos that showed no evidence of Liz or her mother's pregnant belly. Her heart began to beat faster as she searched every album for pictures of her mother's large round belly, a baby shower celebrating Liz's arrival, or a baby being held in her mother's arms at the hospital.

Nothing.

She had a feeling that if she searched the albums at her parents' house, she would come up with the same results. Events that important would have been kept in her grandparents' albums.

I kept this secret from you for far too long.

The room spun around her, and she suddenly felt numb. Was this the secret he had kept from her?

No, he wouldn't have. They wouldn't have . . .

Her mother walked into the living room to find the photo albums sprawled out around her daughter. "Liz, what are you doing?" she asked with a twinge of nervousness in her voice.

"I . . . I . . ." Liz snapped back to reality. "I'm sorry. I was just looking at old albums. I'll put them back," she replied as if she was doing something wrong.

"It's fine. Just make sure you put them away in order, please," her mother commented. Her gaze lingered for a moment as she tightened her lips.

Just as her mother was about to exit the room, Liz called out, "I have a question."

What am I doing? She was sure it was nothing, but she deserved an explanation why there was no record of her mother's pregnancy or Liz's birth.

The color drained from her mother's face. "Y-yes?"

Liz immediately regretted opening her mouth and the photo albums. *Oh, god . . . I should've never done this.* No, she needed to know for sure or the questions would prick the back of her mind forever.

"Are there any pictures from your baby shower?"

Her mother paused to collect her thoughts. "I didn't have a shower. We didn't have a lot of family. Most of our relatives just sent money."

That seemed like a reasonable answer. "Oh, ok. I was just hoping to see a picture from when you were pregnant."

"Oh, well, you know I hate getting my picture taken, and being pregnant, I just never felt my best anyway." Suddenly, her mother was unable to make eye contact with her daughter.

How could they not have one single picture in the nine months her mother was pregnant?

Liz pried further. "What about pictures from the hospital?"

"Oh, we forgot our camera. We were so rushed to get there." Her voice became shaky.

Another valid excuse, but still, someone could've brought a camera to them during their stay.

Liz fidgeted with the corner of the album. "But there's no pictures of me until we were in Florida. No pictures coming home from the hospital. No pictures of the first month or so when I was born." Her voice raised a little. She tried to rein herself in, but try as she might, she couldn't. She was already emotional between her grandfather's death and the funeral today. Now her mother was blatantly lying to her. She was keeping something from her own daughter. *If I am . . . Stop it! I am their daughter.* But she needed to know.

"You know, those, uh . . . those first few months . . ." Her mother stumbled over her words. Her legs moved slightly like a deer waiting to bolt. "What's this about, Liz?" she blurted out in frustration.

Liz pulled out a picture and leaped to her feet. "This was

taken right before I was born." She held it in front of her mother, who inspected it carefully until her breath caught. "Your stomach is *flat*, Mom!"

"Um, the date . . . was . . ." Her mother's excuses were starting to unravel.

I kept this secret from you for far too long. His words kept echoing in the back of her mind.

"You ready to go, kiddo?" her father said as he walked into the living room. Even though she was well past the kiddo stage, he still thought of her as his little girl. He stopped short and glanced between the two women, then at the open photo albums. He let out a defeated sigh. "Is everything ok?" he asked slowly as if he was afraid of the answer.

Liz's mind was spinning so fast that she could hardly think. "Grandpa said he kept a secret from me. Is this it?" she blurted out. Way to ease into it.

Her parents turned to each other, silently communicating. They both knew her grandfather's secret. How long had this been going on? *It's not their fault*, her grandfather's words resonated in her mind.

"You know what it is, don't you?" Liz asked.

"It's been a long day for all of us. Why don't we talk about this later at home?" her father suggested, moving closer to Liz.

With her fists clenched at her sides, she stepped back, distancing herself from him. Her eyes welled up with tears, and she tried to blink them away before her vision became blurred. Her voice shook. "Please."

"It's just . . . you're really emotional right now," her father said.

Liz folded her arms, hugging her body tightly as if that would help comfort her.

"We all are," her grandmother said from the kitchen doorway. "But she needs to know the truth."

Liz's father moved closer to Liz, and his hands fidgeted with the car keys hanging from his belt loop. "Mary, we don't need to do this now."

"I can't do this. Not now. Not after . . ." Liz's mother's eyes welled up. Whatever this secret was, she wasn't ready to share it.

"Yes. We do," her grandmother said as she entered the living room. She carried a glass of water and walked over to Liz, placing her arm around Liz's shoulders. "I'm so sorry, honey," she whispered, then motioned for them to all sit.

Her parents sat on the couch, while her grandmother and Liz sat in separate armchairs across from them. There was a long moment of silence until her father ultimately broke it.

"There's no easy way to say this . . ."

At that moment, Liz wished his next words would be that there was no secret. Or that maybe one of her great-grandparents was a murderer and they were ashamed to tell her. Or perhaps, Grandma's real hair color was brown and she had been dying it this whole time. Anything that would make Liz laugh it off. But it was none of those.

Liz waited for what felt like an eternity until her mother finally revealed what they had all been hiding from her.

"The reason there are no pictures of when I was pregnant, the baby shower, the hospital, or the first few months is because you weren't ours yet."

Liz's heart thrummed so hard she was afraid it would burst out of her chest at any moment and fly across the room. "What do you mean?" There was a part of her that didn't want to know that answer.

"We adopted you," her mother quietly said as she looked up. A tear streamed down her face.

It felt as if Liz's heart stopped. Her voice was barely a whisper. "What?"

"You're adopted," her father slowly repeated.

Liz suddenly forgot how to talk as the words *you're adopted* swirled in her mind. Just like watching her grandfather die in front of her, she tried to convince herself that this wasn't happening.

"We should have told you this a long time ago," her father said in a somber tone, looking at his wife. "And for that, we are both sorry."

The room was silent for a good while until her mother said, "Please say something, Liz."

What was there to say? Liz blinked a few times. She wasn't sure how long she had been staring at the front door. She wanted to feel the cool metal of the doorknob along her hand as she turned it to leave, but she couldn't make her body work.

"I'm adopted," Liz whispered to herself. She wasn't sure if she stated that as a question or not.

"Yes," her grandmother confirmed.

Liz frowned. So her grandmother knew as well. She wasn't sure if her heart could sink any lower. The four most important people to her had been keeping this life-changing secret her whole life.

Liz shook her head furiously. "This is a joke, right?"

She half expected her grandfather to walk through the front door and tell her it was. The same man she had seen being lowered into the ground not a few hours ago. She squeezed her eyes shut, pushing her knuckles into her forehead. Why did she have to look through those albums and question her mother?

"We wanted to tell you so many times," her mother said.

"All this time," Liz said, digging her fingers into the seat cushion. "You all kept this secret from me! Why?"

"Your grandfather insisted we wait," Liz's grandmother explained. "He told us you would understand when the time came."

She remembered her grandfather's words. *Don't blame them. It's not their fault.* But it *was* their fault, as well as his. What made him think that he could keep something so monumental from her?

"Understand? How could I possibly *understand* why you all

kept this from me for so long?" Liz exclaimed. "I'm an adult for crying out loud, not a kid who couldn't handle it. And I don't care what he said. It wasn't his decision to make." She turned to her parents. "There's no excuse for why you didn't tell me! I was your child, not his."

Her mother flinched at the words. Liz knew she was letting her emotions take over, but she didn't care. She had a right to be upset.

"Were you ever going to tell me I wasn't yours?"

Everyone stayed silent.

"In our hearts, you are and will always be our daughter, biological or not," her mother said, lifting from her seat. "We love you just the same." She tried taking Liz's hand, but Liz pulled back. She couldn't even meet her mother's eyes. "We would never do anything to hurt you."

Liz's eyes darkened. "You already have."

Her mother coiled back and returned to her seat, clearly upset.

The front door beckoned Liz. Her feet fidgeted, telling her to run. If she ran, this never happened. She would still be Tess and Patrick's daughter and Mary's granddaughter, not some baby her biological parents didn't want. Or did they? She wondered what had happened to them.

Forcing herself to stay seated, she swallowed down her emotions. "Tell me everything," she rasped.

"Liz, I think we should talk about this at—" her father began.

"No! I want to know! I deserve—" Liz swallowed back tears. Her jaw was so tense that it was beginning to hurt. "I deserve to know everything. Right here, right now." She placed her head in her hands and swiped away a tear.

Her mother nervously clasped her hands together. "There's not a lot to tell. Your grandfather found you abandoned behind a restaurant near their house on Anna Maria Island in Florida."

Liz lifted her head. "Wait." She paused, letting those words sink in. "I'm not even from Ohio?"

Before, at least she could say she was still born in Ohio, but that wasn't even true anymore. Had she been so naïve that she couldn't see it, or was her family just that good at keeping it a secret from her for so long? Over twenty years to be exact.

A thought popped into her mind. Was she still twenty years old or was she now twenty-one? Was she born and hidden for someone to find that same day, or had she already been in this world for some time?

Her grandmother, who had been quietly listening, cleared her throat. "Your parents were visiting us for a week. Grandpa always went out for his morning walk along the beach and returned with the local paper, but this time, he returned with something else."

"Me," Liz whispered.

Her grandmother nodded. "Richard always came home after his walks at the same time each day for breakfast. That day, he ran late. I remembered because he always came home just as I was finishing up making breakfast, and that day, I was already washing the dishes while his breakfast sat on the table. I saw him walk past the kitchen window, but he didn't come inside. He just stood there on the front lawn with a bundle of rags for the longest time until I came to get him. Imagine my surprise when the heap he was cradling began to move. He told me he found a baby. He seemed apprehensive letting you out of his sight, though. From the very beginning, he was so protective of you."

"He didn't even want me changing you at first," her mother added.

"It was like he was waiting for you to crawl away," her grandmother said. "I guess he had already formed a special bond with you."

That wasn't a surprise. She had always felt there was something special between them, as if they shared an unknowing secret. Now she knew what it was and it made her question their relationship.

"Where exactly did he find me?" she asked.

"He told me behind some restaurant." Her grandmother shrugged. "It was so long ago. I can't remember the name."

Liz sighed with frustration. It wasn't like she could go back there and find her actual parents just hanging out, waiting for her.

"Your grandpa, the kindhearted person he is—" Her grandmother frowned. "Was. He thought your parents could take you in."

"He knew how much we'd been trying to have a baby," her mother said. "I never told you this, but before you were . . . before we adopted you, we had a miscarriage." She stared down at her hand that was interlaced with her husband's.

Another secret. However, Liz understood why her mother might not have told her. She couldn't imagine what they had gone through.

"That's why we were in Florida at the time. Your mother and I, we needed a change of scenery. Perhaps it was fate that everything happened the way it did," her father suggested with a shrug.

Liz chewed at her bottom lip. Yeah, fate. Did fate play into her finding out she was adopted so late? She doubted that.

"Everything happened so fast." Her father ran a hand through his black hair. "I walked out and saw your mother holding a baby. Next thing I knew, I was buying diapers and formula without knowing what was going on."

Her grandmother took a sip of water and placed it back on the coaster on the end table. "To his dismay, I had your grandpa call the police. An officer and a social worker came and took his statement. I was in the other room, but I imagined it was mostly what he had told me." She tapped her chin. "I wish I could remember the name of it," she muttered to herself, then waved off the thought. "I think if your parents hadn't adopted you, he would have made it his mission to be a father again." She rolled her eyes. "Thank goodness they did because I was too old to raise another kid."

"But we weren't," her mother added. "I knew right then I

couldn't let you go. The moment I saw you, I just knew. Your father needed a little convincing, though."

"I didn't need convincing," he protested. "I was just worried we wouldn't be able to keep you and that your biological parents would show up. With everything your mother went through, I didn't want her heart to break again." His eyes darkened. "Even now, I'm still worried someone's gonna show up on our doorstep and take you from us."

Liz wanted to promise that no one was going to take her from them, but she couldn't find the words to reassure them. And the truth was, she wanted her biological parents to show up on their doorstep. She needed to know why she had been abandoned. Did they not want her? Was it drugs? Was she stolen from them? Were they even alive? Did she want to know the answer to that last question? Not knowing was just as bad as finding out she was adopted. "Did the police try to find them?"

"They did, but no one stepped forward as your parents or even knew about you," her grandmother replied.

"We told the social worker we wanted to adopt you, so she had us go to her office to fill out the necessary paperwork before we had to head home. Unfortunately, we couldn't stay and wait it out, but it wasn't long before we got the call and our lives changed forever." Her father took his wife's hand and squeezed it.

Liz sat there in stunned silence, wondering what she should do next, when her grandmother uncrossed her legs and leaned forward.

"That story isn't entirely true," she quietly admitted. Liz and her parents all turned their attention to her in bewilderment.

Liz's mother's brow scrunched together. "What do you mean?"

"I don't know," she confessed.

"What do you mean, you don't know?" Liz asked sharply. She was getting tired of all the secrets and lies.

Her grandmother addressed Liz's parents. "After you both

left, I tried asking Richard what else happened. All he told me was that there was more to the story."

Liz's brow drew tight. More secrets? She couldn't take any more. "You never asked him to explain?"

"Believe me, sweetie, I tried. So many times," her grandmother bemoaned. "The more I pushed, the more reluctant he was to answer. He insisted he wanted to tell you himself. He told me he wanted to tell you when you turned eighteen, but when he got sick . . ." She looked down and fiddled with her wedding ring.

Eighteen, that was when the trip to the island was originally planned, but it had been postponed because she couldn't deal with him being sick. *This trip is important.* He was going to tell her everything on the island where she was found. Her fists clutched at her sides. If she had never pulled away, she would have known sooner. Was this her fault?

"And now I'll never know," Liz muttered to herself. She felt sick to her stomach. She needed fresh air. As she rose to her feet, the room spun around her. She clutched the arm of the chair to steady herself, closing her eyes for just a moment.

"Why don't you sit down, dear?" her grandmother suggested.

Ignoring her, Liz straightened herself out, slipped on her shoes, and walked out of the house. No one stopped her.

The crisp spring air blew her hair across her face, causing a few strands to stick to her tear-stained cheeks. She ambled down the same sidewalk she and her grandfather had walked so many times. She had confided in him during their walks and thought he had done the same. Boy, had she been wrong.

Why didn't he tell me? Why did he want to wait until I was older? She wiped the tears from her face as she continued down the path. Where she was going, she didn't know. She just knew she had to get away.

CHAPTER 6
Blending In

Wyatt cried out in fear as he jolted up. His heart pounded frantically as he scanned his surroundings. The sky was a beautiful blue without a dark cloud in sight, while the ocean waves gently washed up along the nearly empty shore. He was still on land.

He peered down, half expecting the usual bright blue scales, yet his legs still remained. It was strange, seeing the fleshy feet and wiggling toes, rather than a tail. A few people were walking along the beach, not paying attention to the disguised mer.

He released a breath and pulled his legs up to his chest. His elbows rested on his knees. The fear in the back of his mind had manifested into what had been a nightmare. He tried to shake off the image of his father's angry face, raising a tidal wave to drag Wyatt back into the ocean. *What if Father did find me? What would he do if he succeeded? He can't force me to go back. I won't.*

His stomach churned, partly from the anxiety he felt thinking about his father but mainly because he couldn't remember the last time he had eaten. He didn't want to go through the pain of transforming just for food. He'd have to figure out how to get a meal on land.

He stood slowly, still a little shaky since he was getting accustomed to his legs. He shook the sand out of his messy mop of brown hair. Now that it was dry, it hung loosely in front of his eyes. He combed it back with his hand, but the ocean breeze blew it right back.

Wyatt heaved a sigh and began walking down the beach. He did his best to avoid eye contact with any locals while taking in as much of the landscape as he possibly could. One thing from the surface world that was different from underwater was the plethora of smells. Being on land, he could now smell the fragrance of the fish, the sea air, and even the dusty sand. He followed his nose as best he could to find food.

It led him first to a café. He walked up the small beach dune to the entrance. Outside there was a sign that read "No shirt, no shoes, no service." Wyatt glanced down at his bare feet, sighed again, and continued walking farther down the beach until he came to a small restaurant. The aroma piping through the open door had to be the best thing he had ever smelled in his whole life! Several tables with colorful umbrellas and chairs were sprawled out on the patio. A ladder blocked part of the entrance with a man standing at the top. He was fiddling with some wiring protruding from the wall. There was an easel holding a decorative sign on the patio that read All Are Welcome. Wyatt stepped in, and a waitress greeted him.

"Just you?" the waitress asked, looking him up and down.

"Yeah, just me," he said with a hint of sadness.

"Nothin' wrong with that! Why don't you have a seat at the bar and the bartender will be with you shortly," she said with a smile.

As he waited, he looked around the quaint restaurant, admiring everything about it. All the mermaid décor should have made him feel a bit anxious, but instead, it gave him a warm, fuzzy feeling.

"You ready to order?" a familiar voice asked, pouring a glass of water and placing it in front of Wyatt.

Wyatt turned to find the surfer he had met yesterday standing behind the bar.

"Hey! I thought you looked familiar! Be honest, you were lured by the sweet aroma of the cinnamon rolls, weren't you?" Liam laughed.

"Is that what that wonderful smell is?" Wyatt inquired excitedly.

"Yup, it's the house special and everyone's favorite! I'll order you one for a starter while you look at the menu," Liam said, handing him a laminated paper.

Wyatt picked up the menu, silently thanked his brother's teachings, and read down the list of meals. Most of them he could pronounce, but he had no clue what they were. As he finished reading, a young woman approached the counter next to him. Her wavy auburn hair was worn in a messy bun. Her long bangs across her forehead nearly hid her seductive hazel eyes. A golden necklace was nestled between her breasts that peeked out from the top of her tight black tank top. Her pockets hung out from the bottom of her jean shorts. She sat at the barstool, and her leg began to twitch with what seemed like exasperation.

"Liam." Her voice was tight.

"Just a minute," Liam called back from the other side of the bar.

She tucked back a few loose strands of hair behind her ears as she waited impatiently. The woman's gaze looked Wyatt over in quiet curiosity. "What happened to you? Your clothes get shrunk in the dryer or something?"

Before Wyatt could even think of something remotely intelligent to reply with, Liam reappeared in front of them.

"I'm running late to the marina," the woman said, glaring at the clock behind the bar. "Can you get my order, Liam?"

"No problem," he answered before leaving them alone.

As she tapped her fingers on the wooden bar top, she shifted sideways so that her legs were inches away from his. "You seem familiar." She seemed to think about that for a moment. "Do I know you from somewhere, maybe the marina?"

"No, I don't think so." Wyatt took a sip of water through the paper straw. "I'm new in town so I'm not sure where that is."

"I volunteer at the marine rescue and spend a lot of time there. I see a lot of people, so I guess I was mistaken." She played with her necklace's pendant.

Wyatt couldn't quite grasp the scent, but she smelled heavenly.

"For what it's worth, I recommend the pancakes." She pointed at the menu as she grazed her hand on top of his.

Wyatt took a deep breath to try to compose himself. "Yeah, I think I'll try those," he stammered.

The scent of her perfume lingered around Wyatt. He didn't know what it was, but there was something alluring about her.

"You got a name, handsome?" she inquired sweetly.

Wyatt gulped. He never felt this nervous around mermaids. "Wyatt."

"I'm Jessica." She put her hand out toward his. He gently took it and kissed the back of it. "Oh." She seemed surprised by his action but didn't recoil either.

"Here you go." Liam dropped the bag of food on the counter, interrupting Wyatt's deep gaze into Jessica's eyes.

"Keep the change," she replied before taking the bag.

"Thanks," Liam said sarcastically, pocketing the piece of paper she had left on the counter.

"Maybe I'll see you again," her smoky voice whispered in Wyatt's ear as she touched his shoulder, then left.

"Well, that didn't take long." Liam chuckled, watching her exit. "She's got you hooked."

"Yeah . . ." Wyatt mused, staring at her backside as she left. "Wait. What?"

"Exactly." Liam put down a small plate with a rather large cinnamon roll on it, breaking Wyatt's trance with its sweet smell.

"What do you mean?" Wyatt asked. He picked up the

cinnamon roll and took a small bite. It was like nothing he had ever tasted before. *Forget finding true love in a woman, I think I found my true love in cinnamon rolls.*

"Nothing, man. She isn't always that, well, personable. I guess she really likes you."

"Maybe," Wyatt said as he wolfed down another bite of the roll.

Liam laughed. "You know what you want to eat, or do you just want me to keep bringing these out?"

Wyatt pointed to the pancakes that Jessica had recommended.

"Do you want bacon or sausage?"

"Uh . . ." Wyatt didn't know what either of those were, but he was sure it was better than kelp for breakfast.

"I personally like the bacon, along with the fresh orange juice."

"Ok, I'll have that then," Wyatt replied. As he finished the roll, he licked the glaze off his fingers, grabbing a napkin. He noticed the wording on it. *The Cove 100 Gulf Dr. N. Anna Maria Island, FL.* "The Cove?"

"Yeah, that's what this place is called," Liam replied in confusion until a lightbulb clicked. "Oh, you must've came in from the patio. We're getting the sign fixed. I wasn't even thinking!"

This is it! I'm on the same island that Mom wrote about, Wyatt thought. *I wonder if this mysterious D is still around.* He'd have to do some investigating.

He sat there pondering the remembered pages of his mother's journal. Before he knew it, Liam came back with a tray full of food. On it was a plate of four large pancakes, and three thin, crispy slices of meat, along with a glass of orange juice and a variety of dark liquids. Liam placed the plate in front of a wide-eyed Wyatt.

"Wow, thanks!"

"Sure thing," Liam replied, walking away to tend to other customers.

Wyatt looked around at all the people enjoying their breakfast, studying how they ate and used the utensils. He needed to try his best to blend in. He picked up his fork and knife and slowly cut the pancakes. He quickly caught on, but not without Liam noticing him staring at the small pitchers of sticky liquid.

Liam walked back. "Is everything ok?"

Wyatt sheepishly stared at the syrup carrier and confessed, "I just don't know which one to pick."

"Oh, sorry! This is maple, apple cinnamon, apricot, and raspberry," Liam said, pointing to each one. "I recommend the apple cinnamon if you want something different."

Wyatt trusted Liam's opinion and poured the apple cinnamon syrup on top of the pancakes. He took his first bite and it did not disappoint.

"Oh my gosh, the food here is so much better than kelp!" Wyatt soon regretted the words that slipped out of his mouth.

"Kelp?" Liam asked with a puzzled look on his face.

"Um, my father is a . . . a . . ." Wyatt stammered.

"Vegetarian?" Liam answered.

"Yes, that's it!" Wyatt was relieved there was a word for crazy or maybe people actually ate kelp on the surface too.

"Does it taste as bad as it sounds?" Liam asked, grabbing a towel to wipe off the bar.

Wyatt laughed. "I think worse." He tried the bacon next. If he had any doubts about leaving the ocean, the food alone was worth the sacrifice.

Liam handed him a slip of paper with a bunch of words and numbers on it. "Whenever you're done," he stated and walked to the other side of the bar where a man had just seated himself.

Money. It was the one thing he had forgotten about. The underwater world only relied on trading if there was a need for an item or service. Wyatt vaguely remembered money being mentioned in his mother's journal. He regrettably wished he had kept her journal on him as a reference.

As much as he hated it, he decided to leave without anyone seeing him. He scanned the restaurant and saw a sign for a restroom next to a back exit. Discreetly, he stood up and walked in that direction, only to bump into Liam, who was exiting the bathroom. Liam held the door open, assuming Wyatt was entering.

Wyatt ducked in before peering out to see Liam walk back to the bar. When he was sure no one was watching, he quickly exited the restaurant. He felt completely awful, especially since Liam seemed like such a nice land-dweller. Hopefully, he was understanding as well.

Wyatt made his way down the shore and sat by the dunes. He was in over his head. There was no way he could survive on land with just these poor-fitting clothes on his back. He sighed and resigned himself to a few more moments on land before turning tail back into the water.

How could he show his face to his father after this? Maybe he was right. Maybe Wyatt should just marry the princess. He would never hear the end of it, though. His thoughts naturally drifted to his mother.

"I miss you so much," he whispered as his eyes welled up. "I wish you were here to guide me."

Just then he saw someone out of the corner of his eye charging toward him.

"You got a lot of nerve doing that!" Liam shouted. "I guess that's what I get for being nice to someone."

Wyatt sighed deeply and used his sleeve to wipe away his tears before turning his gaze back to the water. "I thought once I got here, everything would come into place. My mom did it. Why couldn't I? You know?" he questioned more to himself than the perplexed server. He wasn't exactly sure why he was spilling his guts to this random land-dweller. "She made it sound so easy in her journal. My father doesn't believe in me. I doubt my siblings do, too. I don't fit in anywhere," he confessed. He saw Liam's shoes shuffle next to him. "I'm sorry, you probably want your money, which I embarrassingly don't have."

"I did at first," Liam said with his hands in his pockets, "but now I'm here because you're going through something that is bigger than $10.25 and a tip."

"I don't want to be a burden to anyone anymore."

"If you're referring to your bill, it's fine." Liam shrugged. "Chalk it up as my good deed for the day."

"Thanks," Wyatt replied with a forlorn smile. He tugged the bottom of his jeans that felt like they were cutting off circulation to his shins. Maybe the dress would have been better.

"You don't have anywhere to go, do you?" Liam asked.

Wyatt shook his head and focused on the horizon. Somewhere out there was his family. By now, they must have discovered he'd escaped. The sound of Liam's throat clearing caused Wyatt to come back to reality. He turned to see Liam's outstretched hand. Wyatt stared at it, confused.

"Come on," Liam said. "My parents never thought I could move here and survive on my own either. I proved them wrong and so can you. I'll help you get on your feet."

"Why?"

"Well, I never really got good grades in school, and I always wanted—" Liam mused as Wyatt's brows drew together. "Oh, you mean, why am I helping you?"

Wyatt laughed for the first time since surfacing. "Yes. Why would you want to help a stranger?"

"Someone told me once that people can surprise you. So don't make me regret this."

Wyatt pulled his legs up to his chest. "I'm fine, really."

"Clearly," Liam said, pointing out Wyatt's choice of clothing.

Wyatt turned to him. "Seriously, I don't want to keep you from your job."

"It's fine. I had someone cover me. I can work an extra hour if need be."

Wyatt grimaced. He hugged his knees tightly, refusing the land-dweller's help. All his life, things had been done for him. This didn't seem any different.

"Don't make me stand here all day with my hand stretched out like an idiot. It doesn't bode well with the ladies."

Wyatt should have refused. After all, trusting a land-dweller was unheard of. Yet his mother had trusted one, and so far Liam had been nothing but friendly and helpful. He clasped Liam's hand and was pulled to his feet.

Liam looked the mer over. "First things first, you need some new clothes. Did you wash up on shore and grab someone else's clothes?"

Wyatt laughed nervously as they began to walk back toward the restaurant. "Yeah, something like that."

"I can't imagine not having any support. My parents were never confident that I would make a life here, but at least they helped when I needed to borrow some money."

"I didn't really give my father a chance. I took off behind his back. My sister is the only one I told because I knew she'd keep my secret. Knowing my father, I'm sure he knows what's happened by now."

"I'm sorry you felt that was the only way."

They continued to walk across the side parking area, and Wyatt quietly marveled at the large vehicles. He had seen them in a few of his books, but again, pictures didn't compare to the real thing.

He wondered where exactly they were heading. Just ahead was a long yellow building with two white doors. A few chairs sat on the porch that wrapped around it. A green car was parked in front.

"What's this?" Wyatt asked when they stopped in front of the first door.

"My humble abode," Liam presented.

"Ok . . ."

"I told you I'd help you, so this is my offer."

Wyatt's eyes widened. "Your home?"

Liam gave a slight shrug

"I couldn't possibly. It's too much. Besides, I don't have any money."

"I could use a roommate. And as for the money, we'll figure that out." When Wyatt just stood there in shock, Liam added, "I insist."

Emotions that Wyatt hadn't felt in a very long time bubbled to the surface. He could hardly find the words to express his gratitude. "Thank you! You won't regret it, I promise."

"I'm counting on it," Liam replied as he opened the door to Wyatt's temporary home.

CHAPTER 7
Changing

Liam couldn't stay, as he had to go back to work. However, he did show Wyatt around the apartment. Compared to the palace, it wasn't much, but Wyatt didn't care. He reveled in the plainly decorated space. As soon as he walked in, the kitchen was to his right, while the living room was to his left.

Down the hallway were two bedrooms. Liam's room was at the end of the short hall, while Wyatt's was on the left. A tiled bathroom with a walk-in shower sat across from his room. Liam had taken out a set of towels from the small linen closet next to the bathroom and hung them on the towel rack. Before Liam left, he advised Wyatt to use the shower considering the odor that was emanating off of him.

Wyatt sat on the plush green couch, alone with his thoughts and emotions, worrying about how this would all work out. He took a deep breath through his nose and caught a whiff of his own scent, and boy, was Liam right. Not only did Wyatt reek of fish, but his skin was dry and grimy from the sand and salt water. He knew he had to clean himself up. After all, he didn't want to risk Liam kicking him out over body odor. He just didn't know how to go about that without transforming.

The hallway to the bathroom felt like it was miles away. The mere thought of touching water made his heart race. He reluctantly walked to the bathroom and closed the door. Wyatt turned around and nearly scared himself half to death. Staring back at him was his unfamiliar reflection in a full-length mirror that hung on the back of the door.

Running his hand across his five o'clock shadow, he examined himself. This was the first opportunity he had to fully take in his new likeness. His dry hair reminded him of a clump of seagrass in a tangled mess. *Ugh, I need a haircut.* He ran his hand through it, brushing the locks away from his eyes. The bright blue tint of his pupils had softened to look more like a land-dweller, while the blue strands of hair had disappeared, as well. He unbuttoned his shirt, revealing his sleek athletic physique, and tossed it on the floor.

Wyatt decided that instead of jumping right into the shower, it would be better to start slow and wash his hands first. If he started to change, then he could at least act fast with the towel next to him and dry his hands.

Cautiously pulling the handle forward, he watched the stream of water fall into the basin. His hands trembled as they moved closer to the water. Quickly dipping his right hand through the stream, he tensed up, waiting for something to happen. Nothing. He ran both hands under the water again and again, each time longer than the last, as well as moving the water higher until his forearms were wet. Still nothing. He splashed his face with the water, relishing the refreshing coolness. He licked his lips and noticed a distinct lack of salt. Curious, he cupped his hands under the water and took a sip.

"Ugh." Wyatt cringed. "There's no salt in this water."

An epiphany struck him. *There's no salt in this water!* He immediately turned on the shower, convinced the lack of salt would prevent him from transforming. After stripping the rest of his clothes, he took a deep breath and stepped into the steamy shower stall. Reaching his arms out into the warm water, he was relieved he could do this. He moved his whole body under the cascading flow. The clean water felt so nice as it streamed down his chest. At that moment, everything felt like it should.

However, it was fleeting. As the water flowed down his legs, pain flared through him.

"No, no, no!" Wyatt cried out as his legs gave out, causing him to fall on his knees.

He reached up to try to turn the water off, but it was no use. The torment was excruciating, and there wasn't anything he could do to stop the transformation. Scales began forming on his hips, each one a searing point of pain.

Suddenly, there was a loud knock on the door.

"Are you ok?" Liam's muffled voice yelled through the door. "I came back to get my wallet, and I heard you yell out."

"Uh, yeah." Wyatt panicked as the scales formed faster. He gritted his teeth. "I didn't realize how hot the water was. Everything's fine."

"Ok. I'll see you later," Liam yelled out.

Wyatt lay prone on his back, biting his lip as he was forced to endure the pain. When he felt Liam was truly gone, Wyatt let out another howl of agony. His formerly hairy legs were now covered with the light blue scales of his kind. They began fusing back together in a torturous reversal of his previous transformation. If it wasn't for the shower running, he would have heard the cracking of his bones shifting. His feet and toes melded into a large fluke. Wyatt closed his teary eyes as the pain subsided. A moment went by until he opened them, lifting his head slightly to look at his tail.

"Blowfish," he said, sighing. Laying his head down on the floor, he let the water hit his face. Wyatt became annoyed when the small gills that helped him breathe underwater opened behind his ears. He took a deep breath in from his mouth and exhaled through his nose, forcing the gills to close on their own.

Sitting up, he leaned against the wall, folded his tail, and hugged where his land-dweller knees would be. Mermen were taught to be fearless and show little emotion, but Wyatt had never liked the teachings of merfolk. He allowed hot tears to stream down his face as he quietly sobbed, feeling sorry for himself.

"Come on, Wyatt, pull yourself together. You can do this . . . for Mom," Wyatt whispered to himself as he took a deep breath and shoved any doubts he had out of his head.

He pushed back his wet hair and reached up to the shelf above him, clumsily knocking a few bottles off the shelf. *I might as well clean up since I'm here.* He read the instructions for each bottle and proceeded to take a shower the best he could. Once finished, he reached for the handle to shut off the water but hesitated. He wasn't looking forward to experiencing the pain of changing yet again. However, he couldn't stay there forever.

Wyatt turned the water off, leaned back toward the shower exit, and realized he'd forgotten to grab the towel on the far rack. He sighed in frustration. Using his arms, he dragged himself along the bathroom floor. After grabbing the towel, Wyatt slowly dried his body and tail off. He watched, mesmerized, as his colorful scales dulled. His tail tingled, reminding him of a jellyfish sting, a precursor to the torture that was coming.

Quickly, he rolled up a portion of the damp towel and put it in his mouth. This time he would be prepared for the agonizing pain he was about to experience for the third time in the last twenty-four hours.

The all-to-familiar transformation process from mer to land-dweller began again. The pain of the scales dissolving into flesh was more bearable this time. However, the splitting of his bones made him bite down harder into the towel as he tried to hold back the tears. Then, just as soon as it started, the suffering stopped. Wyatt lay naked on the floor. The cool tile felt good against his legs. It wouldn't be the last time he would feel this horrible pain.

I need to find Mom's necklace.

Wyatt slowly stood on his weakened legs, completely drained from changing twice in the past twenty minutes. He held on to the edge of the sink for balance and was greeted by his reflection. He looked like hell.

Even though he was mentally and physically exhausted, the rumble from his stomach indicated he was more hungry than tired.

Finding shorts, a green T-shirt, and a pair of sandals that Liam had left by his bed, Wyatt changed into them and searched the cupboards for something to eat. He opened everything he could get his hands on, sniffing and sampling them. The peanut butter, while delicious, made him want to drink half the ocean. Unfortunately, a tall glass of dull-tasting water had to do. He continued until attempting to eat a small, yellow square food called chicken bouillon. Spitting it out into the sink, he concluded he couldn't just aimlessly eat land-dweller food. Liam would know what was suitable to consume.

Walking across the parking lot to The Cove was more pleasant with something under his feet. He found Liam sitting at a table. He was on his lunch break. Waving Wyatt over, he motioned for him to sit with him and let him eat the rest of his loaded fries.

"I solved your money problem," Liam announced proudly. "I got you a job here at The Cove."

Wyatt grabbed a fry and bit a piece off. It was a lot better than the yellow cube he had earlier. "A job?"

"You didn't expect to freeload off me, did you?"

"Um, no." Wyatt wasn't sure what Liam meant, but he hoped that was the correct answer.

"I talked to the owner, and she's cool with you working here. On a trial run, of course." Liam leaned in and whispered, "I told her your situation. She said to fill out the paperwork the best you can." He went over to the bar and came back with a piece of paper and a pen.

With the help of his roommate, Wyatt filled out the form while he finished off the fries. Since mers didn't technically have last names, he used Aquana. The address was simple enough, as Liam wrote it down. He had no other past employment unless he wanted to put Prince of Aquana, but that would likely lead to questions he couldn't answer.

"I'm sure that's good enough for now," Liam said.

Wyatt tried to think of the right words to say to show his gratitude. "I'm very well obliged to your kindness during my time of need."

Liam blinked a few times.

Way to stick out like a manatee in the middle of the ocean, Wyatt.

"Um, yeah, anytime," Liam said as he stood up. "I gotta get back to my shift."

"Yeah, um, I'm going to walk down the beach . . . or something," Wyatt stumbled over his words, feeling completely out of place. He decided to leave before embarrassing himself even more.

He hurried out the door and slammed into Jessica, the girl he had met earlier that morning, knocking her to the ground.

Blowfish! Spoke too soon.

"Oh my gosh! I— I'm so sorry," Wyatt stuttered. The scent of her made his heart race as he offered his hand.

"I'm not," Jessica said with a slight smile. She took his hand, and he pulled her up. "It was my fault anyway. I was in a hurry to get dinner. I was so busy today that I ended up skipping lunch." She paused in thought. "If you're not doing anything, why don't you join me?"

"Uhhhh." Wyatt couldn't gather the words to even make a sentence. He hadn't even been on land for a whole day and a girl was asking him out. This was unheard of in the merworld. Mermaids would never ask their male counterparts on a date. He wavered between trying to search for his mother's mysterious land-dweller friend and sharing a meal with a beautiful girl.

"I'm never able to eat everything I order anyway," Jessica said, playing with a strand of her dark locks.

He was still a little hungry. Wyatt looked between Liam, who was shaking his head in disbelief, and Jessica, who was waiting for an answer. Still not able to form any words, he simply nodded.

"Good! I'll get my order. Meet me at that red umbrella down on the beach," she said as she pointed to her spot.

Wyatt nodded again and strolled to where she had indicated. He wasn't sure what was going on with him. Usually, he had no problem talking to females or at least with mermaids. He felt different around Jessica. Maybe because she wasn't forced on him. All his life, everything had been decided for him, even the girls he dated. His father would call princesses from other kingdoms to court. They were always so prim and proper. Just to appease his father, he would entertain these brief dalliances, but they were never a good fit. Jessica seemed the opposite, rough and outspoken. It was refreshing.

Sitting on the beach towel under the umbrella, he nervously watched the distant waves. It was almost silly. Something that had been essential now terrified him. He glanced back to find Jessica nearing him. The gulf breeze whipped her long, dark auburn hair around her face as she kept her eyes on Wyatt.

She took everything out of the bag and opened the containers. "Two bottles of water, a large grilled chicken breast, potato wedges, and a large piece of chocolate cake," she announced. "I hope you're hungry."

For some reason, she could have pulled out a kelp salad and he'd scarf it down if it meant he'd get to spend more time with her. She cut the chicken in half and placed his portion on the container lid along with some of the potatoes.

Jessica handed him his water. "You said you're new to the area. Where are you from?"

"Oh, um, up north," Wyatt replied, not able to think of names of towns or cities besides where he currently was.

"That's a bit vague." She narrowed her eyes. "Like, north as in Clearwater, or north as in Ohio?"

"The second one. Ohio," he said, quickly shoving a bite of chicken in his mouth to get out of any conversation about himself.

"Ah, ok. Well, I don't know much about Ohio other than it has snow."

He twisted the cap off his drink and took a sip, speaking

between chugs. "Yup, that snow is pretty cold and, uh . . . white," he blandly stated, as that was the only thing he knew about snow.

Jessica laughed loudly. "You're funny!" She grabbed a potato wedge and sank her teeth into it. "What made you decide to come here?"

Wyatt blew a breath, relieved he didn't have to think of a total lie. "My mom came here before I was born. I wanted to follow in her footsteps. I think it would be nice to do the same things she did."

"Oh, like what?"

"I'm not exactly sure yet, but having dinner on the beach is a good start," he said with a smile.

"You can't ask her?"

Wyatt's smile disappeared, and he stared out into the horizon. "She died when I was little."

Jessica gently touched his arm. "My mom's dead, too."

Wyatt glanced over in surprise.

Her jaw tensed. "The ocean took her. That's what my dad wrote in his journal. He's dead, too. He died when I was three. Fishing accident. That was twenty years ago, so I don't remember him too much."

"I'm so sorry. That must have been hard." He couldn't imagine not having both his parents. He and his father didn't always see eye to eye, but at least he was still around.

She shrugged as if it wasn't a big deal, but Wyatt got the feeling it was definitely a big deal. "Yeah, I made it through, though. I went from foster family to foster family until I was old enough to be on my own. I reconnected with my uncle recently. He had kept my dad's house." She cut into her chicken. "Even though my uncle left it a shithole, I found some pretty interesting things in there."

"Oh?"

"Journals and stuff about his time on the water. Gives me some insight into his life, you know?"

Wyatt thought back to his mother's journal. He and Jessica had more things in common than he thought.

"Yeah." He took a bite of his potato, and the air felt tense between them. He didn't want to dwell on either one of their parents' deaths. "What about you? Have you always lived here?"

"I've lived here my whole life, that's pretty much it. Nothing to tell, really. It's pretty boring," she said with a monotonous voice as she waved her hand about with her fork.

"You're not boring. I find you enchanting," Wyatt blurted, unable to control himself. He shifted closer to her, their legs nearly touching.

"Enchanting, huh?" she asked as she closed the distance, their lips almost touching. "That's the first time I've ever heard that." She pulled back and gazed at the shore. "What was it like growing up in"—she took a swig of water—"Ohio?"

"Same. It was pretty boring." Wyatt closed the distance on them again. Without thinking, he brushed back a strand of Jessica's hair behind her ear. "I'd really like to know you better."

Jessica turned to him and leaned in close. Her lips grazed his cheek as she whispered in his ear, "You'll just have to keep going out with me to find out more."

A shiver ran down his neck, and his chest tightened. It took all of his strength to keep control. He wasn't about to try to kiss a girl he just met. That wasn't him. Willing himself to pull away from Jessica, Wyatt continued to eat his meal, trying to avoid too much personal conversation.

The rest of the meal passed with idle chat and silly jokes. Before he knew it, the afternoon had slipped into evening. When she turned to him, he couldn't help but stare at her lips. They beckoned him. As quickly as the thought crossed his mind, he pushed it away. Everything in his body told him he shouldn't grow close to a land-dweller this soon.

"Why don't we go for a quick swim?" She leaned her head back on his shoulder. She breathed excitedly on his neck and coyly whispered, "I *may* have a bathing suit underneath."

Wyatt's imagination ran wild. "Yeah, sure," he said in a haze before his subconscious broke through. *You'll change, you idiot!* He needed to get out of there before he said or did anything stupid. He untangled himself from her and stood. "Actually it's getting late. I should probably get going. It's been a long day, and I start my new job in the morning."

Jessica stood as well. "Are you sure?" she asked, placing her head on his chest.

"No. I mean *yes*! Yes, I'm sure. I need to get back. We'll do this again soon, I promise," Wyatt said as he leaned in for a kiss.

Jessica placed a finger on his lips. "Not yet." She held up an unused napkin with a series of ten numbers scribbled on it.

"What's this?" Wyatt asked.

"My phone number, silly." Jessica gathered her belongings, shaking the sand from the towel and placing it in a bag that she swung over her shoulder.

"Oh, I'm just getting started here. I don't have a, um, phone."

"Wow, I don't think I ever met someone without a phone. That's actually really refreshing," Jessica said as she circled behind Wyatt. She leaned in close once more and whispered, "Meet me here tomorrow night at eight." She pulled out the umbrella and closed it.

"Absolutely," Wyatt said, turning around and expecting a kiss, only to see her shapely rear end swaying back and forth as she walked away. Wyatt collapsed, light-headed onto the sand as he gripped his tightening chest. No girl had ever made him feel this way before. There was nothing he wanted more than to kiss every inch of her body, yet at the same time, every neuron in his brain was screaming to run.

<h1 style="text-align:center">CHAPTER 8
Resolve</h1>

After finding out she was adopted and leaving her grandparents' home, Liz continued down the sidewalk to further herself from her family and their lies.

A voice called from behind her. "These old legs can't keep up with you as well as they used to."

Liz stopped and turned to see her grandmother trailing behind. "I just want to be alone, Grandma."

Her grandmother paused next to Liz to catch her breath. "Well, tough."

"Stubborn," Liz muttered with an eye roll.

"I'm not the only one," she pointed out.

"If you're here to tell me to come back—"

Ignoring her, Liz's grandmother continued forward, leaving Liz confused until she caught up to her. Together, they strolled down the sidewalk in silence until they reached the nearby park. Her grandmother sat at an empty bench and patted it for Liz to join her.

"You know," her grandmother began, breaking the silence, "your grandpa used to take you to the park all the time when you were little." She paused and looked over at the swings. "You two had a special bond. Maybe because he was the first person you saw." She sighed. "I'm not sure why he never felt comfortable telling the whole story. Maybe it was because he always said he promised to protect you and would do anything for you. Although, to be honest, it always felt to me like a promise he made to someone else." She placed her hand over Liz's, and Liz didn't pull back. "I'm sorry you had to learn the truth this way."

Liz stared at the brown blades of grass around her feet as more tears flowed down her face. "If he didn't tell you the whole truth, then maybe there's something important he's leaving out. What if he knew who my biological parents were?"

Her grandmother gently placed her soft, wrinkled hand on Liz's face and wiped away the tears. "Whatever it was that he kept, I'm sure he had good reason."

"I just wish I had known sooner."

"I know, but what's done is done. You can't think about the what-ifs. You need to think about what you're going to do now."

Liz felt like she was floundering. "Where do I even start?"

"Your grandfather always said, 'Follow your heart. It will guide the way.'"

"I don't even know what my heart is saying at this point."

"Give it time," her grandmother said, pushing from the bench. She held out her hand. "Come on, it's getting late and you can't run forever."

"I'm not running," Liz protested, only to have her grandmother raise a brow, challenging that statement. "I don't even know what to say to them."

"There's nothing you can say. Your parents, your grandpa, and I made a terrible mistake, and there's no going back. We can only move forward, one step at a time."

Liz took her hand and stood. They arrived back at the house to find her father still seated on the couch. He cocked his head and gave her a somber smile.

"Tess is just finishing up in the kitchen," he told Liz's grandmother.

Her grandmother walked into the kitchen and put her arm

around her daughter, who was clearly upset. Liz couldn't bear to watch her mother crying in the other room.

"We weren't sure how long you'd be gone." Her father stood and began to extend his arms but stopped short, pulling them back.

Liz still wasn't ready to talk to them. She turned around and began to clean up the mess she had made with the photo albums.

"I'll go get her, then we'll leave," he said before joining the rest of her family in the other room.

Something fell from inside the first album she grabbed. It was a postcard from the island. She tucked it in her back pocket, along with a picture of her grandfather holding her as he stood next to her grandmother.

A few minutes later, she had placed nearly all the albums back in order. She picked up the last album, and a small bit of cardboard caught her eye. The missing puzzle piece she had been looking for. It had been next to the shelf the whole time. She stood over the puzzle to find the other pieces had been placed in their collective spots. The only missing piece was the one in her hand. With a sigh, she placed the last one in, finishing the puzzle.

Her fingertips grazed across the pieces of the scenic picture of a sunset along the beach.

You go. I'll be with you in here.

She closed her eyes, forcing tears back.

"You ok?" her mother asked, bringing Liz back to the present.

She wasn't sure if she would ever be ok.

Liz pulled a piece of her breadstick apart and swirled it around the cheesy sauce as she stared at the menu. On the drive home, she couldn't get the words out of her head. *You go.* Did her grandfather really expect her to leave without him? *This trip is important.* What could be more important than telling her about her adoption down in Florida than in Ohio?

"Ok, spill it," Nicki said anxiously, pulling Liz from her thoughts. "I know something's up."

Liz had texted Nicki as soon as they arrived home. She had to talk to someone. That is, someone other than family. Her friend might not understand the situation, but she'd told Liz during the funeral that she would always be there for her. Even if it was to just listen.

"What gave you that impression?" Liz asked surreptitiously and took a sip of water. The restaurant crowd was sparse that evening, but she still felt nervous about spilling her guts out in public.

"Oh, I dunno," Nicki replied, waving her fork around. "You keep staring at your menu like you're trying to decide what to eat when we both know you always get the lasagna."

Liz bit off another piece of her breadstick and placed the menu down. Nicki was right; she was stalling. The last thing she wanted to do was cry in her salad.

Nicki peeked down for Liz to see. "I'm here. You can talk to me."

Liz swallowed hard. She would not cry in her salad. "Remember how I told you my grandpa said he kept a secret from me?"

During the funeral, Liz had sat by herself, confiding in Nicki. She told her everything that had happened just before her grandfather's death. They tried guessing what the mysterious secret could be. Most were ridiculous to lighten the mood. She would have traded being adopted for a great-grandfather who was a serial killer or part of a mob.

Nicki was about to eat a piece of her salad when she stopped just inches in front of her mouth. She placed her fork down, focusing her attention on Liz. "Yeah . . ." When Liz couldn't speak, Nicki reached out her hand. "You found out what it is, didn't you?"

Nodding, she answered, "Yes."

"Do I need to be worried there's a hit on you now?" she asked jokingly.

Liz's lips pursed, and she could barely get the words out. "I'm adopted."

Nicki's smile disappeared, and only the soft sounds of jazz music from the restaurant speakers filled the space between them. "Are you sure?" she said after taking a few moments to process the statement.

Liz exhaled. "Yeah."

She proceeded to tell Nicki about the events from the other night. Piecing the photo clues together, telling her mother that her grandfather had kept a secret from her, finding out she was adopted, and the story that confirmed it.

Nicki stabbed the last piece of lettuce from her salad as Liz finished her story. "God, Liz. I'm so sorry they kept that from you. I can't imagine what you must be feeling and right after . . ."

Liz grabbed a breadstick and ate her feelings. She had only managed to shed one tear into her salad; the rest were wiped away with her extra napkin the waiter provided when he came back to take their order. Liz was only mildly embarrassed.

"I'm still trying to wrap my head around everything." Liz paused as the waiter delivered their food. Once he was gone, she continued. "I came across the plane tickets last night."

"Yeah?" Nicki twirled the pasta around her fork. "You still going?"

"I dunno. I went back and forth so many times I barely got any sleep last night." The debate between staying to be there for her family and leaving to get away from them was nearly consuming her. She couldn't stop her grandfather's words from seeping into her mind. He told her to go. He told her this trip was important. Even though he wouldn't be there to tell her the story of how he found her, it would still be a nice getaway from her troubles. Not to mention, she could try to search for some clues about her birth parents.

"I think you should go," Nicki said between bites.

Liz cocked her head and raised her eyebrow. "*You* think I should go? Who are you, and what have you done to my friend?"

Nicki laughed. "I'm serious. I think a vacation would do you good. You've been through the wringer. I would go with you, but I can't change my vacation dates that late." She took a sip of her tea, letting Liz mull over her words.

"What about my parents?" Liz grimaced at the thought of telling them as she took another bite of her dinner.

Nicki shrugged. "You're an adult. They can't very well stop you."

She made a point. Liz took a few more bites as her head spun. They might not be able to stop her, but they could still be upset with her. "Maybe you're right, but I can't very well leave at a time like this." *Or could I?*

"Just promise me one thing," Nicki said.

"Yeah?"

"If you see any cute guys, bring them back with you, ok?"

For the first time since her grandfather's death, Liz laughed.

The rest of the evening passed with some chitchat, including a job opening at the library. After they finished their meals and paid the bill, Liz followed Nicki to her car to say goodbye. Surprising Nicki, Liz wrapped her arms around her in a big hug.

"Thank you," she said before letting her go.

"That's what friends are for. If you need anything, just let me know. Ok?" Nicki offered.

"I know." Liz smiled, turning back toward her car. She wasn't looking forward to having any kind of conversation with her parents.

On the drive home, her stomach was in knots. She hated confrontation. Was she doing the right thing?

Liz entered the kitchen where her mother was drying dishes.

"How was Nicki?" she asked.

Liz hadn't said two words to either of her parents since yesterday except that she was meeting her friend for dinner. Liz could tell her mother didn't approve of it, most likely afraid Liz would tell Nicki everything.

"She's good," Liz said. "She told me there might be a job opening up soon and she'll put in a good word for me."

"That's wonderful news!" Her mother paused for a moment and placed the last plate in the upper cabinet. "You didn't tell her about . . .?"

Liz bit her bottom lip. "She's my best friend. I tell her everything."

"Liz," her mother said with disappointment.

The past few days had exhausted Liz physically and mentally. She wasn't in any mood to be chastised by either of her parents. "Just because you kept it from me for twenty years, doesn't mean I need to do the same to her!" The words erupted from her before she could stop them. *Crap.* This was not how she wanted to start her conversation about the trip.

Her mother's jaw dropped. Liz had never talked back to her parents.

"Is Dad around? I wanted to talk to you guys about something," Liz quickly said before her mother could yell at her.

"I'm here," her father said from behind Liz. She turned to find him standing in the doorway, frowning. "I'd appreciate it if you'd apologize to your mother."

Apologize? Was he serious? His eyes were stern. He was serious.

"Sorry," she muttered, even though she didn't actually mean it. She was only stating the truth.

"What did you need?" he asked.

Liz cautiously sat down at the kitchen table while they stood on the other side of the counter. "Before Grandpa . . ." She couldn't say the word out loud. "We were planning on taking a trip to Anna Maria Island."

"He talked to us about that a few weeks ago," her mother said, still looking hurt from Liz's words.

"I think he was going to tell me about . . . you know . . . when we got there, since he couldn't tell me the first time we tried to plan it." She was stumbling over her words so much, she wasn't sure if she was making any sense. She was an adult for goodness sake. She shouldn't have been so nervous.

Her father leaned over the counter, staring at her curiously. "What's this about, Liz?"

Liz nervously picked at a piece of skin on her finger. "I was thinking about going."

Her mother's forehead creased. "By yourself?"

"Well . . . yeah." However, the thought of going alone did make her anxious. She had always traveled with her family, and even then, it wasn't that far since her mother had a fear of flying.

"I don't think that's a good idea," her father protested.

Maybe he was right, but something deep down inside Liz kept telling her she needed to go. "I think he wanted me to. His last words were—"

"People say a lot of things when they're about to die, Liz. That doesn't mean that's what you should do," her mother said, still sour over her daughter's earlier comment.

Liz's thoughts moved back and forth faster than a Ping-Pong ball being hit from one argument to another. Was her mother right? Had he just been saying that? *No, he said this trip was important.*

Her father, not one to argue, replied, "How about this? We can check the calendar and all go at a later date. I have a bonus paycheck coming up soon, so we can use that money and all go down."

That sounded reasonable enough, but it didn't sit well with Liz. This trip had already been pushed back because of her. This had been something that she and her grandfather were going to do together. It was supposed to be special. Going with her family wouldn't feel right. Besides, she already had a plane ticket and a house lined up, but she wasn't about to divulge that information.

It's important, her grandfather's voice repeated in her mind. No, she needed to go alone.

"I need to do this," Liz said, practically pleading.

"Do you think that it's necessary to go right now?" her father questioned.

Liz stood up. "Grandpa wanted me to go. We had this whole plan. *He* had a whole plan."

"Grandpa isn't here," her mother said as tears formed.

"You don't think I know that? I watched him collapse. I watched him die!" The images flashed in her mind again. "I have to do this. I could even find out who my real parents are." The words spilled out so fast that there wasn't enough time to take them back. Of course her adoptive parents were her real parents, but that wasn't what she meant. She winced when she immediately saw the hurt in her mother's eyes. This conversation was getting worse by the minute, and her emotions weren't helping. Maybe they were right and she was being rash.

"I know you're an adult, but you still live under our roof, so I'm telling you to wait," her mother said sternly. "We don't need you selfishly running off to Florida so you can have a vacation while your grandma is here grieving like the rest of us. We've already been through enough. I don't need to worry about you traveling alone, too."

Liz clenched her fists at her sides and shook her head in disappointment. They didn't understand. No one did. Her whole life, she had felt like something was amiss, and now she knew why. What mattered was that she had a mother and father somewhere, loving or not. She still wanted to find out who they were and why they'd given her up.

"I'm sorry he didn't get to tell you the way he wanted to and that you found out about your adoption so late," her father said, placing his hand on her shoulder. "We're not saying you can never go. Just push it back."

Liz could go in circles with them all day, but it wouldn't get her anywhere. Instead, she left the kitchen with her father's voice calling out, "We'll go soon, I promise."

. . .

Liz rolled over in her bed and looked at the clock. It was nearly three thirty, and it felt like she hadn't slept at all. Instead of the much-needed sleep she needed, she argued with herself to the point that she had angrily cried into her pillow. She was surprised she hadn't ripped it in two. Maybe Nicki was right. Maybe Liz did need to get away and decompress.

She turned on her lamp and opened her nightstand drawer, pulling out the photograph she had found earlier. *You're more special than you know,* she repeated the words her grandfather used to say. What did he mean by that? *You go.*

I wish you were still here. She closed her eyes and clutched the photo to her chest.

She glanced at the airline tickets, then at the photo again. *Am I crazy? If I do this, there's no going back. Flying alone. I can do this . . .* She took a deep breath. *Yeah, I can do this,* she tried convincing herself.

Her heart sank thinking about her parents. She knew they'd be not only upset but disappointed in her. She couldn't leave without telling them, but waking them up at the crack of dawn wouldn't pan out well. She could see them arguing with her or guilting her to stay home. She didn't want to text them and change her mind on the way there either. She couldn't let them respond back right away. If she was going to do this, she couldn't second-guess herself any longer.

Liz pulled out a piece of scrap paper from a nearby notebook. Writing a note would give her plenty of time to board the plane without a second thought, but it would also let them know what she was doing.

She choked back her tears as she tried to write. After several pieces of crumpled-up paper, she finally finished.

Dear Mom and Dad,

I'm sure by the time you read this, I'll be well on my way to Florida. I've tried to explain how important this is to me. You have to understand that my life has been turned upside down in a matter of days. I know this is the worst time to leave, but I can't wait months to go. This is what Grandpa wanted.

I have faith that I'll find something about my biological parents. Even if I don't, it's something I just need to do by myself. I need to figure out who I am and where I belong.

I'll text you when I arrive. I will always be your daughter, but I'm not your little girl anymore. I'm sorry.

Love,

Liz

She placed it on her nightstand. If she wanted to make her flight, she would have to leave by six. That gave her less than two hours to get ready and pack. She opened up her closet, pulled out her suitcase, and got to work. Half a drawer of summer clothes and a few baggies of travel items later, she zipped it closed. She threw on a T-shirt and jean shorts, then slipped on her shoes.

Leaning over the dresser, she looked at her reflection. *You can do this. Just grab your suitcase and purse and sneak out.* She placed her shaky hand on the handle of her suitcase. What would they think? They were going to be so mad at her. Liz pushed the negative thoughts out of her head. *You're almost twenty-one. You can do this!*

Her parents weren't early risers on the weekends, but with their bedroom being so close, she didn't want to chance waking them up. Then she'd never make her flight.

She felt like a teenager all over again, sneaking out her bedroom window; not that she ever did that sort of thing growing up.

Taking one last look around her bedroom, she slipped outside and closed the window behind her. She hastened to her car in the driveway turnaround and threw the suitcase in the back seat. Turning the keys, she started the engine, only for it to sputter.

"No, no! Come on, start!" she shouted at her car. She kept trying until eventually the battery gave out. "Shit!"

She slammed her hands across the steering wheel. What was she going to do now? Pulling out her phone, she knew exactly who to call. The line on the other end rang several times.

"Pick up. Pick up," she begged.

"Ugh. Hello?" Nicki answered between yawns.

"Hey . . . uh . . ."

"Liz? The sun isn't even up. What time is it?" Nicki paused and then groaned. "It's like six in the morning."

"I know. I'm really sorry," Liz apologized, "but you said if I ever needed anything—"

"Is everything ok?" Nicki asked, sounding concerned.

Liz gulped back tears. She hated asking for help. "My car, it . . ."

Nicki's voice suddenly became clearer. "Are you ok? Where are you?"

"I'm ok. I'm at home."

"You're at home? Where are you going, and why don't you have your dad help you?" Nicki asked.

"I can't. I-I—" Liz began to cry. "I'm sorry. I should have never bothered you."

"I'll be there in like ten minutes." Nicki said before abruptly hanging up.

Just like clockwork, Nicki was there in ten minutes. Liz rushed out from behind one of the tall bushes next to the garage, causing Nicki to shriek.

"Well, I'm awake now. What the hell are you doing?" Nicki called out of the open driver's-side window.

"Shhhh!"

Nicki looked on with wide eyes as Liz placed her suitcase in the back seat before sitting in the front. "So, uh, you have a suit-case," she stated the obvious. "Should I ask where I'm taking you?"

Liz buckled her seat belt. "Um, don't hate me but the Cleveland airport."

CHAPTER 9
Exposed

"Rise and shine!" a voice greeted Wyatt.

"Ugh, just a little longer, Varian," Wyatt complained as he rolled over.

"Varian?"

Wyatt slowly opened his eyes, exposing him to the bright morning sun cascading through the openings between his blinds. He breathed a sigh of relief when he realized he wasn't in Aquana.

Liam stood in the doorway, drinking from a mug. "Who's Varian?"

A pang of sadness went through Wyatt at the mention of his sibling. Wyatt's voice was husky and irregular from just waking up when he replied, "My brother. He used to wake me up earlier than I wanted. Guess I forgot where I was for a minute."

Liam took a sip of his drink and tossed a light blue shirt to Wyatt. "Here, put this on with one of the shorts you got yesterday and get ready."

"What's this?" Wyatt inspected it. The Cove was written on the front right breast, and a mermaid logo was on the back.

"Your work shirt. You have to be at The Cove in half an hour. So get ready and have some breakfast. I left some pancakes on the counter." Liam disappeared into the hallway, then called out, "I'll see you there. It's my turn to open the restaurant."

Wyatt sat up in his bed and looked around. It almost felt surreal breathing in the fresh air and smelling the sweet aroma of pancakes and maple syrup. No one came into his room to get him ready for the day. He was truly on his own. How hard could this be?

He pulled open a drawer and dug through the new clothes. After his afternoon with Jessica, Liam had insisted they go out to a nearby store to buy some clothing. Wyatt almost felt like nothing had changed. Again, someone was taking care of him. That ended today. He had a job now. He would pay Liam back and purchase his own items with his own money.

His chest puffed out with pride. *Poseidon, I'm actually going to work. If Sarah could see me now,* he mused as he got ready for the day.

He hurriedly ate breakfast before rushing out the door, excited to start his first day. As he approached the restaurant, Liam was starting to set up the umbrellas in the outdoor patio area.

"Let me show you how to clock in, then you can help me with the rest," Liam said, leading him into the kitchen area. He grabbed a piece of paper with Wyatt's name printed at the top and showed him how to, as Liam put it, punch in his time. Wyatt wasn't sure why it was called that considering he didn't use his fist.

Afterward, they returned back to the patio. Wyatt was a fast learner and opened the rest of the umbrellas with little difficulty. Maybe secretly being a land-dweller wouldn't be so hard after all.

Other workers began filing in, smiling or nodding at Wyatt as they entered. Liam quickly introduced each of them to Wyatt. Being around this many land-dwellers brought along a twinge of nervousness. Any one of them could expose him if he changed right this second. This wasn't his idea of keeping a low profile, but he'd rather be on land than in the water. Who knew how many soldiers his father had sent out to search for him by now.

Wyatt mimicked Liam's actions of pulling the chairs from the tops of tables and arranging them around each one.

"I'm going to start you off easy," Liam said, continuing with the chairs. "You'll be bussing tables and doing some janitorial work."

"Janitorial?" Wyatt pronounced slowly.

"Cleaning the shitters," Liam put it bluntly, even though Wyatt still didn't completely understand him. That was, until Liam pointed toward where the bathrooms were.

"Hey, Liam," Wyatt said as he helped move the last chair in place. "I was wondering what other restaurants are on the island."

"Oh jeez, there's a lot. Why?"

"My mom used to work at one on the beach, and I wanted to see it."

"Hmmm, there's a handful along the beach." Liam gestured for Wyatt to follow him. "Can you find out the name?"

"I can't." He sighed. "She . . . she passed away when I was really young."

Liam stopped in his place, giving Wyatt a sad look. "Oh, man, I'm so sorry."

"Thanks. I appreciate it. The truth is, I wasn't that old, so I don't remember her," he said sadly. "I found her journal and she wrote about her job, but she failed to mention the exact name or location."

"Maybe you could talk to Mrs. Charleston. She owns The Cove. She's also part of the Rotary and has all the restaurant owners' names and phone numbers in an address book."

Wyatt's eyebrows rose in excitement. "That would be wonderful. Where is she?"

"She lives here in the apartment upstairs. Unfortunately, she's out of town. I'll let her know you want to talk as soon as she gets back," Liam replied.

Wyatt's heart grew heavy. He didn't have the luxury of waiting. He needed that necklace now. The longer he remained on land without it, the more likely he would be found out. Not to mention, he couldn't possibly shower again. Changing was too painful. He had to find that book. It might be the only way to pinpoint where D was.

He was really grasping at reeds here. What if D wasn't even the owner anymore? What if she was already gone, like his mom? All questions would have to wait for the time being as he tried to fit into this new life.

Liam showed Wyatt the ins and outs of bussing. It consisted of clearing the table and prepping it for the next customer. It seemed easy enough when Liam showed him, but when it came time to do his job, he struggled. Multiple times, he dropped the silverware. At one point, he spilled water across the table and jumped back like a fish about to be eaten by a great white, causing customers to stare at him. The water was far enough away, but it was too close for comfort.

He questioned numerous times if he was doing the right thing. Right about now, he'd probably be announcing his engagement to Princess Carmea and being showered with praise. Instead he was slopping food off tables. He had to keep reminding himself that his mother had done the same thing. This was what it was like to live on land.

When he had no tables to clear, he checked the bathrooms, as Liam instructed, to see if anything needed to be restocked or cleaned. The day was a whirlwind of learning how to be *normal* with only a short break for lunch. In no time, the sky went from a bright blue to turning picturesque with colorful hues of red, orange, and pink. When Wyatt asked a coworker what time it was, she revealed it was five minutes to eight. He thanked her and was then startled when he felt a firm hand slap him on the back.

"You did good for your first day!" Liam exclaimed.

Wyatt frowned. "I'm not sure about that."

"Don't be so hard on yourself. You only broke one glass," Liam said, causing Wyatt to grimace. "I broke a glass or two when

I first started out. It takes a few days to get the hang of things. We're open until ten today, but you've been busting ass and I know you have to get out of here for your hot date. Here's twenty bucks for tonight." Liam shoved a folded-up bill into Wyatt's hand. "You can pay me back later."

Wyatt thanked him and ran off to the beach. Jessica was sitting with her back facing him, staring out at the waves that washed up a few yards from her feet. Her hair was in a loose bun, and a few strands floated in the wind. An off-the-shoulder fire-red one-piece swimsuit adorned her toned body, more for looks than for actual swimming.

As Wyatt approached her, she turned her head and lowered her sunglasses down on her nose just enough to show her smokey eyeshadow. "Hey there," she said, patting the spot on the sand next to her.

Wyatt sat down and awkwardly asked, "Beautiful evening, isn't it?"

"I've always loved this spot. The waves crashing against the shore, the sunset, and the smell of the salt in the air makes almost every evening here nearly perfect." Jessica fell silent as she gazed at the great expanse of sea in front of her.

Wyatt sat staring for a few moments, not at the water but at the vision of beauty sitting next to him. He finally broke the silence and asked Jessica, "What would make it perfect?" He felt an overwhelming desire to softly kiss her and shifted closer.

Before his lips could brush the nape of her neck, Jessica quickly stood. "Ice cream!"

Puzzled, Wyatt glanced up at her. "Why would you scream?"

Jessica giggled. "Not *I scream*, silly. Ice cream," she said, pulling Wyatt to his feet.

"Oh, right. Ice . . . cream," Wyatt slowly repeated back to her. "How would that make this evening perfect?"

"Follow me, I'll show you." She threw on a pair of shorts and guided him away from the shore toward the street. She hurriedly led him across, nearly causing an accident in the process, right to the front door of a place called Island Scoops.

Being a mer, Wyatt's body was used to acclimating to different temperatures in the water. However, being on land was a completely new experience. When he walked into the parlor, the crisp air felt foreign but nice against his warm skin, sending a slight shiver down his back. He took in the sight of a dozen or so containers behind a large piece of glass. A wondrous bouquet of smells filled his senses. If cinnamon rolls were heaven, this would be a close second.

"What are all these?"

Jessica raised her eyebrow curiously at him. "Don't you have any ice cream shops in Ohio?"

"Huh?" Wyatt responded distractedly, staring at the selections.

"Ohio? Ice cream shops?" Jessica asked again as she sidled up next to him.

Wyatt looked back at her sheepishly. "Yes, of course. It's just my parents . . . they, uh, never let me have any." He hoped that was convincing enough. *Poseidon, I need to be more careful. I can't believe I almost gave myself away.*

"Aw, you poor thing. That's terrible. Well, let me help you pop your ice cream cherry." She bit her bottom lip, twisting her pendant between her fingers.

Wyatt's head started to swim as he clutched onto Jessica. "Whatever you say, my love," he said in a haze.

She turned to the clerk. "One scoop of cookies and cream and one scoop of the peach passion in hand-dipped waffle cones," Jessica said, placing their orders.

When the clerk finished their order, he handed Wyatt the cones. "That'll be eight dollars."

"Let me help you since your hands are full," she said with a wink. Reaching into the back left pocket of Wyatt's shorts, she pulled out the twenty-dollar bill and tossed it on the counter. "Keep the change."

She grabbed her cone from Wyatt and pulled him outside to walk down the street. Wyatt, still in a slight fog, wasn't exactly sure what to do with his ice cream that had already started to melt down the cone. He glanced at how Jessica was eating it. He cautiously licked at the frozen concoction, savoring the flavor. It was delicious! He took a huge bite, letting the cold substance slide down his throat. As he swallowed the delectable dessert, his head began to ache.

He grimaced in pain, causing Jessica to ask if he was ok. Wyatt nodded. "Yeah, I've never had a headache quite like this," he stated, massaging his left temple.

Jessica looked over, wide-eyed, at the huge chunk that was already gone from his ice cream. "It's probably brain freeze from eating too fast."

Wyatt laughed. "That's ridiculous. How could this possibly freeze my brain?"

Jessica stopped in her tracks and stared at him for a moment, making him wonder if he had said something wrong again. Tilting her head back, she laughed loudly. "That is hysterical! You're full of jokes, aren't you?"

Wyatt gave her a weary smile and shrugged. When he went to take another bite of ice cream, Jessica stopped him.

"Here, let me show you how to properly eat ice cream." Her lips curled. "You have to lick it," she said, placing her hand around his that held the cone, "like this." She rolled her tongue along the edge of the cone to get the melty parts of the ice cream. Her eyes darted to what had melted along his fingers. Taking the cone from him, she pulled his hand to her mouth and sucked on one finger at a time.

The feeling of her lips wrapped around his fingers left his body trembling. He had never experienced anything like that in his life. He wanted to feel them against his lips. Her tongue dancing around and darting inside his mouth. He shook the thoughts from his head. Poseidon, she was driving him crazy.

Once she had stunned him into silence and licked his fingers clean, she handed his cone back to him with a satisfied look on her face. "Shall we?" she asked, walking away from him.

Wyatt obliged and followed her like a pilot fish to a shark.

"So tell me more about yourself."

I grew up in the Kingdom of Aquana. You never heard of it? That's because it's an underwater kingdom just east of here. Oh, and I'm also a merman. The words were on the tip of his tongue. Alarms quickly went off in his brain, shutting the thoughts down. Instead, he said, "There's not a lot to tell. I'm the youngest of three."

Jessica drew closer, sending his head into a fog.

"And my father's a ki—" Wyatt blinked and stepped back. He glanced around. His heart tripled in speed when he realized she had led him straight to the edge of a pier. When did this happen? How had he not realized he was so close to the water? He was letting his guard down too easily around her.

Jessica sat at the edge of the pier and dipped her feet into the water. "You were saying?"

Wyatt tried to remain calm, but he could hardly concentrate on the sound of the soft waves moving about. "What?"

"You were saying that your dad's a . . .?"

"Oh." He placed his trembling hands in his pocket. "He's a kitchen worker." He internally winced. He hated lying to her.

She frowned. "Kitchen worker? Like a cook?"

He looked away from her. "Yup. He loves cooking."

Jessica opened her mouth, but before she could say anything, Wyatt interrupted her. "You said something about a marina when we first met. What's that all about?"

"I volunteer at the county marine rescue. I'm one of a half dozen boat captains that work with their rescue crews in alleviating the human condition on sea life." It was as if she had said that line a hundred times. She looked up at Wyatt. "Why don't you sit next to me?"

Wyatt hesitated. "Um, I'd rather stand, if that's ok."

Jessica pursed her lips in a sexy pout and ran her finger across her necklace and down the seam of her bathing suit. "You've been standing all day at work. Your feet must be tired. Come on, sit."

Feeling the need to please her, Wyatt sat behind Jessica, tucking his legs underneath him. He wrapped his arms around her waist and pulled her gently back against his chest. Her body stiffened for a moment before she leaned into him.

"So what do you do when helping these rescue crews?" he asked. "Have you ever seen anything cool, like whales or dolphins?" Seeing marine life was an everyday occurrence for him, but he figured a land-dweller would find them fascinating.

Jessica casually replied, "Well, obviously I drive the boat, but I also monitor the sonar and depth finder. Occasionally, I help with any endangered marine life they may encounter. I got to swim with a manatee once." She peered over her shoulder, and her face was inches from his. "Did you know that sailors of the past mistook manatees for mermaids? That's where most of the legends started."

Wyatt scoffed. "That's ridiculous. Mermaids are much more beautiful," he offhandedly remarked before realizing he had just stuck his foot in his mouth and quickly correcting himself. "At least they are in the stories I've read."

"What about me?" Jessica ran her hand along the back of his neck. "Am I more beautiful than a mermaid?"

"Uh-huh." Wyatt quivered as he struggled to find any kind of words.

"Mmmm. I just love the feeling of the water tickling my toes." She swayed her legs about, swishing it around her feet. "Why don't you put your feet in?"

Wyatt shook off the seductive haze. "Oh, no, that's ok. I'm good here."

Jessica leaned her head back again and kissed his neck, then whispered, "But the water feels so good against your skin."

Wyatt's right leg slipped out from beneath him, moving toward the water. *What are you doing?* His subconscious kicked in. *You'll change!* His fear of revealing himself cleared his head in an instant.

"I can't!" He quickly jumped up to his feet, leaving Jessica to fall back on her elbows. "I'm sorry. Look, it's getting late, and I'm pretty exhausted from my first day at the restaurant."

Jessica stared up at the moon. "Yeah, it has been a long day."

Wyatt helped her up but kept his distance. "I truly am sorry. Can I at least walk you home?"

Jessica turned her gaze back to Wyatt. "I suppose," she replied, putting her hand in his. In no time at all, they were at Jessica's doorstep. "I'd invite you in, but I've got an early day again tomorrow."

Wyatt leaned in. Even in the merworld, an evening such as this typically ended with a kiss.

She pressed a finger to his lips yet again. "Soon, I swear," she said and kissed him on the cheek.

Wyatt's chest tightened, and his face felt hot. He took her hand in his and brought it to his lips. "Until next time. May the sea forever be on your side."

"I've never met anyone quite like you." Jessica smiled before opening the door to her apartment.

Wyatt's euphoria lasted a good while until he found himself in front of The Cove. After what had happened on the pier, he couldn't waste any more time. He needed to find D, and the only way to do so was to look for that list of restaurant owners in Mrs. Charleston's apartment. With her being gone, this was his only opportunity to do so. Unfortunately, with the restaurant being locked, that would either involve breaking and entering or taking advantage of his newfound friend. The latter seemed to be the obvious choice. He was thankful that Liam had left the door unlocked and was asleep, letting Wyatt take the keys without notice.

Every key looked the same. He clumsily tried each one, with varying degrees of success. He thought he had found the right one when the third key slid in with ease but then didn't turn. He was about to give up when the last key went in, turned, and unlocked the door to The Cove.

Compared to its liveliness earlier in the day, the restaurant was very different. The darkness added an eerie element to the place. The chairs were flipped back on top of the tables. Napkins were neatly folded in preparation for the next day. Bottles were stacked along the back wall of the bar, ready to be poured for happy hour. Everything was quiet except the cacophonous beating of his heart.

Wyatt climbed the stairs leading up to the owner's apartment. A dim glow emanating from the landing of a nightlight threw just enough light to see each step. He quietly made his way up the stairs until he came upon two closed doors. The first door he tried was unlocked, but it was a storage closet. He tried the second door, but it was locked. None of the keys fit. His only option would be to break in. Using his merman strength, he threw his shoulder into the door. The latch broke free from its mooring with a loud snap.

Breaking into an empty apartment didn't sit well with Wyatt. He closed the door behind him as best he could and crept across the wooden floor that creaked ever so slightly. He scoured the apartment for the address book Liam had mentioned, but he wasn't even sure what he was looking for. He turned a lamp on in the living room, then checked the drawers of each end table. Coming up with nothing, he turned the lamp back off and continued his thorough search of every drawer and cabinet he could find with no success.

In the kitchen, next to a pitcher of water, a small, thin book rested on the table. He opened it to find a list of names and numbers. This had to be it.

As he read through the list of names he heard several sounds. The ticking of a wall-mounted clock, the humming of the refrigerator, and something else. It was such a peculiar sound that it made the hair on the back of his neck stand up. He stood still for a moment, listening. In, out. In, out. It sounded like an echo of his breathing.

Someone was there.

His eyes followed the sound to a darkened corner where he caught a glint of a set of eyes from a light outside the kitchen window. Without warning, a figure jumped out from the dark and screamed. They held something in their hands and began thrashing it about, trying to hit Wyatt. He fell against the table, knocking over the glass pitcher. It crashed to the floor and spilled the contents onto his legs. Panic flooded him. He had nowhere to run.

His assailant swung the object at his head, but Wyatt caught it before it struck. He wrenched it from his attacker's hands and threw it to the ground. He needed to get out of there, anywhere, as long as the person couldn't see him transform. He ran toward the busted door, but the individual appeared in front of him, blocking his exit. He turned quickly on the rug, nearly slipping, and ran for another room. His legs burned as he mustered up the strength to stay on his feet.

He launched himself into the first open door he saw and landed on the floor of the bathroom with a thud. The tiles were cool against his forearms as he crawled, clearing the door. He kicked it shut just as the person was about to enter.

Kicking off his sandals, he began to undress, but his scaled legs were already fusing together. The screaming inside his head blocked out the pounding on the door. He held his unchanged feet against the door as long as possible so the land-dweller couldn't get in, but it was no use. His feet transformed into the all-too-familiar blue fluke that fell to the ground. The door opened but was blocked by Wyatt's tail.

This is it. Father was right, he thought.

The light flicked on, blinding Wyatt for a moment.

"I have you blocked. Don't do anything stupid!" a woman's shaky voice cried out. A long piece of wood appeared through the door opening. "When you came into the restaurant, you tripped the silent alarm. The cops are on their way."

"Please, I'm not going to hurt you." Wyatt sat up, lifting the tail from the door. "I don't want any trouble."

"What do you mean, you don't want any trouble? You're the one that broke into my—" She poked her head through the partially open door and gasped. Her weapon—a baseball bat that Wyatt had recognized from one of his books—fell to the floor.

Ashamed of his natural form, Wyatt looked away and curled into a ball. His eyes shut tightly as he waited for her to scream at what she saw. When no sound escaped her, he opened his eyes. Standing in front of him was a woman with tanned, weathered skin. He could tell by the few streaks of silver in her long, jet-black hair that she was older, maybe mid-fifties. Her dark brown eyes scanned him up and down. Suddenly she looked as scared as he felt.

She instinctively picked up the bat, holding it in a defensive stance, and took a step back. "Please, I-I don't know where she is!" she stammered, seemingly not bothered by the fact that a half-man, half-fish was sprawled across her bathroom floor.

"What?" Wyatt asked in confusion.

"She warned me if she were ever found out that soldiers might come for me," she said, her voice quivering. "I never told a soul, I swear! I haven't seen her in ages." Her hands trembled, causing the bat to shake.

Wyatt stared at her, trying to process what she was saying. "What are you talking about?"

"Isn't that why you're here? To find her?" she asked hesitantly.

"Who are you talking about?" he questioned.

"Sarina," she said firmly.

Wyatt's mouth gaped in shock at the realization. Before he could speak, there was a knock on the door.

"Ma'am, are you ok? We're responding to the silent alarm from the restaurant," a male voice called from the hallway.

The woman signaled for Wyatt to be quiet and quickly closed

the bathroom door. The only thing he could hear were muffled voices.

Wyatt's heart raced as he searched for a towel to dry off. The only one was up on a rack behind him. When he tried to pull himself toward the rack to grab it, the door swung open and hit his tail. He groaned.

"Sorry," the woman apologized.

Wyatt turned, waiting for a hoard of land-dwellers to burst through and take him to the nearest aquarium or science lab.

"It's ok, they're gone," she assured him. She stepped over him and grabbed the towel from the rack. She knelt and handed it to him. "You know that name, don't you?"

Wyatt nodded as he breathed heavily, quickly drying his tail off haphazardly. "Are you . . . D?"

The fear she had in her eyes dissipated and was replaced with a look of curiosity. "How do you know that?"

CHAPTER 10

An Old Friend

Wyatt's heart pounded out of his chest as he gingerly towel-dried his tail, avoiding the prying eyes of D. He had waited for this moment since surfacing. He had even practiced what he would say when he found his mother's friend. Now it seemed nearly impossible to get any words out.

"I'm her son, Wyatt," he finally confessed. "Sarina was my mother."

D stared at him for a few moments in silence. She brought her hands to her mouth and blinked back the tears forming in the corners of her eyes. "Oh my god."

She knelt and threw her arms around his neck in a warm embrace. Wyatt awkwardly wrapped his arms around this land-dweller he didn't even know.

She sniffled. "Wyatt."

Hearing his name come out of her mouth felt comforting and familiar, as if his mother was right there with him. His shoulders slumped, relaxing in her embrace. At that moment, he was overwhelmed with a flood of emotions. Before he had time to explore them, his brain sent out a warning, telling him his tail was dry. He pulled away from D. His jaw clenched, and he readied himself for what was soon to come.

Wiping away a few tears, D looked at Wyatt with concern as his chest rose and fell in anticipation. "Your tail . . . I have something that might help the pain." She rose quickly and maneuvered around Wyatt's tail, which took up nearly the entire bathroom floor. "Before your mother had assistance to transform, we concocted a cream when she would come on land. It's not the greatest, but it will help ease your pain." She opened the cabinet above the sink and searched for it. "Aha, here it is!" She held up a small glass jar. She unscrewed the lid and held it out to him. "Rub it on your tail. Hopefully, it still works."

Wyatt placed the tips of his fingers into the pale green cream. It smelled like a mixture of kelp, fish, and some kind of herb that was most likely from the surface world. He massaged it into his scales from his hips to his fluke. He handed the jar back to D and placed the towel over his tail with the familiarity of transformation beginning. However, instead of the horrific burning that came with his tail separating, it was more manageable. He didn't grit his teeth or close his eyes from the pain. He looked down in awe as the scales melted into flesh and his tail turned into legs before his eyes.

"I couldn't bear to watch Sarina go through that pain every time she came on land," D said, returning the jar to the cabinet, "so we experimented with herbs from her world and mine. It sufficed until she found a better way to change."

Wyatt looked up at the woman sitting on the edge of the tub. The corners of her eyes crinkled as she gave a gentle smile.

"Thank you," he said, wrapping the towel around his waist as he carefully stood up. He frowned at the tattered pieces of his once-intact jeans scattered on the floor.

"I might have something that will fit you." She gathered the tattered jeans from the floor before opening the bathroom door fully.

Wyatt grabbed his sandals and followed her out into the hallway to a spare bedroom. A gray distressed dresser sat next to the window. She pulled the bottom drawer open.

"These"—she lifted a pair of khaki board shorts and a navy-blue button-up shirt—"belonged to your father." She gently placed them in his arms, and Wyatt stared wide-eyed at the pile of clothes. "I kept these in case they ever came back. Why don't I leave you to change? I'm going to grab some cinnamon rolls from downstairs to warm up. I have a feeling we both have a lot of questions," D said before closing the door behind her.

Wyatt looked down at the fabric. He couldn't believe these were the same clothes his father had once donned. On land. With legs. He put the shorts on and changed out of his work shirt. His thumb rubbed over the small navy-blue discs that matched the shirt that was once buttoned by his father. Every time he was told how awful land-dwellers were, his father had been hiding this secret. How much had he really enjoyed coming here with Wyatt's mom? What had made him so bitter?

He turned to see his reflection in the vanity mirror. He combed his fingers through his greasy, disheveled hair. His face desperately needed to be shaved, as his five-o'clock shadow had grown out during the course of the day. He turned his head at the sound of metal clanging in the other room.

In the kitchen, D was bent down, placing a baking sheet with two large cinnamon rolls into the oven. Shards of broken glass, small pools of water, and toppled chairs lay in front of him.

"I'm sorry I broke your glass water holder," he apologized, looking at the mess in front of him.

She turned and gave him a once-over with a slight chuckle. Avoiding the glass, she cautiously walked over to him. "I would break that a million times just to meet Sarina's son." She grabbed at his shirt and played with the buttons. "Your father did the same thing the first time he put this very same shirt on." She smiled and fixed the placement of the buttons into their proper holes. Placing her palms on his chest, she straightened his shirt out and stared at his face, taking in all of his features. "There. You look so much like your father. But you definitely have your mother's eyes."

Her words sent a warmth through Wyatt. He had always

known he had similar features to his father, but to hear he had his mother's eyes meant a lot.

"Why don't you help me clean up? I'll grab a broom and dustpan. You can put the chairs back." She disappeared around the corner and returned with the items. "I want to apologize," she began, grabbing a trash can.

"Why?" Wyatt asked, setting a chair upright.

"I feel awful that I nearly knocked you out with a baseball bat," she answered, sweeping the glass.

"Well, I did break into your home. I can't very well blame you for defending yourself."

While Wyatt straightened up the rest of the kitchen, D threw a few towels onto the floor to soak up the remaining water.

"Make yourself comfortable," she said. "I'll put the kettle on. We have a lot to talk about."

Wyatt sat down on the cushioned seat, crossing his arms onto the wooden kitchen table. So many questions raced through his head. He wasn't sure where to start. How did she meet his mother? When was the last time she saw her? How often did his father come on land?

Father . . . His mind drifted to what his father must think of him. Did he suspect that Wyatt had fled to the surface world?

Before Wyatt could ask any questions, D beat him to the punch. "Why did you come here?" she wondered, bringing his attention back to the present. She filled the teakettle with water before placing it on the stove and turning the burner on.

Wyatt fumbled with the cloth placemat. He wasn't exactly sure how to tell her that his mother had died. "I was actually trying to find you. My mom wrote about you in her journal. She only referred to you by D and that you owned a restaurant on the island. Liam said the owner had a book of names and addresses of local businesses. I had hoped I could find this D through you. I guess I didn't have to look far." He shyly gazed up and smiled.

"You're the new hire Liam was telling me about!" she said

with realization as she sat across from Wyatt. "He didn't tell you my name was Denise?"

"He just referred to you as Mrs. Charleston."

"I don't know how many times I've told him to call me Denise," she said with a slight chuckle. "Liam told me about a young man who ran off without paying and seemed to be having some problems. I told him about my experience more or less with your mother. She showed up at my restaurant completely disheveled, clothes that didn't fit, no shoes, and no money. I found it strange she didn't know the simplest thing about the human world, like how to eat with utensils. She could hardly read or write until I taught her."

Wyatt smiled to himself. If it wasn't for Denise, his mother never would have written about her journey to the surface, and in turn, he never would have came to the island.

"At first, I thought she was homeless," she continued. "I guess I was partially right. She didn't exactly have a home at the time. I took a chance on her, and she eventually gave me one as well. She confided in me about everything, and I did the same. She was my best friend." She stared off for a moment until the whistle of the teakettle interrupted her memories of long ago.

"I guess I should thank you for telling Liam to help me. I don't know what I would have done if he hadn't."

"Does he know about . . . ?" She glanced at his legs.

"No. I've been careful."

Denise poured a cup of tea for herself. "Your mother and I would spend many nights talking, snacking on cinnamon rolls, and drinking tea. This kind of feels like old times." She paused in thought again. "Would you like a cup?"

"I've never had tea before, but if my mom liked it, then I'd love some." It felt weird but comforting to talk freely about his mother and to know someone on the surface that knew all the secrets of the merworld.

Denise hesitated with her next words. "When you first told me who you were, you said that she . . . was your mother."

She poured the steaming water into his cup. She didn't have to say anything else, and Wyatt didn't have to answer as they communicated with silence. She quietly brought the two cups over to the table and sat down.

"I knew something happened when she never came back, but I just didn't want to believe it. When? How?" She shook her head as tears threatened to form. "I—I'm sorry. I don't want to bring up something that might be too painful to talk about. You don't even know me." She pulled the string of her tea bag up and down in the water.

"It's fine. I'm ok. I mean, as ok as I can be," Wyatt stumbled over his words. "She passed away when I was about two years old. I don't know much, just that it was because of a fisherman. He captured my sister, Sarah, and my mom risked her life to save her."

"Oh god," she muttered.

He gave her a minute to process the information. She reached out and took his hand, squeezing it tightly.

"I was just a baby so I don't really remember her." He sighed, staring into the brown-tinted water. "I don't even know what she looked like."

With a quick swipe of her eyes, Denise stood and wagged an index finger in excitement. She disappeared into the hallway, leaving Wyatt in confusion.

Returning to the table a moment later, D placed a small box on the table. "This box contains all of our memories together."

She opened the lid, revealing his mother's past. She gave a knowing smile as she watched Wyatt dig through the box. The first piece of paper he pulled out was small with typed writing on it. "*Splash*?"

"That's a ticket stub from an old movie," Denise explained. "It was one of the first things your mother experienced on land. Funnily enough, it's about a mermaid. She found it comical to watch what humans thought of mers. She kept laughing at different parts and commenting that mermaids didn't look like that or that certain things in the movie would never happen. That *probably* should have been my first clue that she wasn't from around here."

She spooned the tea bags out and stirred two spoonfuls of sugar into each mug. Wyatt wrapped his hand around the mug, startled to feel how hot it was. If rushing to eat something extremely cold gave you brain freeze, he didn't want to know what the opposite did.

He carefully took a small sip, savoring the flavor. "Mmm, not bad!"

Placing the ticket outside the box, he sifted through the papers. He pulled out each of the brochures and napkins, and Denise explained their visits to different destinations throughout the island. While he studied each item, she would ask questions about his life.

"You said you have a sister named Sarah. Do you have any other siblings?" she asked.

"An older brother, Varian. I'm the youngest."

"Varian, Sarah, and . . . Wyatt," she repeated their names slowly. "You know, she named you after my husband."

"Really?" Wyatt asked, picking up another brochure, this time to some museum owned by a couple of brothers named Ringling.

"He passed shortly before I met your mother. I always said that he guided her toward me." She reached across the table and gripped his hand. "I think she did the same for you."

"I think so, too." He paused and pulled out another memory from the box. "Poseidon!"

"That's called a photograph. It's—"

"I know what they are." Denise looked at Wyatt in confusion. "I've read a lot of books salvaged and saved from shipwrecks." He shrugged with an impish grin.

She laughed. "You're Sarina's son all right."

He stared at the picture. The color had faded a bit over the years, but there was no mistaking the two women in the photo. Denise, who looked much younger, stood on the beach. The other young woman next to her had light brown wavy hair that swept just past her shoulders. Her lightly tanned arms wrapped around Denise in a friendly embrace as the sun was setting behind them.

"This is my mom!" he cried out with joy, looking back up at Denise.

Denise nodded with a smile. "Seems so long ago. We were just kids. Probably around your age. You remind me of her. Even the color in your tail."

"What color was hers?"

"Like a sky blue, but it had gold along the sides. It was beautiful!" She paused for a moment before the oven timer beeped to let them know the cinnamon rolls were ready. Leaving the table, she took the rolls out and placed them on two plates. "You know, these were her favorite. We ate so many of these while talking about her adventures underwater and my headaches with the restaurant. There are a few more photos in that box," she said over her shoulder.

Wyatt wildly rummaged through the box, pulling several more photographs out. "Oh, wow!" He examined a picture of a man who looked similar to Varian now. The man tried blocking the camera with his hand, but the photographer was able to snap a shot of him. His white teeth shined with his smile. "That's my father. Is he actually having fun?" he joked.

"Oh yeah, he always had a smile on his face when he was with your mother." Denise walked back over and placed the sweet-smelling dessert on the table.

"Not anymore." The only time he'd seen something that resembled a smile was when Wyatt announced he would marry the princess. He sighed heavily, putting the image down.

"I'm sure what happened with your mom has a lot to do with that." Denise grabbed two forks and handed him one. "It took me a long time to find happiness when my husband died."

"He hates the surface world so much." Wyatt began eating the roll, savoring it.

"So . . . I'm guessing he doesn't know you're here, then?" Denise questioned.

With his mouth full, Wyatt shook his head. Finally swallowing he replied, "No. We don't really see eye to eye on, well, anything. I told him I wanted to explore the ocean and be my own mer."

"I'm guessing he didn't react too well to that?" she asked before taking a bite of her dessert.

"He countered by arranging for me to marry a princess in another kingdom."

Denise shook her head in what seemed like disappointment.

"The day before I was to go to the Kingdom of Atalana to announce my engagement, I discovered my mother's journal hidden in the study during my lessons." He paused, realizing that his father had been planning this union for some time. Making Wyatt take lessons on kingly duties was because, in his father's eyes, he was going to be just that one day, King Wyatt of Atalana. "I started flipping through it, hoping she could give me some guidance. I found the entries about the times she was on land and about you. I came up with a plan to escape and come here."

"I'm glad you found her journal, but shouldn't you try talking to your father?"

Wyatt licked the icing off his lips. "I tried. He doesn't understand why I won't just find someone and get married. So he felt he had no other choice but to arrange for my marriage." He shoved another piece of cinnamon roll into his mouth before he grabbed the next photo. His mother, in a yellow two-piece swimsuit, leaned against the railing of a boat while his father was half in the water with his arms crossed, leaning onto the deck. They were staring lovingly at each other. "They looked so happy."

What happened to you, Dad?

"I took that picture. Your father surprised us. That was the first time I saw him as a merman."

Wyatt's brow furrowed. "Why did my mom go back?"

"She stayed on land for a while but would go back to the

ocean to see your father. The king had become very sick, and the kingdom was apprehensive about Taron. He was known as a free spirit, I guess," Denise explained.

Wyatt nearly choked on his cinnamon roll at that statement. "Father? A free spirit?"

"You two aren't that different. When I first met your father, your mother had convinced him to come onto land. He enjoyed himself up here, but with him to be king he couldn't keep coming up on land. The person you describe as your father is someone completely different from who I met and how your mother talked about him. He seemed very carefree and fun-loving. He was even arranged to be married to someone else, but when he met your mother, he fell head over heels for her. I guess between ruling a kingdom and losing the love of his life, he lost himself somewhere along the way."

"You're telling me my father was arranged to be married but rebelled?" Wyatt asked, dumbfounded.

"That's what your mother told me. His father wanted him to marry a princess from a different kingdom. Unite their kingdoms, I suppose." Denise shrugged.

"Just like what he's doing to me now."

"Yet he was in love with your mother. He eventually drew a proverbial line in the sand for his dad, your grandfather. If he didn't let him marry your mother, then he refused to be king. Your grandfather didn't have any other children and refused to have a distant cousin rule the kingdom. So he had no choice."

"Unbelievable. I know I don't have a significant other like he did, but he still knows what a forced engagement feels like." Wyatt wasn't sure if he could be angrier at his father.

"After the king died, Taron needed Sarina by his side. It wasn't an easy decision," Denise explained. "She loved your father very much, but if she stayed on land, she would've never had your siblings or you."

"I guess you're right." He studied every inch of the photograph, committing every feature of his mother to his memory.

He noticed something around her neck. "This," he said, flipping the image around pointing to Sarina's necklace. Denise leaned over. "My mom talked about a necklace that helped her transform."

Denise nodded as she finished her dessert. "She gave them to me the last time I saw her."

"Them? There was more than one?"

"Yes, she had a few made before she even had children. But when she decided to stay underwater, she came back one last time and told me to destroy them."

"Oh." Wyatt's heart sank. Even though his mother wrote that in her journal, he had hoped that somehow it wasn't true. There was no possible way he could avoid water his whole life. He looked down at his nearly empty cup, which seemed to mimic how he was feeling at that moment.

"What would you do if you had the necklace?" she asked, intrigued.

"I want to be my own man. All my life, things have been handed to me because I was royalty, even though I would never be king. I hated it. I have a sense that my mother didn't like that either."

"Independent, very much like her. Stay right here, I have something for you," Denise said and walked into the hallway. A few minutes went by when Wyatt heard her calling him from her bedroom. He walked over to find her sitting on the floor with a screwdriver. She laughed. "I thought I could get this myself, but I might need the strength of a merman."

Wyatt knelt and pried the floorboard up. Denise leaned over and pulled out an old wooden box. She blew a light coating of dust from the top. Wyatt's eyes widened. Seared on the top of it were two waves rising high on each side of a tail fin with a trident above it.

"That's the royal crest of Aquana. What is this?" he asked, puzzled.

Denise stood up and sat on the bed's soft purple comforter.

Wyatt followed suit and sat next to her with weighted anticipation. She handed him the box with a smile.

"Yes, Sarina asked me to destroy the necklaces." She paused for a moment. "But I never did. In my heart, I knew she would be back. And while she never physically came back, her spirit did in you. In some way, I guess I wanted to make sure you were worthy. I know she would want you to have them now."

Wyatt was overcome with a sense of awe as he stared at the precious package. His hands trembled, holding the box his mother once held.

"Well, what are you waiting for? Open it." Denise's eyes twinkled in delight.

Wyatt lifted the golden clasp and opened the box, revealing four simple pendants. Each one glistened with an iridescent turquoise glow. Two of them were a matching set, triangular and similar to an arrowhead he had seen in a book. The third was shaped like a star. The fourth and final pendant was a ring. All four had a thin, braided, black strand of leather rope threaded with two sliding knots to make the necklaces longer or shorter. Wyatt picked each of them up in turn.

After studying them intently, he placed them carefully back in the box. "These are amazing."

Denise picked one of the triangular necklaces from the box and held it up toward him. "May I? This one and its matching pair belonged to your parents. I'm assuming this one is your mother's since it looks a bit worn. If you'd rather have your father's—"

"No," he interrupted. "I'd like my mother's, please."

Wyatt bowed his head as she situated the necklace around him and tightened it slightly so it wouldn't slip off. A warm rush through his body surprised him. The iridescent stone glowed for a few seconds as it took new ownership around his neck. He looked up and stared at himself in the dresser mirror. His eyes glowed bright blue, normally only seen underwater, before dimming back to normal.

"Sarina told me about the power that was harnessed in the necklace. You can access your merpowers but stay true to human form."

"Merpowers?" Wyatt asked in confusion.

"I guess you wouldn't really consider them powers. Did you ever read anything about it in her journal?"

Wyatt sighed. He wished he had brought the journal with him instead of leaving it for his sister to remember him by. "I left it at the palace."

"It's ok. Your mother explained it to me once, but it's been so long, my memory is a bit fuzzy." She took the box and placed it back under the floorboard. "If you don't mind staying a little longer, maybe we can figure this out together."

He smirked. "Only if you cook up another batch of those cinnamon rolls."

"Deal!" She chuckled, rising from the bed. Before she walked out of the room, she opened her nightstand drawer and took out a large wad of cash. "This is what your mother left behind the day she left. I guess you can say it's your inheritance. I never felt right keeping it for myself. It's only right that I give it to you."

"I don't know what to say. I came to this island with absolutely nothing. I had no clothes, no money, and no idea if I would even belong. I have never been treated with such kindness and love as I have now. Thank you, Denise." He wrapped his arms around her in a warm embrace.

CHAPTER 11

Found

Wyatt stifled a yawn from the previous night's conversation with Denise. They had talked into the late hours of the night until both their eyelids grew heavy. Thankfully, he wasn't needed at work that morning, and he and Liam were both on the afternoon shift.

"You coming?" Liam asked, making his way toward the shoreline.

Wyatt's feet were planted firmly on the ground as he took stock of everyone around him. A family of four picnicking, an older couple holding hands as they sat in the shade of their umbrella, a group of teenage girls giggling as they took pictures of themselves in various poses. They all seemed innocent enough, though he couldn't help but hear his father's words seep into the back of his mind.

He shook his head, ridding himself of the distrust. "Yeah, I'll be right there."

He bent down and pulled out his water bottle. Little did Liam know Wyatt had poured some salt into it. He took a big swig before returning it to the cooler. It wasn't quite the same as seawater, but it wasn't horrible either. He stood up and touched his mother's pendant that hung from his neck. It was now or never. He grabbed the white-and-blue surfboard Liam had lent him and walked toward the water's edge.

Liam had insisted the only way to really learn how to surf was by diving right into the water.

The foamy waves rolled just short of the tip of Wyatt's toes. He glanced over to see Liam holding a phone and taking a picture of the group of girls.

"Here you go, ladies," Liam said, handing the phone back to one of them as she stared him up and down. Gripping his bright red surfboard under his arm, he walked back to Wyatt. "Man, I can't believe how different you look."

Wyatt ran his hands through his now short dark brown hair. It was cropped tight on the sides and left a bit longer on top. During his talk with Denise, she had insisted he get a haircut to blend in better. She had taken him out that morning to some place called a salon before treating him to breakfast.

"I'm glad Denise talked you into a trim, but now I'm gonna have to seriously step up my game for the ladies," Liam said, glancing over at the girls who were eyeing Wyatt.

"Thanks. What game?" Wyatt asked in confusion.

"Harsh, man!" Liam replied with a scoff and motioned for them to go in the water.

Wyatt said a silent prayer to Poseidon and moved forward, letting the water roll over his feet. He pinched his eyes shut for a moment, waiting for something to happen. When nothing happened, he glanced down to find his legs still there. Tears pricked his eyes.

"Come on," Liam called out, already sitting on his board.

Wyatt ran into the surf and threw his body on top of his board, paddling his strong arms until he reached Liam.

"You ok?" Liam asked. "You look like you might cry."

Wyatt shook his head with a laugh. "Just some salt water in my eyes," he lied.

"All right. Watch me first."

Wyatt nodded and studied Liam's mannerisms as he caught

the first wave. He rode it until he lost his balance and fell off. Looked easy enough. Just stay on the board.

"Your turn," Liam shouted, bobbing up and down in the water.

When he was tossed over before he could even stand on the board, Wyatt quickly learned that surfing in the water was harder than what he had practiced on land. The sea surrounded him, and he nearly forgot to hold his breath. Swimming wasn't exactly his strong suit without gills or a tail. Thankfully, he could use his powers to push him back to the surface.

"Harder than it looks, huh?" Liam laughed, paddling past Wyatt.

"You have no idea," he muttered.

As the hour passed, Wyatt's surfing and swimming abilities began to improve. Soon, he was able to ride the waves almost as long as Liam. After his last tumble, he walked back to the beach to rest and have a drink of water, even though he had snuck in a few big swigs of seawater already. As he lowered his bottle, he spotted something in the distance, a woman bobbing up and down, staring at him. His eyes widened. She looked like . . .

No, she would never.

A wave rose up, and she was gone, causing Wyatt to question if she had really been there. An uneasiness settled down in his chest.

Liam dropped his board on the beach, startling Wyatt. "You giving up already?" He flipped the lid of his bottle and chugged.

"I'm a bit beat," Wyatt replied, looking back out at the empty water.

"Oh, come on, you got a few more in you."

Wyatt cocked his head. "Don't you think the waves are getting a bit choppy?"

"Those are the best ones."

Wyatt gazed up at the gray clouds that were closing in on the blue sky.

"All right, one last time. But whoever falls off on the board first buys dinner."

Wyatt thought for a moment. "Deal."

"I hope Denise gave you an advance. Tonight's special is steak," Liam teased, running into the waves.

Wyatt followed behind and sliced his hands into the waves, pushing himself farther out. Sitting on his board, he glanced back to see the beach becoming desolate as humans took shelter from the oncoming storm. A few umbrellas that had been left behind trembled from the gusty winds. Thunder rumbled in the distance, and the gentle waves suddenly became violent, jostling Wyatt.

This was fine for any mer, but to a human, the waves could easily carry them out to sea, or worse. They needed to turn back.

He scanned the waters, searching for Liam. Only a few people were in the water, and most of them were trudging back to shore. Soon, he was alone. Paddling back to shore, he looked around, but there was no sign of his friend or his red board. Lightning pierced the sky in the distance.

"Liam!" he yelled, elongating the word, but only the gale winds that whipped around his head replied, whooshing past his ears. Heavy raindrops began to fall from above, hitting his skin.

Something wasn't right.

Throwing his board down, Wyatt dove into the gulf. In mere minutes, the waters from below had darkened. Wyatt concentrated, and just as Denise said he would, his vision sharpened, letting him see clearly as if he were back in mer form. A few small fish swam about, but besides that, the gulf was still.

He swam up and breached the surface just as a wave poured over him. With a gasp, he popped back up. There, in the distance, the same woman he saw earlier was buoying Liam's motionless body.

"No, no, no! Don't die!" She frantically tried to lift Liam onto his broken surfboard. "*Help!*"

"Poseidon." He gasped before diving down. He focused on the water, sending him speeding forward. A familiar blue-and-gold tail swished about as he approached. He wasn't sure what to think. On one hand, her being here could mean the end of his time on land, but on the other hand, if she hadn't been there, Liam might have died.

That was, if he hadn't already.

He surfaced just on the other side of Liam's board to find blood trickling down his friend's forehead.

"He's not breathing! Please, help him," she pleaded, staring down at Liam.

Wyatt gripped the board, trying to keep Liam steady as the mermaid stared slack-jawed.

"Wyatt?" she gasped.

"Hold him still," he instructed, watching to see if Liam's chest was rising. When the board began to float away, Wyatt's gaze shot up. "Sarah, did you hear me? Hold him still!"

Sarah snapped out of her shocked state and nodded curtly.

"If this works, get ready to swim," he said, looking down at his friend. He didn't dare look at his sister. He didn't need any distractions.

"If?" Sarah questioned.

Wyatt held his open hand above Liam's mouth. "I've never done this before." His eyes darted to hers. "I need you to promise me that you'll leave."

"I can't leave you, Wyatt," she croaked.

With a defeated sigh, he went to work, moving the water just like Denise had instructed during their long talk. She told him how she remembered his mother would control the water, shaping it into spheres or long tendrils. If he could do the same thing, there might be a chance he could save Liam.

Concentrating, he pretended to pull an invisible string attached to the water trapped in Liam's lungs. Just as something came out of Liam's mouth, a wave crashed over them, nearly knocking Liam off the board.

"Dammit," Wyatt cursed under his breath.

Sarah held Liam in a tight embrace, clutching his hand. Wyatt moved his hand back over Liam's mouth and concentrated once more. A tendril of water slipped out between Liam's lips.

Sarah's eyes widened in amazement. "It's working!"

Wyatt gave her a knowing look. Liam couldn't see her here, or he'd have questions.

"There's an underwater cave just north of the island. I'll be there."

Before Wyatt could reply, Liam gasped as the last of the water was pulled from him.

"Thank, Poseidon," he whispered and helped Liam to his side as he struggled to cough the rest of the water from his lungs. Wyatt looked over, only to see a gold edge of Sarah's blue fluke dive under.

"Wh . . . what happened?" Liam's hoarse voice asked as his eyes darted around.

"You must have fallen off your board when the waves became violent. I almost didn't find you."

"So did I beat you?" Liam asked with a slight smirk.

Wyatt chuckled. "Sure, buddy."

"Wait." Liam lifted his head slightly and looked around. "There was this girl . . . She . . . saved me."

"No, sorry. It was just me. You must have hit your head pretty bad. Come on, let's get you back on land."

As they made their way to shore, the heavy rain tapered off into a light drizzle. Wyatt helped Liam off the board and to his feet, placing his arm around him. Liam insisted he was fine, but since Wyatt was no expert, he knew he should get a second opinion.

"I wiped out pretty good, huh?" Liam groaned, wiping the blood from his forehead as they arrived at his apartment.

Wyatt opened the door. "I'd say so." He quickly retrieved a few towels and placed them on the couch for Liam to sit on. He handed him a washcloth that Liam held to the gash on his forehead. "It's a good thing I spotted you in the water."

"Yeah . . . I guess so. You sure no one else was in the water?"

Wyatt walked back to the bathroom. "Nope, just your dumb ass that insisted the waves weren't that bad," he called out as he dried his hair. He had learned a few new words while spending time with Liam and the rest of the workers at The Cove.

He caught a glimpse of himself in the mirror. He looked so different, so human. *Human.* He needed to get used to referring to them as just that. Land-dwellers seemed like such a derogatory term to use now that he had spent time with them. He tilted his head, inspecting his clean-shaven face. The one corner of his mouth curled into a half-smile at his rebellion.

"But your dumb ass followed me, so you don't really have a leg to stand on," Liam replied, standing in the hallway.

"I'm going to get Denise to take a look at your head," Wyatt insisted.

"I told you, I'm fine," Liam replied, staggering back to his bedroom.

"Liam, you hit your head and nearly drowned."

He heard Liam flop onto the bed.

"Fine." Liam gave a defeated sigh. "Could you ask her if she has some bandages? All the ones I have are too small."

"I'll let her know."

Wyatt left the apartment to a clear blue sky and blinding sunlight. Besides some palm fronds knocked down and the wet pavement, no one would have guessed a storm had passed. Entering The Cove felt different. Denise assured him he would fit in better with a cleaner haircut, but it felt like it did the exact opposite. He couldn't help but feel more eyes were on him. Especially the women, both working and sitting down to eat. It probably didn't help he was shirtless and dripping wet.

He immediately found Denise and informed her of what had happened to Liam. He couldn't help but beam with pride when he got to the part about controlling the water.

"How bad is he?" she said, unlocking her apartment.

He followed her inside. "Not bad, but he needs a bandage for his head. He has a small gash above his right eyebrow."

"Your mother would have been so proud." With a smile, she touched his arm for a moment before walking into the bathroom. "Thank goodness you found him!"

"Well, I wasn't the one that found him." He leaned against the bathroom doorjamb while Denise grabbed medical supplies. Her head poked from behind the cabinet door, waiting for him to elaborate. He folded his arms across his chest and chewed on his bottom lip. "My sister did."

"Sarah? Did he see her? Why is she here?" she asked, bombarding Wyatt with question after question as she walked back into the hall.

"Yes, but she left before he came to. Although, he claimed a girl saved him."

Denise stiffened and stopped in her tracks.

"Don't worry, I convinced him it was me."

Her shoulders relaxed. "That's good."

"Can I ask for a favor?"

"Sure."

"I know I'm supposed to work this evening, but—"

"Go. I'll take care of Liam."

Wyatt pulled her into a hug. "Thank you, Denise!"

"Before you go, I think you should have something," she said, walking into her bedroom. He followed her, and she motioned to the floorboard. "Those necklaces are your inheritance."

He shook his head. "That means a lot, but you should keep the box here for safekeeping."

"If you insist, but at least give one to Sarah in case she wants to come on land."

Wyatt lifted the floorboard and withdrew the star pendant necklace before returning the box. He stared at it and contemplated. "I'm not sure if she'll take it."

"She might surprise you." Denise opened her closet door and pulled out a sundress, then went into the kitchen and placed it in a small bag. "Just in case she decides to transform," she said, handing it to him. "Go. I have a boy to scold for surfing during a storm."

Denise didn't have any children, but it seemed like Liam was more like a son to her than an employee.

"Thanks again," he said, giving her a quick hug.

Even though Wyatt enjoyed being on land, there was nothing like the feeling of warm salt water wrapping around his body. As much as he wanted to dismiss it, he was a mer, not a human. He kicked his legs, putting space between him and the beach until it was safe. Before, he would have shuddered at the thought of transforming, but now, with his mother's necklace, he wasn't scared. It felt like his mother was swimming right there beside him.

He wiggled out of his bottoms and focused on changing back into a merman. His legs began to tingle, but no pain followed. Scales formed along his legs as they fused together and his feet formed into his wide fluke. He took a deep breath of saltwater in through his nose and out of the gills that formed just under his ears. With a beaming smile and a kick of his tail, he swam north.

Wyatt scoured the area Sarah had indicated until he found a mound of rocks with an opening next to it. That must be it. He kicked his tail, swimming through a long tunnel. He floundered for a moment, admiring the intricate designs carved along it. His hand traced the swirling lines of glowing blues and purples that only mers could see. They guided him to a large underwater cavern. Rays of colored light pierced the clear pristine water, unlike anything he had ever seen before. Sarah was above him, swaying her tail to keep afloat.

He drifted up, soundlessly breaching the air pocket of the cavern before changing back. As he put his shorts back on, his jaw fell open at the sight that surrounded them. This was no ordinary stone cave. Shimmering gems lined the ceiling, creating a spectrum of colors that cascaded around the cave from the small amount of light that filtered through them. Pearl walls with gradients of iridescent purple and light blue swirled toward the ceiling. It reminded him of the inside of a pearl abalone shell he had once found. It was breathtaking.

"Wow." His voice echoed through the cavern.

Sarah twisted around and let out a yelp that echoed throughout the cave. Silence hung in the air. He couldn't believe she was here. The flecks of gold shimmered in her blue eyes as she stared at him for a moment as if trying to figure out if he was real.

"Hey, sis," he finally spoke with a kind smile.

Without warning, she barreled toward him and wrapped her arms around his neck in a tight embrace, nearly pushing him back under.

"I missed you, too," he said with a laugh.

"I was so afraid something happened to you." She pulled away and threw her fist into his chest. "You had me worried half to death!"

"Ow, jeez. I'm sorry!" He rubbed his chest. "Didn't you get my note? I said I needed to be on my own."

"You're my baby brother. I can't very well let you go off and disappear without knowing you're safe around those land-dwellers."

Wyatt stared at her in astonishment. "How did you figure out I was here?"

"My brilliant intuition." Sarah smirked. "And Mom's journal."

"You always were the smart one. But I'm glad you know."

"You look so different." She touched his short hair. "So . . ."

"Human?" he finished her sentence as he climbed out of the water, revealing his legs. He sat on the floor that matched the walls. He raised his right knee to his chest, letting his left leg dangle in the water.

Sarah carefully touched his toes in complete amazement and gawked at him, making him feel uncomfortable.

"I could go back in the water," he suggested dispiritedly.

"No," she said with a smile. "No, it suits you. You look really happy."

Wyatt breathed a sigh of relief. "You don't know how happy that makes me feel."

"When I said you looked different, it wasn't because of your short hair or legs," Sarah began. Wyatt looked down at her in confusion. "It was because I can see the weight lifted from your shoulders. You belong here, Wyatt." She lifted herself to sit next to him.

He wrapped his arm around her for a half-hug. "Thank you. I do feel at home." Wyatt paused. "Does anyone know you're here?" he asked, afraid of what her answer would be.

Sarah shook her head. "Just Lyra." Wyatt furrowed his brow in worry. She threw her hands up in defense. "I know she's Varian's girlfriend, but she was my best friend first, and I trust her. She won't tell him." Her eyes darted down to the shimmering waters.

Wyatt cocked his head. "What's that look?"

"Varian isn't going to find out anyway."

"Why . . . ?"

Sarah moved her tail about, causing ripples. "He went looking for you."

"I mean, I guess that's not surprising."

Turning back to Wyatt, Sarah replied, "Against Father's wishes."

"Seriously?"

Varian had always followed orders. That was what was always expected of him, being the future king and all. If Father said to flip, Varian would ask forward or backward, along with how many times.

"Yeah, a few days ago, actually. Father's pretty upset."

Wyatt rubbed his hands against his face and groaned. If he was ever found, he would be in so much trouble.

"I told him I didn't want to get in the way so I was going to stay with Lyra for the time being as a distraction."

Wyatt raised an eyebrow.

"It's half true!" She shrugged innocently. "He just doesn't know I've been searching for you. I thought maybe I'd find you near the island. I never guessed I'd find you on land, surfing no less!"

"You know what surfing is?"

"Mom wrote about it." She smirked and ran her hand over her tail. "So . . ." She splashed her fluke up and down. "Are you going to tell me how you got those?" she asked, pointing to his legs.

Wyatt smiled and rubbed his fingers between the triangular turquoise pendant hanging from his neck. "With this. It's Mom's necklace."

Sarah's eyes went wide, examining it. Wyatt recounted everything that had happened from the moment he left Aquana until he extracted the water from Liam's lungs.

"How in the Seven Seas did you know how to do that?" Sarah asked curiously.

"Mom told Denise everything, including harnessing our ability to control water in and out of the water with this necklace. Watch." Wyatt reached his arm out and concentrated. A wobbly sphere of liquid emerged from the water and hung in place. He attempted to draw it closer but lost control when he pulled too hard, causing it to splash against his chest.

Sarah burst into a fit of laughter. "Wow, that's amazing," she said with a hint of sarcasm.

"Shut it!" He chuckled, bumping against her arm. "I just got the necklace last night, so I didn't have much time to experiment."

"Looks like you could use a little more practice," she quipped.

"No time like the present." Wyatt conjured another water sphere and threw it toward her.

Sarah closed her eyes and threw her hands up to block the water from hitting her, but instead, the ball floated in front of her.

Wyatt's jaw fell slack. "Unbelievable." He scoffed, rolling his eyes. "You haven't even fully surfaced and you already have more control than me."

"You're just jealous because I'm a quick learner," she bragged, tossing the ball of water at his face.

Wyatt wiped the water from his eyes and glanced over at Sarah with a smile. "Care to put that to the test?"

"What do you mean?" she asked.

He opened up the bag that Denise had given him and pulled out a star pendant necklace.

"Wyatt, is that what I think it is?"

"Mom left several behind. She would want you to have one," he said, dangling it in front of her.

Sarah reached up but stopped short. "I . . . I couldn't." Her hand fell to her side. "You were the one that wanted to be here. Not me. I don't belong here."

"I don't expect you to stay, but I'd rather we visit on land." He waited for Sarah's response. "Just try it. For me. Please?" He wanted her to know the joys of being on land.

"Wyatt, I can't," she said quietly.

"I'll introduce you to Denise. You have to try the food here!"

"I can't," she echoed.

"Why? I bet you'll like it. I promise."

She frowned. "That's just it."

Wyatt placed the necklace down. "You're afraid you'll want to stay," he said, almost reading her thoughts. She nodded. "Aquana is your home. You love being a mer. You're not going to stay on land."

"What if I enjoy it like Mom did?" she whispered, looking down.

"Just like you know me, I know you and you're not going to leave the mer world for the surface. Unless . . ."

"What?"

"You fall in love with one of the humans."

"Yeah, that will *never* happen." She scoffed. Her eyes darted from the necklace to her tail several times. "Fine."

"Great!" He placed the necklace around her neck, then grabbed the bag. "Denise gave me this in case you said yes." He pulled out a green sundress and placed it on the ground. After explaining how to transform, he turned around and waited patiently.

"This feels weird against my skin."

He turned to see her dressed and wobbling on two pale legs. "You'll get used to it."

"Poseidon, this is amazing!" she exclaimed, nearly falling over.

Wyatt caught her in time and helped steady her.

"I feel a bit ridiculous, though." Sarah clung to her little brother as her legs trembled. Wyatt guided her around the cave, then turned. "I think if you were able to do it alone, so can I."

Wyatt rolled his eyes. "If you insist."

He slowly let her go, only for Sarah to fall once more. She huffed in frustration when Wyatt caught her again.

"Don't be stubborn," he said. "I've always imagined myself with legs, so it was easier to adapt. This is all new."

She continued to walk back and forth with his help. "You know this was Mom's cave?"

"Wow. Really?" He took in the beauty of it once more and imagined their mom pulling herself to the ledge, leaning back on her arms and basking in the glow of the filtered light. This was her sanctuary away from everyone.

"I read in one of her entries that she brought D— I mean, Denise here to tell her she was a mermaid."

"Did you read about her bringing Father to the surface as well?"

Sarah stopped walking and held onto the wall. "Yeah. I still can't wrap my head around that."

"He was arranged to be married, too." Wyatt's jaw tensed.

"What?" Sarah exclaimed, nearly tripping over her feet.

"Such a hypocrite," he muttered.

"Well, I can only handle so much right now, so we'll flounder that for later on," she said with a wave of her hand.

"Yes, let's. I'm assuming everyone knows I've escaped. So tell me what happened. How long did it take for Father to find out?"

"I'm guessing the guards raced back as soon as you got away. Cain was not pleased at all. He called you a cuttlefish, which did not sit well with Father. Roka, on the other hand, commented that your plan was a rather brilliant tactic and you would make a good soldier. His words, not mine."

Wyatt leaned against the wall with his arms folded and smirked at the thought of Roka saying that to his king. "What did Father have to say to that?"

"Not much." She took a step by herself with less shaky legs. "He was none too happy with them."

"Is he searching for me?"

Sarah diverted her eyes from him. "Do you really want to know?"

Wyatt shook his head. "Just tell me."

"He's sent half the guards out to find you. I've never seen him this distraught."

Wyatt frowned. Guilt settled into him. *No, I tried reasoning with him. What did he expect?*

"I think I got it!" she cried out, cautiously walking up to Wyatt without faltering.

Wyatt gave a weak smile. "I should probably get back to the island before Liam wonders where I went."

"Wyatt, don't worry about Father. You did nothing wrong. You can't sacrifice your happiness for his."

Wyatt nodded in agreement, pushing from the wall.

"This Liam guy, does he know about you?"

"No," he replied, "and I'm not going to tell him either, in case you're worried."

"I wasn't. I know you'd keep our secret safe," she said, slipping back into the water. Soon, her lush tail reemerged. She pulled the dress over her head and placed it on the floor.

"Hey, um, I was so wrapped up in everything, I didn't get to properly thank you for saving Liam's life," he said, following suit and transforming.

"It was nothing," she replied.

"No, seriously. You risked your life for him. Any other mer would've let him die."

"I'm just glad he's ok," she said.

"He would want me to thank you, as well. That is, if I hadn't convinced him he was just imagining you."

Her eyes widened. "He saw me?"

"I wouldn't worry. He hit his head and was out of it," Wyatt reassured her.

"W-what did he say about me?"

"Oh, nothing really." Wyatt smirked and dove under. He glanced back to be sure Sarah was following him. A look of intrigue crossed Sarah's face. "Just that a beautiful girl saved him."

He didn't say anything more. The flush in Sarah's cheeks as she bowed her head spoke volumes.

He gave a slight grin and kicked his tail toward the tunnel. "I'll come back here tomorrow after work."

"You? Working?" Her laughter echoed behind him. "Now, I've heard everything! I might have to surface just to see that."

CHAPTER 12

Stranded

After Nicki drove Liz to Cleveland and reassured her she was doing the right thing, she guided her through the airport to the security checkpoint where they said their goodbyes.

Before Liz knew it, she was seated in a plane 36,000 feet in the air on its way to Sarasota, Florida. The two-hour flight flew by in a flash, and soon they were beginning their descent. Coming down wasn't anywhere near as stressful as taking off had been, but it was still nerve-racking to say the least.

Liz pulled out the old photo of her grandparents and her. *I'll be with you . . . in here*, her grandfather's words reminded her. She held the picture against her chest and looked out the window, catching her first glimpse of the Gulf of Mexico. Her heart skipped a beat as her eyes were filled with the deep blue of the sea.

"Welcome to Sarasota, ladies and gentlemen. The local time here is eleven forty-five, and the temperature is a warm seventy-five degrees. I'd like to thank you for flying with us today, and we hope you decide to fly with us again," the flight attendant announced upon touchdown as the plane made its way to the gate.

The seatbelt sign that glowed above Liz's head turned off, indicating it was safe to stand. However, Liz was nearly frozen in her seat until the man next to her stood up and handed the blue suitcase to her. She rose slowly to her feet and thanked him. Everyone crowded the aisle, eager to get out of the plane, causing her to feel claustrophobic. Her anxiety spiked even more until the line began to move.

When she arrived at the terminal, she had hoped to be greeted with some Florida warmth, but instead, the cool air conditioning of the airport hit her face, causing a slight chill. She should've brought a jacket. She shivered and looked around, trying to figure out what to do next. *I need to rent a car*, she thought, searching for signs that indicated ground transportation.

She licked her lips as an inviting aroma emanated from a small café she passed. It had been hours since she'd had something fulfilling to eat.

After scarfing down a sandwich and chips, she resumed her walk until she arrived at the rental area.

"Hi. Can I help you?" the woman asked.

"I'd like to rent a car," Liz replied.

"I'll just need to see a valid driver's license, and we can get started."

Liz tugged her license from the snug grip of her wallet and handed it to the woman. Her face took on a perplexed expression as she looked between the license and Liz.

Frowning, she handed it back. "I'm so sorry but you're not old enough."

"Huh?"

"You have to be twenty-one to rent a car," the woman stated.

Crap. Why didn't she know that? Liz gave a heavy sigh. "I didn't realize."

The woman apologized again and suggested Liz get a taxi or ride sharing service before directing her to the pick up area located outside the doors behind her.

"Thanks," Liz said, feeling defeated.

Pulling her suitcase behind her, she walked through the sliding doors to the outside and was enveloped by the thick, humid air. The blinding sunlight caused her to squint. She sat on a bench and took out her phone, noticing it was still on airplane mode. She switched it back to normal. Immediately, her phone buzzed, alerting her of the numerous missed messages. Ten to be exact, one being from Nicki. Liz sighed. She cleared her notifications and shoved her phone back into her purse in frustration.

An older gentleman with an airport identification badge approached Liz and cleared his throat. "Excuse me, miss. Do you need a ride?"

Liz frowned. "I do, but I don't know how to get one."

"Well, this just so happens to be the taxi stand." The gentleman smiled. "Where ya goin'?"

"Anna Maria Island," she answered.

"You want the cab to drop you off at the beach?" He chuckled. "Or do you have a more specific destination in mind?"

Liz pulled out a paper she had printed with the information about the cottage they had booked. She handed it to him. "I'm staying here. This is the address."

The gentleman smiled. "Ah, Bridge Street. I had some good times down there when I was your age."

He placed two fingers in his mouth and whistled. He waved a taxi up to where Liz was sitting. The gentleman leaned his arm in the open passenger window and told the driver Liz's destination before handing the paper back to her.

The driver exited his vehicle and greeted Liz with a smile. "I'm Neil. I'll get your luggage for you." He opened the trunk and placed it inside, then opened the passenger door for Liz. "So Malcolm said you're headed to Bridge Street?" Liz nodded as Neil put the car into drive and began their journey. "Visiting relatives?"

"No, but my grandparents used to live there." She looked longingly out the window, trying not to think of her grandfather.

Neil glanced at her through the rearview mirror. "You won't regret it. It's a beautiful island."

Liz hugged her body as the cold air finally circulated into the back seat of the fast-moving cab. She watched out the window, taking in the scenery. Except for the palm trees that popped up along the way, for the most part, it looked like Ohio in the summer.

"So, where are you from?" Neil asked.

"Ohio," she replied, still staring out the window.

"Ah, up north. Ever been to Anna Maria Island before?"

"No. This is my first time in Florida."

"Oh!" he said with excitement. "If you don't mind, I have some recommendations, if you'd like to hear?"

"That would be great!"

The driver rattled off a list of things to do and places to visit, including the free trolley that passed around the island every twenty minutes and a few restaurants he highly recommended. Liz tried to commit them to memory. She and her grandfather had only written a small list of things to do while they were there and she had seven days to sightsee, not to mention figure out how to research her biological parents.

During the rest of the drive, Liz decided to message Nicki back while Neil made small talk every so often.

> I survived the flight! Yay! I'm just getting a ride to the island now. Text you when I get to the rental.

NICKI

> I told you, you'd be fine. Can't wait to see pics! Have fun!

Liz debated on texting her parents but decided to wait until she got to the rental and placed her phone back in her purse. She began to wonder how much farther it would be until they arrived at the island.

As the car drove over a long narrow bridge, Neil exclaimed, "Welcome to paradise!"

Liz looked out the window to see all the boats anchored in the bay. It didn't look like anything spectacular. She had seen bodies of water before. The car slowed to a stop at the first traffic light on the island.

She excitedly looked out the front window. "Is that the gulf?"

"Indeed it is!" Neil answered as he turned the car left onto Gulf Drive.

"Huh, I knew the island was small, but I guess I didn't expect to see the other side of it so soon."

"Yup. It's not that wide, which is nice because wherever you stay, you're within walking distance of the beach!"

A few minutes later, Neil turned the cab into a gravel parking area in front of a pale green house. The outside was exactly the same as the picture except for one thing: a large real estate sign with the word SOLD plastered over it. Maybe it had been sold before they booked it, and the sign hadn't been taken down yet. However, an uneasiness settled in the pit of Liz's stomach.

"Here we are," he announced, putting the car into park.

Liz opened the door and stepped out into the hot, humid air. It was invigorating after being surrounded by the freezing cold air conditioning for the past half hour. At this rate, she was going to get sick going from one extreme to another.

She took a deep breath and filled her lungs with the salty air. She caught the faint smell of fish, and even though she wasn't a fan of seafood, it still brought a smile to her face. She was home, or at least where she was born.

Neil brought her luggage around. "That'll be thirty-eight, eighty-two."

"Um, you don't take credit cards, do you?" She had taken $120 from her spare money, hoping anything she had to pay for would be charged on her credit card.

"Sorry, just cash," he replied with slight panic in his eyes.

"It's fine, I have cash." Liz handed him a fifty-dollar bill, and Neil gave a sigh of relief. "Thanks for all the advice. Keep the change."

"Thanks! Watch the leaves." He pointed out some large palm fronds on the ground. "A storm blew through yesterday. Looks like they still need to clean up a bit. Have a nice stay!" he said before getting back into the taxi and on to the next customer.

Liz hefted her luggage onto the porch and dug through her purse for her cell phone. There was a keypad to unlock the door, and they were told that the code would be emailed to them that morning.

Alerted by approaching footsteps, she looked up to see a large, middle-aged man with a beard walking toward her.

"Can I help you, miss?"

"I'm staying here for the week," she informed him.

He gave her a confused look. "No one is staying here for a while. I'm renovating it per the new owner's instructions. Are you sure you're at the right house?"

"Uh . . ." She fumbled with her phone and pulled up her email. She hadn't checked it all day, and now she had one from the booking website. It showed a refund for the rental. Her heart dropped. What? She scrolled through her emails, but there was nothing else to alert her of the cancellation. "I don't understand. I booked this last week! They refunded this morning while I was on my way here!"

"Shit," he muttered. He leaned against the porch railing. "This place just sold a few days ago. That's unreal that the previous owners just told you. I'm really sorry about that. I've been hearing that some of these rentals have been doing this. They get an offer from some big business to buy their property, and the owners end up selling it with only a moment's notice to the renter. I don't agree with any of that myself, and I wish I could help you out, but I'm just here to redo the bathroom."

Liz stood in complete shock until panic settled in. Where was she going to find a place to stay now? They had hardly found anything in their budget last week. Even the hotels were booked up. She needed to figure something out, but not here. Lifting the luggage, she stepped down onto the gravel and broken shell drive.

"Hey," the man called out from behind her. "Maybe they

have another rental somewhere that's available? A lot of these owners have more than one."

That wasn't a bad idea. Liz glanced back and thanked the man before dragging her suitcase down the street to a nearby bench. After dialing the previous owner's number, she drummed her fingers on top of her suitcase as the phone rang several times.

The phone clicked, and a female voice was on the other end. "Hello?"

"Hi. Yes, I rented a house from you that was sold. I wasn't told until this morning, and by then I was already on the plane," Liz explained, trying to keep her cool.

"I already spoke to a woman about the property several days ago. We refunded the money. Did it not go through?"

They had already spoken to someone? Of course. Her grandparents' number was on the bill along with their credit card number. Why wouldn't her grandmother let her know? *Because she didn't think I was going.*

Liz sighed. "No, it did. She never told me, that's all."

"Oh, dear. I'm so sorry."

"It's not your fault." Although, who sells a house days before the renter was going on vacation? "Do you have any other properties available?"

"No, I'm sorry. Just that one."

Liz bowed her head, leaning it against the luggage handlebar. "All right. Thank you."

"Have a good day!" the woman said in a cheery voice that made Liz's blood boil.

Seriously? She ended the call and tried not to throw her phone into oncoming traffic. Convincing herself everything would work out, she looked up nearby hotels on the island, which were few and far between.

As she slowly baked under the Florida sun, she called numerous places with no success until a hotel off-island had one available room left. She thanked the island gods. Even though it wasn't exactly where she wanted to stay, it was something.

"Can I have your name, please?" a woman who sounded like she smoked a pack of cigarettes a day asked.

"Elizabeth Brander."

The sound of fingers lightly tapping on a keyboard filled the silence before the woman said, "I'll need your credit card number to secure the room."

Liz rattled off the numbers while her leg pistoned nervously. More typing. The woman asked her to repeat the numbers again. There was a long beat of silence followed by a frustrated sigh.

"I'm sorry, but your credit card has been declined," the woman informed.

"What? I just used this to buy food a few hours ago. Are you sure?"

She tried one more time with the same results. "I'm really sorry. Do you have another card you could use?"

"No," she croaked. She wasn't sure if the heat was getting to her, but it felt like everything was closing in.

"I would suggest calling the credit card company to find out what's going on," the woman said before their call ended.

Liz flipped her card over and dialed the number on the back for customer support. She had never made so many phone calls in a row. After being placed on hold for longer than her nerves could take, she was placed through, only to be told an alert had been sent because the card was used out of state.

"I never received an alert," she explained.

"There are several numbers associated with the account. If we can't contact one, we try another."

The other would be her parents' number. With them not knowing she had left, they had frozen her card, and there was no way for her to reactivate it; a new card number was already in place to be sent.

Liz returned her card to her wallet and shoved it into her purse. After the cab ride, she only had seventy dollars left. Placing her elbows on her knees, she put her head down with her hands behind her neck and closed her eyes, trying to calm her nerves.

Her phone buzzed across the seat. She didn't have to look to see who was calling. She knew it was her parents. They had been trying to contact her all day, and as much as she wanted to, she couldn't keep ignoring them.

Pushing everything down for the moment, she reached for the phone and answered. "Hello?"

"Liz!" Her mother let out a breath she had probably been holding all day. "Oh my god! Where are you? Are you ok? We've been trying to contact you all day. I can't believe you'd leave like this. We discussed this yesterday, and you went against our wishes." Her mother's words went from worry to agitated within seconds.

Liz's voice was shaky. "I know, and I'm sorry."

She was about to tell them that they were right and that she had made a mistake trying to do this alone, but then her father's words resonated in her mind. *I don't think that's a good idea.* Her eyes welled up. If she went back now, she'd just be proving them right.

There was a deep sigh on the other end. "I'm assuming when you made arrangements with Grandpa that you booked a hotel or something?"

Liz lifted her head in surprise. They didn't know the rental had been canceled. Had they not talked to her grandmother?

"Yeah . . . How's Grandma?"

There came muffled voices on the other end. Her father was probably listening in next to her mother.

"She's doing as well as she can be. She decided to stay a few days with her cousin. She doesn't know you're down there. We didn't want to worry her."

"Good idea." Giving Grandma some space meant they wouldn't know Liz was stranded.

Silence hung in the air for an uncomfortable amount of time before her mother said, "The library called. Nicki recommended you for a job. They want you to come down for an interview."

Liz's eyes widened. At least today wasn't a total loss.

Her mother continued. "I think it would be wise if you traded in your airline ticket and came back tomorrow."

"What?"

"You've been searching for a job for so long. You can't pass this opportunity up."

"Did you tell them I was out of town?"

"Well . . . no. They said they needed the position filled right away. I wasn't about to tell them they had to wait for you. That's not how jobs work."

Liz swallowed hard. "I just got here and now you're forcing me to come home?" She jumped up and began pacing.

"No one is forcing you, Liz. You've gone through so much this past week."

Her mother was right. Liz felt like she was breaking at the seams, but coming back home meant dealing with the ramifications of lying to her parents, as well as thinking about her grandfather's death. What was the better choice here?

"You know your father and I love you. We just want you to come back home," her mother added.

Liz scoffed, letting her exhaustion and emotions take over. "You love me? Where was that love all those years when you lied about my biological parents?"

She let the words linger in the silence. Harsh, yes, but it was the truth. If her parents thought she'd just forget the fact that they had kept this secret from her all these years, they were mistaken. Liz pinched the bridge of her nose in frustration, not just with her parents but with herself.

After a long pause, her father's voice came over the phone. "Sweetie, I know you're angry. You've hardly had any time to process everything, and I think we need to sit down and really talk it through."

"You're right. I do need time, and I think this is exactly what I need."

"That's not what I—"

Liz's phone buzzed. She quickly pulled it away from her face and glanced at the low battery notification. "My phone is about to die. I have to go."

She waited for one of her parents to say something back, but all she heard was silence. She looked at the black screen of her battery-depleted phone. "Dammit."

She slumped down onto the bench and leaned forward, placing her head in her hands. Sweat beaded down her face. She needed to get away from this heat, as well as find a place to charge her phone.

She gathered her things and walked across the main road. Between the buildings, the Gulf of Mexico shimmered in the sunlight. The soft lull of the turquoise waves washed over the shore, calming her nerves. The sky was a clear blue with not a cloud in sight. Her heart leaped at the picture. Unfortunately, she had more pressing matters than to prance around on the beach.

With a heavy sigh, she dragged her suitcase behind her as she walked down Gulf Drive until she felt compelled to stop. To her right was a pale yellow restaurant accented with white shutters. A sign hung above the doorway that read The Cove. She bit her lip. She didn't have much money left, and it would be much cheaper, not to mention wiser, to go to the convenience store just ahead. Her eyes darted from one building to the other until her heart made the decision for her.

Without another thought, she clutched her suitcase and rolled toward her heart's destination.

CHAPTER 13

The Encounter

Wyatt wiped the sweat from his brow as he stood over the burners, waiting for the burgers to cook. That morning, Denise had explained that to work at The Cove, Wyatt had to know all aspects of the restaurant, including being a line cook. He had cringed as she instructed him on how to make a fresh burger. The ground meat squished between his gloved fingers as he mixed it by hand. He then put it in a circular mold press to make the patties. He placed one on the hot stovetop and cooked it until the timer went off, then flipped it over until it cooked to perfection.

While the crew in the kitchen made conversation with him, he didn't joke around or freely talk to them as much as he did at the bar with Liam. He glanced at the clock. Only a few more hours until he could see Sarah. He hoped he could convince her to step on land.

Denise entered the kitchen to check on her team as he finished cooking another batch of burgers. He carefully placed each patty on a bun and pushed the plate to the worker next to him who was in charge of the fries.

Denise placed her hand on Wyatt's shoulder. "You're doing good for your first day in the kitchen," she applauded with a smile. "Though I am in a bit of a pickle. I could really use you up front since the only busser I had scheduled had to leave early. Would you mind helping an old lady out?"

"Really? That would be great!" He had been itching to work up front since he started. Cooking didn't come easily to him. The first few burgers were either too thick or too thin, causing them to undercook or be as hard as a dried-up sand dollar. It wasn't until he remembered to set a timer between flipping that he finally got the hang of it.

"Oh, you're a lifesaver!" Denise replied, then motioned for another worker to take over for Wyatt.

With a yawn, he took his apron off and hung it up. He dragged his feet through the kitchen door and out to the table where the cart was left. As he began clearing the table of dirty dishes and silverware, he noticed the rag to clean the tables was missing. He made his way to the bar for a fresh one, walking past a few customers. One couple held hands as they were about to share a large piece of chocolate cake for dessert. Meanwhile, a man sat alone at another table, drinking coffee while he typed on his laptop. Then Wyatt's eyes fixated on a young woman with shoulder-length dirty blonde hair sitting at the bar. Her leg bounced nervously next to a suitcase.

Wyatt walked past her behind the bar to where Liam was working.

"Do you happen to have an outlet I could use?" she asked Liam, holding up her dead phone.

"If you didn't want to talk to me, then you could've just said so," Liam quipped. The woman looked up at him with a blank stare.

Wyatt grabbed a fresh apron and clean rag from under the counter.

"I'm joking," Liam said with a grin. She gave a slight smile, acknowledging Liam's wisecrack.

Wyatt tied his apron and rolled his eyes from behind Liam, causing the young woman to stifle a laugh.

"Why don't we move you to that table by the window?" Liam

said. "There's an outlet under it, and you'll have a great view of the sunset. I'll go check on your food and meet you over there."

Wyatt started to make his way back toward the table when a thud sounded to his left. He turned to see the blonde holding what looked like the handle that had been attached to her suitcase.

"Dammit," she muttered under her breath. A broken handle didn't seem like a huge deal, but tears were forming in her eyes.

Walking up to her, he asked, "Are you ok?"

She fumbled for words as she tried to compose herself. "Yeah . . . I-I'm fine," she stammered. As she bent down to bring the case upright, she quickly wiped a tear from her cheek. "Just having a rough day, that's all."

Wyatt took a step closer to her. "Any way to fix it?"

She stood back up, and her cheeks flushed as she met his gaze. "I dunno. Unless you know a—"

"The handle," he said as he looked at the piece of plastic in her hand. "Any way to fix the handle?"

"Oh! Um, I don't think so. I'll just lug my suitcase around or maybe bend down and push it, I guess." She let out a frustrated sigh.

"Let me at least help you to your table," Wyatt suggested, wrapping his arm around the suitcase and lifting it with ease.

"Or you can always carry it for me everywhere," she muttered under her breath, causing him to smile to himself. She grabbed her purse and followed him. He pulled out a chair, placing her suitcase on top of it. "Thank you," the girl said with a sniffle.

"You're welcome. I'll get the table set for you. You just relax."

"Easier said than done, but thanks," she said as she plugged her phone charger into the outlet below the table.

Wyatt left to procure her napkin, silverware, and water. When he returned, her phone began to buzz and ding. She looked at it, softly groaned, then tossed it to the side.

"Guessing that's not a good sign?" Wyatt queried as he placed all the items in front of her.

She shrugged, looking out the window. "My parents. They weren't exactly supportive of me coming here."

When the woman turned her head to Wyatt, hopelessness bloomed in her eyes. He wasn't sure why, but he felt the need to reach out to her. He leaned down and placed his hand on top of hers, giving it a gentle squeeze. A faint surge of energy flickered in his hand and radiated throughout his body. He'd never felt anything like it before. He looked deep into her blue-gray eyes, and the world seemed to slow for a moment.

"It gets better," he reassured her. "My father wasn't supportive of me either when I wanted to leave home."

"Hi, babe!"

Wyatt jolted back to reality at the sound of a familiar voice coming from behind him. He quickly pulled his hand away from Liz and spun around. "Jessica!"

"When I asked where you were, I was told you were in the back."

"I was, but Denise needed someone to fill in bussing duty for the dinner crowd. I was just helping . . ." He turned to the girl, who was stirring her ice water with a straw.

She peered up. "Liz."

Jessica glanced over at the girl and frowned.

"My suitcase broke,"—Liz motioned to the handle on the table—"and he helped me. Thank you again, um . . ."

"Wyatt," he said with a half-smile. "My name is Wyatt."

She smiled. "Thank you, Wyatt."

The sound of his name leaving her mouth left a feeling he had never felt before. Like jellyfish tendrils moving about in his stomach.

"I'm sure *Liz* is very grateful you took time out of your job to help her with a broken suitcase," Jessica said.

Wyatt ignored Jessica. "Of course. Enjoy your meal, Liz."

Liz smiled, gave a curt nod, and took a sip of water.

Jessica followed Wyatt as he returned to the table he'd been about to clean before he helped Liz.

"I wasn't expecting to see you here," he said.

Jessica furrowed her brow. "Why do you say that?"

He lowered his voice so no one could hear them. "Well, after yesterday, I wasn't sure if you'd want to go out with me again."

Jessica tipped her head up. Her lips grazed his ear. "Of course I'd want to go out with you again. You're a rare catch, Wyatt Aquana."

The sweet smell of perfume drifting up to his nose, coupled with the gentle whisper, brought a shiver down his neck. He cleared his throat and finished wiping down the table.

"Was there something you wanted?" He walked to the next empty table in front of where Liz was sitting.

"Just you," Jessica replied with a wink.

Wyatt stopped midway and stared at her. He couldn't tell if she was joking or not, but she got his attention.

"I wanted to take you out tonight. Since last night didn't go exactly as I had planned. I thought we could see a movie or something."

Wyatt thought for a moment. He had told Sarah he would meet her after work. However, she didn't know what time he would be done and this was something their mother had experienced. To do something she did made him feel closer to her. He could see his sister after the date.

"Can we see *Splash*?" he asked excitedly.

Jessica raised her brow. "What the heck is that?"

"It's, um . . ." Wyatt paused, trying to remember how Denise had described it.

"It's an old movie about a man that gets rescued by a mermaid and she follows him on land," Liz said shyly from behind them.

Jessica scoffed and rolled her eyes. "Seriously? I was thinking more of a movie at the theater, but I suppose I can look it up." She ran her hand up the length of his arm. "It'll be more intimate anyway." She wrapped her arms around his neck, and grazed it with her lips.

"I really need to get back to work," Wyatt insisted. He

grabbed a dirty plate, only for it to slip through his fingers and shatter on the floor. *Blowfish!* He stepped away from Jessica. "Actually I'm pretty tired from work. How about tomorrow we see a movie?"

He was about to bend down to gather the broken glass when Jessica pulled him to her. His eyes went wide as her lips crashed onto his. He leaned into her, feeling her tongue dance around in his mouth. A tiny thought popped into Wyatt's mind; this didn't feel right. Yet as quickly as it came, it faded, but not without seeding itself into his brain. His chest tightened for a fraction of a second before Jessica pulled away.

Jessica moaned softly into his ear. "I'll see you after your shift. There's more of that tonight." With a wink, she turned and walked away.

He wasn't exactly sure if he wanted any more of that.

As he looked around the room, he realized everyone was staring at him, including Liz, who raised her eyebrows slightly before turning to her sandwich that Liam had just placed in front of her.

Wyatt shook the unnerving lustful thoughts from his head and quickly grabbed the rest of the dishes from the table, trying to hide how utterly embarrassing this all was.

Liz gazed out the window at the setting sun, averting her eyes from the public make-out session. Sure, Wyatt was cute, and Liz thought there had been something between them for a millisecond, but he obviously had a girlfriend. Glancing down at her hand, she could still feel the warmth of his skin on hers. She shook her head and continued to eat her sandwich. He was just being friendly. Besides, she wasn't on the island to find a love interest.

Liam casually walked over with a pitcher of water. "Refill, miss?" he said with a fake British accent.

Liz laughed and raised her glass. "Why, yes, Jeeves."

"So are you enjoying the island?" Liam asked, pouring the water.

"I guess so." She shrugged. "I mean, I've only been on the island for a few hours." She gestured to her suitcase across from her.

"Oh, right. Where are you staying? A hotel or rental?"

Liz's gaze fell to her glass of water as her fingers fumbled around the rim. "I, uh, I'm staying at a hotel. It's the one down the road."

"Oh, nice. Right on the beach," Liam said.

Liz looked at Wyatt, who was clearing dishes a few tables away in front of her. She couldn't help but notice that he would glance in her direction every so often. And apparently, Liam noticed it too.

"Quite a display, huh?" he commented.

"Yeah, I was wondering how far her tongue would go down his throat," she said with a twinge of jealousy.

"How do you know I wasn't talking about the sunset?" He flashed a smile and winked.

"Oh . . ." Her face flushed. She turned her attention to the setting sun. Hues of orange and pinks painted the sky as silhouettes of sailboats made their way back to the docks. The calls of birds echoed across the beach. The beachgoers were slowly packing up their gear while a few watched the colorful display of the setting sun. A gentle breeze carried the warm salty air into the restaurant, lifting strands of Liz's hair across her face. Her heart began to beat faster as she stared out toward the gulf. Her fingers fidgeted with her napkin. The water looked so inviting, and she wanted to feel the cool surf against her skin.

"I've lived here my whole life, and I still try to find time to stop and watch the sunset." He paused for a moment. "Hey, my shift is pretty much over, and I was going to grab a bite from the kitchen. You wouldn't want company, would you?"

The impressive seascape before her slowly dissolved as Liam's words echoed in her ears. "I, uh . . ."

Liam picked up the pitcher of water. "I'm sorry. That was rude of me to ask. We just met. I swear, I'm not trying to make a move on you or anything. I just thought that, well, maybe you could use a friend." He began to walk away.

Liz's phone buzzed with a notification, startling her. Realizing how high-strung she really was, she replied, "You know, I could use a friend."

Liam turned back and gave a gentle smile. "Let me just clock out and get my food. I'll add a bonus of chocolate cake for dessert. My treat."

"Thanks," Liz said graciously. She checked her phone to see Nicki had texted. She had completely forgotten to let her know she was ok.

NICKI

Just checking on ya to make sure you're ok.

Hey, I'm so sorry! My phone died and I had to charge it. I'm pretty tired so I'll talk to you later. This place is amazing! One day we'll have to come down here for a girls vacation!

I'm glad you're ok! See, you had nothing to worry about. Oh yeah, I can't wait! Talk later!

"I hope you left room for dessert," Liam said, placing a large slice of cake in front of her.

Her eyes went wide at the sight of it. "Wow! I might be here for a while," she said with a laugh.

Liam placed his dessert and dinner across from her before sitting down. "So where are you traveling from?"

"Ohio," she responded, diving her fork into the massive dessert. She let out a soft moan at the sweet flavor of chocolate that made her taste buds dance in pleasure.

"Never been."

"You're not missing a whole lot compared to living here."

"Meh, it's ok." He shrugged, then bit into a piece of fried

shrimp. He tried to keep a straight face, but when Liz gave him the side-eye, his lips curled. "Ok, ok. You got me. It is pretty great here. Though it would be cool to see snow. So at least you have that."

"Not really. I don't live in the snow-belt region so we don't get snow as often as you'd think. Climate change and all."

"Bummer. So what brought you to this little slice of paradise?"

Liz stuffed a big piece of cake in her mouth and mumbled, "Vacation."

It wasn't a complete lie. This was a nice getaway from her problems, even though some of them were on the island. Just staring out at the waves washing up on the shore took all her worries away. That was, until her phone buzzed for the fifth time since she began charging it. She glanced at the screen and saw it was a text from her dad.

"Do you need to get that?" Liam asked.

"It's just my parents," she replied sadly. Liam raised his eyebrows with a hint of concern. "I don't really feel like speaking to them at the moment." She grimaced at the words. "They didn't exactly want me to come here."

"Oh, I'm sorry. That must be hard."

Liz didn't say anything.

"Or not . . . I don't want to assume anything. Maybe you never liked your parents." He shoved another piece of shrimp into his mouth, piling up the tails in the center of his plate.

"I'm not really sure what to think of them at the moment. I do love them, but they've hidden something from me for so long. It's hard to trust them right now," Liz expressed as she stabbed a piece of the cake. "I'm sorry, you don't need to hear my whole life story."

"It's fine. I get it. I mean, I never experienced that myself, but I understand where you're coming from," Liam said as he grabbed his dessert and started chowing down.

The rest of the evening, they talked about anything and everything except for the real reason why Liz was on the island. Soon, they both looked out at the darkness before them. The restaurant was practically empty, as it was nearing closing time. The employees were wiping off the bar and tables. Liz looked at the time and knew she'd have to leave. She unplugged her phone and stashed it and the charger in her purse.

"Looks like it's closing time," she announced.

Wyatt was leaning against the doorway. She felt his eyes on her, and her cheeks warmed. Taking a sip of water, she watched him leave.

"I'll clean up." Liam piled the plates on top of each other. He smiled as he stood up. "It was nice meeting you. Maybe I'll see you again soon. Are you going to be ok carrying that?" He motioned to her broken suitcase.

"Yeah, I'll be fine. Thanks again for the dessert. It was delicious." She reluctantly stood up, grabbed the side handle of her suitcase, and lugged it through the front door of The Cove. She checked the time on her phone and decided to make a stop at one of the many gift shops on the island. If she was going to sleep on the beach, she would need a few supplies.

After spending fifteen minutes and most of her remaining money on a beach towel, sunhat, sunscreen, and a few granola bars, she left the gift shop and leaned over her suitcase. As she pushed it down the sidewalk, its wheels caught every so often along the way, causing Liz to stumble.

Streetlights flickered on, lighting the path down to the beach not too far from The Cove. She stopped, placed her hands on the small of her back, and stretched the stiffness from her muscles. She gazed up and down the street to make sure no one was watching. When she felt it was safe, she hefted her suitcase and carried it down the path, past the sand dunes.

Darkness enveloped her as the lights along the street began to fade behind her. Her feet shuffled through the sand, causing the coarse grains to shift in her shoes. She cursed herself for not wearing the sandals that were unfortunately packed in her suitcase. The abandoned beach in front of her felt eerie, as the only sounds heard were the crashing of waves along the shore. Farther down the shore, a few silhouettes of people were shuffling back up the dunes.

After walking a few yards, Liz decided she was far enough from public view to make camp. She dropped the suitcase with a muffled thud, then sifted through her purse and pulled out her phone to use the flashlight setting. She sat down and leaned her phone against the suitcase to illuminate the ground. Pulling off each shoe, she let the sand drain from them before taking her socks off and digging her feet into the cool, soft powder. Grabbing the beach towel from the bag, she rolled it up into a makeshift pillow and leaned her head against it.

She had never imagined at the start of the day that she would be sleeping alone on a deserted beach. Was this a mistake? Should she have just waited to go with her parents instead? Would it have been so hard to admit defeat and fly back home that evening?

With a heavy sigh, she turned the light off and stared up at the night sky. A sliver of the moon peeked through the clouds and glistened over the gulf waters that washed onto the shore. She attempted to calm her mind by focusing on the rhythmic pattern of the lull of the waves, but it only caused her heart to race more. It was a ridiculous notion, but she felt drawn to it.

Placing her hands over her head, she took a few deep breaths to regain control, but it didn't help. No matter how much she tried to ignore her feelings, her body wouldn't let her.

A notification dinged from her phone. Liz picked it up to see it was a text from her mother, but she couldn't make herself read it. Even if she did want to text her back, it was nearly impossible with how much her hands were trembling. God, what was wrong with her?

It had been a long exhausting day, and she was sure sleep would be the best way to calm her nerves. She closed her eyes, but try as she might, sleep didn't come. Instead, the roar of the waves grew louder, as if they were beckoning her. She groaned and rolled to her side, trying to ignore it, but her whole body was now shaking as if it was begging for the sea.

"Fine," she muttered, springing up from the ground. Grabbing her phone, she turned the flashlight back on to help guide her. She'd just dip her toes in the water, then go to sleep. Maybe that would calm her down.

Her feet displaced the loose sand as she stepped toward the gulf waters. Liz didn't have to walk far as the high tide rolled in just a few feet away. She turned the light off and shoved her phone into her back pocket. She took a deep breath in, inhaling the aroma of the salty air breezing gently across her face.

The hard broken shells digging into the soft pads of her feet caused her to wince with each step. The gulf was just inches from her, determined to tickle her toes. Her heart fluttered with excitement at the thought of diving in, but it was pitch black and she didn't know the first thing about swimming.

A shiver ran down her spine as the cool water gently licked the top of her feet. The temperature of the water was not something she could normally stand, yet she found herself moving forward. Soon, the waves lapped against her knees.

Liz couldn't help the smile that emerged. She had no money, no place to sleep, and no idea what she was going to do next, let alone how she would even find her biological parents. But for some reason, she had never felt more at ease than she did now, standing in water. She was just about to turn back when a strange sensation shot up her body. It felt like an electric rush of energy surging through her. Her smile quickly disappeared.

Something wasn't right.

A tingling sensation, like what you feel after a limb falls asleep, tickled her feet. Maybe she'd stepped on a jellyfish. She pulled out her phone, flipped the light back on, and scanned the area, but she couldn't make out anything.

The prickling sensation intensified and crept up her legs. She didn't know what a jellyfish sting felt like, but her gut told her this was something else. She tried to pick her feet up to return back to shore, but they were frozen in place, sinking deeper into the wet sand.

Liz fumbled with her phone, trying to place it back into her pocket, when a pain like no other took over. It felt like a hundred tiny needles were piercing her body until a searing pain took over, causing her to lurch forward.

Her teeth gritted, and she half expected to see her legs on fire. When she didn't, she forced her body to cooperate and shuffled her feet, attempting to take a step forward, only to fall. Icy waters mixed with warmth washed over her before she had a chance to hold her breath. She coughed up the salt water.

Liz's arms shook as she tried to push herself up. The wet sand enveloped her hands, making it more difficult to move. Pain radiated from her abdomen and shot down her legs. She desperately wanted to release her anguish into the night, however, she bit her bottom lip and held it in so as not to draw attention. With a whimper, she pinched her eyes shut as tears streaked down her face. Pushing through the agonizing spasms, she lifted her legs until she was able to stand, but it didn't last for long, and she collapsed back to the sandy floor with the waves crashing at her back.

Her whole life, she had dreamed of seeing the ocean, feeling the sand between her toes as the water lapped at her feet. Now in a matter of minutes, those dreams were taken away by the burning sensation coursing through her body as the dark waves ran their cool fingers over her, trying to pull her back in. Exhaustion overtook her, and it felt as if dry land was a hundred miles away.

Come on, get up! Get up, dammit! her mind shouted. *I didn't come all this way to fail! I can do this!*

Liz lifted her head. Water dripped from the soaked tendrils of hair clinging to her face. Her eyes stared hard at the shadow of her suitcase just ahead. With gritted teeth, she gripped the sand and clawed her way out of the sea, pulling with all her might. Her feet pushed through the anguish, slipping along the sand. She breathed hard as she reached the strip of broken shells the tide had washed ashore. The jagged pieces dug into her flesh as she dragged herself out of the water and onto the soft dry sand. Her head felt as if it was floating out of her body, and the world started to spin through the darkness.

She was nearly there.

Just a few more feet, she told herself just before she collapsed into the inky black nothingness.

CHAPTER 14

Unanticipated Kindness

Liz stirred awake as a muffled voice called out over the rhythmic sounds of waves lapping the shore. She felt her body being rolled over. She opened her eyes, squinting at the brightness of the morning before it was suddenly blocked by the upper torso of a shirtless man. Startled by his presence, she quickly sat up, causing the world to spin around her.

"Whoa, slow down." The man gently steadied her shoulders. "It's me, Liam. Remember, from The Cove?" He sat back on his heels, giving her space.

"Liam . . . What are you doing here?" she rasped, wiping away the sand from the side of her face.

"I was on my morning run and saw you on the ground," he explained. "What happened?"

Liz looked around the secluded beach with a furrowed brow, trying to recall how she had ended up face-first on the beach. Memories flashed through her mind from the previous night. She remembered she couldn't sleep, so she had walked out to the water's edge and felt a sense of calm before unimaginable pain engulfed her body. Now what was left was a ghost of the pain.

She shifted her legs as her face twisted in discomfort. She was unsure if they ached from the night before or from sleeping on the hard ground. There was something else, though, that she couldn't place. She felt different, as though something in her body had changed. She lifted her knees toward her chest and looked down at her feet. She had never been so relieved to see her toes wiggle in the sand.

"Liz, what happened?" he asked again.

"I, um . . ." Liz paused, trying to figure out what to say. "I was waiting for the sunrise. I must have fallen asleep," she lied.

Cocking his head, he raised his eyebrows. "Facedown on the ground?"

Liz stared out at the ocean as she remembered the waves crashing over her body while she tried to crawl back to shore.

"Did you sleep here last night?" he asked with worry.

She snapped to attention. "No." She scoffed. "Of course not. I was staying at that hotel down the road." She brushed the sand off her hair and body.

"Something tells me that's not the case," he disagreed, eyeing her makeshift campsite with her blue suitcase and rolled-up towel behind her. "I know we don't know each other that well."—he paused for a moment—"but when I find someone lying on the beach, I get concerned. Please tell me what happened."

Liz sighed and wrapped her arms around her legs, hugging them tightly. "It's just that it's . . ." She pushed her feet into the sand, trying to think of her next words. She wanted to save him the sob story of her grandfather's death. It was too personal. Instead, she confessed her current situation: the canceled rental home, the declined credit card, and leaving only a note for her parents.

"Why leave a note? I mean, you are an adult," Liam pointed out.

"Yeah, but it was just the timing of it all. They wanted me to wait, but I couldn't. This trip is important to me. I left a note and got on a plane so they couldn't persuade me to stay. It was shitty of me, I know."

"Do they know you don't have any money?"

Liz shook her head. "If I tell them, it would just prove them right, that I couldn't do this alone." She didn't dare look at Liam. She couldn't imagine what he must have thought of her. "But I don't think I'll have a choice now. I only grabbed the cash I had on me. I . . . I barely have enough to get by." She blinked back tears. "I'm sorry."

"Don't be. I get it."

Liz turned her head, wiping her eyes with the back of her hand.

"Really, I do. My parents didn't think I could move down here. It was a struggle at first, but I proved them wrong. I'm sure they were just worried about you."

"That's an understatement. They've called and texted a dozen times since I last talked to them."

"Maybe you should shoot them a text to at least let them know you're ok," Liam suggested.

"You're probably right." Liz reached for her phone but only felt her empty back pocket. "Shit! Where's my phone?" She panicked, checking all of her pockets. She scrambled to her purse and dug through it.

Liam scanned the area. "I don't see it. Where did you have it last?"

Liz thought about the night before. "Oh, no! No, no, no! I think I dropped it in the water!"

She quickly stood up and raced toward the water's edge but stopped just short. Her heart quickened at the thought of what happened the last time she touched the sea.

Liam followed behind her, looking at the waves. "If you dropped it, it's probably to Sanibel by now. Not that there's any saving it if we did find it."

"Dammit!" She kicked the sand in frustration.

"Honestly, you should be more worried about a manatee using up all your data," he joked. Seeing Liz scowl at his improper joke caused him to backpedal. "I'm sorry. Maybe you can get a new one?"

Liz raised an eyebrow. "And how would I go about that without money?"

He grimaced. "Oh, right. Well, you could borrow mine if you'd like." He pulled his phone out. "That is, if you want to call them."

Liz thought for a moment. "I'm not sure if I really want to talk to them." Her voice was cold.

"Why? I mean, no offense, you're an adult and have every right to come here, but you're pretty much living on the streets . . . Or rather the beach."

"They lied to me my whole life and . . . and . . ." She shook her head. "I'm sorry, this is too much information. We just met. I'll be fine, really. I'll figure something out." She began to walk back toward her suitcase.

Liam chased after her. "It's not too much. Really. We all have baggage. Some a little more than others. You obviously need a friend right now."

Liz didn't say anything, but instead she unraveled her beach towel and shook the sand out.

"What did they lie about?" Liam pried, grabbing the end of the towel to help her fold it.

"I don't wanna talk about it. Especially with someone I just met." She met his steel-blue eyes. "No offense," she added. Taking the towel from his hands, she knelt, packed it in the bag, and unzipped her suitcase, searching for her sandals.

"You're wrong, you know," Liam stated, kneeling next to her. Liz looked over at him, puzzled.

"We met yesterday. So that doesn't count as *just met*." He smirked and nudged Liz a bit, causing her to smile. "Come on. This is a safe space. You can trust me. I know that doesn't mean a lot coming from someone you barely know."

With a deep sigh, she tipped her head down and softly confessed, "I'm adopted."

The words hung in the air for a moment until Liam asked, "When did they tell you?"

"A few days ago." She sniffled. "If I hadn't pieced everything together, I'm not sure I would have ever known." A salty tear fell onto her right leg, causing a familiar sting akin to what she felt last night.

"Wow," he uttered. "I can't imagine how that would feel."

Liz looked over to see a few people along the beach. She zipped her suitcase back up and slipped on her sandals. "I'm sorry I unloaded this on you."

"Sometimes it feels good to get things off your chest, no matter who the listener is," Liam offered.

"I appreciate it, I do, but I should go." She stood up, grabbing her purse and bag from the gift shop.

"So what are you going to do now?" he asked.

Liz looked around, disheartened. "I'm not really sure, but I'll be ok." The truth was, she had no clue what she was going to do, and it terrified her that she might have to admit defeat. "Thanks for listening. I'll see you around." She hefted her suitcase from the ground and walked down the beach even though she had no place to go.

"Hey, wait up!" Liam called from behind her. Liz stopped and turned, allowing him to catch up. "Look, I can't imagine how you're feeling right now, but you said it yourself that you're almost out of money. Why don't you come to the restaurant with me and I'll introduce you to Mrs. Charleston's famous cinnamon rolls?"

"Thank you, but I'm fine."

"Come on," he insisted. "You gotta eat."

Liz contemplated a bit until her growling stomach didn't give her much choice to argue.

Liam chuckled. "That sounds like a resounding yes to me."

"Fine," she relented.

Liam took her suitcase and led the way up the coast until they arrived at the patio of The Cove. He placed her suitcase down at a table and pulled out one of the aqua chairs, motioning her to sit.

"Stay here, I'll get your food. What would you like to drink?" Liam asked.

"Water is fine," she replied, not wanting him to spend any more money on her.

"Orange juice it is." He grinned.

She groaned. "You're persistent, aren't you?"

Liam shrugged. "I try. I'll be right back," he told her before disappearing into the restaurant.

Liz leaned over, peering through the open door. The restaurant wasn't open yet, but the workers were bustling inside.

"You never told me work shirts were optional," a familiar voice rang out from inside, causing Liz's stomach to flutter.

"You're just jealous, Wyatt, because I'd be getting *all* the tips if I worked like this," Liam yelled back.

"Uh-huh, sure," Wyatt replied.

"Maybe we should make this a thing. What do you think, boss? Shirtless Men Mondays to see who gets the most tips," Liam suggested.

A woman laughed loudly. "Pretty sure we'd be shut down for health violations."

Liz couldn't help but laugh at their banter. Ten minutes later, Liam came back with a to-go cup and two bags. She looked at him in confusion, as she had thought she was going to eat there.

"So . . . don't be mad," he began, handing her the cup, "but I talked to the owner, Mrs. Charleston—"

"How many times do I have to tell you? Call me Denise," an older woman scolded as she walked out of the restaurant. Her sun-kissed skin gave her the look of a lifelong island resident. "Hello, dear. I'm Denise Charleston." Her smile was kind as she extended her hand.

"Liz." She stood and shook her hand. "I had dinner here yesterday. Your food is delicious."

"Thank you!" Denise leaned in. "The cinnamon rolls are my specialty."

"I can't wait to try them." Liz glanced between Denise and Liam, trying to piece together what was going on.

"Liam said you needed a place to stay," Denise stated.

"Oh, no! I'm fine, really," she said, firing a quick glare at Liam.

"Nonsense! I have a spare apartment that we use for extra storage. It's just sitting there. I'd be happy to let you stay for as long as you need," Denise offered.

Liz's eyes went wide. "What? No, no. I . . . I couldn't. That's very generous of you, but . . . but no."

"I insist." Denise picked up Liz's suitcase and started walking away, leaving Liz no choice but to follow her.

"Liam," Liz whispered, "why did you tell her I needed a place to stay?"

"Because it's true and I knew that Denise had a spare apartment just sitting there," Liam replied as they made their way across the parking lot. "As beautiful as our beaches are, they're not the most comfortable places to sleep."

Liz continued to glare at him as they approached the cute little yellow cottages that were attached to each other. The one farthest from The Cove looked like it was occupied since there was furniture on the porch. The other one, however, was vacant.

Denise turned a key to unlock the empty cottage. The door creaked as she pushed it open to reveal a living area that had not been occupied for some time. Both Liam and Liz followed her through the entrance.

A thin layer of dust lay everywhere. To Liz's left was the living room. Old worn sheets covered a couch and two high-backed chairs while cobwebs adorned a fake plant that sat in the corner.

To her right, several boxes were stacked throughout the kitchen, and another set labeled napkins sat on the island counter. Denise walked into the living room and pulled the curtains open, letting the sun pour through the dingy windows. Dust drifted throughout the room, causing Liz to sneeze.

"Bless you." Liam placed the broken blue suitcase down onto the hardwood floors next to the doorway.

Denise opened a window to let the salty air breeze through. "Forgive me for the dust. This place hasn't been used in years except to store some extra supplies for the restaurant."

"It's ok, but, Mrs. Charleston—" Liz began.

"Please, call me Denise," she replied.

"Denise," Liz corrected. "I really appreciate this, but I can't stay here. You don't even know me." She didn't understand why someone that she had never met could be so kind by offering an apartment rent-free.

"You're right, I don't know you, but I know Liam and I trust him," Denise stated as she pulled some of the sheets off the furniture.

"What, um, did Liam tell you exactly?" Liz inquired, looking down at her shoes.

"He told me you needed a place to stay since you lost your credit card," she said, giving Liam a knowing look.

"Don't worry, I didn't tell her much," Liam whispered to Liz.

"I can see your hesitation, but I assure you that I want to help," Denise said. "I won't take no for an answer, young lady."

"She can be very persuasive," Liam joked, picking up the dusty sheets and throwing them outside.

"Thank you," Liz said graciously. "I'll repay you once I'm back home and have access to money."

"Oh, there's no need. Frankly, it would do this place good to have someone living in it for a bit," Denise insisted as she fluffed the dusty pillows on the couch.

"I already tried to pay her, but she wouldn't hear it," Liam told Liz.

"And I told you, I don't need the money." Denise made her way to the door. "I'll have someone drop off some supplies and fresh linens later, as well as pick up some of the boxes, if that's ok?"

"Yeah, that's fine," Liz replied.

"I have to get back to the restaurant. Are you going to be ok, Liz?" Denise asked, handing her the keys.

"Yes. Thank you again! You don't know how much I appreciate this."

"It's my pleasure. I'll see you in a bit, Liam," Denise said before leaving.

Liam propped himself against the doorway. "So I guess we're going to be neighbors for a bit."

"Neighbors? You live next door?" Liz asked in surprise.

"Yup." He smiled. "I would stay and help but duty calls at the bar."

"Right. Well, thank you. I would have been fine on my own, but . . ." she trailed off because she knew exactly how she would have been on her own.

"Let's just leave it at thank you. And it was nothing. Denise is the one with the apartment. I just didn't want my run to be interrupted again." He winked.

Liz crinkled her nose in annoyance but gave a slight laugh. "I'll try not to disrupt your run again." She stretched her back and yawned just as Liam was about to leave.

Liam looked back at her, contemplating. "Look, I'm going into work and you don't have a clean bathroom or bed. You're more than welcome to wash up and crash at my place until Denise has your fresh linens."

"No, it's fine. I should probably start cleaning," she replied. Her eyelids felt heavy as she tried holding back another yawn.

"Uh-huh. If you change your mind, there's a spare key under the flower pot. You can crash on the couch or the bed. I don't really care. Make yourself comfortable."

"Thanks. We'll see." Liz looked around the room. "There's a lot to do here."

She hated how it felt like Liam and Denise were taking pity on her. She had no money, no place to sleep, and no idea who her parents really were. Who wouldn't pity her? On top of all that, she had no clue what happened to her the previous night, but that wasn't something she was going to publicly discuss with anyone. She pushed the thought out of her head while making excuses for what happened. It was food poisoning or maybe a jellyfish sting. Whatever it was, she hoped it was a one-time thing.

"Ok. Just as long as you promise not to steal anything. I'm not sure if I could live without my knock-off version of Lucky Charms cereal," he stated with a straight face.

Liz stifled a laugh as she nodded in agreement. "*If* I go, I swear I won't steal your cereal, but I can't promise anything if there's chocolate there."

"Oh, well, in that case, maybe you shouldn't go."

She smiled. "Your chocolate is safe."

"Come by The Cove later. Lunch and dinner are on me," he quickly added, leaving before she could argue with his gracious offer.

Liz shook her head in defeat at Liam's kindness. Closing the door behind him, she leaned against it. She suddenly felt utterly alone in the emptiness of the dusty apartment. Taking a deep breath of stagnant air, she went into the kitchen, pulled the curtains back, and opened the window up.

As the humid air washed over her face and she stared at the distant waves rolling into the shore, anxiety rippled through her. It felt like time stood still while the water slowly retreated into itself. Liz felt every muscle being drawn toward the ocean like a weak magnet, but terror flashed through her mind.

Deciding to wash up, she turned the handle of the sink, only to find it didn't work. It made sense that the water wasn't turned on. The apartment hadn't been occupied. Liam's words echoed in her mind. She looked back around the room at everything she had to clean up, but her eyelids were so heavy that it felt as if she could pass out right then. Giving a heavy sigh, she grabbed the to-go bag, drink, purse, and her suitcase in case she needed anything and headed over to Liam's.

After grabbing the spare key and unlocking the door, Liz entered Liam's apartment. She sat at the tall barstool in the kitchen and set her purse next to her, only for it to fall to the ground and spill out all of its contents. Just great. After gathering everything, she returned to the island and opened the container to reveal an enormous cinnamon roll. It was delicious, although the quietness of the room felt deafening.

Soon, her subconscious took the opportunity to fill the void. *What are you doing? You have no money. What do you have to show for yourself anyway?*

She closed her eyes for a moment, trying to push the negativity away, and took a few more bites. *You had to sleep on the beach. What kind of person ends up like that? Are you seriously going to live off these people's pity?*

She clutched her fork tighter. *The only reason Liam even talked to you was because he felt sorry for you. That's the only reason a guy would ever talk to you. Just like Wyatt only talked to you because he felt bad for you. Just like the owner felt sorry for you.*

Her jaw tensed as she stabbed the fork into her breakfast so hard that it nearly went through the box. *Mom and Dad would be so ashamed of you right now.* She shoved the piece into her mouth and angrily chewed longer than she should have until her jaw hurt. *Is this how you treat your parents?* The fork snapped in half.

With tears in her eyes, she cried out, "They're not my parents!"

She pushed her food aside and closed her eyes, trying to compose herself. She took a sip of orange juice before deciding she was no longer hungry and reluctantly determined sleep might be a better option.

Lying down on the couch, Liz curled up into a ball, clutching one of the throw pillows. *You're so damn stubborn. You should have stayed in Ohio and gotten a job like a normal person. Just go back home. Your real parents didn't even want you in the first place.* She rolled over, trying to turn her back on her negative thoughts. Her fists clenched so hard that her nails dug into her skin. *They left you in an alleyway to die, for god's sake!*

She threw her fist into the pillow. *Admit that you were wrong and call the actual people that care about you and raised you!* Her head began to throb as the subconscious voices grew louder. *Go back home. GO BACK HOME!*

She punched the pillow harder, several times until she couldn't hold the pain in any longer. Her chest heaved as her body shook, gasping for air between each uncontrollable sob. She licked her lips, tasting the saltiness of her warm tears.

Soon, she calmed down, and her fists relaxed. Utterly exhausted, she closed her eyes and tried to sleep, but the couch was too hard for her liking. There were two bedrooms. She wasn't sure if it mattered which bed she took, and frankly, she didn't care.

CHAPTER 15

Paths Crossed

"Couldn't convince Denise on Shirtless Men Mondays?" Wyatt asked from behind the bar as Liam, donning his work shirt, walked through the patio entrance.

"Meh." Liam shrugged. "I don't think the ladies could handle us." After he clocked in, he returned to the front, behind the bar. "Thanks for taking that customer. I had to deal with something this morning or I would've been here sooner."

"No problem," Wyatt replied, placing strawberries in the blender to make a smoothie. "I'm starting to get the hang of working here." He bent down, searching under the counter. "Where's the top of this mixing thing?"

Liam laughed. "Yep, you're getting the hang of working here all right. The top of *the blender* is probably still in the back," he said, shaking his head in disbelief. "I'll go grab it."

"No, I'll get it. I need to get some more bananas anyway," Wyatt said before walking to the kitchen.

After Liam greeted his first customer, he caught sight of the young woman walking in. Her messy, light brown hair swayed slightly in the breeze, brushing past her shoulders. A faded green sundress that had seen better days clung to her toned body, and she wore a star pendant that hung close to her breasts. Grains of sand covered her arms and legs. Her eyes met Liam's as he stood pouring a glass of water until it crested over the rim and spilled onto the counter, causing her to giggle at the sight.

"Dammit." Liam quickly grabbed a rag to clean up the mess. "Sorry about that." He handed the man his drink before continuing to sop up the spill. A shadow loomed over him. "I'll be right with you." He looked up to meet the woman's gaze. "Oh, um . . . hi." His voice hiccuped. He cleared his throat. He was so entranced by the woman's beauty his brain felt like it had quit functioning properly. He stuttered over his words until he finally managed to choke out. "Welcome to The Cove. What can I get for you today?"

Get it together, Liam!

She gazed into his eyes until she finally said, "Wyatt."

"Oh." Liam's heart sank a little. How many girls did this guy have? "He's in the back, but he'll be right out. Why don't you have a seat here and I can get you something to drink?" The woman stared at the seat next to her for a moment, then apprehensively sat at the bar. "What would you like?"

"I'd like to speak to Wyatt," she replied, seemingly annoyed.

"Yes, I know that. I just figured you'd want to have something while you waited." Liam handed her a menu, folded out to the drink section. She leaned forward, nearly inches away from him. She smelled like the ocean. "We have. . ." He swallowed uncomfortably and stammered through the list. "Water, orange juice, apple juice." Her blue eyes darted up at his. Something felt familiar, causing him to pause. "I'm sorry, but you look really familiar. Have we met?"

"No." She shifted her gaze to the menu. As a man sat on the stool next to her, she quickly turned her head and anxiously moved herself to the edge of the seat, trying to put distance between her and the man.

"Are you sure?" Liam asked again. "Maybe on the beach or in the water. I'm always out surfing."

"No!" she snapped.

Liam stepped back in surprise. "Ok."

"I don't swim. So there's no way you've seen me in the water." She crossed her arms. "Besides, I just arrived here, so it's impossible we've met," she said in a firm voice as she stood up and walked behind the bar, stunning Liam.

"What are you doing?" he said in a hushed tone, not wanting to draw too much attention. "You can't be back here."

"You asked if I wanted anything to drink. I am very much capable of getting it myself." She opened cabinet after cabinet until Liam pushed his hand on one before she could open it.

"It's kind of my job to get your drink." He grabbed a glass from the shelf and filled it with ice water. "Here." He gently extended the now-full glass to her but quickly withdrew it before she was able to take it.

Her face became flushed. "Thank you."

"You're welcome." He smirked, handing her the drink. "Look, I'm sorry, but you can't be back here," Liam repeated, gently putting his hand on her shoulder, trying to guide her out from behind the bar.

The woman jerked away, clearly irritated by the contact. She spun around and squared her shoulders back, standing as tall as she could just inches away from Liam's face. She did her best to assert her presence, even though she was half a foot shorter than him.

"You really don't like being told what to do, do you?" Liam couldn't help but chuckle. Her frustration made her sexy as hell.

"What's so funny?" she demanded.

Liam stifled another laugh, "Nothing. It's just . . ."

"*What?*"

Liam grinned. "It's cute that your nose crinkles up when you're mad."

~

With the blender lid in tow, Wyatt nearly tripped over himself at the sight of his sister sizing up his friend. *What in the trenches?* he thought, quickening his pace. "Ah, Sarah, what are you doing here?" Wyatt interjected, unsuccessfully trying to lead her away from the bar.

"I was worried. I remembered you said you worked at The Cove so I came on—" Sarah stopped short. "To the island to find you."

"Clearly, I wasn't behind the bar," Wyatt stated.

"Obviously." Sarah carefully took a sip of water, grimaced, and placed it back on the counter. "Ugh! This *water* is disgusting."

Liam picked up the water and sniffed it in confusion.

"I just wanted to see what this job of yours involves." She glanced around behind the bar. "What is this?" Her finger roamed over the purée button on the uncovered blender.

"Sarah, no!" Wyatt ran up to the blender, and Sarah jumped back. However, it was too late. The reddish-pink strawberry banana smoothie mixture erupted from the pitcher, covering Wyatt. "It didn't have the top." He held the lid up and flicked a piece of strawberry from his cheek as Liam stifled a laugh.

"It's not my fault!" she said defensively with her hands on her hips.

Wyatt rolled his eyes. "Then whose was it? You're the one that started messing with stuff."

"Well, Liam never told me—" She snapped her mouth shut.

"How do you know my name?" Liam asked in surprise. "I never told you."

"I . . . I . . ." Sarah stammered, looking at Wyatt for help.

Wyatt enjoyed watching his sister squirm a bit until he spoke up. "Liam, this is my sister, Sarah. I told her I worked with you behind the bar. I guess her curiosity got the best of her, or rather me," he explained, doing his best to wipe his shirt clean from the fruity concoction.

Liam handed Wyatt a towel. "She just walked back here like

she owned the joint," Liam whispered to him. "I'm sorry. I tried to get her to leave, but she's a bit stubborn."

"That's my family for you." Wyatt sighed as he threw the rag on the counter and gently took Sarah's arm.

"Hey!" she yelled as Wyatt guided her from the bar.

"Stop yelling! You're going to draw even more attention," he hissed, looking around at the few morning customers who glanced up from their meals.

"I wouldn't draw attention if you would have just shown up last night!" she scolded.

Wyatt winced. He had completely forgotten he was to meet her in the underwater cavern. He had planned on going after seeing Jessica, but he had been so exhausted after work that he canceled his date with Jessica and fell asleep as soon as his head hit the pillow.

"It's my fault," Liam said, trying to take the fall. "I had him work late and then he had a date with—" he began, causing Wyatt's eyes to widen.

"Date?" Sarah shouted. Wyatt flung his head back in exasperation.

Liam's face shifted into a grimace. "Crap," he muttered.

"I didn't go—" Wyatt started.

"You're going out with a lan—" Sarah began spouting off before she was muffled with Wyatt's hand on top of her mouth. She stared daggers into Wyatt as he slowly removed his hand.

"Are you going to stop yelling at me so we can talk like two civilized *humans*?" Wyatt asked.

"Yes," Denise said from behind them. "Let's take this upstairs to my apartment."

"Denise, it's not her fault," Liam pleaded. "I was just showing her the bar. Don't blame Wyatt."

"Denise?" Sarah asked in shock. "Is that—"

"I didn't exactly imagine you meeting Mom's friend like this," Wyatt muttered.

Denise patted Liam on the back. "It's fine, Liam. Get back to work and I'll have someone clean up this mess." She turned back to Sarah and looked her up and down with a smile. "You remind me so much of your mother. Follow me, dear."

Liam leaned over the bar. "Well, it was nice meeting you, even if you were about to punch me." He winked.

Sarah's cheeks blushed as she scrunched up her nose at him.

Wyatt gave a confused look between Liam and Sarah before she turned around and walked away from him. "Is there something going on here that I don't know about?" he inquired, playfully nudging her as they walked up the steps.

Sarah tripped over her own feet, necessitating Wyatt to catch her. "No!" She straightened herself. "That dumb land-dweller was irritating me."

"Person," Wyatt said. "That dumb *person* was irritating you. Mom hated the term land-dweller."

"Plus, if you refer to them in that way, people are going to start questioning you," Denise explained, turning the key to her apartment.

"Also, that dumb guy seems to have a crush on you," Wyatt teased.

"Well, I don't like him." Sarah pushed past Wyatt through the entrance to the apartment.

Denise closed the door behind them and guided them to the living room. "Please, sit."

Sarah sat on the worn green couch.

"I'll stand, thanks. I wouldn't want to dirty your couch with smoothie," he said, glaring at his sister.

Denise nodded before disappearing into the kitchen for a moment.

"Admit it, there's an inkling of interest for him," Wyatt egged on.

Denise reappeared and placed a few glasses and a pitcher of water on the coffee table. "Water?"

"I already tried your water, so I'll pass," Sarah said with a look of disdain.

"I promise, this will taste a lot better." Denise poured the drinks.

Sarah studied it for a moment before taking a sip. "Mmm. I will admit this tastes delicious, but I won't admit I like him. I mean, he isn't the ugliest land-dweller." She paused. "Sorry. Human I've seen, unlike you." She playfully stuck out her tongue.

Denise laughed. "Your mother was a spitfire, too." She went back to the kitchen and returned with a bottle of water. "I prefer filtered water instead of salted." She sat across from them in a yellow, floral high-backed chair and slipped off her sandals, stretching out her legs.

"You really knew our mom?" Sarah asked.

"I did. She was my best friend," Denise answered. Her gaze fell to the floor. "I am so sorry to hear she passed."

Sarah's voice shook when she spoke. "She didn't pass. She was—"

"Wyatt told me. That must have been horrible."

"I don't remember much, but what I do still haunts me like it was yesterday. Yet at the same time, it feels like a lifetime ago," Sarah said, fumbling with her hands.

"I can't imagine." Denise shook her head. "I'm sorry you had to go through that at such a young age."

"I barely remember what she looked like." Sarah sniffed and touched her wet cheek. She looked up at Wyatt with a confused expression.

"It's ok," Wyatt said, rubbing her back. "Those are tears. We don't feel or see them underwater."

Denise stood up and handed her a tissue. "Here, I have something you should see that I think will help," she said and left the room.

The ticking of a clock in the other room filled the void of silence between Wyatt and Sarah.

"You doing ok?" he asked

"We can trust her, right?" Sarah wrung her hands nervously.

"Yes. She kept Mom's secret for this long. She'll keep our

secret. Don't worry." He knelt and took her hand, gently squeezing it.

The floor creaked as Denise walked back into the room, placed the same box she had shown Wyatt before on the table, and opened the lid.

"What's this?" Sarah curiously looked down into the box. "Ow, Wyatt, my hand!"

Wyatt looked down to find his hand clenched tightly around Sarah's. "Sorry," he apologized, quickly releasing it. "I didn't realize I was squeezing so hard."

"Wyatt, why don't you go back to work? Let us girls chat and maybe do a little bit of shopping." Denise winked and looked him up and down. "You might want to change into a clean shirt, too."

Wyatt turned to Sarah. She was already diving into the box of their mother's memories.

She peered up. "Go. I'll be fine."

"You know where to find me," he said.

After leaving the restaurant, Wyatt walked back to Liam's apartment, where he noticed a pair of small sandals outside the front door. The last time he had checked, Liam's feet weren't that small, and he knew Sarah hadn't left them.

A strange slight pull tugged at his chest. He turned the doorknob to find it unlocked. Odd.

Wyatt quietly entered the apartment. "Hello? Anyone here?" he called out, with only silence replying back.

He scanned the area. His eyes narrowed at a half-eaten cinnamon roll that was sitting on the island counter, along with a drink and a to-go bag from The Cove.

He closed the door, revealing a blue suitcase with a broken handle. His breath caught at the sight of it. Liz. Her blonde hair, pale skin, slight smile, and the way her skin felt underneath his hand filled his mind. Wyatt tried to push the thoughts aside. He was just getting to know Jessica; he couldn't be that kind of guy.

He took off his shoes and walked around the seemingly empty apartment. Was she still here? Slipping through the hallway, he noticed the door to his room was slightly shut. He peeked through the crack to see Liz curled up in a ball, fast asleep. What was she doing in his bed? Sleeping, obviously. But Liam never told Wyatt she was crashing here. Maybe he didn't know. Though he doubted she'd break into the house just to sleep. He'd have to ask Liam when he went back to work.

He was about to turn around when he remembered why he had come there in the first place. *Blowfish, I need a clean shirt! I'll just go in really quick and grab it.*

Wyatt crept into his room and carefully tried to open the dresser drawer, but not before the wooden floor creaked under him. She stirred and let out a small whimper. He held his breath as his body stiffened. She let out a slight snore, reaffirming that she was still asleep.

Glancing over his shoulder, he noticed her tear-stained face. His heart sank knowing she had been upset, and he felt the urge to comfort her just like the night before. Pushing the feeling aside, he slipped his stained T-shirt off, exposing his back to her. He balled up the shirt and set it on the dresser, accidentally knocking down a small wooden turtle figurine in the process. His reaction time wasn't fast enough to catch it before it clattered to the ground.

Shit!

As Wyatt knelt to retrieve it, he turned to see Liz staring back at him.

"Um . . . hi." Wyatt wasn't exactly sure how to greet a person who had been sleeping in his bed.

"Wyatt?" Liz lifted her head slightly off the pillow, and her locks stuck to her face from the dried tears. She craned her neck and looked around in confusion until a realization hit her. "Oh no, is this your room?"

"Yeah, but it's fine." Wyatt sat on the floor. Propping his arms along the bed. Resting his chin on his forearm, he met her gaze. "Are you ok?"

Her eyes darted down. "Yeah, just tired," she replied, brushing her hair from her face.

He furrowed his brow. "You've been crying."

She slowly sat up and hugged one of the pillows, hiding her face behind it. "Is it that obvious?"

Wyatt gently pulled down the pillow, revealing her blue-gray eyes. "Just a bit." He smiled, gesturing with his thumb and pointer finger nearly touching.

Wyatt stood and put his clean work shirt on. As he pulled the hem down, he spied her watching him and her cheeks turned a rosy pink. The bed dipped under his weight as he sat on the edge, inches from Liz's bare feet.

"I'm just having a bad day, that's all," Liz confessed, lowering the pillow.

"It wouldn't have to do with your parents, would it?"

She bit her bottom lip as if she was trying to hold back what was on her mind. "I'd rather not talk about them."

"I understand. If you ever need to talk to someone, I'm here for you. I'm a pretty good listener." The words tumbled out of Wyatt's mouth before he could even comprehend them. He hardly knew this girl, but something about her made him want to open up.

"Thanks," Liz replied with a weak smile.

Wyatt cleared his throat, fidgeting in his seat. "Can I ask why you're in my bedroom?"

Seemingly embarrassed, Liz looked around for a moment before her words quickly flowed out of her. "I'm staying next door, but I'm waiting for clean sheets and the water to be turned on. Liam was kind enough to let me stay here if I needed to rest. I tried sleeping on the couch, but it wasn't that comfortable. I swear I didn't know this was your room, or I would have stayed on the couch and—"

"It's fine. I don't blame you for wanting to sleep in my bed. I mean," he stammered, "in a bed compared to the couch." He internally grimaced at his words. "So you're, uh, with Liam, huh?"

"With Liam?" She raised her eyebrows. "No, no, I'm not with him. I mean, maybe we're friends. We literally just met. I didn't come here to hook up with someone." She let out an exhausted sigh.

"Oh, that's good. I mean, it's good to focus on whatever you came here to do." Wyatt's words flew out of his mouth. *Why am I rambling? Focus, Wyatt.*

Liz rubbed the back of her neck. "Yeah, I guess so."

"I just came by to change my shirt. You probably want to get back to sleep. I'm sorry for waking you."

"Well, you weren't really expecting a girl in your bed." She blushed before looking away. "At least not me."

"I'm glad it was you." Wyatt stood and gently touched her hand for a moment. A surge of warmth shot up his arm. "I, um . . ." He paused, curious about what just happened. "I gotta get back to work." He felt guilty leaving Liz alone in the apartment since she had clearly been upset earlier. "Maybe I'll see you later."

"Maybe," she replied with a gentle smile.

CHAPTER 16

Becoming

When she heard the front door close, Liz buried her face in Wyatt's pillow from embarrassment. The scent of the ocean drifted up to her nose, causing her shoulders to relax.

Deciding to stop sulking, she picked herself up, wandered into the kitchen, and reheated the rest of her cinnamon roll. After finishing her breakfast, she brushed her teeth, then left Liam's.

Gazing out at the gulf before turning the key to her temporary home, she couldn't help but feel entranced by the aroma and the sound of the sea. Ignoring the lure, she sighed and entered. She scanned the room, trying to figure out what to do first. Deciding to start with her suitcase, she lugged it down the hallway to the bedroom.

She examined the simple room. Light bled through the window to her right, revealing the beige walls, hardwood floor, an older dresser, and a full-sized bed. A large mirror hung on the back of the door.

She knelt and began to unzip her suitcase only to be interrupted by a knock on the front door. Liz returned to the kitchen and answered the door, revealing a man holding a large box.

"Denise said the water should be on now and sent me over here with new sheets, towels, and cleaning supplies. I'm also supposed to pick up the boxes for The Cove," the man explained.

"Oh, thank you! You can set that one on the counter over there," she said, gesturing toward the kitchen.

After the man dropped it off, he made several more trips to remove the restaurant supplies, and then left her alone.

Most of the day was dedicated to cleaning and tidying the apartment, with a break for lunch. Thankfully, Denise had included a loaf of bread and a jar of peanut butter, as well as a few bottles of water in the box. After nearly half a roll of paper towels later, she was done cleaning the kitchen and living room. She made the bed and thoroughly wiped down the bathroom.

Exhausted and a bit hungry, she plopped on the couch and looked at the clock. Seeing it was nearing dinnertime, she remembered what Liam said about coming by The Cove. She hated being a freeloader, but her stomach was craving more than another peanut butter sandwich.

The sun was descending toward the horizon as Liz walked the short distance. The soft sounds of the waves beckoned her toward the beach. Everything in her body screamed to veer off toward the water. She forced herself to move to the patio, but she gazed one more time to the shore, causing her skin to crawl. What was going on with her? The feeling terrified her as her hands twitched.

A cold blast of air kissed her skin as she walked through the back entrance, sending chills down her body. It wasn't anything new, as she was usually cold in any setting that was below seventy degrees. She proceeded to sit at the bar and look over the menu while she waited for Liam to take her order.

"Hey!" his familiar voice greeted her. "Taking a break from cleaning?"

Liz peered over her menu at Liam's eyes that seemed to smile back at her. "Yeah, I didn't want to but my stomach argued otherwise. Plus, it doesn't help that the apartment is next to the restaurant. I'm pretty sure I could smell the burgers inside the apartment."

"Hence why I try to get a morning run in once in a while," he said, patting his stomach. "Speaking of which, do you know what you want? Or do you want me to give you some time? Our special today is jumbo fried shrimp."

"Meh, no thank you. I'm not a fan of seafood. The turkey bacon club sandwich looks good, but you don't need to be spending any more than a couple of bucks on me. How about a small appetizer?" She placed her menu back down for Liam to take.

He frowned. "If you're worried about the price, it's not a big deal. I get a discount because I work here."

"Are you sure? An appetizer would be fine."

"Nope, I've made up your mind. You're having the sandwich. Would you like fries?" Liam asked.

With a slight chuckle, Liz defeatedly replied, "Yes, please."

"And what would you like to drink?"

"Water is fine," she insisted.

"Ok, but I told you not to worry about the price," Liam said.

Liz couldn't help but notice Wyatt's absence from the bar. "I thought Wyatt was working today?"

"He just left. His sister is in town," Liam quickly answered before turning to the next customer a few seats to her right to take their request before leaving to put their orders in.

She looked over at a man a few seats to her left who was already halfway into his meal. The smell of his shrimp and fish wafted to her nose. Normally, she couldn't stand the aroma of seafood, but something about it smelled delicious. She convinced herself it was the seasoning or the way it was prepared. Her right leg bounced furiously against the railing of the barstool. She fumbled with her hands as they began to shake again. *I just need some food*, she tried convincing herself. *I did a lot of work.*

Liam returned and grabbed a cup, filling it with ice and water. Liz's throat had become so dry that she couldn't even swallow her anxiety.

Liam's eyes darted to Liz's folded arms that were shaking. "Are you cold?" he asked, handing the glass of water to her.

"A little," Liz lied in a raspy voice. She was a bit cold but not enough to make her tremble so much. She leaned down and took a sip of the ice water through the paper straw, savoring it. She continued to suck the water down while Liam talked.

Liam chuckled a bit. "I don't think I've ever met someone that was cold on an eighty-five-degree day! Why don't you sit out on the patio to warm up?"

Liz nearly choked on her water. "No!" she blurted out. The thought of staring at the gulf sent chills down her spine. She quickly composed herself, realizing she might have come off a bit harsh. "I mean, I'll probably be too hot out there. I'm either too hot or too cold. I don't really have a happy medium." She plastered a smile on her face, then immediately went back to her water.

"All right." He shrugged, then noticed her drink was nearly empty. "Here, let me top you off," he said, grabbing the pitcher of water to refill her glass before returning to his other customers.

Liz quickly drank the full glass of water within seconds, immediately noticing her jitters calming down. She must've been dehydrated.

"I guess you were pretty thirsty!" he exclaimed in surprise when he later returned. "I'll just leave the pitcher here."

Liz played with her straw, twirling it around the water as she waited for her food. It wasn't long before her meal arrived. When she was done eating, she thanked Liam, who unfortunately wasn't able to chat much since the restaurant was bustling from the dinner crowd.

As Liz left The Cove, the orange glow of the sun radiated out of the horizon, sending beams of light into the darkening sky. She looked up to see the tiny dots of starlight dimly appear and wondered how her parents were. What were they thinking at this very moment? Were they worried? Disappointed? Angry? Should she use Liam's phone to call them? Would they only try to convince her this wasn't a good idea and that she should come home?

Her eyes welled up at the thoughts, but she held back her emotions, pushing them deep down, and entered the apartment to finish unpacking.

After placing the last articles of clothing in the dresser, she stretched her stiff back. Her hair felt dirty and oily from being out in the sun. Deciding not to let her fear from what had happened last night get the best of her, she gathered her pajamas and a towel. In the bathroom, she stared at the walk-in shower for longer than she desired.

She scoffed to herself. It wasn't like the water could actually hurt her. It was just leg cramps last night, anyway. Yeah, really bad leg cramps.

She turned the knob, letting the water fall from the showerhead, and stripped out of her dingy clothes. Entering the shower, she let the warm water cascade down her sore and tired body as she hung her head. For a moment, she let go of her feelings and cleared her mind, letting nothing penetrate her thoughts. And for that moment, she was completely at ease and free from all stress.

That was, until the tops of her feet started to tingle.

The water was probably just too hot.

However, it soon changed into the pinpricks from the night before that crawled up her legs. Memories of feeling helpless on the beach flashed through her mind. She pressed her right hand against the wall in front of her as her heart beat rapidly. Her eyes tightened as the feeling rose up to her waist.

No. No, not again!

She screamed in agony. Pain seared her right thigh as if she was being branded with a hot iron. Her legs gave out from beneath her, and she fell hard to the tile floor, scraping her knees. This couldn't be happening again.

She needed to either turn off the water or get away from it. The first seemed impossible. With as much pain as she was in, standing or even trying to sit up wasn't an option, and the valve to shut it off was near the entrance. Either way, she had to move.

Just like last time, she couldn't get her legs to work properly. She wasn't about to repeat the other night and continuously fall back down on the hard floor. Using her arms, she pulled herself toward the lip of the shower. If she could just get herself out of the water, then maybe the pain would go away.

She was halfway out of the shower when there was a knock on the door. She peered up to see it cracked open.

"Liz?" Liam's voice called from the other side of the door.

Her eyes went wide. He couldn't be here. He couldn't see her like this.

"It's Liam. I heard you scream from my apartment. I had an extra key and let myself in. Are you ok?"

Liz was lying completely naked and sprawled out between being in and out of the shower and in excruciating pain; she was not ok. There was no way she could hide it from him.

Her right thigh radiated, causing her to cry out again. The door creaked open. She had to admit defeat.

"It . . . it burns." She squeezed her eyes shut. "I can't move. It hurts too much."

"I'm coming in, ok?" It wasn't so much of a question but a warning. Before she could answer, the door flung open and he was standing on the other side of the room with his right hand barely covering his eyes.

Liz lowered her head against the cool tile. If she wasn't in so much pain, she would have felt the heat rush to her cheeks in embarrassment. No other male had ever seen her naked before, and now, here was this man to see her in all her pale glory.

"Oh god! What happened?" Liam shut the water off.

The white linen towel she had desperately tried to crawl toward was now draped over her. Liz turned her head to the side to see Liam kneeling beside her.

"Can you stand?"

She tried desperately to push herself up. If she could stand, then maybe she could run away from all of this. However, she was too weak. A sob she had tried to hold back came out of her mouth as she shook her head. His warm hands began to roll her over, and she quickly grabbed the towel to wrap it around her wet body, securing it as best as she could. Her chest tightened as if someone was slowly squeezing her insides.

She turned her head the other way so he couldn't see her as he gently lifted her in his arms and set her on the fluffy bath mat outside the shower with her back against the wall. She still refused to look at him as he sat in front of her and pushed the wet tendrils of hair from her face. She wasn't sure if the droplets of water along her cheeks were from the shower or her tears.

"Are you ok?" he asked again. He shook his head. "I mean, of course not." His eyes scanned her over, stopping at her scraped knees. "What happened?"

Liz took a deep breath. She needed to say something, anything, so that maybe he would leave. "I, um, I fell."

Everything was silent except for the dripping of water from the shower. She grimaced as she tried to pull her legs up to her chest.

He narrowed his eyes, seemingly not believing her lie. Instead of asking for the truth, he asked, "Where does it hurt?"

Her eyes darted down, and she felt herself pulling away from him.

"Liz, you can trust me." He placed his hand under her chin and lifted her head so her eyes met his. "Let me help you. Please."

"Here," she whispered and pointed to her upper thigh.

"Is it ok if I move the towel so I can see? It's not something I haven't seen before." He cocked his head to the side. "Have you seen all the middle-aged men strutting about with their Speedos on?"

Liz's lips curled slightly as she tried not to smile at his joke, but it quickly faltered when his hands reached for the towel. "Wait."

She undid the towel and pulled it away, doing her best to

maintain her modesty. She wasn't about to let Liam see any more of her body than he needed to.

When she tried to expose her right thigh, she hissed. It felt like peeling off a Band-AID that was stuck to a scab. When crimson appeared on the fluffy white material, she froze and looked away, afraid to see what was underneath. Had she cut herself when she fell?

Liam placed his hand next to hers to help peel back the towel and gasped. "Oh my god."

She looked down and suddenly felt light-headed from the gruesome sight of her leg. It was as if her flesh had been burned away, leaving a four-inch oval of she didn't know what.

"We need to get you to a hospital," Liam urged.

Liz's eyes went wide. If she went to the hospital, they would run all kinds of tests and call her parents. She didn't even know how to explain what had happened to her. "No!"

Liam stared at her in confusion. "No? Look at your leg. There's blood all over you, and you're in pain. If that doesn't scream emergency room, I'm not sure what does."

"Please," she begged.

With a defeated sigh, Liam leaned in closer to inspect it. "Did you get a tattoo? I think it may be infected."

"I-I don't have a tattoo," Liz stammered. Something glistened underneath all of the blood, and she forced herself to examine her thigh closer. The edges of the skin around the outside of it were scabbed. "Can you get me a wet towel?"

Liam grabbed a washcloth from the cabinet and ran it under water. When he returned, he lightly placed it over her wound. Liz flinched as he cleaned the area.

"Does it still hurt?" he asked, letting the cool water run across her wound.

She relaxed a bit. "Not as much." It felt like the water was helping her now, instead of hurting her. It made no sense.

"You need to tell me exactly what happened," he said with a stern voice.

There was no lying to him at this point. "I don't know. I went into the shower, and then my legs started to tingle just like—" Her mind flashed back to being on the beach.

"Just like what?"

She blinked and looked at him. "It was just like last night," she murmured. "Except worse." She turned her attention to the bloodied towel and moved Liam's hand away from it.

"Last night? Does this have something to do with how I found you on the beach yesterday?" His voice was far off as she stared at her thigh. She couldn't quite make out what was underneath the smeared blood, but it wasn't normal.

"What . . . what is that?"

Liam furrowed his brow, studying her leg. He carefully wiped off the remaining blood and removed the thin layer of necrotic skin to reveal an iridescent aqua pattern that blended with her flesh. "Are those . . . ?"

Liz shrieked and immediately looked anywhere but at her leg. It was just a really nasty bright bruise, right?

Bruises aren't aqua and shimmery!

Her breath quickened until she was nearly hyperventilating. Suddenly, she didn't want to be there anymore. Her leg twitched. Good, at least they were working now.

"I . . . I . . . Oh god!" she stammered.

Liam inched closer to her, but she pulled her leg farther from him and curled into herself. "Breathe. Just breathe."

"Breathe? Breathe? What the hell is on my leg?" she shouted at him.

Liam swallowed hard, which wasn't a good sign. "They look like . . . scales," he said more calmly than Liz had liked him to be.

"What do you mean, *scales*?" she exclaimed.

He continued to stare at her thigh. "Scales, like you'd see on a fish."

"I know what scales are, Liam! And stop staring at me!" She hid her leg back under the towel and leaned her head against the wall. Was this some kind of punishment for coming here? "I don't know what's happening to me," her voice croaked. Closing her eyes, she choked back tears.

When Liam wrapped his arms around her slender body in a warm embrace, it broke down the wall she had built around her since her grandfather's death. Tears flowed freely down her face as she sobbed uncontrollably into his shoulder. Her hands clutched his shirt, and she never wanted to leave, even though an ache was forming in her chest.

"Shh, it's going to be ok," Liam tried reassuring her the best he could. "But you have to breathe, ok? Can you do that?"

Liz sniffled, nodding. Liam slowly pulled away from her. She wiped the tears from her face with the palm of her hand and continued to take short breaths, gasping for air every so often.

"Deep breath in." Liam inhaled with her. "And deep breath out," he said and exhaled. "Good. Again."

They continued the breathing technique until Liz had calmed down.

"Let's take it one step at a time, ok?" He pulled himself up. "Why don't we wash the rest of your leg off and get you dressed?"

Liz looked down at her leg, and while he had used the cloth to clean it up, there was still blood that had run down her leg. "What if this gets worse?" Liz recoiled, her breath quickening.

He held out his hand. "I won't let anything happen to you."

"You can't promise that."

"You're right. But you have to trust me. Can you stand?"

Liz moved her legs around. "I think so."

She took his hand, and he pulled her to her feet. She cinched the towel around her tighter and reluctantly walked into the shower, holding his bicep for support. He turned on the water, diverting the flow to the handheld sprayer and grabbed it from the wall. She pulled the bottom of the towel just high enough to reveal her thigh.

"Doing ok?" he asked, letting the water wash away the remaining blood and loose skin.

Liz nodded. He turned off the tap, and water dripped from the bottom of his shorts.

"Let me get some fresh towels." He disappeared into the hallway before returning and handing her one. "I'll give you some privacy." He closed the door behind him.

Liz stood still, holding the dry towel. What was she going to do now? Call her parents? Go home? And then what? She pushed the thoughts from her mind. One step at a time.

She let the bloodied towel drop to the floor and dried herself off with the new one. She put on her pajamas, which consisted of a slightly oversized shirt and fluffy socks. Why hadn't she brought something more modest? Because she hadn't thought she'd be wearing PJs in front of a guy. She stared at herself in the mirror. Her tired, bloodshot eyes blinked a few times before she hung her head. She couldn't stay in there forever; Liam was waiting for her.

With a sigh, she left the room and found him in her bedroom, sitting on a towel on the edge of her bed. She sat down a few feet away from him and fidgeted with the hem of her shirt, trying to pull it down farther. He turned to her with a half-smile, and her cheeks flushed in embarrassment.

"You good? I mean, as good as you can be," Liam asked.

She remained quiet and shrugged. The silence hung between them for what felt like hours before Liam finally spoke.

"You said before that this was like last night. What exactly happened?" he asked.

She closed her eyes for a moment, reliving the nightmare over again. "The start of this." was the only thing she could reply as she looked at the scales on her leg.

CHAPTER 17

Diving In

The alarm clock on top of the nightstand flashed eleven forty-five. Liz ran her fingers through her now-dry and slightly wavy hair. She curled her legs under her and leaned back against the headboard as she waited for Liam to speak. She had laid all her cards on the table, hoping she could trust him. Something was wrong with her, and as much as she wanted to deal with this on her own, she couldn't.

Liam sat back on his elbows with his feet dangling off the bed, still trying to process everything she had told him about the previous evening. He opened his mouth to say something but quickly shut it as if he was carefully calculating his next words.

"I wish you would have told me what happened when I found you lying on the beach," he said, breaking the silence. He turned his head to her with pity in his eyes. She hated it. She had seen it too many times at her grandfather's funeral.

Liz cocked her head to the side. "And have you look at me the way you are right now?" she replied, causing Liam's eyes to dart away. "Besides, you would have made me go to the hospital."

He shifted in his seat. "Yeah, you're probably right. I don't blame you for not sharing that with a complete stranger."

"I thought since we talked earlier, you weren't a stranger?" she quipped, playing with the hem of her shirt, trying to hide the pattern on her thigh.

Liam smiled for a moment before his gaze turned to the scales that peeked out. The vibrant colors had dulled since drying. Swallowing her fears, she slowly glided her fingertips across each smooth scale that overlapped the other. It felt strange but oddly familiar, like they had always been there. She caught Liam watching her and saw his hand fidgeting.

"If you want to feel them, you can," she said, exposing the scales.

He moved his hand over them, hesitating for a moment before letting his fingertips glide across them. She never imagined the first guy touching her would be like this.

He quickly withdrew his hand. "I'm sorry."

Liz furrowed her brow and pulled the fabric back down, hoping it would ease her worry if she couldn't see the scales. "Why are you sorry? It's not like this is your fault."

"It's not your fault either. You didn't ask for all of this to be dumped on you. Finding out you were adopted, not knowing who your birth parents are, your rental being sold, your credit card being frozen, and now this."

"You forgot about my suitcase handle breaking. I'm pretty sure that one takes the cake." She smiled weakly.

"Very true, I forgot about that important detail." He playfully nudged her shoulder. "I'm not sure how you're handling all of this."

"I'm fine," she said with a shrug.

"You know what FINE means, don't you?" he asked.

"What's that?"

"Freaked out, insecure, neurotic, and emotional," Liam said with a smirk. Liz promptly grabbed one of the pillows and flung it at Liam. "Hey!" He laughed, throwing his hands up in defense.

Liz lowered the pillow and hugged it, playing with one of the corners.

Liam's face was drawn as he said, "You know, I was really scared for you back there."

"Me too," Liz said. Her eyes felt heavy as they sat in silence for a moment. "It's late. Don't you have work in the morning?"

"I'm fi—" Liam stifled a yawn, and Liz raised an eyebrow. "All right, I might be a little tired." He pushed off the bed, and Liz followed him out into the hallway toward the living room. He paused, and his gaze darted down at her leg before meeting her eyes. "Maybe I should sleep on the couch."

"I'll be ok," she replied. Now it was Liam's turn to raise his brow at Liz. She let out a sigh. "As ok as I can be. I'm pretty exhausted from everything, so I shouldn't have any problem getting to sleep tonight."

He opened the door and turned around. "You'll come get me if something happens, right?"

"I promise," she assured him.

He leaned against the doorjamb with his arms folded. "So now what?"

"Now, you go to bed and go to work in the morning." Liz pushed him out the door.

"I know that!" He lightly chuckled. "I mean, what do we do about you?"

She shrugged. "I don't know. We can discuss it after you're done with work tomorrow," she suggested, hoping nothing else would happen in the meantime.

"Sounds like a plan. I only work until three tomorrow," he said, then headed toward his apartment.

Liz panicked. "Liam?"

He turned to her before opening his door. "Yeah?"

"You won't tell anyone, will you?"

He walked back to her and placed his hands on her shoulders. "You have my word," he replied with a serious tone. "I won't tell anyone. I promise."

"Thank you. Get some sleep."

"You, too."

～

Liam glanced at the time. Three o'clock on the dot. He untied his apron and left the bar to clock out.

"See you tomorrow," Wyatt called out to Denise before walking into the back with Liam. They had both opened the restaurant.

"Got any plans today?" Liam inquired, waiting his turn to clock out.

"Yeah, Jessica's picking me up. I'm not really sure what we're doing."

"I'm not trying to be rude, but she is totally out of your league. You know that, right?" Liam playfully elbowed him. "I mean, you wash up on shore and not even a few hours later, you've landed the hottest chick around here."

Wyatt turned around, cocking his head slightly. "Is that a hint of jealousy I'm hearing?"

"No." His voice pitched up an octave. Wyatt crossed his arms and leaned against the wall while Liam clocked out. "Ok, maybe a little," he admitted. "But not because you're dating Jessica. She seems way too high maintenance or something."

"Or something." Wyatt clocked out before they exited. "Don't worry, you'll find someone out of your league soon." He slapped Liam on the back with a laugh. "What about you? Any plans?"

"I'm meeting a friend," Liam replied, opening the door to the patio and exiting into the muggy ninety-degree air.

"Oh? Could it be the same friend you were out with late last night?" Wyatt nudged Liam's arm.

Liam laughed. "You checkin' on me now?"

"I just noticed that you weren't home when I went to bed last night."

"You're giving me flak for being out late? What time did you get back?" Liam asked.

"Apparently not as late as you. Soooo, who's the lucky girl?"

"She's just a friend. I was helping her with something, and I guess time got away from us," Liam explained, walking past Liz's apartment. He turned to see Wyatt standing in front of her door. This wasn't the first time Liam had noticed his friend's eyes drifting in her general direction. Interesting. "You coming?"

"Huh?" Wyatt turned his head to Liam. "Oh yeah." He continued to their apartment and through the door.

Liam quickly changed from his work attire into cargo shorts and a red tank top that showed off his arms. He walked out of his room and met Wyatt, who had donned a pair of jean shorts and a light blue T-shirt.

"So you and Jessica . . ." Liam began, locking the door. "You guys getting pretty serious?" When Wyatt didn't answer, Liam turned to find him gazing toward Liz's apartment once more.

"How's Liz getting along?" Wyatt asked, completely oblivious to Liam's question.

"Good, I guess," Liam answered.

"Did she say how long she was staying?"

"Oh, I dunno. So . . . you and Jessica?" he asked again, trying to get away from any subject matter that dealt with Liz.

Wyatt turned his attention back to Liam and began to walk toward The Cove parking lot. "Oh yeah. Sorry." He thought for a moment, then shrugged. "I dunno."

Liam followed him. Even though he was meeting Liz at her place, he didn't want Wyatt to think something was going on between the two of them, not to mention why he was helping her.

"Do you like her?"

Wyatt rubbed his hand along the back of his neck. "She's cool and all, but there's just something about her. I'm not really sure how to explain it. It feels like I'm being pulled in two different directions. One minute she's distant from me. The next she's devouring me in front of the whole restaurant."

"Maybe give it some time?" Liam suggested, trying to be supportive as they sat on one of the wooden benches. Frankly, he wasn't exactly sure why Wyatt was dating Jessica. She certainly wasn't the nicest person Liam had met, but then again, maybe there was a soft side under all that makeup and high heels.

"She's mesmerizing, but I'm not sure I feel a real—"

Before Wyatt could finish and Liam could give him any more advice, a midnight-blue Jeep sped to a stop in the parking lot. Jessica lowered her shades and stared at the two men. Her fiery red lips curled up. "Hey, sexy. Ready?"

"Oh, thanks but I'm waiting for someone else," Liam joked. Wyatt chuckled but soon composed himself when Jessica's smile disappeared immediately.

She narrowed her eyes at Liam. "Who would go out with you anyway?"

"Jessica—" Wyatt began to chastise her as he walked around to the car's passenger side.

"You know I'm only kidding." Jessica pouted her full lips, waiting for Wyatt to enter the car.

I'm sure you were, Liam thought to himself, internally rolling his eyes. He waved, watching them peel out onto the main road. "So much for that softer side," he muttered, feeling sorry for his friend.

When Jessica's vehicle was clearly out of sight, he trekked back to Liz's. He lifted his hand to knock, and before his knuckles could land on the wood, the door swung open.

"Hey!" Liz greeted. "I heard you leave and saw you were talking with Wyatt."

Liam walked through the doorway. "Yeah, he asked how you were doing."

"He did?" she asked coyly.

"Yeah, but don't worry, I changed the subject. I didn't want him asking any more questions about you," Liam replied, making his way into the kitchen.

"Oh." Her shoulders fell. "That was a good idea." She closed the front door, then spun around. "Wait, more questions?"

As he sat at the island, his eyes narrowed on his laptop and the multitude of browser tabs open. That morning, as he was getting ready for his run, Liz had asked to borrow it so she could email her parents that she was ok. He had tried to convince her to borrow his phone to call, but she still didn't feel comfortable talking to them.

"So, what's going on here?" he asked, ignoring her question about Wyatt.

Liz grabbed a glass of water from the counter. "I've been trying to figure out what's happening to me," she answered, lifting the edge of the glass to her lips. She took a few big swigs before taking a seat next to Liam.

"Make any headway?"

She twisted her mouth. "Not really. Searching 'blue aqua scale skin condition' just brings up something called"—she glanced at a piece of paper next to the computer—"ichthyosis vulgaris, which looks nothing like what I have."

Liam leaned over the table and studied her findings. Listed on the paper was everything that had happened to her with a different diagnosis next to each symptom, but combined with the scales, nothing came up.

She was staring at her glass of water, deep in thought. Her mouth opened, then closed a few times as she tried to bring herself to speak.

"What is it?" Liam questioned. He could tell something was eating away at her.

She placed her forearms on the counter and leaned forward. "Remember how I said I was adopted?"

Liam gave an exaggerated shocked face. "You are?"

"Stop it." She nudged his shoulder. "I think I need to find my biological parents. Maybe whatever's going on with me is something genetic that they can help me with."

"Does that mean you're going home then?"

She shook her head. "I wasn't adopted in Ohio. I was adopted here on the island."

"Whoa, seriously? Wait. Wasn't this trip planned before you knew? What are the odds?"

"It's not a coincidence. I hadn't planned on going alone. My grandpa was going to go with me. He was going to tell me." Her eyes darted away, and she lifted the glass to drink the last of her water.

Liam frowned. "I'm sorry he never got the chance to tell you in person, but at least you know."

"Yeah, I guess so. I'm not even sure where to start."

"Well, let's start from the beginning. Did anyone ever tell you exactly what happened?"

"My grandpa—" Her breath caught for a moment, and she cleared her throat. She stood and grabbed her glass to refill it with tap water. "My grandpa was on his morning walk along the beach when he found me abandoned behind a local restaurant." She downed the rest of her water before placing the glass on the counter a little too loudly.

"You've been drinking a lot of water, are you ok?" he asked.

She filled her glass once again and quickly spun around with a smile. "Yup, just a bit parched."

He studied her as she returned to her seat. He wasn't sure if she was being completely honest, but he decided not to push it. "Do you know which restaurant it was?"

"No, just that it was near their home." The corners of her lip pulled down as Liz played with the rim of her glass. "Why couldn't he have just told me sooner?" she whispered, wiping away a tear from the corner of her eye. She straightened and turned to Liam. "After my parents revealed the truth, my grandma confessed that my grandpa had told her there was more to the story. But he never told anyone what that was, not even her. She said he had promised to protect me." Her fists clenched. "How is this protecting me?" she snapped, getting out of her seat.

Liam turned around and watched her pace. "Look, I can't tell you why he did what he did, but he must have had his reasons. We'll figure this out, but getting angry about the past isn't going to help you. Is there anything else you can tell me? Or something he told you that might help?"

Liz gave a deep sigh. "Other than him telling me I was more special than I knew, nothing comes to mind." She paused, then walked over to her purse in the living room, dug through it, and returned to her seat. She placed an old postcard on the counter in front of him and turned it over. "I do have this. My grandparents' old address."

Pulling the laptop in front of him, he brought up a map and typed in the address. "This is just around the corner from us. There are a few other restaurants nearby as well."

Liz frowned. "I can't very well go to each restaurant and ask if they found a baby twenty years ago."

"True. Though, not all of the restaurants were around back then. I know The Cove has been around for some time. I'll tell you what, Denise might know more about the area. Let's start there," he said, closing the laptop.

Unfortunately, Denise wasn't much help since it was so long ago. They told her Liz was writing a research paper on the history of the island. It turned out that The Cove was the oldest restaurant in that area. However, Denise had no recollection of a baby being found there. Instead, she suggested they research the local library for old newspaper articles.

"Are you sure he found you behind a restaurant?" Liam asked, scrolling through the articles that appeared on the library's computer screen. Liz was sitting next to him, doing her own research.

"That's what my grandpa told them, but now I'm wondering if he made that up," Liz said despondently.

"Why would he lie about where he found you?" Liam wondered. "He said he would protect you. Do you think that's part of his reason? Maybe your parents are actually, like, the mafia and they paid your grandfather to take you."

Liz gave him a side-eye. "The mafia?"

"You're right. I haven't seen anything about the mob in any of these articles."

"I don't know." She frowned. "There's so much of my life that doesn't make sense to me anymore." She scrolled to a front page-news article and stared at it.

"Is that anything?"

Her face twisted as she read through the text. "No. Just a fishing trawler named *The Fortuna* that caught on fire during a storm. Only one person on board, but the weird thing was that he didn't die from the fire."

Liam leaned over and saw a picture of a large, bearded man, Bill something. Since the article was older, the text wasn't as clear and some of it was smudged. Liam skimmed the article to find out that the man had been punctured with a harpoon and his skull had been fractured in several places.

"Jesus," he muttered.

"Wonder how that happened."

"Says here the police believe he was standing at the top of the wheelhouse and fell. There was a storm that day, so makes sense if the boat was rocking a lot. Guess that's better than being burned alive."

"Still, though."

"I think it's safe to say *that* guy isn't your father. Looks nothing like you," he said, pointing to the picture, and Liz nodded in agreement.

"Sorry to interrupt," a woman said from behind them, "but the genealogy center is about to close."

"Thank you," Liam replied before the librarian left.

"Dammit," Liz muttered.

They had spent over an hour combing through articles and had gotten nowhere.

"We can come back. Sometimes the police blotters are a few days or a week behind. I'm sure it would list a baby being found."

"Maybe, but even knowing where I was found isn't going to give me a solid lead on who left me there." She gave a defeated sigh. "I'll print off the police blotter on the next page to read later. I doubt I'll find anything."

"You never know." Liam logged off the computer and turned his chair toward her as she stared across the library. "Hey, we'll figure this out. Together."

Liz searched his face. "Why are you doing this?"

"What do you mean?"

"You could easily just walk away and wash your hands of this situation, but instead, you're here, being supportive. Why?"

He leaned forward and interlaced his hands. "I suppose if I went through something similar, I would hope someone would be there for me. I couldn't imagine going through this alone."

She smiled. "You're a great friend."

He smiled back at her words because that was what she was to him. He had never had a sister, but if he had, he imagined she would be exactly like Liz.

"All right." His voice became chipper. "Since our plans didn't pan out, why don't we go explore the town? Maybe get your mind off this. Even if only for a little bit."

"Ok, I could use some distraction," Liz replied. They stood, and she grabbed the printed newspaper article. "Ugh, I printed the wrong page. Let me try again and then we'll go."

A few seconds later, she grabbed the correct page and walked out to the parking lot toward Liam's green Toyota Corolla. Liz pulled at the bottom of her shorts to hide the scales.

"How about I take you to get new clothes, too? That way you don't have to worry about anyone seeing your legs," he suggested, opening the passenger side door for her.

"I don't have any money, though."

"Don't worry. I worked a lot of hours this week, so all that extra cash is burning a hole in my pocket."

"Liam—"

With a smirk, he closed the door on her before she could protest.

CHAPTER 18

Torn

Wyatt's eyelids grew heavy as his body sank farther into the plush couch of the small boutique. When Jessica stated she had something fun for them to do, this wasn't exactly what he had imagined. However, since he'd canceled their last date, he owed her that much.

She sauntered out of the dressing room with the tiniest red bikini on, her breasts nearly spilling from her top. If this was her way of trying to entice him, it wouldn't work. He stifled a yawn as she posed. An older gentleman shopping with his wife looked like he was about to have a heart attack as his eyes widened at the sight of Jessica.

Wyatt rubbed his hands over his face. Was he supposed to be attracted to this? It felt like a desperate attempt for attention.

"Well, what do you think?" she asked, spinning around. Her auburn hair swayed back and forth from her high ponytail.

"Yeah, looks great," he replied without a glance. It probably looked like the last five. Why had he agreed to this? He hoped this would be the last suit she tried on. It wasn't that she wasn't beautiful, though he had anticipated getting to know more about her during their time together.

She chewed her bottom lip and studied him. "You seem bored. Why don't *you* try on some swimsuits for me? I know this great secluded spot where we can go for a swim. Just the two of us." She walked over to a rack of men's swim trunks and rifled through the clothing.

Wyatt remained silent, trying to think of an excuse. Even though he was now perfectly capable of wading into the water without the fear of changing, something just didn't feel right about swimming with Jessica. Water was a part of his life, and he wasn't sure if he wanted to share the joy he had for it with her.

"Here, try these on," she said, holding up a piece of black cloth. What they were exactly, he wasn't sure, but there was no way in the Mariana Trench he was putting them on.

Wyatt stared wide-eyed at the tiny briefs Jessica waved in front of him. "I'm good, thanks."

"You know, living on an island, you'll have to go in the water sooner or later. What better way than to experience the pleasures of the gulf than with me?" she coyly suggested.

"Maybe another time."

She frowned. "You know," she began, straddling him, "you don't have to be afraid of the water. You can tell me anything." Her necklace swayed back and forth, almost hypnotizing him. His hand grazed across her thighs, causing his breath to hitch.

"I . . . uh . . ." He hesitated for a moment until a blonde woman walking on the other side of the street caught his attention from his periphery. He blinked a few times, glanced out the window to see she was gone, and looked back into Jessica's eyes. "There's nothing to tell."

He shrugged and took his hands away from her. Jessica pushed herself off him with a sigh.

"What if we do something different instead? Maybe that place across the street?" He pointed, even though he had no clue what it was exactly. He at least knew it didn't involve trying on clothes.

"Well, I think you should at least try these on. You might

surprise yourself and want to dip your toes in the water," Jessica badgered him again, placing the swimsuit in his lap. She walked back to a rack of clothes, picked out a coverup, and held it against her body in front of the mirror.

Wyatt scowled at the dainty lump of fabric that was draped across his thighs. For far too long, decisions had been made for him, and now, it seemed Jessica was trying to do the same thing.

"I don't want to do this right now," he said, quickly feeling guilty for the words that spilled out of his mouth. He sighed, tossed the trunks aside, and stood up. He was about to apologize when she slammed a hanger back onto the rack.

Jessica folded her arms and glared at him. "How dare you! Where do you get off talking to me like that?"

Wyatt was struck with a mix of surprise, hurt, and anger. He thought about his next words, yet held his tongue. The small boutique felt like it was suffocating him. He needed to get out of there before he said something else he'd regret. Without saying another word, he exited the store, leaving Jessica standing half-naked.

Feeling a peculiar tug in his chest, he followed it to the wooden structure across the street. A sign hung at the top of it that read The Fish Hole. Greenery and palm trees surrounded it, almost as if it had been there first and the island grew up around it. Unfortunately, the clicking of high heels followed behind him.

"Wyatt," Jessica huffed, adjusting her black low-cut tank top as she ran after him. Her lips pouted. "I'm sorry, I didn't mean what I said. Please forgive me." She wrapped her arms around his neck, letting the sweet smell of her perfume entice him.

Words escaped his mouth before he could even think. "No, forgive me. I shouldn't have gotten mad at you. All you wanted to do was show me how beautiful you looked."

He blinked. *What am I saying?* It seemed he had been apologizing more times than he could count since he met her.

"Of course, I forgive you!" Jessica replied and pulled closer to him. She looked up behind his head at the sign hanging above them. "I suppose we can do something you want to do. But you'll owe me. Perhaps a swim?" Her lips were about to nibble on his ear when his knees buckled, causing him to nearly fall into her.

"I'm sorry," he apologized once more, pulling back.

"It's fine." She shoved her hand into her purse and sifted around. "I left my phone in the dressing room. You go ahead and pay for our round. I'll be right back."

He kept his eyes on her as she sauntered back across the street. He combed his hands through his hair, trying to figure out what was wrong with him. His mood swung back and forth so many times it was becoming nauseating. As he walked through the entrance to assess his surroundings, he tried to make heads or tails of what he had just gotten himself into. Thankfully, it appeared to be a game. Easy enough.

He stood in line at the cashier's counter. A man in front of him tapped his foot impatiently, and the brim of his backward baseball cap bobbed up and down. Once the couple at the head of the line paid for their game, the man went next.

"Two waters, please," the familiar voice stated.

"Liam?"

The man turned around to face Wyatt with surprise. "Hey! I didn't know you'd be here." He looked around, puzzled. "Where's Jessica?"

"She left her phone at the store across the street." Wyatt leaned in. "Please, you gotta help me. She wanted me to try on some sort of tiny swimsuit," he whispered, quickly looking behind him in case Jessica was there.

Liam laughed. "I dunno, man. I think you could pull those off. I'll even come with you to take pictures," he joked. "I'd like to help you, but I don't think we're sticking around. Liz doesn't—" His mouth snapped shut as Liz walked up to them. She wore capri-length leggings that had a green scale pattern on them. Her light purple tank top had two metallic violet shells printed on her chest.

Wyatt chuckled to himself and couldn't help but picture her

as an actual mermaid. His heart fluttered at the sight of her, but it was short-lived when he realized the girl Liam had talked about meeting was Liz and they were most likely on a date. He felt a pang of jealousy but quickly shook the thoughts away. *Liam deserves to be happy. Besides, I'm with . . . Jessica*, he thought. Still, it was hard to set his feelings aside.

"Liz, what are you doing up? I thought you were going to stay at the bench while I got water," Liam said with concern.

"I'm feeling a lot better," she replied, taking the water from Liam, who narrowed his eyes at her. Her putter slipped from her fingers as she suddenly realized Wyatt was present.

"Hey, Liz." Wyatt smiled warmly, bending down to pick up her club. When he handed it back to her, her fingertips lingered over his hand for a moment, and a warm sensation swelled in his chest.

"Did you pay yet?" Jessica asked as she appeared around the corner. She immediately frowned at the sight of his friends.

Wyatt quickly broke his connection with Liz. "I was just about to when I bumped into Liam and Liz." He turned to Liam. "Would it be ok if we joined you?"

"I'm sure they're too busy," Jessica stated, looking Liz up and down.

"We were actually just leav—" Liam began.

"Yeah, that'd be fun!" Liz interjected. "We were just killing some time before dinner." She cracked open the bottle of water and took a sip.

"Sure, why not?" Jessica replied sarcastically as she grabbed a long metal rod and a yellow ball.

"Hi. I'm Liz, by the way," Liz greeted Jessica, trying to be cordial.

"That's nice," Jessica replied curtly, then promptly walked away.

"She's in a ripe mood today," Liam said quietly before leaving Wyatt to pay.

Wyatt grabbed the items that everyone else had and met them

at the first hole. "You can go first," he said to Jessica, hoping to study her movements.

She sat on the nearby bench and crossed her legs. "Gentlemen first."

He glanced at Liz and Liam.

"We played the first three holes, so we'll join in on the fourth hole," Liam said.

Great. Wyatt clutched the rubber part of the rod and placed a red ball on the ground with a shaky hand. Now what? He scanned the area, trying to see what everyone else was doing. Ok, easy enough. Just hit the ball into the hole. He took a deep breath and bent his knees, ready to hit the ball, when Jessica scoffed behind him. He glanced over his shoulder to find her silently judging him with her arms folded across her chest.

"If you can hit your ball in the hole with the end of your putter like that, I'll give you twenty bucks," Liam said with a chuckle.

Thankfully, Wyatt's back was turned to them or they would have seen the panic in his widened eyes when he realized he was holding the putter the wrong way. He swallowed, drew a deep breath, then struck the ball. It didn't get far, but at least he didn't miss.

Turning around, he plastered a smile on his face and gave a shrug. "I figured we could make it challenging."

Jessica took her place at the green. "Well, we're already wasting an afternoon as it is. I don't need to waste an evening, too." She smacked the ball and followed it to the other end near the hole.

"I would have played your way, but I wouldn't want you to wait forever for me," Liz said.

The corner of Wyatt's lip curled at the thought. "I wouldn't have minded."

By the time he finished the fourth hole, Wyatt had caught on how to play mini golf. It reminded him of a game he used to play as a child using sea urchins.

Standing out of the way, he watched Liz finish hitting her ball.

He whipped his head around when Jessica wrapped her arm around his bicep, causing a sudden pain in his chest. Wincing, he rubbed his palm across his chest, hoping to ease his discomfort.

She leaned over and whispered, "If you want to leave right now, I wouldn't be against it."

"I . . ." There was a part of him that wanted to take her by the hand and leave.

As Liz walked past him, her eyes connected with his, causing that seed of doubt to grow. *What am I doing? Do I truly want to be with Jessica?*

He furrowed his brows. "I paid for 18 holes. I'm having fun. Aren't you?"

"I thought we could have more fun in the bedroom." She spun around and wrapped her arms around him, bringing back that ache in his chest once more. Her breasts pushed against his chest, and she ran her hands through his hair.

He quickly pulled away. "I think our ideas of having fun are completely different," he said, leaving her aghast. Her mouth opened and closed so many times that it reminded him of a fish. A beautiful, deadly fish.

As the game progressed, Wyatt tried to avoid Jessica's advances, not just because it was becoming increasingly annoying, but also because it was becoming increasingly uncomfortable. By the last hole, it felt like someone had punched him in the chest. *Poseidon, what is going on with me?*

"Thank God this is the last one," Jessica muttered, swiping her hair from her glistening face.

"Not for us," Liam announced. "Liz and I are doing two rounds."

Liz was finishing her last putt.

Wyatt didn't want to leave. Who knew what else Jessica had planned for their date. "Hey, Jessica, how about we do another round?"

"Ugh, pass." She rolled her eyes, then leaned against his chest, letting the scent of her perfume linger. "Why don't we look at a few more bathing suits for me to try on? Then I have somewhere special I want to take you."

Wyatt's mouth began to open. He wanted to tell her yes. He wanted to take her to all the stores, buy her anything she wanted, and shower her with love and affection. She deserved it, right?

At that moment, Liz's soft voice cried out in excitement, causing his mood to shift.

"I got a hole in one!" she cried out with glee, bounding across the path to them.

"Awesome!" Liam said, giving her a high five.

Wyatt spun around from Jessica's body. "That's great, Liz!" He imitated Liam, extending his hand up in the air for Liz to slap. He turned to Jessica and tried to compromise with her. "I'm having a lot of fun, but if you'd like to go, you can. You can show me what you bought later."

Truthfully, he had no intention of another dreadful fashion show.

Jessica blew out a frustrated breath and folded her arms. "Fine. I'll go shopping and meet you at the vegan restaurant down the road."

With Wyatt's perplexed look, Liam leaned over and whispered, "Think kelp salad but worse."

Wyatt's eyes widened.

"We were going to eat at the Oyster Bar if you guys want to join us," Liam suggested.

"I think Izzy—" Jessica began.

Wyatt gave her a hard look. "Liz," he corrected.

Jessica shrugged. "Whatever. I think she'd agree that they've interrupted our date enough."

"I don't mind," Liz's small voice spoke up. Her eyes stayed on Wyatt for a moment before darting back to Jessica. "I like hanging out with you."

"Please?" Wyatt gave her a half-smile.

Jessica blew out a defeated sigh. "Ok. But I'll meet you there. I'm not about to melt away playing any more of this childish game."

"We should be done in, like, half an hour," Liam estimated.

Without another word, Jessica turned away and left The Fish Hole.

Liam waited until Jessica was out of earshot before he spoke. "You sure you want to hang out with us? There's still time to catch up with her. I know you're dying to model those banana hammocks," he quipped, nudging an elbow into Wyatt's side.

Wyatt scoffed. "Why would I need a hammock for my banana?" he asked curiously.

Liam burst into a fit of laughter. "Oh, you're a riot!"

Returning to the front counter, Wyatt paid for another round of golf. While he waited for his change, he couldn't help but admire how beautiful Liz was as her hair fell over her face while looking down at the koi pond in the middle of the course.

Wyatt grabbed the money and headed toward the bench where Liz seemed lost in thought. He could have sworn he saw her wipe away a tear from her cheek. He searched the area. "Where's Liam?"

Surprised, she looked up at Wyatt, quickly composing herself, and sniffled. "Restroom."

Wyatt sat next to her, their legs nearly touching. "What's wrong?"

She turned her head away, taking a deep breath. He swore he could almost feel her about to break down. Reaching out, he gently took her hand in his. Her shoulders relaxed as if his touch washed away all of her sadness. "Your parents?" he inquired.

She nodded. "Among other things."

His thumb caressed the top of her index finger.

"If you need to talk about it," he began but quickly stopped. *She already has someone to talk to*, he scolded himself. To both of their disappointment, he pulled his hand away. As an excuse, he took a quarter out of his pocket and walked over to a machine that was labeled Fish Food.

"Thanks, I appreciate it," she replied behind him.

He placed the coin in the slot and turned the lever until the food fell through. Gathering them in his hand, he looked at the tiny pressed brown pellets in confusion. This was supposed to be food for the fish? They didn't smell horrible, but he wasn't about to try them himself, although, for a moment, curiosity nearly got the better of him.

Liz brushed up against his arm as she stood next to him. He held his hand out, letting her toss the food to the eager fish. To his surprise, they went crazy over the food.

"Did you know that there are over twenty-four different types of koi fish in the world?"

"Wow, I didn't know that," she answered, throwing a pellet on the other end of the pond for the smaller ones that couldn't get through the large group.

"Yeah, they're actually pretty intelligent. Although manta rays are smarter," he said in a matter-of-fact tone, sprinkling a few pieces of food on to the surface of the pond.

"I thought maybe dolphins were the smartest fish in the ocean."

Wyatt chuckled to himself. If only she knew that the most intelligent species in the Seven Seas was standing right next to her. He couldn't tell her that, though. "They're one of the smartest mammals in the ocean. They can even feel compassion and empathy."

"You know a lot about your sea life, huh?" she asked.

"You could say I grew up around them," he said with a shrug. There was something about Liz that made him feel at ease. It had always been hard for him to open up to girls, but that could have been the fact that they were usually set up by his father. Jessica was no different, and he might have even built his walls up more. However, with Liz, he wanted to destroy those walls, even though it would be dangerous to expose who he really was.

"You guys ready to get your butts whooped?" Liam asked, coming around the corner.

Liz threw the last of the food into the pond and turned toward Liam with a smirk. "You mean by me, right?"

"Oh, it's on!" Liam exclaimed.

Over the next forty-five minutes, Liam overtook the lead from Liz and finished in first place, while she finished in second and Wyatt in a close third. After they finished the last hole, they each placed their ball in a homemade Plinko board. The balls dropped and hit the wooden pegs until they landed on one of the prizes. Liz received a free game, Liam got to pick out a shark tooth, and Wyatt received a dollar off his next round.

"That was a close game," Liam stated. "Who's ready for some food?"

Leaving The Fish Hole, they walked down Bridge Street to find Jessica in a heated conversation with another man. He was a foot taller than her, and his muscles bulged under his tight shirt. Wyatt couldn't make out exactly what they were saying, but it had something to do with a fishing trawler. The man's voice sounded oddly familiar. Though he didn't recognize him, perhaps he had been a customer at The Cove.

"I'm close. I'll get the information even if I have to—" Jessica stopped short as Wyatt, Liam, and Liz approached. "Next time, call me," she hissed.

The man nodded curtly before leaving her.

"It's about time! I've been here forever. This heat is killing me." Jessica's anger read across her sweaty face.

Wyatt couldn't quite put his finger on it but something about the man seemed peculiar. "Everything ok?" he asked her.

"Just something for work," Jessica replied, shoving her phone into her purse.

"You could have sat inside," Liam said, holding the door for them. Jessica narrowed her eyes at Liam as she tried to follow behind Wyatt into the restaurant but was blocked by a couple exiting.

Wyatt squeezed his way into the crowded waiting area behind Liz to make room for Liam and Jessica. A group of eight waiting to be seated shifted, leaving Liam and Jessica stranded in the back. A large man moved behind Wyatt, causing him to stumble toward Liz. He placed his hand up, catching himself against the wall. Their bodies were so close, he swore he could feel her heartbeat.

He lifted his head, staring into her eyes for what felt like forever as everything and everyone around them came to a standstill. Electric energy seemed to charge the air between them, drawing them closer to each other without a single thought. Liz's breath quickened as Wyatt drew closer.

"Finally!" Jessica declared as the party of eight moved to their seats. Oblivious to the chemistry between Wyatt and Liz igniting, she grabbed Wyatt's hand and dragged him to the front, breaking the connection.

"Hi, welcome to the Oyster Bar!" the hostess said in a musical tone. "How many are in your party?"

"Two," Jessica stated.

"Uh, that's four, Jessica," Liam called out as he walked up to Liz. He looked between Liz and Wyatt several times.

"What?" Liz said sheepishly. If her cheeks were any redder, she would have looked sunburnt.

"Nothing," Liam replied with a smile.

"Oh, yeah. Silly me! I'm just used to it being the two of us," Jessica said, playing with Wyatt's hair before he slicked it back in place.

"Is outside ok? All of our tables inside are full," the hostess stated.

Jessica folded her arms in disgust. "Seriously?"

"There are plenty of outdoor fans on our patio, but if you'd like to wait for an indoor seat, it will be about fifteen to twenty minutes"

"The patio is fine," Wyatt said.

"Great! This way," a waitress said, grabbing four sets of utensils from underneath the hostess stand.

The waitress made her way to the back of the crowded restaurant. The smell of fish, shrimp, and oysters filled the air. People of all colors, shapes, and sizes sat around wooden tables while music played in the background. Instead of napkins, a paper towel roll sat in the middle of each table.

"If I knew you were going to pick such a *fancy* establishment, I would have dressed nicer," Jessica said facetiously.

The waitress opened the back door to the half-full patio before she placed the utensils down on a high-top table surrounded by barstools that overlooked the bay. Liz hoisted herself up on the stool, letting her feet dangle above the floor.

Jessica looked at the stool in front of her. "Wyatt, could you make yourself useful and help me up?" she asked, running her fingers down his arm.

"Sure," Wyatt said and took a deep breath.

As he lifted her into the seat, he tried to push away the pain in his chest. Something wasn't right. While he spent time with Liam and Liz, he had felt a weight lift from him and a pull toward Liz. Maybe his heart was trying to tell him something. He knew he should end things with Jessica before she had deep feelings for him, but for some reason, he couldn't bring himself to say the words.

A different waiter walked up to them and introduced himself, placing four glasses of ice water in front of each of them. "Would you like me to put in any appetizers while you look over the menu?"

Liam passed out the menus that sat next to the paper towel roll. "You guys want to share an order of coconut shrimp?"

"I'm good. I'm not a fan of shrimp or coconut," Liz replied.

"I'll try it," Wyatt stated, as it sounded intriguing. Since being on land, he was willing to try anything. So far, nothing had disappointed him except the bland taste of tap water.

"One order of coconut shrimp then. Even if the girls don't eat it, we'll devour them," Liam told the waiter.

"Ok. Would anyone want anything besides water to drink?" the waiter asked.

"Root beer for me," Liam replied.

"I'll have a strawberry daiquiri," Jessica said.

"I'm ok with water," Liz said, placing a paper straw in her glass.

"I'm good with water as well," Wyatt said as he watched Liz use the straw and proceeded to do the same.

"Ok, I'll be back with your appetizer and drinks," the waiter replied and left the group.

Wyatt stared at the list of entrees. He had no idea there would be so many choices of meals on land. It was almost overwhelming. "So what are you guys having?" he asked to get ideas for what food would be good.

"Gulf shrimp," Liam said first.

Jessica smiled. "I'm having a baked stuffed lobster tail."

"Of course, she'd get one of the most expensive things on the menu," Liam muttered under his breath.

Wyatt glanced over to see Liz stifling a laugh.

"What was that?" Jessica asked.

"I said, that's the best thing on the menu," Liam replied, trying not to laugh.

"What about you, Liz?" Wyatt asked before Jessica's sharp tongue got the best of her.

Liz placed her menu down. "I think I'll have a grilled chicken sandwich."

"Who gets *chicken* at a seafood place?" Jessica asked, rolling her eyes.

"Sounds good. I think I'll get that too," Wyatt said over Jessica.

"I heard their chicken is *egg-cellent*!" Liam exclaimed, and everyone cringed except for Wyatt, who didn't quite understand the joke.

Liz laughed. "Wow."

Liam shrugged. "I try."

The waiter walked up to the table with a warm plate of freshly made coconut shrimp, as well as Liam's root beer and Jessica's cocktail. He set the food and drinks down, then refilled Liz's water that she had already drained.

Once they made their menu selections and the waiter had left, Liam was the first to place a few shrimp on a small plate. The smell of the delicious appetizer wafted in the air. Liz stared at it for a good minute before deciding to take one. She savored the first bite, then quickly loaded her plate with a few more.

Wyatt cocked his head at her with a grin. "Not a fan of shrimp, huh?"

He chuckled and grabbed a few for himself. Liz shyly gave a half-smile. He began to eat one and nearly ate the tail before Jessica gave him a suspicious look. Observing the table, he realized his friends had placed the uneaten tails on their plates. Usually, he would eat the whole thing underwater, but apparently, it was customary not to eat the tail on land.

"This is so good, I nearly ate the tail." He laughed it off so as not to draw suspicion to his behavior. Jessica only smiled back as she sipped her drink.

While they waited for their food, the guys made small talk about work while Liz kept to herself. Jessica had turned her back on the men, completely ignoring them as she stared out at the bay and drank her daiquiri.

Ten minutes later, Liam reached out to the empty plate in front of him while he was talking to Wyatt. "Hey! Who ate all the shrimp?" he inquired, looking around until his eyes landed on the multiple tails on Liz's small plate. He laughed as she hid her face in embarrassment.

Just then, the waiter walked out with their food, placing each steaming plate in front of them.

Liam nudged her playfully. "Guess you found a new food you like."

"I guess Florida shrimp is better than Ohio's," she admitted, moving her straw around her glass.

Jessica raised her eyes to Liz for the first time since they had arrived at the restaurant. "How funny! Wyatt's from Ohio, too!" she exclaimed, violently cracking her lobster tail.

Wyatt nearly choked on his sandwich. Shit!

CHAPTER 19

Follow Your Heart

Liz stirred the ice around her glass. No matter how much she drank, the plain taste of the tap water didn't quite quench her thirst. She looked at the plate of discarded shrimp tails and regretted not ordering shrimp as her meal. Although she hadn't realized how much she liked the small crustaceans until recently.

All her life, she had never cared for the taste, let alone the smell, of any kind of seafood. Yet, for some unknown reason, the aroma of the coconut shrimp made her mouth salivate so much that she couldn't resist trying one. After the first bite, her taste buds came alive, inviting her to eat more. She tried to tell herself that it was just the coconut that masked the smell and taste of the shrimp, but that wasn't the case when the waiter placed Liam's shrimp dinner in front of him.

Her curiosity was piqued upon hearing Wyatt was also from Ohio. "Really, what part?" she asked him. The thrumming against her chest quickened into a panicked beat.

He flipped the question to her. "Um, what part are you from?"

"I'm from northeast Ohio, about an hour southeast of Cleveland."

Shoving a handful of fries into his mouth, he responded with a mumble, "An hour north of there."

Jessica leaned back in her seat, folding her arms. "Are you telling us that you live underwater?" she quipped. Wyatt turned his head, looking at Jessica in panic. "An hour north of Cleveland, you'd be, like, floating in the middle of Lake Erie."

"Oh, I meant . . ." He paused in thought.

Something told Liz he wasn't exactly from Ohio. She pretended to wipe her mouth with a napkin so Jessica wouldn't spy as she mouthed, "West," to Wyatt.

"West. An hour west of Cleveland." He looked to Liz again for help. "Sand . . . husky?"

Liz jumped in to save him. "Oh, Sandusky! That's a nice place."

Wyatt cleared his throat. "Yeah, *Sandusky*. I'm a bit direction-ally challenged. It must be from the heat." He shoved some more fries into his mouth, trying to avoid any more questions.

Liz silently giggled at Wyatt, who resembled a chipmunk storing food in its cheeks.

"I've never been that far north," Liam added to the conversa-tion. "I've been to Tennessee, but that's as far as I've traveled."

"Have you been to Nashville?" Liz asked.

"Oh yeah! I love that city." Liam proceeded to tell them about his travels to the Volunteer State, from the Country Hall of Fame to the Jack Daniels Distillery.

"Sounds like a fun place to visit," Wyatt commented.

"We'll have to go there one day," Liam suggested.

"Would your ratty car even make it that far?" Jessica chortled as she sipped the thick strawberry mixture through the wide straw.

Before Liam could retort, the waiter walked over to their table to check in on them and refill their drinks.

Out of the corner of her eye, Liz could see Liam's jaw tense. She decided a change of subject was in order. "So, Jessica, what do you do? For work, that is," she asked before taking another bite of her sandwich. It was good, but she couldn't help but leer at the large pile of shrimp on Liam's plate.

"I work at the marina. I'd explain it to you but you probably wouldn't understand," she replied and took another sip of her daiquiri.

"Oh, um, do you see a lot of dolphins?" Liz asked, trying to make some kind of connection with the intimidating woman.

"I live on an island. Of course I see dolphins," she said curtly.

Well, I tried, Liz thought as her eyes darted to Liam's plate.

Liam whispered, "Do you want some of my shrimp?"

"I saw a small pod of dolphins the other day," Wyatt stated. "Looked like a mother and baby."

Liz shook her head at Liam before turning her attention to Wyatt. "Aw, that must have been awesome to see."

Jessica said, rolling her eyes. "I'm sure he sees them *all* the time."

"Sure, but I never tire of seeing marine life," Wyatt stated and began to talk about what other ocean life he'd seen around the docks. At the same time, Liam grabbed half of the chicken sandwich from Liz's plate and traded it for half of his shrimp.

"Liam," she whispered in protest.

"Don't argue. I can almost see the drool coming out of the corner of your mouth. Besides, your sandwich smells really good," Liam whispered, then turned his attention back to the rest of the table. "I saw a fever of rays by City Pier not too long ago."

"A fever? What's that?" Liz asked curiously.

"It's what they call a group. It was pretty cool. I think I have a video of it on my phone," Liam replied, digging out his phone from his back pocket to show her.

"Wow!" Liz said in amazement.

"The other day I saw a manatee," Wyatt began.

Liz listened intently as Wyatt and Liam shared their stories. However, she noticed Jessica ignoring them. She watched the eyes of Wyatt's date linger on another man sitting across the patio. To be honest, it seemed as if Jessica's gaze was drawn to every tall, tanned, muscle-bound brute strutting in and around the patio.

Jessica gave an audible yawn, begrudgingly turning her attention back to the group. "Do you even care about this?" she spoke up, directing the question to Liz, stopping the conversation.

Wyatt interjected. "You have to remember, Jessica, that even though we've seen dolphins and other fish before, it's still a treat to people that don't live on the island. Instead of shrugging it off, it might be better to share your experiences."

"And just how do you know so much about the inhabitants of the ocean?" Jessica asked, raising her brow. "Didn't you just move to the island?"

"That doesn't mean I've never visited before. Besides, I've studied marine biology most of my life."

"Well, you never told me that," Jessica stated, flabbergasted. "Frankly, I thought you were as uneducated as Liam."

"Wow," Liam muttered before finishing the sandwich.

"Oh, lighten up. I'm kidding," Jessica replied, but something told Liz she wasn't a person who jested.

Wyatt shrugged and took a bite of his sandwich. "You never bothered to ask," he replied between chews.

"And did Liam care to ask you?" Jessica asked with disdain.

Liam dropped a shrimp tail on his plate. "I'm not the one dating him." He brought his straw to his mouth and muttered under his breath, "Although, if I did, I'd sure as hell treat him and his friends a lot better than you have."

Liz stayed silent, feeling like a fly on the wall in the midst of a weird, awkward conversation. She had every intention not to let Wyatt's date draw her into the discussion. It wasn't her and Liam's fault Jessica didn't even know her own boyfriend. Was he her boyfriend? She glanced over at Wyatt, who looked completely defeated. He deserved better.

"Does anyone need a refill?" the waiter asked from behind Liz. Everyone shook their head, except Liz, who held up her once-again empty glass. After the waiter refilled her drink, he asked if there was any interest in dessert.

"No, you can bring the check," Jessica announced without letting anyone speak.

Wyatt furrowed his brow. "You didn't even let us answer, and I'm not done with my sandwich."

"And some to-go boxes," Jessica called out to the waiter, who was beginning to walk away. She turned back to her date, scooted closer to Wyatt, and caressed his bicep. "You know Liam and Liz would rather be alone. We'll take our food to go and eat on the beach. Then we can go for a dip in the water."

"We told you we didn't mind you joining us. Although I'm having second thoughts," Liam said.

Jessica glared at Liam. "I think Wyatt would rather be with me than hang out with a freeloader and a girl that dresses like a fairytale princess," she stated, pointing out Liz's clothes.

Liz glanced down at her outfit and began questioning her fashion sense.

Jessica pushed herself off her stool, nearly tumbling down before Wyatt caught her. Wrapping her arms around his neck, she quickly hoisted herself onto his lap before he could protest.

The briny air breezed through Liz's hair, and without warning, she felt all the oxygen leave her lungs like someone had punched her in the chest.

Liam's voice sounded muffled in Liz's ears. "I pay my rent and there's nothing wrong with Liz's . . ."

The only thing she could hear was the sound of her raspy breaths and beating heart. Gripping her hands tightly around the edge of her seat, she squeezed her eyes shut and tried to compose herself. Something echoed in her ears until she realized it was Liam's voice.

"Liz, are you ok?" he asked again.

Liz's eyes snapped open. "I . . . I need to use the restroom," she announced abruptly as she bolted from her seat.

"I guess the shrimp didn't agree with her," she heard Jessica state with a chuckle as Liz rushed off.

Making her way along the outside of the restaurant, she sprinted toward the bathroom, nearly knocking into several customers. She wasn't sure if she was going to be sick or have a heart attack, but she needed to get away from everyone and fast. She passed the front of the Oyster Bar and stopped in front of the women's single-stall bathroom behind a gift shop. Occupied.

Dammit! This can't be happening!

She had felt this way earlier during the beginning of their mini golf game, but it hadn't been as bad. Now, it felt like someone had reached into her chest and was squeezing her heart. Leaning forward, she pushed her hands against the worn wooden railing, digging her nails into the paint, and hung her head between her forearms while closing her eyes.

Breathe, Liz, breathe.

Everything around her quieted as she focused on the sound of the bay's water lapping at the pier. Her eyes opened, and she leaned over the railing to stare at the water below. What she wouldn't give to feel its warm embrace. She glanced around, noticing there was nobody nearby.

I could jump. No one would notice. She shook her head, trying to break free from the sway of the water. *What am I doing?* She took a deep breath, inhaling the salty air. It was almost euphoric. *Maybe the water will stop the pain. Yeah, that'll help me. I need to be in the water.*

Unable to control herself, she placed her feet on the bottom railing.

Pain radiated through Wyatt's chest, and he could hardly manage to get any words out. "I need some air," he blurted out, nearly shoving Jessica off his lap.

"We're outside." She waved her hands about, stating the obvious. Wyatt ignored her and hastily walked away as calmly as he could. "Where are you going?" she exclaimed, causing several customers to turn their heads toward them.

Poseidon, I can't take this anymore!

"Away from you!" he cried out in anger.

He could faintly hear Liam arguing with Jessica, preventing her from chasing after Wyatt. He'd owe his friend later.

It took everything in Wyatt not to double over from the ache searing through his chest. With each stride he took distancing himself from Jessica, the torturous feeling dulled. He checked behind him to make sure the lamprey of a woman wasn't following him.

When he was sure, he continued on his path as it wrapped around the back of a small store. That was when he saw Liz standing on the lower part of the wooden railing. Her body leaned over, and her hair fell around her. If he didn't know any better, she was either going to get sick or dive into the water to swim away. He wouldn't blame her. This day had been a disaster.

Clearing his throat, Wyatt approached her and paused to catch his breath. "Are you ok?"

Liz jumped and turned to him. Her eyes looked him up and down for a moment. "I could say the same about you." She carefully planted her feet back on the floorboards of the pier.

Wyatt straightened his back, running his fingers through his hair. "I'm fine, really. What about you?" he asked again. "You took off like a sailfish." Liz gave him a puzzled look. "They're really fast."

"I'm on your team if we ever play a fish trivia game." She smiled, causing him to chuckle. "I'm all right. I think it was just some indigestion. The sea air helped, though. I'm feeling a lot better." Her eyes glanced past his shoulders. "Did you, um . . ." She glanced down. "Did you come here to check on me?"

Wyatt's head teetered to and fro. "Yes and no." He blew out a deep sigh, leaning his forearms along the railing next to her. "I needed to get away from her. I felt like I couldn't breathe."

Literally. "I'm not exactly sure what to think at the moment." He stepped closer to her. "Honestly, I was more worried about you."

Liz bowed her head, letting her hair fall to hide the rosy blush that was spreading across her cheeks. The quietness between them lingered for a moment as Wyatt watched her index finger run along a carving in the railing of M+B 4EVER. He stared at the lettering when a tidal wave of emotions hit him. Something tickled the back of his mind, almost like a whisper he couldn't hear. Liz seemed to be more lost in thought than he was.

Without hesitation, Wyatt placed his hand on top of hers, bringing her back to the present. "You sure you're ok? You seem distracted."

The pad of his thumb moved back and forth against her smooth skin. The ache in his chest had since gone away, and now he felt a sense of calm.

Liz's eyes met his as she lifted her head. "I . . ."

She wanted to tell him something. He could tell it was on the tip of her tongue, but before another word came out, she pulled her hand away from his.

"I should get back and let Liam know I'm ok." She hastily walked back toward the patio, passing Jessica along the way. She glowered at Liz, and Wyatt thought for sure she was going to throw her into the bay at any minute.

Blowfish.

Jessica strolled up to him, blowing out a sigh of frustration as she folded her arms across her chest. "I hope the next words out of your mouth is an apology. There was absolutely no reason for your little outburst."

"I . . ." He felt himself ready to say he was sorry for what seemed like the tenth time today, but then he caught Liz looking back at him just before she disappeared behind the corner. He blinked and took a few steps away from Jessica as a crease appeared between his brows. "No."

"No?" she asked, baffled by his response.

"No. I think *you* owe my friends an apology. You have been

nothing but rude and condescending to them. And I'm the fool for not saying anything in the first place."

Jessica scoffed. "Your friends? I doubt those people are your friends or ever will be. They don't know you like I do." She closed the distance between them and lifted her hand to his cheek. "You know I'm right. You want to be with me."

Quickly dismissing her, Wyatt pulled back. "I think you should go. I'm sorry. I should've realized this sooner, but it feels like we're two completely different people. I'm sure you'll make someone very happy one day, but it's not going to be me."

She stood there with nothing but a blank expression on her face. "You don't mean that. We can make this work. Just come with me and I'll show you."

Before he could stop her, she wrapped her arms around his neck and thrust her head into the crook of his neck, causing him to hold back a painful groan.

He gently pulled away from a seemingly weeping Jessica and looked her straight in the eye. "I'm truly sorry, Jessica."

Leaving her, Wyatt walked back to their table, feeling numb from the situation and unsure if he should feel remorse. They had only gone out a few times, yet she clung to him like a suckerfish.

When Wyatt sat back down at the table, Liam looked around. "So . . . ?"

"It's over," Wyatt said in a definitive tone.

They all stayed quiet for a few moments. With Wyatt no longer having the stomach to eat and Liam and Liz finished with their meal, they decided to split the check and leave. Liam led the way through the crowded restaurant with Liz and Wyatt following behind. As they exited the front doors, an arm hooked under Wyatt's bicep.

"Jessica, what are you doing?" Wyatt questioned.

"Listen, the man said it's over," Liam stated.

Ignoring Liam, Jessica tugged Wyatt's arm toward the parking lot. "Please, let's talk about this while I drive you home."

"I know you might not be used to rejection, but Wyatt can get a ride home with us. He is my roommate after all," Liam said from behind them.

Jessica spun around on her heels. "Stay out of it!" she hissed. "He's coming with me."

"I can speak for myself," Wyatt addressed both of them. He glanced at Liz, who awkwardly waited next to a nearby gift shop and ticket office. He then turned his attention back to Jessica. "I have nothing else to say to you. I'm going with Liam and Liz."

Jessica spun around, glaring at Liz. "You!" she shouted, marching toward her. "This is your fault, you bitch!" Before Liz could speak, Jessica grabbed a piece of paper that was sticking out of her purse. "What the hell? Where did you get this?" She angrily waved it in front of Liz's face.

Shaken, Liz replied, "I— It's just stuff I'm researching."

"Research. Something. Else," Jessica said through clenched teeth as she ripped up the paper into tiny pieces, letting the wind carry it away. Snatching a plastic cup from a bystander, Jessica hurled the cup's contents toward her. In a few quick steps, Wyatt leaped between the two women, preventing Liz from getting doused. The amber liquid drenched his upper body.

Wyatt clenched his fists. "That's enough! Liz doesn't deserve this. You can't tell me what to do. We're not together. We never were. I'm going home with them, not you."

A few people along the edge of the pier yelped as a small rogue wave rose and splashed along the wooden deck. *Poseidon, I have to calm down, or I'm going to muster up a tidal wave*, he told himself, letting his emotions get the best of him.

Jessica narrowed her eyes at him. "This isn't over." She turned and disappeared into the parking lot.

Wyatt ran his hands through the top of his hair, tugging at the roots in frustration. A warm touch radiated down his right arm. He lowered his arms to find Liz comforting him. She didn't say anything, only looked at him with concern.

He sighed, wringing the liquid out of his shirt. "I feel like I should be the one apologizing for her."

"Don't," Liz replied.

Liam walked up to them and handed Liz a few pieces of the paper Jessica had destroyed. "I tried to save as much as I could. Sorry."

Liz fumbled through the pieces and shrugged. "It's fine. That was the extra article that printed anyway. I didn't need it."

"What was it?" Wyatt asked.

"Just an old news article about a boat that caught on fire and the guy that died in it," Liz replied.

"No offense, but I'm glad you dumped her," Liam said as Liz threw out the pieces of paper in a nearby trash can.

Wyatt leaned over to Liam. "Are all females that crazy?" he asked quietly so Liz couldn't hear.

Liam chuckled. "No, but if they were, Liz would be the exception," he replied with a smile.

Wyatt looked around to see that the majority of the crowd waiting to get into the restaurant was staring at them. "We should go before we attract any more attention."

As they walked toward Liam's parked car, Liam stopped in his tracks. "You know, I completely forgot we need milk and bread. You'll be able to get to the apartment quicker if you walk," he said with a sly wink at Wyatt.

"Liam—" Liz started to protest.

"Besides, I don't want to hold you guys up and um"—he sniffed the air—"no offense, Wyatt, but I don't want my car smelling like beer."

"That's fine. You can take Liz with you and drop her off. I'll walk," Wyatt suggested. After all, it would be the proper thing for Liam to do for his date.

"The store is the other direction from our apartment, so I can't and it's about to close, so . . ." Liam hurried into his car and started the engine. "You guys have fun," his muffled voice called out from behind the driver's side window.

"Ok then," Wyatt muttered to himself, baffled by his friend's abruptness. Both he and Liz watched the green car drive down the street before it disappeared around the corner. He looked over at Liz and shrugged. "Shall we?"

They walked side by side, following the crushed-shell cement sidewalk, all the while sharing shy glances with each other.

"So . . ." Wyatt began, nervously fumbling with his hands before shoving them into his pockets. "You and Liam, huh?"

Liz furrowed her brow. "What about us?"

"I just want to apologize for crashing your date," he said, stumbling over his words.

"You weren't crashing anything. We're just friends."

So he wasn't lying when he said he was meeting a friend, Wyatt thought, relieved. Suddenly, a realization hit him, and he abruptly stopped in the middle of a crosswalk. "The grocery store wasn't about to close, was it?"

She chuckled, shaking her head. "No."

That sneaky sea urchin. Wyatt shook his head, smiling to himself as they continued down Bridge Street. Voices grew louder as they walked toward a crowded bar. Music blasted as a man took the stage to sing a drunken rendition of a song about piña coladas.

"What in the Seven Seas is this?" Wyatt asked. The tune was so off-key that he couldn't help but grimace.

Liz laughed. "You've never heard this song?"

Wyatt shook his head.

"It's an older song called 'Escape' by Rupert Holmes."

"That's Rupert Holmes?" he asked, astounded by how awful his singing was.

Liz tried to hold back another laugh. "That"—she pointed to the man shimmying on stage—"thankfully is not Rupert Holmes."

Wyatt listened to the words as they stopped to watch. "It sounds like it's about two people that actually have more in common than they thought."

She glanced over to Wyatt. "Hmm, I guess so. I always thought it was about piña coladas." She shrugged. The man belted out the chorus, causing her to recoil.

"Are you regretting not going with Liam?" he asked with a chuckle.

"Nah, I think this is more exciting."

"I have to admit, it is a catchy tune," Wyatt confessed, bobbing his head along with the beat.

They watched as the man grabbed the mic stand, placed it between his feet, and gyrated his hips around to the music.

"Yup, definitely more exciting!" Wyatt exclaimed. They both burst out in laughter, leaving the overly pitchy karaoke singer behind them.

They took their time walking down the street, getting to know each other. Wyatt found himself wanting to know anything and everything about her, while it seemed Liz felt the same, asking him different questions. While he had to twist his answers, he tried to stay as honest as he could with her. In the short amount of time just walking down to the end of the street, he learned more about Liz than he ever did about Jessica.

When they crossed the main drag, Wyatt paused. "Would you like to walk along the beach?"

Liz hesitated, biting her bottom lip. "Sure, I'd like that."

They slipped off their shoes as they walked down the path and over the dunes. The sun had just dipped below the edge of the sea, while the gentle waves hugged the shoreline. A dark orange glow was painted just above the horizon, with the sky taking on a purple haze as night softly came upon them.

"This is beautiful!" Liz said in awe.

"It sure is," he said, keeping his eyes on her.

Liz turned her head to him. "How do they compare to the sunsets in Sandusky?" she asked, shooting him a knowing expression.

Clearly, she had seen right through him during dinner. "Yeah . . . about that. I'm actually from an hour or so south of here. Thanks for saving me, by the way. How did you figure it out?"

"Well, for one, you said you grew up around fish. I thought for a moment that maybe your family worked at an aquarium, but then you didn't know where Cleveland was, so I determined you never lived in the Buckeye State." She smirked. "Why did Jessica think you were from Ohio?"

Wyatt, feeling embarrassed, rubbed his hand along the back of his neck while they walked close to the shoreline. "I guess she must have heard me wrong or something. I didn't feel like correcting her." He shrugged, hoping that was as good an excuse as any.

"I don't blame you. She looks like the kind of person that doesn't want to be corrected." Liz frowned. "Is that awful to say? I'm sorry. I don't know her. Maybe she's a great person and was having a bad day," she said, her words hurriedly spewing out.

"No, she definitely wasn't having a bad day. I'm not sure what I saw in her anyway."

Liz shrugged without saying anything, but her presence gave him comfort. He drifted a little closer to the wet sand, stopping for a moment to let his feet sink in.

"Do you mind if I take a quick dip in the water? This beer stinks. I'm sorry you had to deal with the smell this long," he said.

"No, go ahead." She motioned toward the water. "Thank you for diving in front of me. You didn't have to."

"I couldn't very well have you take the brunt of her anger for me," he stated, wading out into the water until he could dive under the waves.

If Liz wasn't with him, he would have felt inclined to take all of his clothes off and transform. As much as he enjoyed living on land, the sea still called to him. He missed pumping his tail and gliding through the water at top speeds.

He swam around for a quick minute, then surfaced and made his way back to the shallows. He walked up the shore to find Liz plopped down on the sand, hugging her legs against her chest. Her eyes were fixated on the water behind him, her breath quickened.

"Did you want to dive in too?" he questioned, wringing out

his shirt. A few tendrils of wet hair fell haphazardly across his forehead.

Liz's gaze lingered on him until she snapped back to reality. "Huh?"

"I didn't think you'd want to get your clothes wet, but the way you're staring longingly at the water says otherwise," he observed as he sat next to her.

"I would, but it's just . . ." Her eyes flickered to the waves, and her brow furrowed.

Wyatt waited patiently, giving her as much time as she needed. She seemed lost in thought. He placed his wet hand on her forearm, bringing her back to him.

"Something happened to me in the water. I'm not exactly comfortable talking about it, but—" She bowed her head and pushed her feet deeper into the sand.

"It scares you," he finished her sentence. She nodded, pulling her legs tighter to her chest. "I could see how the ocean can be a terrifying place. If it helps, I'll be with you the whole time if you'd like to go in."

"I appreciate it, but I . . ." She sighed in frustration.

"Or I could bring the ocean to you," he said quickly, trying to lighten the mood by tousling his hands through his wet hair and spraying seawater onto Liz.

She held her hands up and squealed. "All right, all right," she surrendered, wiping the water from her face. "Maybe I can dip my toes into the water while we walk back."

"I think that's a great idea," he said, standing up. "Start off slow and maybe in time you'll want to go deeper."

He extended his hand out to her. She slipped her hand into his, and he pulled her up from the ground so quickly that it nearly caused her to fall into him. She gazed up at him, and for a moment, he could have sworn he saw a flicker of light in her eyes when she blinked.

Wyatt cleared his throat. "Ready to go?"

"Um, yeah." She quickly let go of his hand and distanced herself.

Wyatt picked up his shoes and guided them toward the water's edge. Liz flinched as the waves neared her feet. It was as if she was waiting for it to grab her by the ankles and take her. *Poseidon, I wish I could comfort her more.*

"It's ok. I won't let anything bad happen to you. I promise." He took her hand and rubbed the top of her knuckles with his thumb before she interlaced her fingers between his.

Liz nodded, took a deep breath, and slowly crept farther in, letting her feet sink into the wet sand. Her hand clutched his in anticipation, sending tingles up his arm. He wondered if she felt the same sensation. Closing her eyes, she let the waves crash into her legs. As the water rolled back, she relaxed as if all her fears were washed away into the gulf. Wiggling her feet free from the sand, she let the surf wash over them once more. Her eyes fluttered open, and a smile crept onto her face.

"You're doing great!" Wyatt exclaimed.

Liz's smile disappeared. "I feel like a wimp for being so afraid."

He squeezed her hand. "Don't be. In fact, just yesterday I got so scared of a bug that I nearly fell off the kitchen chair."

"How big was it?"

"This big," Wyatt explained, barely separating his thumb and index fingers.

Liz stifled a laugh. "That's pretty terrifying."

He playfully pushed up against her shoulder. "Ha. Ha. Luckily I was by myself or I would've never heard the end of it from Liam."

"Pretty sure it was a gnat."

"Well, those can be pretty scary," he said, trying to make her feel better. "It's getting dark. We should head back."

He reluctantly released her hand as they strolled down the shoreline. The beach was nearly deserted with only the glow from the businesses lighting the way. As The Cove came into view, a twinge of pain on the bottom of his foot startled him. He didn't think he stepped on anything. Before he had time to look, Liz hissed.

"Are you ok?" he asked with concern. They had started walking through the broken shells that lined the shore. It hadn't been a problem for him before, but this time felt different.

Liz stopped and lifted her leg to check the soft pads of her feet. Her body swayed back and forth as she tried to keep her balance. Wyatt quickly stepped in to help steady her.

Dropping her foot down, she pulled away from his touch. "I just stepped on a broken shell, I'm fine," she said defensively.

Liz ran her hands over her face in frustration. Her body had tensed up once again, and Wyatt couldn't help but feel like it was his fault.

Wyatt gave her space. "I'm sorry. I didn't mean—"

"No." She sighed. "I'm sorry. I didn't mean to lash out. I just feel like the last few days have been an emotional roller coaster. My brain is telling me one thing, and my heart is telling me another," she confessed, dropping her arms to her sides. "And I really don't know why I'm oversharing."

"Because you need to vent." He took a step toward her. "Before I came here, I felt the same way. My brain was telling me I had to stay with my family and do what my father said. But my heart guided me here."

"Do you ever regret listening to your heart and not your brain?"

Wyatt looked out at the vast waters. "Never. Sometimes your heart leads you to unexpected places. If I never followed mine, I wouldn't be here walking along the beach with you." He turned his head to look into her eyes. There was just enough light left in the sky to see the slight blush tinting her cheeks. "Close your eyes and listen to your heart."

She looked at him curiously for a moment before her eyes closed.

"What is it telling you to do?"

Liz breathed in the salty air, then opened her eyes. Her gaze darted from the water and back up to Wyatt. Throwing down her shoes and purse a few feet inland, she bit the bottom of her lip and gave a devilish grin.

"It's telling me to do this." She slipped her hand into his hand, and a warmth spread through his chest that he couldn't explain.

The next thing he knew, they were both waist deep in the water, laughing and splashing about.

CHAPTER 20
Regret

Sand clung to Liz's feet as they trudged up the dunes. She took one last glance behind her, but the only thing she could see was darkness shrouding the beach, only leaving the alluring sounds of the waves calling to her.

The glow of the parking lot greeted them, but Liz hesitated to continue. She stood frozen in place, wanting to turn back around and dive back into the water. Letting her guard down and running into the surf with Wyatt had been exhilarating. He made her feel so at ease, like she could take on anything. All of her troubles had floated away while they waded and splashed each other. She wasn't sure what scared her more, the water or her feelings toward Wyatt.

"You ok?" Wyatt asked, peering over his shoulder.

She turned back to him and tucked a wet tendril of hair behind her ear. "Yeah." She smiled, slipping her sandals on.

He escorted her to her front door, where they awkwardly stood, unsure how to end their day.

"This was fun," he said, fumbling with his hands. "It really turned my day around, all things considered." He wiped the droplets of seawater from his face.

"I'm glad," Liz replied with a shiver. The warmth of the sun was now gone, and the breeze from the gulf brought goosebumps down her arms. She gestured toward the door. "I should get inside."

"Liz?"

With butterflies in her stomach, she found him right in front of her. His arms extended out to hug her, but instead, she panicked and took his left hand in hers, awkwardly shaking it.

"Have a good night," she blurted out before breaking their connection and hastily entering her apartment, closing the door on a puzzled Wyatt.

Liz leaned against the door, thumping her head back. *A handshake? Really, Liz? God, he'll never want to see me again.*

Liam nearly choked on his chocolate cake as he stared at his drenched friend who had just walked through the door. "Why are you dripping water all over the floor?" he asked, hopping off the barstool and went to the linen closet.

"She shook my hand. Is that normal? Maybe I misread her feelings."

Liam peeked his head around the door. "What?"

Wyatt's forehead creased as he stared at his left hand. "I went to hug her, and she shook my hand instead."

Liam closed the door, shrugged, then threw a beach towel at him. "I dunno, but you still didn't answer my question of why your clothes are soaked."

Wyatt moved the towel across his body before walking any farther. "We went into the water."

"Oh." Liam sat back down and was about to take another bite when his fork slipped from his fingers with a clang. "Wait. What do you mean *we*?" he asked, dumbstruck. "You and Liz went into the water?"

"Yeah," Wyatt said dreamily. He stopped in the middle of the living room, seemingly lost in thought as a smile crept over his face.

Liam rotated on his barstool and crossed his arms like an overbearing father. "Anything else happen?"

"Not really. I'm going to take a shower and get ready for bed."

"Uh-huh." Liam threw his dessert into the fridge. "I'm going to see if Liz needs any more towels."

Even though he knew she had plenty, he needed an excuse to check on her. Concerned, he grabbed a towel and his keys and rushed out the door. He stared at the woodgrain of her front door and wondered what he would find on the other side. He knocked several times, each one louder than the previous. The door swung open, revealing Liz, completely soaked with a puzzled expression on her face.

"Liam! What's wrong?" she asked as a drop of water from her hair slid down the side of her face.

"Oh, I don't know." He pushed the towel toward her. "Maybe the fact that the last time you were in the water, you collapsed on the ground. What if something happened?" He looked her over. "*Did* something happen?"

"Shhh! Just get in here." She quickly ushered him inside. "Yes, but I kind of wish it didn't."

"What do you mean?" Liam's eyes grew wide as he shut the door behind him.

"He went to hug me and I gave him a handshake. A handshake! Who does that?" She hid her face in the towel.

"I meant, did anything, you know . . . ?" Liam glanced down at her legs.

"No. I'm fine." She rubbed the towel along her body, trying to soak up the seawater. "Let me change out of these clothes, then we can talk, ok?"

"Yeah, go ahead." He followed her into the hallway and leaned against the wall while she went into her bedroom and closed the door behind her. "When I left you two to walk home together, this wasn't what I had in mind."

"I knew it!" Liz shouted from the other side of the door. "You *were* trying to set us up, weren't—"

"Liz?" Liam frowned in concern. "Everything ok?"

"I'm . . . fine." Her voice was an octave higher.

Liam sighed. "You're a horrible liar. Can I come in?"

She shuffled around the room and then quietly replied, "You can come in now."

He slowly cracked open the door and peeked in to find her sitting on her bed, looking pale and distraught. Not only were there more scales on her right thigh, but now they were on her left, blending seamlessly with her porcelain skin.

"Something felt off when I went into the water, but I didn't think anything of it." She bowed her head. "How could I be so stupid?" Her voice shook. A lone tear fell onto her leg, causing the scales to glisten slightly.

Without saying a word, he sat next to her, and they both stared at the array of shimmering scales.

"What's happening to me?" she asked with a shaky voice before she broke down in tears.

Not knowing what to do or say to bring her comfort, Liam placed his arm around Liz and held her tightly. She winced in pain and quickly stood, distancing herself from his embrace.

"And why does it hurt so damn much when we touch?" she cried out. She grabbed the nearest thing, which was her purse, and threw it across the room with such force that it nearly punched a hole in the wall. She sank to the floor and hugged her knees as her body trembled from her uncontrollable sobs.

Minutes ticked by as he sat by her without saying a word. When it seemed like there were no more tears to shed, he convinced her to lie in bed. Maybe tomorrow would be a better day for her. He stayed with her, pulling the covers over her frail body as she continued to softly cry herself to sleep. His heart shattered into a million pieces.

"I don't know what's happening to you, but I'm going to do

everything I can to figure this out. I promise," he whispered in her ear before leaving her for the night.

Liam entered his pitch-black apartment and tiptoed back to his bedroom. After laying in his bed for what seemed like hours, it was nearly impossible to turn his brain off. His alarm clock glared back at him, the blue-white numbers reading one o'clock.

Pulling the sheet away from his body, he got up and slipped into the hallway, passing by Wyatt's closed door. He sat on the couch, stroking his five o'clock shadow while his eyes stared at the bright light illuminating from his laptop screen.

For nearly an hour, he contemplated how to help Liz, diving into one rabbit hole of medical websites after another. Unfortunately, everything that showed up on his search engine was nearly the same as what Liz had found. He finally grew weary of looking at the blinding screen. As he closed his laptop, something tugged at the back of his mind. It was the same thought that had crossed him when he first saw her scales. He had dismissed the idea because it was not only impossible, but Liz would think he was crazy for even suggesting such a thing.

Curious, he reopened his computer and typed in *M-E-R-M-A-I-D-S*. Fairy tales for sure, but what if they were real? What if her grandfather had found her behind The Cove? The beach was behind it. He told her she was more special than she knew. Could that be what he meant? Did he know?

Rubbing his hands over his tired face, Liam pored over the myth and legend of the fantastical creatures with a renewed purpose to stay awake. The more he thought about it, the more it made sense. The emerging scales, her newfound taste for shrimp, the inordinate amount of water she had been drinking. Nothing else seemed to fit what was going on with her.

Nothing except . . . *This is crazy. There's no such thing as mermaids. Is there?*

Wyatt stumbled over his feet, nearly falling to the ground. The world spun so fast he couldn't discern his surroundings.

"Tell me where it is," a deep male voice echoed through Wyatt's haze.

"You fool, you gave him too much. He won't be able to tell us anything now," another voice hissed.

"W-what the hell is that?" the first voice cried out in agony.

"That is the proof we need," the other voice said as it faded into the darkness.

An inky black void shrouded Wyatt. It was a comforting feeling, unlike the sliver of light that bled through the slits of his eyes. Each time he tried to open them, searing pain encompassed his head as if he was in the deepest trench in the ocean. Mers could go to great depths, but even they had their limits. Something didn't feel right.

A groan escaped his cotton mouth as Wyatt rolled over. The last thing he remembered was feeling the warmth of Liz's hand as she pulled him toward the water. His hand curled, gripping something soft, but it wasn't Liz's hand.

I'm in bed? How did I get here? he thought, only making the ache in his head worse. He felt like he had been tossed around by a humpback whale. He just wanted to go back to sleep, which was unusual for him. Mers didn't need as much sleep as humans.

He forced his heavy eyelids open, letting in more of the harsh light. His clothes were skewed about the floor. A few memories slowly came back to him. He remembered telling Liz good night, the handshake, and then taking a shower before bed. No, something else happened after he got out of the shower. No, before he went to bed . . .

"Ugh. Jessica," he said with a slight growl, running his hands over his face.

Slowly, the events of last night trickled back into his mind. There had been a knock at the door, and all that happiness he felt with Liz had faded away with the turn of the knob. On the other side of the door had been the woman pleading for his forgiveness.

After some persuading from Jessica, he had conceded and gone with her to talk on a nearby bench. What happened next became hazy.

He sensed something behind him move, and the sheets shifted, causing him to whip his head around.

"Well, good morning, handsome," Jessica's voice purred as she traced a finger down his spine.

Wyatt's heart plummeted to the pit of his stomach. A weird sensation he had never felt before came over him. The contents of his stomach twirled around like they wanted to escape. *Poseidon, what's happening to me?* He steeled his eyes shut and closed his mouth tight as if that would stop his body from acting on its own. Water began to seep from every pore of his body.

"Ugh, if you're going to throw up, do it in the bathroom," Jessica ordered.

There wasn't enough time to escape the room, especially with the world around him in constant motion. Falling off the bed, entangled in the sheets, Wyatt grabbed the nearby trash can and released the contents of his stomach into it. It was the most horrid experience he had ever had. Mers hardly ever got sick, and when they did, nothing of this magnitude ever happened.

Tears formed in the corners of his eyes while his stomach continued its attempt to pump out more, leaving him to dry heave.

"What did you do to me?" Wyatt cried out, his head still bowed above the can.

"Me? I didn't do anything, honey. You were the one that insisted on drinking like a fish last night at the club," she simply stated.

"Drink? Club?" he muttered to himself. The putrid smell of his insides was enough to cause him to heave one last time.

"Why don't I get you a glass of water?" she snidely offered before slipping out.

Wyatt tried unraveling the sheet around his waist, only to find himself completely naked. Before he could question why in the

Seven Seas he had no clothes on, Jessica returned and sprawled catlike on the bed behind him. She stretched her hand in front of him, offering the glass of water. He sipped it slowly, expecting it to taste utterly bland.

"Salt water?" he asked in surprise. He should have panicked, but he had little energy left, and the salt seemed to help his stomach.

"I've heard it's a good hangover remedy. Just not in large amounts. Thankfully, unlike you, I know how to handle my alcohol."

He took another big swig and placed the glass down. He could have downed a few glasses of it, but he didn't want her to start questioning him. Leaning his head against the side of the bed, he finally took in his surroundings. Not only were his clothes spread out all over the floor but so were hers. The pace of his heart quickened.

"What are you doing here?" he inquired, not sure if he wanted to know the answer.

"Don't act so surprised. Did you think I was going to sneak out after the amazing night we had?" She pushed up on her elbows. Her cleavage hung out of a lacy, black bra nearly inches from his face.

He looked at her quizzically. "Wait . . . Are you saying we . . . you know?"

She bit her bottom lip. "And then some." He stared at her blankly for a moment before she frowned. "Don't tell me you forgot."

No, no, no! This can't be happening! Having sex, or mating as the mers called it, was only done for procreation after they were joined in union. The thought that he not only mated with a human before marriage but did so without having any feelings for her was unfathomable.

His stomach roiled once more. "I think I'm going to be sick," he said, lurching forward and loudly vomiting into the trash can again. This time it wasn't just the water he had drunk that spewed from his mouth but also shame and regret.

"Shhhh, you'll wake Liam," she scolded.

At that moment, Liam walked past the open door. "Too late." He yawned, then quickly backpedaled. "Jessica?" he exclaimed, pushing the door open farther to find her resting seductively on Wyatt's bed. Her rear end hung out of a matching black lace thong while her legs swung back and forth. "What the hell are you doing here?"

"Nice to see you, too. Do you mind? We're having an intimate moment. So stop staring at my ass, perv, and get out!" she barked.

"You know, you have a strange way of describing intimate moments." He looked over at Wyatt, who was resting the side of his head on the top of the trash can. "I'm more concerned about my friend than your assets. What did you do to him?"

"He's just peachy." Jessica pushed herself up and sauntered over to Liam. "You don't need to worry that pretty little head of yours." She mussed up his sandy blonde hair. "I'll take care of him. Trust me."

"That's what I'm worried about," Liam said before continuing down the hall.

Jessica closed the door and turned on her heels, smiling back at a sickly Wyatt. "Now where were we?"

"Why?" Wyatt spat out in confusion. "Why are you here? I broke up with you." Not that they had ever been a couple.

"It was a true test of our relationship, and while it took some convincing, I eventually forgave you," she said matter-of-factly

"Forgave me?" Wyatt cried out, questioning his own sanity at that point. *Poseidon, what have I done?*

"Of course. You practically begged me to come back here after we went to Club 21," Jessica replied, gathering her clothes off the floor.

"Club 21?" Wyatt clutched the sheets tighter and leaned his head against his bed.

"You seriously don't remember? You were the center of attention on the dance floor."

He didn't even know how to dance. Maybe it was a good thing that he didn't remember.

Wyatt opened the drawer in front of him and fished out his boxer briefs and then a yellow work shirt and beige cargo shorts from the drawer below that one. He awkwardly dressed under the sheets while Jessica shimmied into her tight skinny jeans and low-cut black tank top.

Jessica took out her phone, and her mouth curled slightly at whatever she was reading on the screen. She tapped her fingers to it, then shoved it back into her purse.

"Well, as much as I'd love to stay and revisit last night's workout, I have something at work I need to deal with," she announced, slipping her shoes on. She walked over to Wyatt, wrapped her arms around him, and stroked the hair on the back of his head. "Why don't you come with me? You can see what I do."

This was the first time she had offered a glimpse into her life. It was tempting. Maybe he could salvage their relationship. No, he didn't want to be with her. He never had.

He blinked a few times, then forcefully pulled her away. "Stop!" he snapped.

"That's not what you said last night," she said seductively as she tried to advance toward him once more.

"I don't know what happened or why I even went out with you last night, but it was a mistake. This whole thing was a horrible mistake."

"But you told me you loved me," she blurted out.

"Love? I hardly know you. How could I say I love you? You've never shared anything about yourself with me," he scorned her in frustration.

"You don't want to know the real me," she spat out, seemingly regretting the words.

His eyes narrowed at her. "What is that supposed to mean?"

"I have to go," she said, looking at the alarm clock on the nightstand. "This conversation isn't over." She grabbed her purse and stormed out of the room. Stopping in her tracks, she peered over her shoulder at Wyatt, who had his head poked out from the doorway. "You'll soon realize what you said was a mistake."

Wyatt watched her intently to make sure she actually left.

"Have a great day!" Liam called out to her as she fumbled to open the locked door. Jessica stared daggers at him before throwing her middle finger in the air and leaving through the front door.

Once out of sight, Wyatt slammed his door shut and growled in frustration. He grabbed the pillow she had been lying on. Her scent still lingered, and he took out his anger on it.

"Freakin' lamprey. She thinks *I'm* squiddish," Wyatt muttered.

There was a knock on the door. Wyatt flung it open, half expecting Jessica to be in front of him instead of his roommate, who was raising an eyebrow while sipping his coffee.

Liam lowered his cup. "So, I'd ask how your night was, but judging by the yelling and—" He looked over Wyatt's shoulder. Pillow fluff was scattered across the bed. His mer strength, unfortunately, had gotten the best of him in a moment of anger. "Damn, man. I guess I should be lucky you didn't punch a hole in the wall."

He sighed. "I'm sorry. I'll buy another one."

Liam leaned against the doorjamb. "Don't be. Besides, I have more in the linen closet. Just take care of the trash can. I don't deal with bodily fluids," he said, grimacing.

Wyatt nodded and sat on the bed, rubbing his thumb and index finger across his aching forehead.

"I guess that's the last time I leave you alone," Liam said, trying to lighten the mood. "What the hell happened last night? I heard her say you forgave her? Look, if you want to sleep with Jessica, that's your prerogative, but you can't lead Liz on like that."

Looking Liam dead in the eyes, Wyatt replied, "The last thing I want to do is hurt Liz. Jessica aside, yesterday was perfect. Walking along the beach with Liz was wonderful. I felt like I could tell her anything. I've never been like that with anyone before." There was a long beat before he added, "Thank you. I know what you did."

Liam waved his hand. "I didn't do anything. You two did that all on your own. I just stepped out of the way. I saw the looks you both were giving each other during dinner." He took a sip of his coffee. "You really like her, don't you?"

"Yeah," he said quietly with a smile.

"Then why was Jessica over here?" Liam questioned.

"I have no clue. I would never purposely get back with her. I just wish I had a clearer idea of what went on after you left."

"Come on, let's try to recall last night's events." Liam motioned his head toward the kitchen. "There's coffee if you need it."

"Thanks, but I have water." Wyatt grabbed the glass off the floor and proceeded to follow Liam to the kitchen island.

Liam grabbed a bowl and spoon for each of them and sat them on the island counter. "I suggest you get some food in your stomach." Wyatt reluctantly nodded, and Liam poured cereal for the two of them. "So, what's the last thing you remember?" he asked, grabbing the milk from the fridge and pouring it over the cereal.

"Jessica showed up shortly after you left, right around the time I got out of the shower. She asked if we could talk, but I said no."

"Because you're a sane person," Liam quipped as he pushed the cereal toward Wyatt and sat down next to him.

"Thanks." Wyatt took a small bite. "She somehow coerced me to go outside and talk. We sat down on that bench along the path to the beach. She smelled really good. After that, things get a little fuzzy. Only bits and pieces are coming back to me. It almost feels like a dream."

"Or a nightmare."

"Yeah, really." Wyatt took another bite of cereal, as his stomach was beginning to feel better. "I remember getting in her car. She drove us to this brick building with bright lights out front." He thought for a moment. "She mentioned we were at this club. Um . . . Club 21."

"I've only been there once myself. Not really my scene. I don't drink like that anymore. It's not fun blacking out. It sounds like that's what might have happened to you," Liam explained.

Memories flickered as he tried to cast his mind back to what happened next. He was met with flashing lights of every hue as loud music enveloped them. To the left was a large open area where hundreds of people crowded in the center and danced along. Jessica said something to him, but the music was so loud he couldn't make out her words.

"She dragged me to the bar and had the bartender give me this tiny glass. I thought it was water at first," Wyatt confessed. However, it was quite the opposite. It had the putrid taste of octopus ink and burned the inside of his throat. He had tried to wave off the bartender, but somehow Jessica had persuaded him to have another one.

Liam stifled a laugh. "Yeah, they don't put water in tiny glasses at the bar. What happened after that?"

"The room began to spin and then everything went dark."

"How many did you have?"

"Two."

Liam stopped his spoon midway to his mouth. "And nothing else before that?"

Wyatt shook his head.

"Have you ever had alcohol before?"

"No." Wyatt shoveled a spoonful of cereal into his mouth.

"Even if you were a lightweight, I don't think you'd black out just from two shots. Are you sure you can't think of anything else?"

Wyatt thought for a moment, letting the cereal crunch

between his teeth. He stopped mid-chew when he remembered the bartender. Swallowing, he replied, "Remember the man that Jessica was talking to in front of the restaurant?"

"Yeah."

"He was the bartender."

Liam wiped the corner of his mouth with a napkin. "Maybe she knows every brute at the place?"

Wyatt chewed at his bottom lip. "Something just doesn't add up about last night."

"A lot of things don't add up with that chick," Liam pointed out.

"She even claimed that I professed my love for her."

"Seriously? Do you believe her?"

"I don't know." He stirred his spoon around in his cereal. "Is that something I could have said when I was out of it?"

"It's possible if you weren't thinking straight. Or she could be lying."

"Like when she said we had sex?"

"You don't remember?" Liam finished his cereal and placed it in the sink.

"No. After I blacked out, I woke up here." Wyatt shook the thought of mating with her away as he placed his head in his hands. "If I don't remember it, does it count?" He tried to hide his pain through a laugh.

"Wish it worked that way." Liam shrugged as he grabbed his shoes. "I'm going for my morning run. I suggest a cold shower to help wash off the shame that you're obviously feeling."

Wyatt scoffed. Liam couldn't have been more right.

"And anything else she may have given you," Liam joked before heading out the door.

CHAPTER 21

Fish Out of Water

Liam's feet rhythmically smacked the wet sand at full pace. His run had started out later than usual, mainly from sleeping in a bit from his late night researching, but maybe that was a good thing considering who he was about to run into. There, along the dunes, sat Sarah in a yellow two-piece bathing suit. Her wet light brown tendrils of hair hung over her shoulders, likely from an early swim. She massaged her right calf muscle before stretching out her legs to lean back on her elbows.

Liam unknowingly slowed down his pace, admiring her beauty. He caught a slight glance in his direction before she turned back to watch the waves.

"Hey," he greeted breathlessly. When Sarah didn't respond, he continued. "So . . ." He paused, trying to make conversation. "You staying out of trouble?"

Sarah turned her head up toward him. He wiped away the sweat from his forehead and rested his hands along his hips. He swore he caught her gaze lingering longer than she should have.

His mouth turned up into a smirk. "I've stunned her into silence, I see. Next time I'll wear a shirt."

"I've seen plenty of men without shirts on," she retorted.

Liam raised an eyebrow. "Have you now?"

She quickly stood. "That's not . . . I didn't mean . . ." Sarah said, flustered, causing Liam to chuckle.

"Relax, we're on a beach. Even I've seen plenty of bare-chested men. Some of their images are burned into my brain, and not in a good way," he said with a shudder. Sarah failed to stifle a laugh. "Hey, look at that."

"What?"

He beamed. "I made you laugh."

Sarah crossed her arms over her chest and wrinkled her nose at him. "Is my brother awake?"

"Yeah, he was just stepping in the shower when I left." Liam dug into his pocket and pulled out his key. "Here, take it."

She snatched it and studied it as if it was the first time she had held a key in her hand.

"You do know how to use that, right?" he questioned jokingly.

She looked back up and scowled. "Yes, of course I know how to use it! I was just—"

"Lost in thought?"

"Yeah."

"Wanna talk about it?" Liam asked.

She dusted the sand from her legs. "No. I'm fine, really." Her face softened for a moment. "Thank you." She turned and began walking toward the apartment.

"Sarah?" Liam jogged over to her.

She stopped and turned around. "Yes?"

His eyes darted down, looking at the sand as he tried to figure out what to say next. "Are you having dinner tonight?" he asked, then winced at how terrible that sounded.

She stared at him, puzzled. "Yes . . ." she replied slowly. "I always have dinner."

"If you'd like to have dinner at The Cove later, I'll be there."

"Are you serving the food?" she inquired.

"Yeah. I mean, no," he stammered. He moved forward, nearly tripping over his loose shoelace. *Smooth.*

"So, you aren't serving the food?" Sarah asked with a slight smirk.

"I will be serving food," he said as he bent down to retie his shoe, "but I meant after, when I'm not working."

"So, you'll be gone."

Ugh, this woman is infuriating. Liam stood. "No! I'm trying to ask you if you would like to have dinner with me!" he said breathlessly.

"Oh. Why didn't you just say that?" she asked with a slight grin, knowing exactly what she was doing to him.

"I dunno."

Sarah turned and began walking toward the apartment again while Liam stood dumbfounded until he was able to muster up his courage once again.

"You never gave me an answer on dinner," he called out.

Sarah peered coyly over her shoulder. "No, I didn't."

Liam cupped his hands to his mouth and yelled out, "Woman, you drive me nuts."

She laughed. "You make that sound like a good thing."

He shrugged. "Maybe it is."

Wyatt sat sprawled out on the couch, still reeling from what had happened earlier. After he cleaned up the horrors of last night and took a shower, he had decided to mindlessly watch television.

His ears perked up at the sound of the doorknob moving about. He stood and peeked out the window to find Sarah leaning over, trying to work the key. He smiled to himself and sat back down, waiting for her to come in.

When the door finally opened, Wyatt leaned his arms on the back of the couch. "Good job! Took you long enough."

Sarah scowled at him. "How long were you sitting there listening to me trying to get this stupid key into that stupid hole?"

she asked, slamming the key on the small table next to the door. "Liam should have specified how to use it."

He chuckled. "Every human knows how a key works. Asking him to explain the fundamentals of it would make you stick out like a manatee in the open ocean."

Sarah scoffed as she examined all the items around the living room. "Humans have too many things," she stated, picking up a throw pillow, then tossing it back.

"Hence the need to lock the door," Wyatt explained, flipping aimlessly through the channels. "Nice bathing suit, by the way. It looks similar to what Mom wore in that one picture. Where'd you get it?"

"Denise took me shopping. I have a bunch of clothes at her place."

"Look at that, already embracing being human," he teased.

"Ha. Ha," she mocked, inspecting the fake plant in the corner. Wyatt still wasn't sure why someone would have something like that in their home.

"I didn't know you were coming back so soon. I figured you would have stayed back and told Father." He paused his finger on the remote and sat up straight. His eyebrows raised up high. "You didn't tell him, did you?"

She turned back and looked him dead in the eyes. "Yes. The guards should be here any minute to take you back."

Wyatt's eyes scanned her face before she broke into a grin.

"I'm a bit offended that you seriously think I would do that to you."

"Sorry. I guess I'm still working on my trust issues. This is the longest I've been away from home without a soldier dragging me back." His gaze returned back to the television. Wyatt didn't pay much attention to his sister inspecting the items along the coffee table.

"Well, you might be right not to trust people," she stated.

"Why do you say that?" He pulled his eyes from the winner of the baking show to find Sarah staring wide-eyed at Liam's glowing laptop screen.

"Your friend is a mer hunter," she said, spinning the device toward Wyatt.

He leaned forward, his eyes moving back and forth as he read the text in front of him. A smile crept on his face, and he shook his head. "No. Liam couldn't hurt a sea slug."

"Explain, then, why he has documents pertaining to mermaids."

"Maybe he's just interested in mythology. I wouldn't worry about it," he stated, leaning back.

"This magic box tells our secrets though!"

"That's called a laptop." He had watched Liam plenty of times to piece together exactly what the contraption was. "Humans use it to find information about anything they want. They can even communicate with each other or play games. It's truly fascinating."

"How many humans use these . . . laptops?"

"I'm not sure, but plenty have a phone that shows the same information. I've seen Liam use his plenty of times."

"What if they all know our secrets?" She gasped. "We should warn Father!"

Wyatt had to keep himself from laughing. "Calm down. Not everything on there is true. There are plenty of made-up stories. Humans have tales about us but there are no facts to prove we actually exist. Here, just read this," he told her, pointing to an article about how merfolk lay eggs.

Sarah studied it, then declared, "This doesn't prove you're right, though. If Liam is searching for information about us, then he could be a danger."

"He's not. I know Liam. He's harmless," he assured her. The only thing Sarah had to worry about was falling for his friend's charm.

"Maybe I should do some digging around during dinner," she mused.

"Oh? Is my big sister going on a *date* with a human?" he asked with surprise.

"It's not a date! He suggested I eat dinner at The Cove after he's done working."

"Whatever you say." He nudged her playfully. "Since you have some time on your hands before your . . . whatever you want to call it," he said, and Sarah scowled, "why don't we explore the island? I don't work until later."

"Sure. I'd like that."

"Great! Why don't you go change, and I'll meet you outside." He pushed himself up from the couch and gathered supplies while Sarah went to Denise's apartment.

Fifteen minutes later, Wyatt sat at one of the patio tables outside The Cove with the extra book bag Liam had given him that contained water bottles of salt water and a beach towel.

"Ready?" Sarah asked, approaching him. She had changed into jean shorts and a loose dark green tank top.

Wyatt stood up and slung the book bag over his shoulder. "Yeah."

As they walked over to the trolley stop, he couldn't help but wonder about their brother who had gone out alone to look for Wyatt. "Have you heard from Varian?"

"No, but Lyra told me he had checked in with her. He promised he'd be back yesterday to try to smooth things over with Father."

"Oh. Well, hopefully he'll give up on his search."

Sarah shrugged. "He cares too much to give up."

That's what I'm afraid of, he thought as the trolley pulled up to its stop.

Sarah followed Wyatt onto the bus. It was her first time experiencing public transportation, and Wyatt could tell she was nervous by the way she tensed each time a human entered or exited at each stop. It was as if she was waiting for them to strike her down with a harpoon. Wyatt motioned for her to look outside at the buildings passing by as a distraction. Soon they approached their stop and walked to a small café.

"This is amazing!" Sarah exclaimed, sucking down her mango smoothie.

Wyatt finished chewing his ham and cheese sandwich before replying. "I told you you'd enjoy the food here."

"I have to admit, it is better than back home. There are so many options up here."

"And not a kelp salad in sight," he added.

After they finished, they walked over to a small boutique, where Sarah looked for a dress to wear for dinner that Wyatt still insisted was a date.

"If it wasn't a date, you wouldn't be so concerned with your outfit," Wyatt stated, waiting for Sarah to try on her fifth dress.

"Forgive me for not wanting something so constricting against my legs," she stated before finally settling on a flowery off-the-shoulder dress. It was shorter in the front but flowed past her knees in the back.

Wyatt paid for it before they hopped back on the trolley to the City Pier. From there, they walked toward the northern tip of the island, Bean Point.

"You know, it would be quicker if we swam," Sarah suggested during their walk.

"What would be the fun in that?" Wyatt smirked and ran down the beach.

"Hey!" she shouted, chasing after Wyatt.

He slowed his pace at the edge of the shore. Two dark figures floated a few feet from him in the water. Wyatt had never seen them before, but there was no denying it was a manatee mother and her calf.

Slipping his sandals off, he waded into the shallows. "Come out here," he instructed his sister.

Sarah dropped her shopping bag and sandals in the sand and followed him. "Oh wow! Is that—" she exclaimed, walking farther out into the water.

"Manatees. They might not come to you since we look like humans."

Sarah stepped forward and bent down, letting the hem of her shorts touch the water. Holding her hand out under the surf, she patiently waited. Soon enough, the calf swam up, letting her caress its tough, wrinkly, gray skin. The mother followed, pressing her snout against Wyatt's leg.

"They are adorable," she said, peering over her shoulder at her brother. She laughed as Wyatt was nearly bowled over by the adorable sea cow.

"They sure are friendly."

"Because they know they can trust us," Sarah stated.

Wyatt looked around, realizing they were drawing curious eyes while playing with the manatees. Turning to Sarah, he quietly said, "We should go before the locals suspect something."

"All right, sweetie, go to your mama," she told the calf.

Wyatt followed Sarah back to the beach and handed her a water bottle. "So now that you know I'm safe, are you going to return home?"

Sarah leaned back, letting the warm sun caress her skin. Her initial reason for coming was to make sure Wyatt was safe before returning to Aquana, but it seemed as if she was now contemplating leaving for good.

"Not until I make sure Liam isn't a concern." She took a sip of water. "Are you still seeing that human?"

"No. You'll be happy to know I ended things with her last night," he answered.

Sarah furrowed her brow. "I'm not happy in the least."

"Yet, you relaxed as soon as I said it," Wyatt said with a lifted brow.

"Ok, so you dating a human concerned me."

"I went out with her a few times. For what reason? I'm not sure. Maybe I was subconsciously rebelling a bit." He shrugged, taking a sip of water.

Sarah laughed. "A bit?"

"All right, a lot," he confessed with a smirk.

"And what happened to finding your soul mate?" she questioned.

Wyatt turned to look at her with skepticism. "Oh, so you believe me now?"

"Mom might have convinced me in her journal. She didn't elaborate on the details, but she was very adamant that Mara and Mercer were soul mates." She lifted her water once more, then asked, "So?"

"The mistake with Jessica aside, I'm still hoping."

"Well, if you're to continue living here, unless she walks straight out of the ocean, I doubt you'll find her on land. Still, it seems rare for a mer to find their true mate. I don't want you focused on searching for someone that is nearly impossible to find," Sarah expressed.

Wyatt stretched his legs and gazed back out at the sparkling aqua-blue waters. "I know she's out there and who knows, maybe she's human." A smile crept across his face. "The stories were never specific in saying a mer would find a mer soulmate."

She sighed. "I would much rather you open up to someone from our world. Dating on land is too dangerous."

Wyatt turned his head, looking at her incredulously. "And you going out with Liam tonight is any different?"

Sarah shifted her body toward Wyatt, curling her legs under her. "Yes," she answered definitively. "I'm keeping you safe. If there's nothing to worry about, then I'll stay away from him."

"If you can honestly tell yourself that's the only reason you're meeting him for dinner, then I don't need your protection," Wyatt voiced. "I promise you, he's no hunter. The only mer he has his eyes on is you."

Sarah scoffed at his observation.

"He likes you, Sarah, and I can see you don't completely hate him either. Maybe take your own advice and try to keep your heart open to the possibility of finding love. It may be unconventional love, but it's still love."

~

Liam was finishing pouring a glass of water for a customer when Sarah walked through the patio doors.

"You're early!" he exclaimed in a chipper voice as she approached the bar. He flashed her a smile, causing her cheeks to blush.

"Yeah, we came back early so Wyatt could get ready for work." She looked around. "Where's Denise?"

"Oh," he said with disappointment. "I think she's in the back. I'll go get her."

"I can wait until she comes back out. I don't want to take you away from your customers. I just need to talk to her and change for dinner."

Liam leaned his arms over the bar top, inching closer to her. "So, is that a yes to our dinner date?"

"No," she blurted out.

He drew back, confused. "No?"

"It's not a date," she said definitively, "but I will have dinner with you."

"I'll take that. Just a casual meal between two people," he reiterated with a wink. Not giving Sarah a chance to second-guess herself, Liam waved his hand in the air, flagging Denise, who had just left the kitchen.

"Whatcha need?" Denise asked Liam, drumming on the countertop.

"I was wondering if you could help me," Sarah spoke up.

"Sure thing. Let's go to my office," Denise replied, motioning up toward her apartment.

As Liam tended to his customer, the minutes ticked by until he heard sandals coming down the stairway. His mouth gaped at the sight of Sarah standing at the top of the landing, completely transformed. Her hair was pulled back in a half-up, half-down hairdo. Her dress hugged her body in all the right places, flowing behind her. Gracefully, she descended the stairs and headed to the bar as Liam was mid-pour. He blinked a few times, coming back to reality, and handed the customer her iced tea.

Liam's eyes outlined her body. "Not a date. Got it." He smiled. "I still have fifteen minutes on the clock. Why don't you sit here and I'll get you a glass of water?"

"No, I really don't care for tap water," she replied.

"Hmmm, I got just the thing." Liam grabbed a glass and began adding things to the mixer. A few minutes later, he handed her a glass of pink liquid. "Strawberry lemonade."

Sarah sniffed it before taking a sip through the paper straw. "Mmmm! This is so much better than water!"

Liam leaned his forearms along the counter. "I thought you'd like that." His eyes glanced over at the patio doors to see Wyatt walking through. "Oh, hey, there's your brother," he stated, giving him a wave before Wyatt disappeared in to the kitchen.

"What's that smell?" Sarah asked, twisting her face as if a skunk had just walked into the restaurant.

Liam tilted his head up slightly and sniffed the air. "I don't smell anything. I don't think it's me." He quickly sniffed each of his armpits, then shrugged.

Sarah leaned over the bar, smelling him up and down, getting inches from his body. A shiver ran down his spine. "No, it's not you."

"Are you sure? Maybe you should take another whiff?" He moved closer with a smile.

Before Sarah could even reply, a woman pushed up alongside her. Shit, what was she doing here?

"Where's Wyatt?" she demanded, scanning the whole restaurant for what seemed like her next prey.

"Oh, hey, Jessica!" he exclaimed loudly as Wyatt was about to exit the kitchen. His roommate spun on his heels and dove back inside. "I don't know. Did you check the apartment?"

Her eyes narrowed in on him. "You're a poor liar, Liam. I know he's working a shift today. Where is he? In the back?"

"Why does it matter to you?" Sarah questioned, nearly gagging from whatever stench she insisted she could smell.

"I'm his girlfriend," Jessica replied flatly.

"That's not what I heard," Sarah muttered under her breath before taking another sip of her drink.

Jessica lifted her chin, looking Sarah up and down. "And who the hell are you?" she asked, clenching her jaw. A few customers and staff were beginning to stare.

"She's a paying customer that you don't need to harass," Liam said, inserting himself between the two women before it escalated further.

"What's going on here?" Denise asked with her arms folded in front of her chest. Her chipper demeanor was gone just like Jessica's dignity.

"I'm here for Wyatt and your employee refuses to tell me where he is," Jessica said with her back to Liam and Sarah.

Liam shook his head frantically with wide eyes in hopes to influence Denise's decision to state Wyatt's whereabouts.

With a subtle nod, Denise replied, "I'm sorry, Jessica, but he's not here."

Jessica spun back around to face Liam. "Liars!" she yelled, pounding her fist on the bar, then turned back to Denise. "I know he's working right now!"

Sarah held the back of her hand up to her nose. "Oh my gosh, she reeks!" she whispered to Liam. "You can't smell her?"

Liam leaned over the bar. "It's probably the stench of desperation," he replied in Sarah's ear, causing her to let loose a chuckle.

"What the hell is so funny?" Jessica hissed.

Sarah stood up. "Maybe the fact that—"

"That she finally got the joke I told her right before you came in," Liam interrupted before Sarah could poke the seductive bear any more.

"Whatever. You're not worth my time." Jessica looked Sarah up and down before returning her attention to Denise. "Now tell me where he is. I have a right to know where my boyfriend is!"

Within that moment, the whole restaurant got eerily quiet except for the bustling of the kitchen.

Denise kept her cool. "You're correct, he is working. However, I sent him on an errand to pick up some supplies. I can let him know you stopped by. Now I suggest you leave, as you're causing a scene in my restaurant," she strongly recommended, guiding her toward the exit.

"I'll be back tomorrow," Jessica promised before storming out the doors.

Denise walked back up to the bar. "Are you two ok?"

"Yeah. I could have taken her, though," Sarah stated bluntly. Liam stifled a laugh "What? You don't believe me?"

Liam put his hands up in defense. "Oh, I believe you."

"Ok, you two." Denise placed her hand on Sarah's back to return to her seat.

Just then, Wyatt walked behind the bar, nervously looking around. "Is the coast clear?"

"Yeah, you're safe," Denise assured him.

"Oh my god, she's back!" Liam cried out, causing Wyatt to dive behind the bar. Laughter erupted between him and Sarah.

Wyatt stood up to see Jessica was nowhere in sight. "Very funny!" he said, shooting a glare at Liam.

"You're horrible, Liam," Denise scolded him with a light smack on the arm when she walked behind the counter to check the register.

"So, that was the girl you went out with?" Sarah inquired in disbelief.

"Unfortunately. She wasn't like that when we first went out," Wyatt replied. "Thanks for not telling her where I was."

"She's, um . . ." Sarah began, trying to think of the right word.

"Crazy? Psychotic? Downright certifiable?" Liam finished her sentence as he cleaned the counter.

"I don't know the girl that well, but there's definitely something off about her lately," Denise said, closing the cashier drawer. "I'm glad you decided to break up with her, Wyatt."

"We had a few dates, but we definitely weren't a couple. There was never anything special between us," Wyatt affirmed.

"Not unlike you and Liz," Liam said, lifting his brow with a smirk.

"Oh?" Denise asked curiously, turning to Wyatt.

"Don't you have things to do?" Wyatt narrowed his eyes at both Liam and Denise.

"What? You have to admit you two certainly had a moment yesterday," Liam stated. Wyatt shook his head as he knotted his apron around his waist.

"What happened yesterday?" Sarah inquired, taking another sip of her drink.

"Besides Jessica losing her shit? I might have staged a little romantic walk between the two of them," Liam replied. Sarah gave Wyatt a worried look.

"It wasn't romantic," Wyatt butted in.

"Says the guy that held her hand," Liam stated, wagging his eyebrows.

"Liz is a nice girl. She's very sweet. There's nothing to worry about," Denise told Sarah, then turned back to Wyatt. "Before you start cleaning the tables, can you take that person's order?" She motioned toward the patio.

"If it'll get me away from listening to all of you talk about my love life, then yes, I'll gladly tend to them," Wyatt said, hastily walking away from the conversation. He pushed past the patio doors and headed to the only customer who had yet to order.

Her back was turned to them, but Liam could definitely tell who it was by her dirty blonde hair. He shared a knowing look with Denise.

"What are you both smiling about?" Sarah asked suspiciously.

"Denise is being diabolical." Liam chuckled, untying his apron, as his shift was at an end.

"I am not! I only told the girl to sit at the table and you would take her order. It's not my fault I *forgot* your shift was ending," she replied innocently.

The three of them watched Wyatt greet Liz with a pleasantly surprised expression. His face beamed as he took her order. Liam placed the apron under the counter and walked around it to sit next to Sarah.

"Who is that?" she asked Liam.

"That's Liz," Liam answered.

"He looks so happy," she said quietly to no one in particular.

Denise quickly busied herself, cleaning off a nearby table when Wyatt walked back into the restaurant. He shook his head in disbelief. "You knew she was here, didn't you?" he asked Denise and Liam, walking behind the bar to fill Liz's drink order.

"She might have told me she was coming here for dinner earlier today when I dropped off her phone," Liam admitted.

"You bought her a phone?" Denise asked in surprise. "Liam . . ." She sighed.

"Before you say anything," Liam began, "yes, I am too nice, but also her phone was busted and she didn't want to worry her parents. I picked up a prepaid one for her to use."

While that was true, he also wanted to make sure she had a way to communicate with him if something happened to her again.

"That was nice of you," Denise commented.

"I'm going to bring Liz her drink," Wyatt said, grabbing her water. "So, if you could all not stare, that would be great." He was out the door before anyone else could comment.

"I should change clothes for our *non-date* date," Liam said, peering down at his stained work shirt.

"I've never seen my brother act like this," Sarah observed.

"Happy?"

"Yeah. Maybe he was right."

"About what?"

Sarah seemed deep in thought before she waved the subject away and smiled. "Nothing. Liam," she said, stopping him from getting up.

"Yeah?"

"You seem to be close with Liz. Why didn't you ever date her?" she inquired.

"We have more of a sibling-like relationship. Plus, I think she might be getting asked out very soon." He gestured toward Wyatt, who was now sitting next to Liz, his fingers fidgeting nervously. Liam stood up from his seat, leaned down by her cheek, and whispered in her ear, "Also, I might have had my eyes set on someone else."

CHAPTER 22

Disbelief

Liz added to the ever-growing pile of discarded shrimp tails. Just a few days ago, she never would have touched them, and now she couldn't get enough of the delectable crustaceans. She chugged down her third glass of water, making this her eighth total glass for the day. Her nails scratched at the top of her Bermuda shorts that barely hid her spreading aqua rash. She had made the mistake of taking a shower that morning, causing the outbreak to creep farther over to the front of her right thigh.

Rummaging through her purse, she pulled out her new prepaid cell phone to check the time. Liam had unexpectedly stopped over earlier that day to drop it off. She should have scolded him for spending more money on her, but the truth was, she needed some way to communicate, especially with how the rash was progressing. Thankfully, he had already put his number in, along with Denise's, in case of emergencies.

As a concerned friend, he requested that she call her parents as soon as possible to let them know she was ok. She knew he was right, but the guilt settling in the pit of her stomach made it nearly impossible to dial their number. The closest she got was saving it in her contacts. She had emailed them a quick note from

Liam's laptop to let them know she was ok, but she knew that wasn't enough.

Her hands shook so much, she was afraid she would drop the new phone. She quickly plunged it back into her purse, along with any thoughts of home.

"You must be thirsty," Wyatt commented, startling Liz. "Sorry. I didn't mean to scare you." His hand touched her bare shoulder for a moment. There was something about his touch that made her feel like she was being wrapped in a blanket of comfort. She never wanted him to let go.

"No, it's fine. I've just had a lot on my mind," she said. Her gaze lifted to his as he refilled her water.

"Would you like to talk about it?" he asked with sincerity, placing the pitcher of water down. "Or do you want to drown yourself in some more shrimp?" He chuckled, observing the giant pile of discarded tails.

"I, uh . . ." she stumbled over her words. There was nothing she could think of that would excuse the large amount of seafood she was eating, along with the countless refills of water. At this point, he probably thought she was dumping the water on the ground just to get him to come back. She hid her face in her hand. "I don't know what's wrong with me," she muttered into her hands.

"Don't be embarrassed," Wyatt said, pulling out the chair next to her to sit down. He took her hands and lowered them to see her face, sending warm energy throughout her body. "Frankly, I like a girl who can down her weight in shrimp."

"Better shrimp than lobster tails. Liam would have a fit," Liz said, trying to force a smile.

"Oh?" Wyatt asked.

Her head dropped as she tried to hide from even more embarrassment.

"It's ok," he whispered, taking her hand in his once more. He grazed the pad of his thumb across her knuckles.

Liz gulped down the lump that was forming in her throat.

"He's been paying for my meals and extra clothes. It's a long story, but my credit card is useless and I don't have any cash. On top of that, the house I had rented was canceled on my way here. Denise was kind enough to let me stay at the apartment she owns for free." She hung her head, afraid of what Wyatt thought about her. "I feel so ashamed that they felt the need to do that for me. I should have just swallowed my pride and traded in my later flight and returned home as soon as I got here. My parents don't even know." Tears threatened her eyes but she held them back. "I'm not sure why I keep pouring my heart out because now you're just going to pity me like everyone else has." The words spilled out of her like a broken dam.

"Liz . . ." The way he said her name felt so familiar, like he had said it a million times before. "I would never pity you." He squeezed her hand, and she lifted her head to meet his sky-blue eyes. The butterflies in her stomach were beating their wings furiously. "If anyone knows where you're coming from, it's me. When I arrived here, I had absolutely nothing in my pockets, so to speak." He chuckled to himself as if it was an inside joke. "Both Liam and Denise helped me get on my feet. I felt the same way as you. Sometimes, I still do."

Liz felt better knowing she wasn't alone. "I guess we're both pretty lucky to have found them. I did promise them I'd pay them back once I returned home."

Wyatt's shoulders slumped from her words. "I forgot you were going home soon."

Liz hesitated as if it was an option to go back to Ohio. "Yeah, I guess."

"You seem unsure."

She sighed. "I don't know anymore. I know I should go back, but I . . ."

"You what?" he urged her on, pulling his chair closer.

She tucked a strand of hair behind her ear. "I feel like I belong here. It feels weird saying it, but truthfully, I never felt like I belonged in Ohio."

Because I never really did. I was adopted. She thought about telling him exactly why she was here, but she had already divulged enough information. He didn't need to hear her life story.

"I don't know if it was the allure of seeing the gulf for the first time, but ever since I got here, problems aside, I felt like this is where I was meant to be." She shook her head and ate another piece of shrimp. "That sounds silly."

"It's not," Wyatt told her, placing his hands on the table inches away from hers. "I know how you feel. That's exactly why I left home. I never felt like I fit in with anyone there." He promptly stole a shrimp from her plate, removed the tail, and popped it into his mouth.

She raised an eyebrow, playfully nudging his shoulder. "You, not fitting in? I don't believe that for a second."

He smiled back. "You'd be surprised." He stared out at the gulf, and his smile faded. "I always felt like a dolphin in a herd of manatees, always wanting to play in the wake of passing boats but everyone telling me I can't."

Liz couldn't help but laugh a little.

He turned back to her. "What?"

She grinned. "You and your fish references."

"What can I say? I'm a regular fish out of water." He shrugged, stealing another shrimp from her plate. There was a brief pause as he finished chewing. "To be honest, I actually came over here for a reason."

"And what was that? To help me finish the rest of my shrimp?" she asked with a smirk.

"That too." He laughed. "I was wondering . . . would you like to hang out tomorrow?"

Silence hung in the air as Liz contemplated how to answer. She only had three more days on the island, and what had she done? Sleeping on the beach and catching some kind of weird rash wasn't on her list of things to do while on vacation. She had wanted to fulfill what her grandfather had planned, yet when she had searched her purse last night, she couldn't find the paper he had written their activities on. That was the last piece of him she had held on to and now that was gone.

This trip is important. Tears threatened her eyes.

Wyatt cleared his throat, snapping Liz out of her pseudo-argument with the voices in her head. "It seems like there's something else on your mind."

"I'm sorry. It's just . . . I'm probably leaving in a few days and I don't want to . . . um," she fumbled over her words, trying to think of the right thing to say without hurting his feelings. The last thing she wanted to do was lead him on.

"Let's just call it a tour of the island before you go home."

"And if I decide to stay?" she asked, the words coming out of her mouth without her even thinking. Stay? Why would she say that? She couldn't possibly stay here . . . could she?

"Then I hope tomorrow is one of the reasons you're convinced." He placed his hand on top of hers, causing the butterflies in her stomach to flutter toward her heart.

Before her inner voice could protest, she replied, "Ok."

"Ok?"

Her smile said it all. "Yeah, I'd like that."

"Let me go check my work schedule for tomorrow." Wyatt lifted her hand up to his lips and kissed the back of it before standing up, causing her heart to nearly float away.

While she waited patiently for Wyatt's return, she wondered if she had made the right choice. *It's not a date,* she assured herself. *He's just going to show me around the island.* She finished her dinner as Wyatt hastily walked back to the table.

"Good news, Denise gave me the whole day off. I'm all yours." He beamed.

She might never want to leave after tomorrow.

Liz screamed as she jolted up from bed. Her chest heaved as she tried to catch her breath. The last thing she remembered from her reoccurring nightmare was running through a wall of flames and diving into the water. Since coming to the island, her nightmare had progressed where she was trapped in a small room as smoke began to fill. This time, she must have escaped, but how?

"I'm so sick of these nightmares," she growled in frustration. Grabbing the glass of water she kept on her nightstand as of late, she took a sip to quench her thirst, then returned the glass back to its place on the coaster.

A glance at the alarm clock and she grimaced, falling back into the plush mattress. *Ugh, only four in the morning.* She began to roll over when her phone dinged. Sighing, she rolled back over and checked it.

LIAM

Is everything ok? I thought I heard you yell.

I'm fine. Just a bad dream. Sorry if I woke u.

Don't sweat it. Night.

Liz returned the phone. She was grateful for it. However, she didn't need Liam constantly checking in on her. But it was better than him banging on her door. She closed her eyes and tried to fall back asleep, but it never came. Only one thought filled her mind, and as much as she tried to resist the urge, she was too exhausted to fight it.

Flinging the sheets off her, she slipped out of bed and got ready for the day. It was still dark outside, but she didn't care.

After cautiously making her way down the dunes, she spread her towel along the cool sand, hoping that would satisfy her need to be near the water. She lay there, staring up at the tiny stars that grew dimmer as the sun rose behind her to greet the night sky. The lull of the waves provided a feeling of calm, yet it wasn't enough.

Before her subconscious could rationalize staying on dry land, she stood and walked toward the edge of the foamy waves. She stayed there, stock still, letting the water caress her toes, and watched the silhouettes of a few sandpipers scuttle across the sand as they tried to outrun the waves.

Without hesitation, she stepped even farther into the surf until the bottom of her shorts kissed the water. She could hear Liam's voice in her head, scolding her from going in, but the rash on her legs felt so dry and itchy. Water was the only thing that seemed to help. It took everything in her not to dive underneath.

Her fingertips grazed the surface of the water, and she closed her eyes, taking it all in. Within seconds, a stinging sensation prickled along the tops of her feet, causing her to hiss. She moved them about, freeing them from the grip of the wet sand before hobbling back to her towel to examine them. Each toenail had an aqua sheen to it. If no one knew any better, they could say she had painted her nails. However, on the top of her right foot, you could clearly see the aqua pattern that matched the rest along her thighs. Thankfully, the only thing different about the left was the faux nail polish.

How much worse was this going to get? And how much longer could she put off getting medical attention?

"Hey!" a familiar voice called out.

Liz snapped her head up to see Liam running down the shore. She had forgotten he went on morning runs to avoid the heat and crowd. She hurriedly buried her feet into the sand.

"You're out and about early," he huffed. "The nightmare keep you up?"

"Not really. I just couldn't get back to sleep."

"Nervous about today, huh?"

Liz looked at him, confused.

"I heard about Wyatt asking you out." Liam pulled up the bottom of his tank top to wipe the sweat from his face, revealing his toned abs.

"He's just showing me around town."

"Uh-huh, sure." He drew out the last word. "I saw the way he was looking at you and how he kissed your hand."

Liz turned away, feeling heat rush to her cheeks.

"When do you head back to Ohio?" He knelt on the sand.

"In two days. I wish I could stay, though."

"You should," he said.

"If only it was that simple." But what was holding her back? Liz turned her head back to see him exercising. "What are you doing?"

"Push-ups. I have to get some kind of workout done instead of cutting my run short."

Liz laughed. "I didn't make you stop. You chose to."

"You can always join in," he suggested, holding himself up between reps.

"It looks super fun, but I think I'll pass," she said sarcastically.

"Suit yourself!"

"So, wait. Were you spying on us yesterday?"

"No," Liam replied. Liz pushed him over before he could finish his last push-up. "Ok! But in my defense, it was hard not to notice you two staring into each other's souls." Brushing the sand from his body, he shifted and sat next to her.

"How was your date with Sarah?" she asked, trying to change the subject.

A smile crept across his face. "It was nice. She insisted it wasn't a date, even though she was wearing a dress and makeup. If that's a casual outfit for her, I'm not sure if I'll be able to handle an actual date with her." He chuckled. "She did ask me a lot of odd questions, though."

"Like what?"

"Like if I fish."

"That's not odd," she pointed out.

"Or if I liked to see the guts of a defenseless fish spill out after I killed it with a harpoon."

Liz lifted her eyebrows. "Um . . ."

"I told her I only like to eat fish. I can barely catch a guppy. I'm not sure if she was testing me or what, but I think I passed."

"Maybe she's just really passionate about sea life," she suggested with a shrug.

"Apparently. But the girl sure can eat them. We went shrimp for shrimp in a sort of unofficial eating contest. I let her beat me."

Liz gave him a look.

"Ok, she beat me. I could have kept going, but I don't think she would go see me again if I threw up on her."

"That would definitely be a no-go for a second date if that happened to me."

"Ah, remember, this wasn't a date," he corrected her. "So, it would be a first date, not a second."

"She was wearing a dress and makeup. Pretty sure it was a date, even if she didn't want to admit it."

"That is true. But don't tell her that." Liam pulled his right leg up toward his chest, hanging his arm over it. "So, have you called your parents yet?"

Liz looked down at the sand as she scrunched her toes around.

"You didn't, did you?"

She shrugged. "I'm just trying to come up with the right words."

"I get it, but you really do need to call them. What if you get worse?" he asked, his voice laced with concern.

Liz sat silently, pushing her feet farther into the sand.

He blew out a sigh. "It's gotten worse, hasn't it?"

Again, she remained quiet, staring out at the water. She didn't owe him an explanation. Out of the corner of her eye, she could see Liam scanning her body to spot anything out of the ordinary. His gaze stopped at the hem of her wet shorts.

"Did it spread?" he asked.

The sand slowly sifted from her feet as she lifted them. Before Liam could lean over to touch her foot, Liz jerked them away, hiding them back in the sand.

"Dammit, Liz," he muttered. "You know it gets worse when you go in the water."

Liz shrunk back. She couldn't help but feel like a child being scolded. "I know," she whispered.

"I don't suppose you packed aqua nail polish."

Liz shook her head.

"What were you thinking?"

"I wasn't! Ok?" She pulled her knees up to her chest and fought the hot tears that begged to escape her body. "I knew the consequences, but I didn't care." She buried her head between her knees. "I don't know what's happening to me. Between the rash, the chest pain, and the mood swings . . ."

"Chest pain and mood swings?"

Liz swallowed her emotions down. "The first time it happened, I just figured it was something I ate. Bad heartburn or something. But it's happened multiple times now. Sometimes it happens when you touch me. My chest will feel like it's on fire. The last time was the worst. It literally felt like a knife digging into my heart." She grimaced, remembering the searing pain.

"That's when you ran out at dinner the other day," he speculated.

Liz nodded while she hid behind her arms that hugged her legs tightly.

"And the mood swings?"

She lifted her head, wiping away a tear from her cheek. "I've been feeling different emotions that come on rather suddenly."

"Like panic attacks?"

"No. This is different. It almost feels like I'm channeling someone else's emotions." She tilted her head back to the sky. "God, I sound crazy."

"You're not crazy," Liam said.

She pulled away as he went to comfort her.

"I'm sorry. I wish there was more I could do," he said, letting his hand fall back.

"I think, at this point, I should just admit defeat and go to the hospital."

Liam sat silent for a moment, and Liz could see the wheels in his head turning. "I think . . ." he began but stopped short.

"What?" she asked.

He ran his fingers through his hair, and his jaw tensed, as if the next words out of his mouth were difficult to say. "I think you should hold off on going to the hospital."

"Why? I'm clearly getting worse." She opened up her water bottle and took a swig, trying to hide her grimace at the taste.

"I don't think it would be a good idea," he answered, rubbing his hand against his stubbled jawline. His eyes focused on the waves washing in and out of the shoreline.

"Well, the other option is to keep searching for my biological parents. Maybe we could go to the library again today or call some of the adoption agencies. I'll tell Wyatt that something's come up."

"I don't think you'll find anything at the library or any agencies."

Liz cocked her head at him. "What aren't you telling me? Did you find something?"

Liam took a deep breath and shifted his body to look at her. "I've been doing my own research and might have come across something. It's just a theory, though."

"What is it?" She had done hours of research, but nothing remotely close to what was happening to her had shown up. For Liam to find something was certainly a step in the right direction, theory or not.

"You have to keep an open mind, ok?" His hands fumbled around nervously.

"Ok . . ." She looked at him curiously.

He bit his bottom lip. "I don't know how to say this without sounding completely nuts."

"Just say it," she said firmly, becoming frustrated with his hesitance.

His eyes met her, and with all seriousness, he answered, "Mermaids."

Liz blinked a few times, trying to register what came out of his mouth. "What?" she asked, hoping she'd heard him wrong.

"Mermaids," he repeated. "It kept nagging me in the back of

my mind, but I didn't want to think that because it's completely absurd. But what if they're real?"

Liz scoffed and turned her attention back to the painted sky that was brightening from the sunrise behind them. "There's no such thing as mermaids. There must be a perfectly good *medical* reason for this. I just—"

"Believe me, this wasn't the first thing I jumped to. I stayed up for hours trying to figure it out, but you have scales on your legs and now your feet."

"It's a rash," she retorted.

"You said you didn't like shrimp but then started craving it the other day."

"I like the shrimp here. It tastes different. So what?"

Liam jumped to his feet. "What about being drawn to the ocean?" He motioned toward the gulf, then pointed to Liz's water bottle. "Or the fact you've been drinking water like crazy even though I can tell you hate the taste of it?"

"I don't care for the taste of water anywhere. It's Florida, and it's hot. I need to stay hydrated," she said defensively.

Liam paced in front of her, shaking his head. "Stop making excuses!" he snapped.

Quickly, he turned on the balls of his feet, leaned down, and snatched her water bottle, dumping its contents on the ground before hastily walking into the surf.

"What are you doing?" Liz exclaimed, running after him, stopping just short of the tide.

He knelt and filled the bottle up with seawater. "Try this." He held the bottle out to her.

Liz looked at it, completely perplexed. "I'm not drinking that nasty water. I'm not a—" She stopped, looked around, and lowered her voice. "I'm not a mermaid."

"Humor me," he insisted, pushing the bottle closer to her.

Liz clenched her fists. "No! This isn't some kind of joke, Liam!" She yanked the bottle from his hand, rolled up her towel, and stormed back toward the apartment.

"Liz!" Liam called out, keeping pace with her. "Please."

"Stop! Just stop! I don't need your help. I'll figure this out myself. Don't follow me," she huffed, then returned to her trek up the dunes to her apartment.

I can't believe him! Liz entered her apartment and slammed the bottle of seawater on the kitchen island. Clutching the edge of the counter, she hung her head and squeezed her eyes shut. The one person she had opened up to now thought she was some freak of nature. A tingling sensation ran down her arms and into her fingertips as her grip tightened. Her anger broke at the sound of frantic pounding on her front door.

Liz began to yell as she flung the door open. "I told you, I didn't—" She stopped short when the man in front of her was, in fact, not Liam. "Wyatt!" she greeted in surprise.

His body was rigid, and his mouth sat in a hard line. She turned to look at the clock. She wasn't expecting him for a few hours.

"What are you doing here? I thought you weren't coming until later."

He stood silent, looking her over as if she was injured. *Oh no, did the rash spread more?* she wondered. Before Wyatt's gaze went to her feet, she quickly placed her left foot on top of her right one, balancing the best she could.

His demeanor quickly relaxed, and his eyes softened with a bit of worry. "Are you ok?" he asked, looking at her clenched fist. He placed his hand on her shoulder.

The anger Liz had felt soon melted away under his touch, but in its place, a new emotion stirred in her. She tried to blink back the tears that were beginning to form.

"Hey, it's ok," Wyatt comforted her. He let himself in and guided her toward the couch. His body sank into the cushions, causing Liz to lean into him before shifting a few inches over. "What happened?"

Liz crossed her feet and curled them under the couch. "Liam

and I got into an argument." She did her best to suppress her emotions. "Why am I such a freak?" she whispered.

"I'm not sure what you two argued about, but he told me you're like a sister to him. I'm sure whatever he said he didn't intend to hurt you. And if he did, then I'll go over right now and beat him up for you."

A quiet chuckle bubbled out of Liz. She lifted her head, looking into his comforting eyes.

"And you are not a freak. You're beautiful." He wiped away a rogue tear from her warm cheeks.

Liz wasn't sure how he knew she needed him to be there, but she was glad he was on the other side of the door.

Breaking his gaze from hers, Wyatt took both of her hands into his. "Since I'm here, would you like to start our day a bit sooner and have breakfast? Unless, of course, you already ate."

"Sure. I could use a distraction anyway," she replied.

"Good, because I have the whole day planned," he said with a boyish grin.

CHAPTER 23

Connection

Liz excused herself while Wyatt waited patiently on the couch. To her dismay, her toenails and foot weren't the only things to be affected by her dip in the water. Her left thigh was nearly covered in the aqua rash. She changed and pushed the looming thoughts of her health aside. She would deal with it later. Today, she just wanted to have fun before she had to go back home.

A few minutes later, she returned wearing navy-blue capri-length leggings with a light blue swirl pattern along the sides and a flowy light blue tank top. The look in his eyes was like nothing she had ever experienced before. No guy had ever looked at her the way he did at that very moment.

He quickly cleared his throat and stood up. "Ready?"

She grabbed her purse and slipped on her shoes before replying. "Yup."

They walked to the trolley stop not far from their apartments and sat on the bench.

"Have you ridden the trolley yet?" he asked.

"This will be my first time. Where are we going for breakfast?"

He gave a sly grin. "It's a surprise. You're going to like it, though."

Soon, the two-toned green trolley bus came to a stop in front of the bench and opened its doors to them. Wyatt let Liz board first. They walked toward the back of the crowded bus, where they found one empty seat.

"You take it. I don't mind standing," Wyatt offered, motioning to the lone seat in front of them.

"That's ok," she said, clutching the metal pole.

Wyatt nestled in behind her, placing his hand above hers.

The trolley quickly lurched forward, causing Liz's balance to falter. She stumbled back into Wyatt, and he quickly placed his hand along her hip to steady her. Her back leaned against his hard chest.

Liz reluctantly stepped forward, planting her feet firmly onto the floor as she clutched the pole tighter. "Sorry," she apologized, peering over her shoulder.

His hand fell to his side. "I didn't mind," he replied with a smile that caused her cheeks to burn before she turned back around.

After a few stops, the people sitting in the bench next to them exited, allowing Wyatt and Liz to sit. She sat by the window, looking at the different buildings and palm trees that passed by. If someone had told her a week ago that she would be on an island, riding in a trolley with a guy, she would have said they were crazy.

"You know, this is the farthest from home I've ever been." Staring out the window, she felt a pang in her chest at thinking about her family back in Ohio.

Wyatt shifted in his seat. His arm brushed against hers, sending a warm electric sensation down her arm. "Do you regret coming here? I know you said your parents didn't exactly agree with you leaving."

Liz thought for a moment, pondering her response. Turning her attention away from the outside world, she looked at him and finally answered. "I don't regret coming here, but I didn't exactly leave on the best terms with them. In fact, I was so afraid they would say something to get me to change my mind that I left a note and snuck out of the house." She picked at a piece of skin along her fingernail. "God, that sounds awful when I say it out loud. I feel like a horrible person for putting them through this."

Was this trip so important that she had to leave her family during such a difficult time, or was she just running away from having to deal with the fact that her grandfather was gone? She pushed the thought aside.

"You're not a horrible person. When I left my father's king—um, home, I didn't even leave a note."

She tilted her head in surprise. "Really?"

"Mm-hmm. I didn't leave on good terms, either. I got into an argument with my father," he replied. "He wanted me to be something I'm not."

Liz furrowed her brow."What about your mother? Does she agree with him?"

Her own mother came to mind. A wave of sadness startled her, and she bit her bottom lip, trying to keep her emotions in check. Wyatt's eyes stared past Liz's shoulder and out the window as the gulf passed them. He took a deep breath. "She died a long time ago."

"I'm sorry," she whispered. She cast her head down and spotted Wyatt's hand clutching the bottom of the seat. A longing to comfort him seeped into her. Her fingers tiptoed next to his with uncertainty.

Wyatt's gaze broke as he noticed her melancholy. "I'm fine, really. I was so little, I don't really remember her. Although I do feel closer to her than to my father. He always did say I took after her."

"That's nice to know."

He gave a slight chuckle. "Not for him. She was . . . How does the phrase go? A free soul?"

"Free spirit," Liz corrected him as the bus slowed to a stop to pick up the next group of people.

"Yes. A free spirit." He smiled.

Liz cleared her throat and shifted in her seat, feeling the

sadness dissipate. "So, how much farther is this secretive place you're taking me?"

Wyatt leaned into the aisle, looking ahead. "Not far."

A comforting silence remained between them the rest of the way. As the bus slowed near an upcoming stop sign, Wyatt instructed Liz to pull on the rope above them. A bell rang, signaling the driver to drop them off at the corner bus stop. They exited and approached a purple, yellow, and aqua building. A sign above the awning read "Ginny's & Jane E's Café, Bakery & Store at the Old IGA."

The entrance led into the store first. It was filled with a variety of products from the floor to the ceiling. Most were items made by local artisans. As they made their way to the bakery in the back, Liz's eyes grew wide at the contents of the glass case.

Liz inhaled the delectable smell of large cinnamon rolls. "Oh, I think I know what I'm getting!"

"I have a feeling it's the same thing I'm ordering. Don't tell Denise," he said with a wink, walking toward the counter. "Would you like to split one? I figured we could stop at a few places and try a sampling of the island foods."

"Sure."

After Wyatt ordered their breakfast, they both sat at a small table in front of a bookshelf and dived into their sweet roll. As Liz finished her portion, she couldn't help but feel like they had done this a million times. Everything felt so natural with him.

Liz scraped the remaining frosting from her plate, savoring every last bite of it when she felt a tickle in the back of her mind. It sounded like an echo whispering across a canyon. She looked around to see everyone nearby engaged in private conversation.

"What did you say?" she asked Wyatt, figuring she had missed something he said.

"Hmm? I didn't say anything."

She must have been hearing things.

There it was again, like a feather softly moving about in her mind. She concentrated, trying to make out the words. *Can't . . .*

tell . . . not yet. Again, she looked around, confused where the voice was emanating from. She must be losing her damn mind.

"Are you ok?" Wyatt asked, bringing Liz's attention back to him.

"Yeah. Um, you ready?" she said, brushing it off.

"Sure. I'll gather our things and meet you up front," he said, taking her plate.

She started walking around the shopping area, and a few moments later, Wyatt joined her.

"These are beautiful," Liz exclaimed, strumming her fingers across all the necklaces that hung on a large pegboard.

Wyatt examined each piece and picked up a necklace Liz was admiring. A handmade nautilus shell pendant hung from a brown leather band. "What do you think? Is it me?" he joked, holding it up.

Liz laughed. "I think this would be more your style," she stated, picking up a simple braided leather bracelet. She clasped it around his wrist.

"I like it." He moved his wrist about before returning it to the table. "And I think this is more you," he said, giving her the necklace. He watched her hold it up, letting the shell rest along her chest. "Do you want it?"

"I love this, but I could probably find something similar online when I get back home and have money," she said with a frown, placing it back onto the pegboard.

Wyatt snatched it back up. "You deserve it."

"You already paid for breakfast. I can't let you pay for this too," Liz protested, bounding after him as he placed it on the counter.

"If you go back to Ohio, I want you to take a piece of this day with you as a reminder." He smiled, then paid for the necklace.

Pulling her hair up, Wyatt placed the necklace around her. His fingertips gently grazed the nape of her neck as he fastened it, bringing the warm tingles of energy down her spine.

"Thank you so much!" she said, looking down at the shell pendant, then back up into his warm welcoming eyes. "I love it!"

"I'm glad." He motioned toward the door. "Ready to go?"

Liz reached into her purse. "Oh, I forgot my phone. You go ahead. I'll just be a minute."

"Ok. I'll meet you at that table right outside the door."

A few minutes later, she walked out of the store. "So now where are you planning on taking me?"

Wyatt, who looked deep in thought, whipped his head around in surprise. "Do you like ice cream?"

"You're going to get me fat by the end of the day," she teased, sitting next to him.

"I don't think that's possible," he replied with a chuckle. "I was thinking we could hang out at the City Pier first to give our stomachs some time to digest. Hopefully, we'll see some manatees or something else around there. Then we'll get some ice cream to cool off."

"You're pretty on top of things today," Liz stated, impressed he had put so much thought into it.

"I can't take all of the credit. If it wasn't for Liam, we would probably waste half a day trying to find everything."

"Liam helped you plan this?" she said quietly, feeling completely awful for walking away from him.

Wyatt's smile faded as they sat down at the bus stop. He tipped his head to look at her. "Hey, don't worry. Everyone has disagreements. I'm sure the two of you will work it out," he assured her as the trolley slowed to a stop in front of them.

"I hope so." She sighed and climbed the steps onto the bus.

It didn't take them long to get to the Anna Maria City Pier. While they walked the length of the pier, Liz watched the shimmery turquoise waters lap around them. With each swell, they teased her to dive in. She wrapped her shaky arms around herself. *Maybe this was a bad idea*, her mind swirled in a thought-inducing panic. *I shouldn't be near the water . . . should I?*

"Are you ok? You're trembling," Wyatt said. He almost looked as anxious as she was.

"Yeah," she lied, gripping her biceps tightly, trying to pull herself together. What was wrong with her? She felt like she was going to jump out of her skin. "I guess it's just nerves. There's no railing. I don't want to fall in."

Wyatt gently placed his hand on Liz's upper back, causing all her worries to immediately melt away. "I won't let you fall in. And if you did, I'm a pretty good swimmer."

She coaxed a smile in response. Hell, now she really wanted to dive in.

"Why don't we sit and see if we can spot anything in the water." He gestured to the empty wooden bench in next of them.

He situated himself, curling his right leg under him, and patted the seat next to him. Liz cautiously sat down, shifting her body to let her right arm rest along the back of the bench.

Wyatt pointed to a dark cluster swimming just under the surface of the water. "See those coming toward us? That's a fever of cow-nosed rays."

"Wow!" She gasped in amazement. The sea creatures cut through the water like a hot knife through butter. "There's so many of them! Are they dangerous?"

The rays swam closer toward the shore, where a few beach-goers waded in the water.

"Well, they do have a venomous spine at the base of their tails, but they're really shy, so they won't bother humans," he replied. "They've never bothered me at least."

"You swam with them?" she asked in awe.

He gave her a warm smile. "A few times."

Those same whispers from earlier took hold of her head again. *Love . . . see . . . underwater.*

She scanned the area, yet no one was close enough for their voice to carry in her direction. She could have sworn it was Wyatt, but he clearly didn't say anything. Not wanting to dwell on it, she focused on the rays darting in and around the pilings of the pier while Wyatt enlightened her with a few more facts until the creatures moved farther south along the shore.

The sun was now glaring down on them, and sweat was beginning to bead down her neck and back. "I think I'm ready for that ice cream."

"Sure! Do you know what time it is? We have to be somewhere at a certain time, and I don't want to lose track and be late."

Liz pulled out her phone. "It's eleven o'clock."

She stared at the screen longer than she wanted, as if a text from her parents would magically appear, even though they didn't know her number.

"Have you talked to them yet?" he asked.

Liz shoved her phone back into her purse and shook her head. "I emailed them, but I haven't checked if they replied. I'm a bit nervous. What would I even say?"

"I know how you feel. If my father walked up to me right now, I'd be nervous too," he said as they walked across the street to the ice cream parlor. "I'm the last person that should be suggesting you call your parents, but for what it's worth, I think they'd just be glad to know you're safe."

Liz tapped her fingers against her purse, contemplating. She knew in her heart that he was right. She had waited long enough. After fishing the phone from the bottom of her purse, she clutched it to her chest and nodded as they approached Two Scoops Ice Cream Parlor.

"I'll go get us some ice cream and let you have some space, ok?"

"Thank you," she replied softly.

"What's your favorite?" he asked.

Liz sat down at a small table outside the shop. "Anything with peanut butter in it," she replied.

"You got it. Take all the time you need," he said before entering.

Liz's heart raced as she looked down at the contacts. Her

parents were at the top of the short list of numbers she'd saved on her phone. Peering up into the windows of the store, she could see Wyatt waiting in line. He glanced back, giving her an encouraging smile. Her uneasy half-smile reflected off the glass before she returned her attention to her phone. Her hand trembled as she touched the call icon for her parents. The phone rang for what seemed like forever until a voice answered on the other end.

"Hello. You've reached the voice mail of . . ."

Liz quickly ended the call before the robotic voice could finish. Her mind wandered to dark places, picturing her mother staring at the caller ID and refusing to answer. *She couldn't be that upset with me, could she?*

Hoping they were just out of the house, she tried her mother's cell phone. It only took two rings before her mother answered. "Hello?"

Liz felt slightly relieved that her subconscious wasn't right.

"Hello?" her mother repeated.

Liz's throat suddenly felt dry, and she had to force the words out of her mouth. "I— it's Liz."

"Liz?" Her mother sighed with what Liz hoped was relief. "We've been worried sick! Why didn't you answer your phone?"

"M-my . . ." She squeezed her eyes shut. She had to get it together before Wyatt came back out. "My phone stopped working." That was a lie, but admitting her phone was in the middle of the Gulf of Mexico would just solidify that her parents were right and she wasn't capable of being out on her own. "I had to get a replacement. I emailed you to let you know I was ok."

"Oh, I haven't been on my computer lately."

She should have known that her mother wouldn't have gotten her email. She only checked it on the computer probably once a week.

"How did you get a new phone?"

She pinched the bridge of her nose. "It was under warranty." Another lie to add to the pile of why she was a horrible daughter. She was thousands of miles away from her mother, yet she could still feel the tension through the phone. "I'm sorry I left without telling you or Dad."

There, it was out in the open.

Inside the store, Wyatt waited in line and gazed at Liz with worry. Her hair lifted from the breeze, letting him see her face. She was breathtaking. Although, she could have been wearing a paper bag and she still would have been just as beautiful.

He moved forward and read all the various flavors of ice cream. She said she liked peanut butter. *Why do I feel like I knew that?* He furrowed his brow when his mind wandered back to that morning. He still wasn't exactly sure what made him rush to her apartment. Just a coincidence.

Then there was the warm electric sensation he felt each time their skin touched. Surely he was just imagining things. Not to mention the sudden emotions he had been feeling lately. *Perhaps I'm more worried about Father than I thought.*

"Next," the worker announced.

After he paid for the ice cream, Wyatt stepped to the side and watched the worker scoop it into a cup. Waves of anxiety struck him with such force that it nearly caused him to stumble backward.

Something didn't feel right.

Panic coursed through his body, and his breath quickened. He felt everything close in around him. He looked down at his unsteady hands. *What's happening to me? Why am I—*

His thoughts immediately turned to Liz. He walked toward the window and saw her shaking hand holding the phone up to her ear. Her face was pale, and tears were beginning to form in the corners of her eyes. *It's her*, he realized. *I'm channeling her. But how? How am I feeling her emotions?*

"Here you go," the worker said to Wyatt, holding out the cup.

Wyatt snatched it up without a thank you and rushed out the door.

"I didn't run away from my problems!" Liz's voice shook before she stopped at the sight of Wyatt.

"Are you ok?" he whispered, pulling his chair next to hers.

Liz responded by shaking her head with discontentment. He gently took her soft hand and caressed it. She took a deep breath and squeezed his hand.

The volume wasn't high enough for Wyatt to discern the conversation, but he could faintly hear a woman's voice, who he presumed was Liz's mother, on the receiving end of the phone.

"I grieved during the funeral. What more do you want me to say?" Her hand tightened around Wyatt's so hard that he swore she had the strength of a young mer. "This isn't an escape. He wanted me to go. I told you that was his last . . ." Her voice cracked. "His last words to me." Liz bowed her head, letting her hair shroud her but not before Wyatt caught a glimpse of the tears that were threatening to escape her glassy eyes.

"It's ok." He rubbed her back in a circular motion. Her fingers began to loosen their grip around his other hand.

"Yeah, I'm here," Liz said over the phone. She lifted her head and met his gaze. "Look, I-I have to go." She paused while her mother replied. "I can't. I love you." She barely got the words out before her trembling hand placed the phone down. She kept her focus on the table. In a voice barely a whisper, she said, "I should have never called."

Wyatt cocked his head so she could see him. "Liz, please, look at me."

She looked away, shaking her head. "I can't. I don't want to cry in front of you again."

Shifting his seat closer to her, he placed his hand on her cheek and gently tilted her head up so he could peer into her beautiful eyes. "It's ok. I'm not going anywhere." He wiped a tear from her cheek with his thumb. "You can talk to me."

Liz let out a soft sniffle before she poured her heart out about her grandfather's untimely death and how coming to the island was his idea. Wyatt's heart shattered into a million pieces at knowing there was nothing he could say to give her comfort.

"They don't understand." Liz's bottom lip quivered. "This trip was . . . He was . . ." A sob escaped her as she pinched her eyes shut. "I miss him so much."

Wyatt didn't know what to say, so he did the only thing he could do and gathered her into his arms. She melted into his chest as she cried, letting the tears flow.

"Shhh, it's going to be ok," he tried reassuring her as he caressed her back.

"No, it's not," Liz whispered against his neck. "I don't know where I belong. I can't stay here. I have nothing, nobody."

Wyatt pulled her away and wiped a few more tears with his thumb. Moving her hair away from her face, he looked deep into her eyes and stated with all his heart, "You have me, Liz." A warm comforting energy fluttered in his chest, and he wondered for a split second if she felt it too.

Her hand pressed against his cheek, rubbing the scruff along his jawline. His gaze darted to her lips that moved closer to him. She was so close, he could feel her warm breath quickening. Tingles shot through his body as his lips grazed hers.

"Wyatt! There you are!" a female voice called out.

His heart sank. His sister arrived at the worst possible time.

Sighing, he pulled back. "I'm sorry. Let me go see what she wants. Will you be ok for a minute?"

Liz nodded with a sniffle.

"Why don't you start on the ice cream, ok? I got us peanut butter fudge to split." He kissed the top of her head, then walked toward the parking lot where Sarah looked on with concern.

"I wasn't expecting you to be back so soon," he said, approaching her.

Ignoring his statement, she shifted her eyes from Liz, then back to Wyatt. "Is everything ok?" she asked in a whisper.

"Yeah." He glanced back at Liz, who was drowning her

sorrows in ice cream. Sarah cocked her head, clearly not believing him for a second. "Just some family issues she's dealing with. Nothing that has to do with us, in case you're worried I spilled our secret."

"I'm not worried. I trust you."

It felt nice to hear her say that, even if it was getting harder to keep their secret from Liz. There was a desire deep within him that wanted to whisk Liz away into the water and show her his world. Which world did he even belong to anymore?

"Wyatt?" Sarah's voice brought him out of his self-reflection.

"Yeah?"

She frowned. "It's Varian."

"What about him? Is he ok?"

"I'm not sure," she began. Wyatt gave her a puzzled look. "Lyra sent me a message via dolphin that he hasn't returned. Father's getting worried."

Wyatt half listened. His attention returned to Liz, whose head hung low as she shoved another big spoonful of ice cream into her mouth. Suddenly, soft whispers echoed around him. No one except for Sarah, who was still talking, was around him. He concentrated on the words but could only make out a few, which didn't make any sense. *How . . . I . . . go . . . back*

"Wyatt? Wyatt, did you hear me?" Sarah punched him in the shoulder, snapping Wyatt out of his haze.

He crossed his arms in front of his chest. "When was he supposed to be back?"

"Yesterday, I think."

Wyatt's brow arched. "It's been one day. I'm sure he's fine. He probably just stopped to rest or get food. He's Captain of the Guards. He's capable of taking care of himself."

"Varian's a fast swimmer. He should have been back by now. And if Lyra's worried . . ."

Even though Wyatt had assured Sarah their brother was ok, he couldn't help but feel Sarah was right. The ocean alone was a vast world to explore. Who knew where Varian had ventured to.

"Could you look for him?" Sarah asked.

Wyatt's eyes widened at the thought. "You know Father has guards searching for me. If I swim too far out, I'm bound to run into one of them."

She sighed. "I know."

Running his finger across his eyebrow, he weighed his options. If something did happen to Varian, it would be because of Wyatt running away in the first place. But if Wyatt left the island and was brought back to the kingdom, he would never see Liz again.

None of that would matter anyway if she returned home.

"Ok, if we don't hear that he's home by tomorrow, then I'll go search for him." It was the least he could do.

Sarah hugged him. "Thank you!"

"Let me know if you hear anything. I should get back to—"

"Your date?" Sarah finished his sentence.

He rolled his eyes slightly. "It's not a date. I'm just showing her around the island."

"So, that's what you're calling your lips now? The island?" she asked, wagging her brows. "I saw what you two were about to do." She smirked but then her expression turned serious. "Be careful, Wyatt."

"I will be." He began to walk away but stopped short. "How did you know I was here?"

"Liam." She coyly smiled. "I told him I'd have dinner with him again if he told me. He said you'd probably be around here getting ice cream."

"Should have known he'd give in to you. I better get back. My ice cream is either melting or Liz ate it all. We can talk later, ok?" Wyatt turned and made his way back to Liz. He hated leaving her alone when she was so emotional. *It was probably a good thing we didn't kiss anyway. If she's leaving then . . . I don't even want to think about that.* He pushed the uncertainty aside.

"Everything ok?" she said, pushing the cup of ice cream toward him.

"Yeah, just my sister and her horrible timing. I'm sorry I left you alone." He glanced down. "To apparently eat most of the ice cream," he said with a slight chuckle, seeing the soupy remnants at the bottom of the cup.

"Sorry." Liz dipped her head, blushing a bit in embarrassment. "I think your sister owes you some ice cream." She stifled a laugh.

"I'm glad you found that funny," he mused, pointing to her smile with his spoon.

She frowned. "I'm sorry I ruined our day."

"What are you talking about?" he asked, scraping up the last bit of melty ice cream with his spoon. "You didn't ruin anything. We still have the whole day left."

He slurped down the rest of the ice cream from the cup before standing up and holding his hand out. Without hesitation, Liz placed her hand into his.

CHAPTER 24

Flying High

After leaving Two Scoops, Wyatt escorted Liz back onto the trolley and they got off at the second stop. They visited the Anna Maria Historical Society Museum where they took turns in front of the old island jail posing for pictures with Liz's phone. While Wyatt was leaning against the jail, a passing couple offered to take a picture of both her and Wyatt.

"You two make a cute couple," the older woman stated, handing the phone back to Liz.

Liz blushed but didn't say anything to correct the woman.

"Come on. We still have plenty of time before our surprise activity," Wyatt said as they walked across the street to a clothing store. "I figured we could browse a little, grab some lunch, and then get back on the trolley."

He held the door open for her, and she walked through to an array of men's and women's apparel. She casually sifted through the clothes while Wyatt remained close by. Her mouth thinned as she glanced at the swimsuits. She pulled out a purple two-piece before shaking her head in dismay and turned with the suit in hand.

Wyatt's lips pursed together. "You know, I wanted to take you swimming, but after what Liam told me—" he began.

Her eyes narrowed. "What did Liam tell you?"

"He said it might be a bad idea since you don't like the water. I tried telling him you were fine with it the other night, but he insisted you were . . . um, how did he put it? Being a good sport?"

"You know what? Just forget it," she said defeatedly, shoving the bathing suit into his chest before leaving Wyatt to wonder if he had said something wrong.

He returned the garment to the rack when whispers interlaced with the store's music echoed around him. He looked around but didn't find anyone nearby. He focused on the words, hearing only bits and pieces. *Can't believe . . . look . . . my decision.*

Deciding to deal with the phantom voices later, he hastily followed Liz, who was angrily muttering under her breath and pacing outside.

Placing his hands on her shoulders and stopping her mid-step, he dipped his head to look her in the eyes. "Hey, if I said something wrong, I'm sorry. I didn't want to ask you about swimming in case it was a sensitive subject. I know you were reluctant before. If I pushed you to do something you weren't comfortable with—"

"Stop," she interjected.

Wyatt released her shoulders and straightened his back.

"I should be the one apologizing, not you. I'm sorry I stormed out. For Liam to tell you that I was just pretending to have a good time in the water with you was wrong." Her breath caught for a moment. "You didn't make me uncomfortable. In fact, it was the complete opposite. I loved every minute splashing in those waves with you."

Something deep within him stirred at her words, causing him to grin. He wanted to make her feel like that every moment he was with her, even if it would be short-lived.

"Ok, let's start this over. Would you like to go swimming with me?"

Liz paused for a long beat. "I'll . . . let you know," she replied, her lips curling up.

"Sounds good. What do you say we go back inside and search for a bathing suit? Even if we don't go swimming, I'd hate for you to get drenched if we decide to play around in the water again." He gave her a wink.

"All right." She followed him back inside and to the swimsuit section, yet she looked dissatisfied with each suit she picked up. "I'm not exactly comfortable wearing something so revealing."

He pulled a pair of women's bottoms from the rack that looked to be as thin as a fishing line. "Yeah, me neither," he joked, modeling it in front of his shorts. Her laughter was infectious. He returned the item back to its place, then gazed at her, admiring her enchanting smile.

"What?" she asked coyly.

"I like seeing you smile," he replied, causing a slight pink tint to appear across her cheeks.

Before Liz could respond, a female clerk approached them. "Hi. Are you two finding everything ok?"

After asking the woman if there were any other suits for Liz's liking, they followed her into another section specifically for surfers.

"We have shorts, or if you're looking for more coverage, we just received a new shipment of these," she said, showing a rack of surfer leggings. "We have capri and ankle-length. You can match them with a rash guard shirt or any bathing suit top. The changing room is right over there. If you need anything, just let me know."

"Thank you." Liz took a few pairs off the wall to try on along with some halter bikini tops.

Wyatt patiently waited while Liz tried on the clothes. Unlike Jessica, she didn't prance around to model for him. He wouldn't have complained if she did, though. Before he knew it, she emerged with one pair of each length of leggings. The ankle-length pair were a muted teal color, while the capris were swirls of different shades of aqua, both of which were paired with matching tops. She also picked out a pair of sporty water shoes. She peered down at the price tag of each item.

"Are you all set?" Wyatt asked.

"I'm just trying to figure out which one I can afford. Liam let me borrow some money that I promised to pay back after."

"Here, let me see." He took the items from her grasp and headed to the front of the store.

"What are you doing?" she questioned, bounding after him.

He glanced back with a smile. "Don't worry about it."

"You can't buy all of this. It's too much." She frowned. "At least let me pay for part of it."

He promptly placed them on the cashier's counter and swung around to see her digging through her purse. Wyatt's fingers gently pull her wrist up, denying her access to her money.

"It's fine." He released her. "Denise gave me an advance, so I have it covered. Besides, I already paid for our next activity, so it's not like I don't have enough for the rest of the day."

"I'm not having you pay for anything else for me after this," she said with a wave of her finger. "We can eat PB and J sandwiches on the beach for all I care."

Wyatt chuckled at her persistence. "Fine, you can pay for lunch as long as I pick the place, but dinner is still on me."

She pursed her lips together, then replied, "Deal."

Wyatt pulled out the wallet Denise had given him and proceeded to pay as the clerk bagged the clothes. "You know, I'm happy you changed your mind about swimming."

"Well, we'll see."

"No, no. I'm buying these, so you owe me a swim," he said with a smirk. "I think we should go back to the apartment after we grab lunch and change into our suits for our surprise activity. It's ok, we won't be going in the water."

She gave him a worried expression. "But why do I need to change?"

"Trust me," he replied, then thanked the clerk and grabbed the bag of clothes.

"So what are we doing about lunch?" Liz inquired after they exited the short trolley ride down the road.

Wyatt stopped in front of a building called The Donut Experiment and opened his arms with a grin.

"Really?"

"You said it was my choice, and I choose donuts."

Liz scoffed. "That you did."

Soon, they were savoring each bite on the bench outside.

"You have a little . . ." Liz pointed to Wyatt's cheek.

"Oh." He grabbed a napkin and tried wiping it clean. Liz chuckled. "Did I get it?"

Shaking her head, she took a fresh napkin and poured water on it. Leaning forward, she carefully cleaned the smudge of glaze from his face. It seemed to be something she'd done countless times before. He gazed into her eyes, and the corner of his mouth curled up slightly. Her eyes dipped down to his lips.

"I think I got it all," she said, quickly pulling away from him.

"Thanks." He gathered up their trash before they walked to the nearest trolley bench. He watched Liz out of the corner of his eye. "I'm glad you like that." He pointed to the necklace she was fumbling with.

Liz's mouth lifted. "What's yours?" she asked, noticing the leather rope around his neck.

Wyatt pulled out the triangular, iridescent turquoise pendant that he usually kept under his shirt. "It was my mother's."

She studied it intently. "It's beautiful," she whispered.

"It makes me feel close to her." He returned the necklace back under his shirt.

"It's nice you have something to remember her by."

During the rest of their time on the trolley, Wyatt recounted some of the stories Denise had shared with him about his mother, leaving out any mer references. Liz asked him about his upbringing, which he tried to keep as human as possible, and he reciprocated. He was surprised to find her listening intently when he spoke about his life. It was a breath of fresh air compared to how

Jessica treated him. Why he ever fawned over her, he would never know. But he was thankful she was out of his life.

Once they arrived at their stop, they walked back to their apartments. Wyatt quickly threw on his swim trunks and sandals before going back outside to wait for Liz.

"You're back soon," Liam observed as he approached the front porch for his lunch break.

"We stopped to change into our bathing suits."

Liam scowled. "But I told you she didn't like the water."

"Apparently, you were wrong," Wyatt replied, leaving it at that as Liz walked out of her apartment in the capri-length leggings and a matching bathing suit top. Running her fingers through the side of her hair, she smiled from ear to ear.

"Liz, can I talk to you for a second?" Liam asked from behind Wyatt.

Her smile quickly disappeared. "We'll talk later."

"Please, Liz," Liam pleaded.

Wyatt looked back and forth between his two friends. "Why don't I let you two have a minute?" he announced, then leaned close to Liz. "I'll be right over there." He motioned to a bench by The Cove.

He sat down and waited patiently. It didn't take a manta to see that Liz's conversation with Liam wasn't going well, and Wyatt could feel every emotion she was going through. Irritation, anger, and hurt radiated from her into his body. The physical pain that ached in his chest the moment Liam tried to stop Liz from turning away took him completely off guard. Whatever this was, he couldn't tell her. Not yet, anyway. She had too many other things on her mind, and she didn't need that right now. Not to mention that if he told her what was going on, he would have to tell her who he really was.

Would that be a bad thing?

Liz waited until Wyatt was out of range. She was about to open her mouth when Liam beat her to it.

"What do you think you're doing?" Liam asked with concern. "You can't go swimming."

"I can't believe you told him I didn't like the water!"

"What else was I supposed to say?" He looked around, leaned in, and whispered, "That the next time you go in the water, you might sprout a tail?"

Liz shook her head furiously, feeling the hurt of his words all over again. "I can't believe you're still on that. I'm not some fairy-tale creature." She attempted to walk past him, but he grabbed her arm in protest. Her head whipped back, and she winced in pain.

Liam quickly let her go. "I'm sorry."

Liz rubbed her chest. "I have nothing else to say to you," she replied with disdain before storming off.

As she approached him, Wyatt stood with a frown, clearly observing how hurt she was. "I'm sorry."

"I'm just so tired of people telling me what I can or can't do," she huffed, years of anger bubbling to the surface. Before her emotions could boil over, her fingers laced between Wyatt's. Who was first to take the other's hand was a mystery to both of them. Her shoulders immediately relaxed.

"I understand," he said, squeezing her hand.

Somehow she sensed he knew exactly how she felt. "Liam and I just aren't seeing eye to eye at the moment. I'm not sure if we ever will."

His forehead crinkled in thought. "Do you want me to talk to him?"

Liz shook her head as they began to walk. "No, but thanks for the offer. I'll talk to him tomorrow. Right now I just want to enjoy the rest of our day together."

While they walked toward Bridge Street hand in hand, Liz tried several times to guess what they were going to do. Soon enough, they arrived at a shop next to the Oyster Bar, where they had previously dined. A couple blocked the entrance, looking at a few T-shirts, so Liz opted to sift through the local brochures. She pulled out one that read *The Mystic Mermaid: Dolphin Tours with Captain Reed.*

"I wanted to do that one, too," Wyatt stated, noticing the brochure, "but the woman said the captain was out of town for the week."

Placing it back in the holder, she replied without thinking, "Maybe next time."

He smiled. "Definitely."

Once the couple left, they entered the tiny store filled with fishing gear, trinkets, and other souvenirs. A middle-aged woman sat at the counter, her nose buried deep in a book. Wyatt cleared his throat to get her attention.

"Oh, I'm sorry! How can I help you two?" she asked, placing her book on the counter.

"We're here for the one o'clock."

"Oh yes. Wyatt! Why don't you fill out these forms and I'll let the guys know you're ready. You're our only customers for that time so you have the boat to yourselves. Have either of you been parasailing before?" she inquired, handing them each a clipboard with a survey of general questions.

"No, this is my first time," Wyatt answered. "You haven't parasailed before, have you?"

Liz's mouth gaped before she shook her head.

"Aw, first-timers! It's fun! I'll be right back," the woman said before stepping out with a walkie-talkie.

"We're going parasailing?"

Wyatt nodded with a smile as he filled out the form. "I have to admit, I'm a little nervous. I've been under the water plenty of times but never above it. I thought it would be fun."

There was a pang of sadness in her chest at a memory that flashed in her mind of when her grandfather gave her the list of activities they had planned to do. One of them was parasailing. She had asked if he realized he was nearing eighty. *Are you saying I'm too old to have a little fun?*

"If you don't want to do this—" Wyatt began.

"No, I do. I was just thinking back to when my grandpa and I planned this trip. This was on his list and—" She stopped short as realization hit her like a tidal wave. She couldn't remember what he had written on that small piece of paper before, but as she thought about the day, it came back to her. Having cinnamon rolls for breakfast, going to the pier to look for marine life, getting ice cream, going shopping, getting donuts, riding the trolley, and now going parasailing; they were all on his list. She held her hand to her mouth and prayed she wouldn't break down for the third time in front of Wyatt. "How?"

Wyatt dropped his pen and turned to her. "How what?"

"How did you know? Everything we've done today was what my grandpa wanted to do with me."

Wyatt took her hand, and just like magic, a sense of calm washed over her. "Remember when I said I had some help planning the day?" He pulled out the crumpled paper from his back pocket and handed it to her. "I found this the same day I found you sleeping in my bed."

Liz unfolded it with shaky hands. There, on the paper, was her grandfather's handwriting. Her vision blurred from tears forming once again.

"I had no clue what it was. I asked Liam if it was his, and when he said no, I figured it belonged to you. I just thought it was things you wanted to do. I was going to give it back to you, but then I figured I would surprise you by helping you cross everything off your list. I didn't know it had such a special meaning. I hope I didn't overstep and—"

Before he could finish his sentence, she wrapped her arms around his neck and hugged him tightly. "Thank you, Wyatt," she whispered into the crook of his neck. "This means so much. You have no idea."

"I'm glad I could do this for you." His soft lips brushed against her ear, and she melted into him.

"All right, the guys are ready for you," the woman said, returning to the shop.

Liz pulled back from Wyatt, and they both handed over the clipboards.

The woman looked over the forms and nodded. "Alrighty, you guys are set and you're already paid. Just head down to the first dock and have fun!"

"Thank you!" Wyatt said.

"I'm nervous, too," Liz said as they walked back to the intersection before turning the corner where the boats were docked. "My parents weren't exactly thrilled when my grandpa suggested the idea."

"Oh yeah? They were worried about him?"

"I think both of us. It's certainly nothing they would ever do."

"Oh no, I'm already starting off on the wrong fin with your parents."

Liz laughed. She stopped just short of the narrow dock, nervous energy swirling around her stomach. Wyatt immediately took Liz's hand, letting his arm extend behind him as he walked out first to the bright yellow speedboat with a navy-blue phone number printed on the side.

Two men were busy readying the ropes and towline. Of the two, a larger man with a gray goatee stepped out of the boat to greet them as their captain.

"Welcome! My name is Sam, and that's my assistant, Leo," the captain addressed, indicating the other man with long blonde hair that was tied back in a ponytail.

After introductions, Sam helped them into the boat. Up front, Wyatt and Liz took a seat, and Leo gave them each a life vest to wear before helping the captain with the ropes. Wyatt fumbled with the fasteners of his life preserver.

"Let me help you," Liz said, assisting him with the clips.

Slowly, the boat backed away from the dock and made its way out through the bay. It wasn't long until they were beyond the

Longboat Pass bridge and into open water. The engine kicked into its higher speed, causing Liz to slide into Wyatt.

"Whoa!" Wyatt yelled out over the motor. "You good?"

Liz laughed excitedly. "Yeah, this is great!"

Without warning the boat jumped a small wake from another passing boat, and Liz and Wyatt popped out of their seats.

Realizing any effort to move back to her original seat was futile, Liz let her body rest into Wyatt. He wrapped his arm around her, and ribbons of tingling energy swirled through them. As the yellow speedboat glided across the water, the spray of the sea misted across their faces. Liz's mouth salivated as she licked the salt from her lips.

Between the roar of the engine, the wind rushing past their ears, and the music playing loudly from the radio, there was no point in conversation. Most of the ride was spent admiring the vast expanse of the Gulf of Mexico. Every so often, Wyatt would spot something in the water and point it out to Liz.

"Dolphin!" he shouted, pointing out a small dorsal fin popping out of the water behind the boat every few seconds.

Just when Liz wondered how much longer it would be, the captain idled down the engine, and the boat slowed until it came to a stop. While Captain Sam set up the parachute, Leo stepped down to help them into the harnesses and explained all the safety procedures and what to do if something should happen.

With the boat now swaying back and forth, Liz's breath caught at a sudden realization; she was now confined to this tiny floating metal island. If something were to happen to her, she was trapped. Her fingernails scratched at the dry aqua patches under her leggings. What she wouldn't give to dive into the water at that very moment.

"You guys get all that?"

Liz snapped back to reality at Leo's question.

"Yeah, we're good," Wyatt replied before Leo returned to help Sam. Turning his attention to her, Wyatt placed his arm around her. "Hey, it's ok."

His voice brought her comfort. She dipped her head in embarrassment. "I think my nerves are getting the better of me today. I didn't really hear everything he said."

"So, you probably shouldn't be in charge of pulling the red cord in case something goes wrong, huh?"

Her lip curled slightly. "Probably not."

A loud *swoosh* drew their attention to the back of the boat. A large yellow-and-blue striped parachute billowed out in the wind like an umbrella. Both Wyatt's and Liz's eyes widened at the sight.

"Ready?" Sam called out over the music that played from the speakers. "You can leave any belongings and shoes under the seats. Wyatt, you're up first."

He stepped up to the large platform, and Liz nervously removed her shoes, placing them under the bench, along with her purse. The aqua scales stared back at her, pushing the reminder that she needed to find her biological parents before she got any worse.

No one had seen her feet before. If they asked, she'd just say it was a tattoo. That was believable, right? What had she gotten into? Without Wyatt by her side, her leg began to piston nervously until Sam called her up.

Sam held out his hand to help her up to the platform. Her chest tightened slightly but not as bad as when Liam touched her. She planted her feet on the rough surface of the platform, and the captain guided her next to Wyatt, who gave her a comforting smile. Leo finished with Wyatt and then attached Liz's harness to the long bar affixed to the chute.

"Sit down with your feet out in front of you," Sam instructed after Leo finished double-checking their restraints.

Liz sat, rolling her right foot to the side so Wyatt wouldn't be able to see the top of it. Nervousness set in even more, as there was no turning back now. *God, I'm so scared. I don't think I can do this.*

Wyatt gripped his harness so tightly that his knuckles turned white. If he wasn't sitting down, he would have collapsed through the onslaught of fear that slammed into him. He looked at Liz, who was doing the same.

The quiet whispers he had heard softly before were now echoing loudly in his head, still disjointed. *Scared . . . can't . . . this.*

If Wyatt's jaw wasn't so tense, it would have dropped. Could it be that he was hearing Liz's thoughts? Before he could even try to figure out what was happening, Leo crouched down and readied his camera.

"Here we go!" Sam called out.

In the next instant, Sam threw the boat in gear and gunned the engine. The sudden blast of wind caught the parasail, pulling Wyatt and Liz into the sky. She shrieked as they left the platform, slowly moving farther and farther from the boat. The sudden fear that had taken over was now beginning to fade away as the vessel became smaller by the second. His own fear, however, was still causing his heart to beat rapidly.

"Oh my God, this is incredible!" she exclaimed as her grip loosened on the straps.

Wyatt gawked in surprise. "You're not scared?"

"I was, but now that we're up here." She paused, looking at the beauty around her. "It's just so . . . peaceful." She looked at him with the biggest smile on her face.

She was right. The feeling of being hundreds of feet above the surface of the water was indescribable. Never in a million years would he have thought he'd be flying above his very own home.

"This is a lot higher than I anticipated!" he said in amazement.

After a few minutes, the rope seemed to finally stop, letting them dangle in the air while the boat continued to move. He could just make out the tiny yellow boat gliding along the shimmering aqua waters beneath them. The shadow of the parasail seemed to float on the surface of the sea.

"I know I already said this, but thank you," she said, releasing her grip on the harness and spreading her arms out like one of the seagulls flying below them.

"I honestly thought you were going to hate me after this," he replied.

"I could never hate you," she said softly.

Wyatt released his grip from the harness and took Liz's hand. "I'm glad." He looked around and took a deep breath in, exhaling it slowly. "It really is peaceful up here."

"So what's better, being above the water or below it?"

Wyatt thought for a minute. "At the moment? Being with you, up here." He squeezed her hand. "I don't want this to end."

If the harnesses and life jackets weren't in their way, this would have been an opportune moment for him to lean over and kiss her. But not wanting to make it awkward, he instead gently kissed the back of her hand, letting his lips linger for a moment.

"Me neither," she replied.

They continued to take in everything around them and watch the other tiny boats move about below. A small aircraft flew in the distance. Thankfully, it was higher than the parasail. Soon, a tug came on the rope, and it slowly reeled them back to the boat. When they were nearly a whale's length away, the rope halted, and the boat slowed down to a stop.

Wyatt and Liz drifted down, slowly making their way toward the water. She squealed in delight as their legs and bottoms dipped into the warm sea just as Sam cranked the engine back into full, letting the sail catch the wind and once more lift them up.

"The captain asked me earlier if we'd be interested in doing that. I was hoping you wouldn't mind," Wyatt explained.

Liz beamed. "That was amazing! I guess it's a good thing we wore our swimsuits then."

As they neared the platform, Leo yelled over the motor, "Ok, you're going to put your legs out and your hands up on the bar."

Once they arrived back on the hard surface, Leo quickly unhooked their harnesses from the overhead bar and guided them back up front so he could help Sam gather the chute and ropes. Liz and Wyatt removed their harnesses and sat down.

"So . . . do you have anything else planned for today?" she asked. "Or should I consult the list?"

"I don't really have anything else planned." He smirked. When Liz looked at him with disbelief, he threw up his hands. "Ok, I don't have anything else *big* planned for our date."

Unless . . . Could I tell her the truth?

Liz stared out at the glistening water in front of them. "So, you consider this a date? I thought you said you were just showing me the island," she asked, tilting her gaze slightly back toward him.

"Well, it's whatever you want it to be, but I wouldn't protest if you said it *was* a date," he confessed.

She turned back to him and smiled coyly. "I'll let you know by the end of the day."

"Fair enough," he replied with a smile, but he already knew what she really thought about this.

A date, her voice whispered in his mind, causing his smile to grow.

CHAPTER 25

Interrupted

After docking and thanking the captain and his assistant, Wyatt suggested they play a round of mini golf at The Fish Hole since it was too early for dinner. He didn't care that Liz won, as long as she was having a good time. It was his goal to keep Liz distracted as much as possible from any thoughts about her return home.

"You're pretty good at this," he commented, watching his ball come up empty in the Plinko game.

"You're not that bad, either." She dropped her ball in next, winning a free game.

"You're being too kind." He chuckled and returned their clubs. "She won a free game," he informed the cashier. After being handed the prize coupon, Wyatt passed the ticket to Liz. "Guess we get a rematch."

She stared at it for a moment before handing it back to Wyatt. "Here, you'll be able to use it before I will."

Wyatt put his hand up, refusing her offer. "No, it's yours."

"I don't know when I'll be back," she replied softly.

Turning to the clerk, Wyatt asked, "Does this have an expiration date?"

"Nope. As long as we're in business, you can use it whenever," the man replied.

"See? It's settled. You keep it." He placed the ticket in her purse. "And the next time you come back, we'll play a round."

Before she could say another word, he put his hand up to prevent further protest.

She sighed in defeat. "Fine, but just so you know, you might be waiting a while. Who knows how long it'll be before I'm back."

Wyatt took her hand and squeezed it, letting the heat run up his arm. "You're worth waiting for." A hint of pink highlighted her cheeks as she bashfully smiled. His stomach rumbled, letting him know it was time for their next venture. "Come on, let's go grab some dinner."

"I have a feeling it won't involve PB and J sandwiches," she said as they exited.

He didn't reply, only giving a sly smile. During their walk, Wyatt kept their conversation going, avoiding any talk of her home or parents.

"Beach House Waterfront restaurant? This is where you're taking me?" she asked Wyatt when he guided her toward a beige and gray building with hard angles and a gray roof that jutted out at the entrance.

"I figured it would be better than sandwiches." He shrugged as they approached the covered entrance. He held the door for her, then followed her inside. A small gift shop was on either side of them, while a large bar that was twice the size of the one he worked behind could be seen in the back.

"This feels like too much. I can't have you—"

"Uh, uh, uh," he tsked. "We agreed you'd pay for lunch but dinner is on me."

Liz playfully rolled her eyes. "Fine."

Wyatt left Liz to wander the store area while he checked on their reservation. When the hostess looked for an open table, a slight wave of anxiety crawled up him. He glanced back to see Liz nervously wringing her hands. She caught his stare and smiled. The emotions he felt slipped away.

"It'll be just a few minutes, sir," the hostess informed.

Wyatt pushed through the crowd, wondering how the end of their date would go. Something inside of him kept driving the desire to be completely honest with her.

"It won't be long," he told Liz.

He bit his bottom lip in thought as they waited. His mind raced a mile a minute. What if he told her the truth? Would she even believe him? Would she decide to stay? If he told her, he risked exposing his kind. Did she also feel whatever this connection was between them? What if she didn't share the same feelings?

For all he knew, this could be some merpower Denise didn't know he could harness. But this didn't happen with Jessica. What if Liz was his . . . ? No, she was human. Although, the stories never specified . . .

Liz's eyes darted around the crowded waiting area as if she was searching for something. She pinched her eyes shut.

"Are you ok?" Wyatt asked, causing her eyes to snap open.

"Yeah. I think I'm just dehydrated from being out in the sun," she replied.

"We'll get you some water soon," he assured her.

"Wyatt! Party of two!" the hostess called out.

They followed the waitress out the back doors to the outdoor patio and down into the area that was surrounded by sand. A large cluster of rocks created a barrier from the rest of the shoreline, lending a sense of privacy to watch the sunset. Hues of purple, gold, and blue cascaded across the sky, and beams of light spilled behind the clouds. Soft waves washed against the shoreline.

Wyatt pulled out the chair for Liz at the circular table shaded by a navy umbrella. Soon the waitress arrived with two glasses of water and took their orders. Wyatt decided on the seafood gumbo while Liz got fish and chips.

The gumbo was more than he bargained for and commented

that it was delicious, yet deadly. Liz laughed at his statement and tried a bite.

"It's a bit spicy, but I wouldn't call it deadly. Having some bread will help, or I'll trade you if you can't handle the heat," she offered.

"No, no. It's good," he said confidently, taking another piece of bread from the basket.

Half a loaf of bread and six glasses of water later, they rested their stomachs as the sun began to dip into the horizon.

Leaving . . . days . . . her voice whispered in his mind.

He internally sighed. The end of their day was coming to a close, and he knew what she was thinking.

"You've been pretty quiet," Wyatt observed, finishing the last piece of bread.

"I don't want this to be over."

"Come on," he said, placing money on the table, "let's go for a walk along the beach." He picked up his sandals and stood. Hand in hand, they walked down to the beach.

"I can carry your shoes if you'd like," he offered.

"I'm good," she said with a slight frown. Her free hand twitched as she watched the waves lick the sand.

Hate . . . becoming . . . Wyatt heard the soft words echo through his head.

He toyed with the idea of telling her. He opened his mouth before snapping it back shut. Would she think he was crazy? Would she run away? Would she exploit him? Liz would never do that . . . At least he didn't think she would.

Before his mouth opened again, Liz suddenly stopped and freed herself from his hand. "I almost forgot." She reached into her purse. "I have something for you," she said coyly.

Wyatt's brow raised in surprise. "You do?"

Liz pulled out a small bag and handed it to him. Without saying anything, he carefully opened it and pulled out the same bracelet she had picked out for him back at Ginny's and Jane E's.

"When did you get this?" he asked, completely baffled.

"When I went back because I *forgot my phone?*" she said, putting the last few words in air quotes. "I thought you should have something to remember this day as well." She took his left wrist and carefully placed the bracelet around, clasping it in place.

Wyatt beamed, staring at the band wrapped around his wrist. "Liz, I don't know what to say."

"You don't have to say anything. This is my thanks to you. This date has been amazing."

"So it's a date, huh?" he asked, his eyes darting up to Liz's.

She shrugged with a smile that quickly faded. She crossed her arms in front of her and stared out toward the Gulf of Mexico.

"I need to tell you something," Liz and Wyatt said in unison.

Wyatt smiled nervously and rubbed the back of his neck. "You go first."

Liz ran her hands along her upper arms. "You know, this reminds me of the puzzle my grandparents were working on," she reminisced, admiring the hues of orange, pink, and purple emitting from the setting sun. "My grandpa never finished it."

A feeling of melancholy washed over Wyatt. He wasn't sure what else to say except, "I'm sorry."

"I was over at the house after he passed and put the last few pieces in, but one piece was missing. I thought it fell between some old photo albums. One thing led to another and soon I was surrounded by old photos." She blinked hard, clearly trying to hold her emotions at bay. "My grandpa had told me this trip was important, and that day I found out why. He kept so much from me. My whole life feels like it's been a lie."

"How so?" Wyatt inquired.

Liz turned away, and he sensed she was arguing with herself, not to mention the jumble of words spewing in his mind that made no sense. Frustrated, she went to spin around, only to trip and lose her balance. Wyatt caught her just in time, pressing her body against his.

"You can tell me anything, Liz," he whispered, his face just mere inches from hers. He stared into her eyes. He knew right then that he would tell her everything. She needed to know. He would show her his tail before she was gone forever.

"I . . ." she began but was cut off when Wyatt's name was shouted by someone. They both turned in surprise to find Jessica running toward them.

"Wyatt! I'm so glad I found you!" Jessica exclaimed, trying to catch her breath.

"Jessica, wh— How did you find me?" Wyatt asked in confusion.

"I need to talk to you," she said, ignoring his question, then glared at Liz before adding, "In private."

"There's nothing you can say that I want to hear. C'mon, Liz." Wyatt took Liz by the hand and began to walk away.

"Please, it's important," Jessica pleaded. "I'm only here because Liam sent me to tell you that your father is looking for you."

Wyatt stopped abruptly and turned back to Jessica. A rush of panic enveloped him. "Liz, can you give Jessica and me— "

"Of course. I have to use the restroom anyway," Liz stated.

Wyatt nodded in appreciation and reluctantly released her hand, hoping it wouldn't be long before he felt her touch again. When she was out of sight, he returned his attention back to Jessica. "Ok, you have me alone. What do you want?" He folded his arms across his chest, waiting for the next lie to spill out of her mouth.

"I told you why I'm here," she said, stepping closer to him.

He stared at her for a moment, then took a step back. "Yeah, right." He cocked his head. "I don't believe you. Liam would never tell you anything."

"I suppose he wouldn't." She began to strut around him. She tiptoed her fingers along his shoulders and across his back. "I just needed to get you . . . all . . . to myself," she said, and her index and middle finger finished their walk along the opposite shoulder.

Wyatt shook his head and batted her hand away. "I should've

known. Look, I'm not sure how many different ways or times I have to tell you, but it's over."

Jessica placed her hand on her hip and tilted her head to the side. "Oh, I think you'll want to be with me after you hear what I have to say."

"I doubt that," he retorted and walked toward the restaurant.

Jessica grabbed his forearm. Her nails dug into his skin and sent an ache up his arm to his chest. "I wouldn't walk away if I were you," she sniped with venom in her voice.

Wyatt pulled out of her grasp, narrowing his eyes. "Are you threatening me?"

"Not you," she replied, then peered up at the patio of the restaurant.

"Liz."

"I have a friend up there," she stated before nodding curtly at a large, bearded man dressed in black that was sitting at a table by the stairs.

"You were talking to him yesterday in front of the restaurant," Wyatt pointed out. "And he was the bartender when I blacked out."

Jessica rolled her eyes. "Good job, Sherlock. He's keeping tabs on her. If you don't comply, well . . ." She shrugged.

Gritting his teeth, he hissed, "What do you want?"

As he stood completely rigid, Jessica wrapped her arms around his neck and leaned in close, causing pain to radiate from his chest. "Hmmm, what do I want?" she whispered into his ear, curling his hair around her finger. "Your money? We both know you don't have any. Your love, perhaps?" She paused for a moment. "I'd rather gouge out my eyes."

Wyatt's brow furrowed in confusion. If she'd never liked him, then what did she want from him?

"I want something much more . . . satisfying." Her tongue darted out to lick her lips. "I want to *destroy* you. All—of—you."

"You're insane," he said, trying to pull away, but her fingers were still entangled in his hair.

She gripped the back of his head and pulled him close, switching to the other side of his face. "I know what you are," she whispered, her hot breath feeling like fire in his ear, "merman."

His heart dropped to the depths of the ocean in a matter of seconds. Jessica pulled back with a sinister grin and released her grip.

Wyatt stumbled back. "How?"

"Oh, it wasn't that difficult. The first time I saw you, I was waiting in a truck by the docks."

Wyatt recalled the two men standing above him when he first surfaced.

Come on, the boss is waiting in the truck.

I still don't understand why the hell we need these chains. What is this job anyway?

"I watched you stagger down the dock in nothing but a towel. Then you stole one of my men's clothes. So when I saw you at the bar the next day, I had to investigate further. Not to mention, this necklace was surprisingly helpful. I really didn't think it was anything special. But then, here you are," she stated, moving the gold pendant back and forth across the chain around her neck. "I assume it releases some type of pheromone."

That explained why all sense of reason disappeared when he was close to her. Poseidon, how could he be so stupid?

She sauntered closer to him. "That woman at the bar, who I presume is a mermaid, nearly outed me. Apparently the scent doesn't work for mermaids and does the exact opposite."

Sarah. He glared at her.

"Ah, so you know each other. I should have figured." She tapped her chin. "A sister, perhaps?"

"You stay the hell away from her!" he growled, grabbing her arm. He didn't care how painful it would be to touch her. All this time, his body had been telling him he couldn't trust her, and he never listened. Not that he'd had much of a choice on what he did around her.

"Uh, uh, uh," she scolded, raising her other hand in the air. "One signal from me and your precious girlfriend is dead."

"We're surrounded by people," he said, stating the obvious.

"Oh, he has his ways." Her lips curled into a wicked smile, and Wyatt released his grip. "You're lucky he didn't try to kill you after he drugged you."

Wyatt furrowed his brow. "Drugged?"

"My guy gave you something to make you sleepy when I brought you to Club 21. Although"—she glared back up at the man—"since it didn't affect you right away, he ended up giving you too much. But nonetheless, you did what I had hoped for."

He was almost afraid to ask. "What was that?"

"Proof that you were a mer. Although, I was eighty percent sure I was correct. But just to be on the safe side, I needed confirmation. Once you saw he was threatening me, you didn't hesitate. Such a gentleman." She lightly slapped the side of his face. "However, Kyle didn't care to be nearly dragged into the depths of the sea. Everyone thought my father was crazy, and I almost did too. With all the ranting and ravings about mermaids, who could blame them? But after reading his journals and finding you, well, I guess we both know the truth."

"You're never gonna get away with this," he said through gritted teeth.

"Oh, but I will if you want Liz to stay alive. Come with me and she'll be spared."

Wyatt's jaw clenched. Waves crashed up against their legs in response to the anger that consumed him. For a split second, he thought about pulling her out into the ocean long enough for him to take off, but there was still the man watching Liz, along with everyone else on the beach.

"Time's ticking, and my patience is wearing thin," she stated.

"Jessica, please don't do this," he begged.

She raised her hand in the air, reminding him of the power she had at the moment. He looked back up to see Liz walking out the door and maneuvering around the tables toward the steps.

Don't come any closer. Please stop, Liz, he thought in his mind, knowing she wouldn't be able to hear anything. For a moment, he thought maybe there was a chance she'd heard him as she paused.

"Now, we don't need her following us or wondering what happened to you. So, let's put on a little show for her, shall we?"

"What?"

"Kiss me," she instructed.

Wyatt recoiled. "You don't even like me. Why would we kiss?"

"I thought you were smarter than that, merman. We need to make it believable. She needs to think we're still together," Jessica explained, wrapping her arms around his neck. "We can't have her following us."

Wyatt's eyes darted over to Liz, who continued walking toward them. His heart shattered at what he was about to do, but he had to protect her. Burning pain radiated throughout his chest as his lips met hers in a gentle kiss.

He began to pull back when Jessica clawed her hand around the back of his head. Her hot breath whispered against his lips, "Not good enough. Kiss me like her life depends on it."

He pinched his eyes shut. *I'm sorry, Liz.*

His lips engulfed Jessica's, and the flame in his heart spread across his entire body. He groaned in agony. Surely she was done, but she kept her hold on him. Her tongue plunged deep, dancing around his mouth. On top of the pain, he felt mentally and physically sick to his stomach. Wyatt hated every ounce of himself. He couldn't bear to look for Liz and was sure she had run off.

Without warning, Jessica pushed him to the ground. He gasped, clutching his chest. He looked for the knife that Jessica had surely plunged into him, yet nothing was there.

She scowled and spat on the ground next to him. "You disgust me, freak."

True to Jessica's word, the man left Liz alone and was now crouching by Wyatt. "Get up," he ordered.

If he wasn't in an unbearable amount of agony, Wyatt would have relaxed knowing that Liz was safe. But he couldn't walk, let alone stand. Was he dying? He hoped so, then at least Liz would be safe.

"I . . . can't," he rasped.

A few choice curse words were muttered under the man's breath as he lifted Wyatt up and threw his arm across his back. "Swallow this," the man ordered, handing him a pill.

Wyatt shook his head. "What—"

"Just take it or I'll go looking for that pretty little chick that ran off."

He did what he was told and forced the small capsule down his throat. It didn't take long for the haze to take over.

How did I swim so far off the ocean's current? Father tried to tie me down to someone I didn't even know, only for me to come to the surface and date a human I have no feelings for. Now look where it's got me.

Wyatt's legs stumbled behind him as he was dragged through the restaurant's open patio, the exact opposite way he was hoping the man would have gone. He could have easily taken him out, being close to the sea. But now, there were too many people around. As they walked past the bar, the man commented to a few lingering beachgoers that his friend had too many drinks.

Wyatt's vision began to haze as Jessica's midnight-blue Jeep came into view. He felt himself being lifted into the car, and his body slammed to the floor. He lifted his head, and the world spun.

A green car peeled into the parking lot. He knew that car. It was . . .

His eyelids drooped. He shook his head. He needed to stay awake. He needed to get out. He needed to get to that car, Liam's car.

He opened his mouth to shout, but instead his eyes rolled back and his head fell to the floor with a thud.

CHAPTER 26

Breathless

Begrudgingly removing herself from what would surely be an awkward situation if she stayed, Liz made her way back to the restaurant. There was something about Jessica that didn't sit well with her. She glanced over her shoulder while walking up the steps, resulting in her face meeting the chest of a large man with a beard.

"I'm so sorry," she apologized to the man dressed in a black T-shirt and dark jeans before composing herself. He seemed oddly familiar.

He didn't say a word. His dark brown eyes scanned her up and down, making her feel uneasy. She quickly continued to the restroom. While washing her hands, she noticed her fingernails now had an aqua sheen, similar to her toenails. She drew in a breath and let out a deep sigh, staring at herself in the mirror. *I have to tell Wyatt everything.*

Once finished, she exited the bathroom and weaved around the tables until she arrived at the edge of the stairs that led down to the beach. Suddenly, her body launched into a fight or flight response, and her heart began to race. She gripped the railing tightly, confused at first, and then blinding fear washed over her. Something wasn't right.

She bounded down the steps, running toward the beach. She didn't know what was happening, but she knew she needed to get to Wyatt fast.

Stop . . . a voice whispered in her mind, causing her feet to slam to a halt.

She looked around to find no one nearby except the man she had bumped into earlier sitting at a table at the top of the steps.

Shaking the voice from her head, she continued on a few more feet until her body froze at what she saw next.

Wyatt glanced mournfully at Liz before Jessica's slender fingers caressed his cheek, pulling his head back to her. She slowly wrapped her arms around his neck.

I'm sorry, the whisper echoed in her mind as Jessica placed her hand around the back of Wyatt's neck.

. . . everything for her.

She finally understood that the whispers were merely her internal self-doubt. She watched in misery as Jessica pressed her body against Wyatt, their lips meeting in a deep, passionate kiss. Sharp pain pierced through her chest, and Liz gasped.

"No . . ." she whispered. Her knees gave out, and she collapsed onto the coarse sand.

There was no other way to describe it, other than it felt as if someone had sliced her flesh wide open and ripped out her heart. It overwhelmed her so much that when she opened her mouth, all that came out was a silent scream. As anger and fear consumed her, she clutched at the boulder next to her and pulled herself up from the ground before anyone could question her. She couldn't bear to look back at Wyatt, so instead she made her way north through the sand, guided by the retaining wall.

Liz stumbled along the formation that, unfortunately, jutted out toward the high tide. Her feet sloshed through the water. Darkness clouded her vision as she staggered toward the parking lot. She collapsed once more on the cool sand and leaned against the jagged rocks. She grasped her head in her hands.

How could she be so stupid?

Hot tears escaped down her cheeks. In a fit of rage, she clenched one of the smaller boulders until it cracked under the pressure.

She wouldn't be able to make it back to her apartment alone. She had only one option. Reaching into her purse, she pulled out her phone and tapped the screen with her trembling fingers until she found Liam's number. With ragged breaths, she closed her eyes and listened to each ring, praying he would answer.

"Hey," Liam's melancholic voice emanated from the receiver. "Look, I'm sorry about earlier. Can we—"

"Liam." Liz groaned. "I . . ."

"Is everything ok?" Liam asked, his tone shifting to concern.

The best Liz could muster through the overwhelming pain was a sniffle and short heavy breaths. She could hear fumbling on Liam's end, followed by muffled whispers.

"What's going on? Are you ok?" he asked in a quiet tone.

"You need—" She winced. "You need to come get me. I can hardly move. The pain . . ."

"Oh god. Is Wyatt with you?" he asked.

"Just come get me!" She gritted her teeth, trying not to crush her phone into a million pieces.

"Where are you?"

"The Beach House, shore side of the dunes, near the parking lot."

"I'm on my way," Liam said and immediately ended the call.

Leaning her head back, she let her hand fall to her side and closed her eyes.

What felt like only a moment later, a voice echoed her awake. "Liz . . . Liz, wake up."

Her eyes fluttered open, blinking several times until the blurry images focused to reveal Liam's face in front of her. The sun had now disappeared below the horizon, and lights were beaming throughout the parking lot. She shifted her body and tried to stand.

"Whoa. Take it slow," he cautioned, slowly rising with her, his hand extended in case she needed it. Once they were both standing, he looked her over. "What happened?"

The images of Wyatt's mouth pressed against Jessica's slammed into her mind. Ignoring Liam's question, she climbed up the dune toward the parking lot and leaned against the rocks.

"Liz, stop." He shifted in front of her. "You need to talk to me. Where's Wyatt?"

She glowered at him. "I don't want to talk about him. I just want to go home."

"Ok." He held his hands up in defense. "I'll take you back to the apartment."

"No! I want to go *home*! I wanna go home to Ohio, to my family. I wish I never came here! I wish I never found out I was adopted!" she snapped.

The adoption, the secrecy, her grandfather's death—the anger of it all had been building up inside Liz for so long, it was at its boiling point. Her hand balled up into a fist, and she punched the boulder next to her, cracking it in half.

Liz crumbled to the ground and sobbed. "I just want to go home."

Liam stood in stunned silence for a moment before crouching beside her. "Well, I, for one, am glad that you came here. Let's get you back to the apartment and go from there, ok?" he suggested, and she nodded in response. "I don't want to cause you any more pain. How can I help you?"

Liz wiped the tears from her cheek with the back of her hand. "I don't care anymore," she replied defeatedly.

The lines in Liam's already furrowed brow became more defined with worry. After hesitating at first, Liam scooped her up into his arms and maneuvered around the rocks to the parking lot. She flinched under his touch but welcomed the pain. Maybe she wouldn't feel so numb. Opening the passenger door, he sat her down inside the car. He closed the door and ran to the driver's side before starting the engine.

"You ok?" he asked, turning the air vents in her direction.

She lifted her gaze, refusing to answer. He stared at her a little too long for her liking. Had something else changed? She didn't want to know.

His mouth thinned, and for a moment, she thought he was going to say something. Instead, he fumbled with the seat belt and put the car into reverse.

Liz sniffled and leaned her head to the side, staring out the passenger window. She heard the click of the glove box. Liam had grabbed a few napkins as they waited for the midnight-blue Jeep in front of them to turn onto the main road.

"Here," he said, handing them to her. "You wanna talk about it?"

She turned away from him, refusing to answer.

Liam remained quiet with only the hum of the AC filling the void as he turned the car.

Liz huffed, glaring back at the Beach House restaurant through the car's passenger-side mirror. Being betrayed by Wyatt was a horrible feeling, but this felt like something more. It felt like rage was consuming her. Her knuckles became white from her fists clenching tighter. The veins in her arms felt oddly hot. Suddenly, a burst of light, like a flashbulb, lit up the car.

"What was that?" Liam exclaimed, looking between her and the road.

"Nothing," she lied. She closed her eyes and tried to calm herself, slowly unclenching her hands. *Great, something else I have to deal with.*

"Liz, that wasn't—"

"Don't." She held her hand up. "Just don't, Liam."

He snapped his mouth shut and focused on the road. The disconcertment was palpable during the remaining, thankfully short drive. Liam parked in front of his apartment, and before he could even reach his hand to turn the engine off, Liz unfastened her seat belt and grabbed the door handle.

"Liz," he began, but nothing else came.

Without so much as saying a word, Liz exited the vehicle. The last thing she wanted to do was explain what happened at the restaurant or what that spark of light between her fingers was. The agony had nearly faded away, but her heart still felt like it had shattered into a million pieces. She entered her apartment and slammed the door shut behind her.

Placing her purse on top of the kitchen island, she pulled out her phone to find a missed call from her mother's cell. Scoffing at the thought of talking to her parents, she haphazardly tossed her phone on the kitchen island. Leaning her elbows on the counter, she ran her hands over her tired face.

She peered between her fingers to see the bottle of water Liam had filled with seawater taunting her. Snatching it up, she walked over to the sink to pour the contents out. She paused as the salty water began to spill out. Lifting it to her nose, she smelled it with curiosity.

Liam's theory about her being a mermaid swirled in her mind. *No, no. This is insane. I'm not drinking this stuff.* Her hand shook, spilling more of the water. With a growl, she slammed the bottle down onto the counter. Grabbing the edge of the countertop, she bowed her head in frustration, squeezing her eyes tight. She was not a freak of nature.

Taking a moment to compose herself, she noticed some of the water had landed on the back of her hand. She was about to dry it on the dish towel when her mind pressed her to taste it. Determined to prove Liam wrong, she darted her tongue out, and her taste buds came alive. She shook her head. It was just her mind playing tricks on her.

She took a quick swig from the bottle and swished it around in her mouth, ready to spit it into the sink. However, the water took hold of her, and she let it slide down her throat, savoring the unique taste. The thirst she had been yearning to quench so much these past few days was finally being satisfied, and she hated it.

Her hand continued to tremble as she set the water back on the counter. She turned away, folding her arms across her chest, and stood for a moment as her brain and heart argued with each other.

Listen to your heart. Wyatt's words resonated in her mind.

Without a second thought, she spun around, snatched the bottle with both hands, and feverishly chugged the water. Before she knew it, she had emptied over half of the bottle. With a gasp, she threw it into the sink and stared as its contents trickled out.

"What am I doing? What's wrong with me?" she whispered. Tingles ran down her arms as she clenched her fists at her sides.

Mermaids. The word swirled in the back of her mind.

"There's no such thing as mermaids," she muttered under her breath and maneuvered around the front of the kitchen island. "I'm going home."

When she opened her right hand to grab her purse, a spark snapped from her fingertips, and Liz jumped back in alarm. She held her hand close to her chest. It had to be from static electricity. Right?

On the verge of a panic attack, she tried to compose herself, but with each inhale she took, the air thickened, making it harder and harder to breathe. Her eyes darted back to the sink where she'd left the bottle. Even though she didn't want to admit it, she knew she needed more. When she took a step toward the sink, her legs gave out unexpectedly, and she grabbed onto the seat of the barstool, taking it down with her.

Her side slammed against the ground. She pushed herself up, wheezing with each breath, and her vision blurred from lack of oxygen. A panic-inducing thought consumed her.

I'm going to die. I'm going to die right here on this floor. Alone.

A knock emanated from the other side of the door just a few feet in front of her. Liam's voice was muffled from behind the door. "Liz? Liz, I'm sorry. Can we talk? I know you want to go back home, and I don't blame you."

With as much energy as she could muster, still gasping for air, Liz reached for the barstool and lifted it a few inches off the ground.

"I just don't want to lose you as a friend."

The stool hit the ground with a soft thud.

"Liz? What's that noise?" he asked. "Please answer me!"

The skin under her ears burned like someone had sliced her with a hot knife. She let out a raspy scream.

The door swung open and Liam dropped next to her. "What happened?" he asked.

"Ca . . . can't breathe," Liz replied, barely a whisper.

The lights dimmed as her eyelids grew heavy. She just needed to sleep. That was all.

"Stay with me!" Liam lifted her in his arms for the second time today. She felt herself become weightless, and the air breezed past her. Was he running? Where were they going? Hopefully to her bed so she could rest. She was so tired.

She sensed Liam lowering her to the floor and then felt a cool hard surface under her. Not the plush mattress she had hoped for. Sounds echoed through her ears as he shuffled about. Then she heard the squeak of a handle, followed by the pitter-patter of water droplets as they cascaded onto her lower torso.

"I'm sorry it's cold," he apologized. However, to Liz, it actually felt quite warm. "Just stay with me, ok?" His voice sounded distant in her ears.

Liz forced her heavy eyelids open to assess her surroundings, catching sight of Liam rushing out of the room. She leaned her head back against the shower wall. Each breath came with a wheeze.

Within moments, Liam was back with a glass filled to the brim with water. He knelt down next to her, and the water sprayed the right side of his body. "Here, drink this."

Liam placed the smooth glass against her bottom lip and tilted it up. The disgusting tap water slid down her throat, resulting in her gasping and sputtering. It didn't help much, but she no longer felt like she was breathing through a narrow straw anymore, nor did she feel as tired.

Liam withdrew the glass, but his gaze was fixated on her neck, where she felt a stream of water trickle down. Without saying a word, he carefully pushed back her hair, and his eyes widened in disbelief at what he saw.

"What is it?" she tried to ask, even though she was afraid of what the answer might be.

Her trembling fingers reached up and felt the skin just below her ears. There was a small opening nearly two inches long, angling up toward her hairline. It was as if someone had cut open her skin and forgotten to stitch it back together. It shuddered and closed. *Oh god! What is that?* She didn't know if she was going to be sick or pass out.

"It's going to be ok," Liam tried to reassure her, but the sentiment was wasted.

"Ok?" her voice croaked as if she smoked a pack a day. She looked at him in horror. "This is *not* ok! I'm not ok, Liam! What are those?"

"If I'm still correct"—his face cringed a bit—"I think those are gills."

Liz swallowed hard and shook her head several times. "No. No, you're wrong! I am not some kind of fish!"

Standing up, Liam blew out a sigh of frustration and ran his hand through his sandy blonde hair and tugging at the roots. He stepped out of the shower and turned back to her. "You have scales on your legs, your nails changed color, and now you have gills," he said, gesturing to each part of her body. "Not to mention how much water you've been drinking, your newfound love for shrimp, whatever the hell happened in the car, and I'm pretty sure your eyes weren't aqua earlier, either."

"Are you done?" she barked, her voice slowly coming back.

He shook his head with a scoff and turned to exit the bathroom, but his sandal slipped on the smooth tile floor and spilled him backward. In an instant, Liz could see that the back of his head was about to land on the raised lip of the shower entrance. She reached out in a futile attempt to stop his fall. Squeezing her eyes shut, she waited for the sickening thud of his head against the hard surface. However, no sound followed, not even the white noise of the running shower.

Liz peeked through the slits of her eyes and was shocked at the sight in front of her. A tendril of water snaked around the shower wall, holding Liam up just a few feet from the ground.

"Holy shit!" He gasped, tilting his head around in astonishment.

Liz stared at her outstretched arm for a moment before she let out a small shriek and pulled her hand to her chest, releasing the hold she had on the water. As a result, Liam's rear end fell to the ground, along with the water. He stared at her in disbelief. Her heart felt like it was about to burst from her chest with how hard it was beating. When Liam reached out to her, she scurried back.

Liam stood up and turned the water off with a heavy sigh. "And you can control water," he added to his growing list of reasons why he believed she was changing into a mythical creature.

"I thought you were my friend." Her voice shook. She cowered in the corner, holding her trembling hands. She wanted to run, but she couldn't run from herself.

"I am," he replied defeatedly.

"Then why do you think I'm some kind of freak?" Her teary eyes glared at him.

"Liz . . ."

"What?" Liz snapped.

"I am your friend." Liam did his best to stay calm. "If I wasn't your friend, I wouldn't have been by your side through all this. I wouldn't have stayed up late at night researching ways to help you, only to find the one thing that makes any sense is completely outrageous. It was so crazy, in fact, that when I suggested it to you, you pushed me away. But still, even when you called, I came running. Would someone that isn't a friend pick you up when you were nearly unconscious and bring you to the shower to save your life?" He began to walk out the door but paused with his back to her. "I care more about you than you know. God help me, I don't know why, but I do."

Then, just like that, Liz was left alone, soaking wet, with only her thoughts. She pulled her knees up to her chest and sobbed.

"What have I done?" she whispered.

CHAPTER 27

Restless

With his head in his hands, Liam sat on the towel he had draped across the couch. His once-smooth hair was now a tousled mess, and his shorts were soaked. Minutes ticked by as he debated going back to Liz. However, guilt prevented his feet from moving.

His emotions had gotten the better of him, and he'd taken it out on her. She may have done the same, but he didn't blame her. She had no one else to talk to or guide her through this. And now, because of him, she was closing herself off even more.

He raised his head at the sound of wet shoes sloshing down the hall. Liz looked like hell as she braced herself against the wall. Her head hung low, and water dripped from her hair to the floor.

"I can't do this on my own," she quietly admitted. She peered up with a look of despair. Even though her eyes were bloodshot, they were a mesmerizing aqua that reminded him of crystal clear gulf waters on a sunny day.

"I'm scared, Liam." Her voice cracked as she blinked a few times. Her eye color faded back to a blue-gray, but he could still see flecks of the color trying to shine through.

Liam stood slowly and cautiously approached her, afraid she would bolt like a rabbit among the dunes in the early morning hours. "I'm scared too. I'm sorry I walked out. You deserve better, especially with whatever happened between you and Wyatt." She flinched at his name.

What did you do to her, Wyatt?

Nearing her, he could see she was close to breaking down. Water from the shower and her own tears mixed together along her cheeks. What he wouldn't give to pull her into a hug and tell her it was going to be all right, but truthfully, he just didn't know. There weren't any easy answers or explanations. All he could do was be there for her, if she'd let him.

He opened the linen closet, pulled out a large towel, and draped it over her shoulders. Running his hands up and down her covered arms, he realized she was only in pain when their skin touched. With that, he wrapped the thick towel tighter around her and pulled her into his arms.

"I'm sorry. I was just so angry and . . ." She pulled away from him, suddenly taking in his attire. He was wearing a now-wrinkled button-down dress shirt and khaki shorts that were half-wet and half-peppered with sand. She blinked several times in confusion. "I interrupted something when I called, didn't I?"

"You don't need to apologize." He took a few steps back to let her dry off. "I was kind of on a date with Sarah," he said, rubbing the back of his neck

Liz stared at the wood grain on the floor.

"Hey." He tilted his head so she could see his face. "It's fine. Really. She completely understood. Sarah knows we're friends and that you were out with Wyatt."

Liz raised her head slightly. "What did you tell her?" she asked, her voice still a bit gravelly.

"I told her you weren't feeling well and needed to get back to the apartment. Since you guys didn't have a car, you called me. There was no need to say anything about her brother since I didn't know what was going on."

"I'm sorry I ruined your date."

"You didn't ruin it, and don't be sorry. It was nearly over. I just missed out on a good night kiss. Which probably wouldn't have happened anyway. I have a feeling she wants to take things slow. She still insisted we were just sharing dessert, like two regular humans. Her words, not mine. Quirky." He shrugged. "But I like quirky." He paused. "Why don't you finish drying off and maybe we can talk about what happened?"

"Ok," she agreed.

He clapped his hands. "You go do that, and I'll grab us some drinks and dessert."

A slight smile crept across her face. "Yeah, I'd like that."

Liam made a pit stop at the beach before heading back to his apartment to grab dessert and a drink for himself. When he returned to Liz's apartment, she was still behind closed doors, giving him cause to worry.

Liam leaned against the wall, holding their drinks. "Everything ok?"

"Define ok," she answered back.

"Upright, not lying on the ground."

"Then I'm just peachy," she replied, moving around the room.

When the door opened, Liam took her in. She wore a pajama tank top along with gym shorts that showed the scales had crept down, covering both thighs and some of her knees. He felt helpless seeing how bad her scales had gotten.

She lifted her arms to dry her hair, revealing a few aqua scales along her waistband. She was either embracing what she was or she didn't care if he saw her changes. Either way, it made him feel good that she was at least more comfortable around him. Her hair was slightly wavy as she lowered the towel from her head and tossed it to the bedroom floor.

"I thought you didn't drink?" she inquired, observing the alcoholic beverage in Liam's hand as she stepped into the hallway.

"I keep a beer or two in the fridge for emergencies." He handed her a water bottle.

"So your friend turning into a freak qualifies as an emergency?" She arched an eyebrow, following him toward the living room.

He stopped at the end of the hall and turned to her. "First of all, you are not a freak. And second, yeah, I'd say this qualifies. I better stock up if this is going to be a regular thing." He popped the top on his beer and lifted it. "Cheers." He clinked it against her plastic bottle and took a pull, letting the smooth liquid relax him. "Sorry, yours is nonalcoholic."

Liz took a sip. "This is salt water," she noted, sitting down on the couch.

Liam sat next to her. A plastic container of chocolate chip cookies and several napkins were on the coffee table. "I saw it in the sink. Was it wrong of me to assume you wanted more?"

"No, you weren't wrong. It's . . . delicious," she admitted, sheepishly turning away.

"Is that what caused . . . ?"

"After I left your car, I ended up drinking the water you had filled earlier. I did it out of spite to prove you wrong." She scoffed. "I guess it backfired on me."

"I didn't want to be right, you know."

Liz tucked her hair behind her ear and touched both sides of her smooth neck. Her shoulders relaxed. "Huh, they're gone."

"I wonder if they only appear with salt water," he pondered. "It would make sense or else you would have a hard time breathing."

She tilted the bottle up, stopping mid-chug with panicked eyes. She felt the sides of her neck. A relieved breath escaped her.

"That's not to say that drinking the seawater was the only reason the gills manifested," he elaborated.

Liz shot him a look. "Then why are the scales still here when I'm dry?" she asked, gesturing to her legs.

He lifted his hands in a shrug. "I don't know how this all works," he said with a raised pitch in his voice. "The only way to find out is to pour water on your neck."

"Yeah . . . no, I'd rather not test that theory today," she said, placing her water bottle on the coffee table.

"I agree. It's already been a long day." He took a swig of beer. "At least you still like chocolate," he joked, watching her dig into the dessert.

With a mouth full of cookie, she mumbled something incoherent. His brow ticked up. She swallowed and continued. "Sorry. How was your date before I interrupted it?"

Liam smiled to himself. "It was nice. There's something unique about her. I can't quite put my finger on it, but I really like her."

"I'm glad." She smiled before leaning over to pick up a crumb that had fallen to the ground.

He inadvertently noticed something through the low-hanging collar of her tank top. There, more of the aqua scales flecked along the top of her breasts. When she caught him staring, she quickly sat back up and adjusted her top.

"Sorry, I didn't mean to stare," he apologized.

She placed her dessert on a napkin and rested her elbows on her knees. "I should have listened to you. The water is only making this spread."

"It's not your fault, and frankly, nothing I said would've mattered. I think you're drawn to it," he said, watching her stare intently at her water bottle.

"It's getting worse," she admitted. "Not just the scales but the need to be in the water. It took everything in me not to jump in every time I was near it with Wyatt." She paused. "What if I wake up one day with . . . ?"

"A tail?" he finished her sentence.

Liz took a deep breath and succumbed to her desire, grabbing the bottle once more and taking a swig. "I'm not going to admit that I'm . . . a mermaid, but I will admit that there's something not exactly human going on."

"Fair enough." He went to reach for a second cookie when he realized Liz was reaching for one as well. He pulled his hand back.

"Go ahead." He noticed the sheen on her nails that matched her toes. His eyes looked her over, taking in every change that had occurred. Aqua scales, eyes, toenails, and now fingernails. "You have to admit that color suits you."

She lifted her hand, admiring the glint from her nails. "I do like it. I love any shade of blue, but aqua was always my favorite."

"You know, for everything you've gone through, it could be worse."

"How so?" she inquired between chews.

"Your scales could be your least favorite color." Liam took another gulp of his beer.

"Ugh, pink," she said with disdain.

"Or mustard yellow." He chuckled as Liz made a gagging face.

"Or pea green," Liz added, and they both laughed.

A silence crept between them for a beat before Liam broke it. "I really am sorry I walked away when you needed me. It's nice talking to you like this."

"Yeah, it is. And even though you were kind of a jerk—" she began.

"That's an understatement," he muttered.

"I did deserve it. I just really wanted to ignore everything and go back to a time before I even knew I was adopted," she admitted.

"You don't mean that, do you?" he questioned. "You wouldn't have come here, we wouldn't have met, and then there's Wyatt."

Liz turned away at the mention of his name.

"Are you going to tell me what exactly happened between the two of you earlier?"

Liz closed her eyes for a moment and took a deep breath before she spoke. "Well, the whole day was absolutely wonderful."

She recounted the events of their date, including how Wyatt had confessed to finding her grandfather's list and how Liam had helped him.

"What can I say? I'm a romantic at heart. Although, I wasn't keen on the parasailing part." He finished the last of his beer and placed it on the coffee table. "So, it ended with you guys strolling along the beach. It sounds like you had a perfect evening. I'm still not clear on what went wrong."

Her eyes narrowed at Liam. "What went wrong was you telling Jessica where he was."

Liam's brow scrunched together. "What are you talking about? I didn't even see Jessica today. The only person I told was Sarah, and that was because there was an urgent family matter, and she promised to have dinner with me if I told her . . ." His voice trailed off. "But that's beside the point."

"So, you don't know anything about his father?" she asked. Liam gave her an even more confused look. "Jessica told Wyatt that you said his father was here looking for him."

He slowly shook his head. "No. What else did she say?"

"I don't know. I got the impression that she didn't want me to be part of the conversation. Being the kind person I am, I gave Wyatt some privacy and went to the restroom. When I came back"—she choked back a sob—"they were kissing."

Wyatt had just told Liam he would never hurt Liz. "Maybe she forced herself on him. She was pretty persistent when she showed up at the bar the other day."

Liz shook her head with dismay. "I don't think so. It looked to me like he was enjoying it."

"It just doesn't sound like him. I'll talk to him."

"You don't have to. I'll be leaving soon anyway. It was never going to work." Liz placed the last bit of her cookie on the table. It seemed she had lost her appetite after replaying the images back through her mind.

Liam stared off, thinking long and hard. "Do you think leaving the island is the best thing for you?"

"I'm not sure. I don't know what I'm going to do." Liz sat back against the couch, leaning her head on the cushions, and looked up at the ceiling. "God, what am I going to tell my parents?"

"How 'bout the truth?" Liam suggested with a shrug.

Liz's head tipped to the side with her brows furrowed together. "Oh yeah, I'll just walk up to them, if I can by then, and tell them that their little girl isn't actually a girl but rather a vicious sea monster."

Liam grabbed the throw pillow that was between him and the arm of the couch and threw it into her stomach, catching her off guard. "Mermaids aren't monsters, they're beautiful," he said matter-of-factly.

"Ugh, I'm not a mermaid." Liz playfully threw the pillow back at him.

"Whatever you say, but you're using that magical power of yours to clean up the bathroom," he said jokingly with a yawn, pushing himself into the corner of the couch.

Liz raised her hands in front of her and moved her fingers about. "I didn't even know I could do that!"

"That was . . . pretty incredible," he said, trying to stifle another yawn.

"I guess," Liz replied and continued to inspect each finger, waiting for something to happen. "But it's scary. I didn't want to admit it, but the light you saw was a spark that came out of my fingertips. It happened again before—"

A loud snore interrupted her, and she turned to see Liam sleeping soundly. She felt bad he was sleeping on the uncomfortable couch instead of a bed, but she was glad he was nearby.

Letting her friend be, she quietly turned the light off and slipped away to the flooded bathroom. If she could control the water back into the shower, then cleaning up would be a piece of cake.

Extending her hands, she concentrated, but the water didn't even ripple. She thrust her hands out again, imagining it moving in her mind. Still nothing. Following several failed attempts, she gave up and walked back out in the hallway to grab a large towel.

After fifteen minutes of soaking up water and wringing it out in the shower, she had hardly accomplished anything. Frustrated, she let the heavy towel fall to the ground with a *thwack* and decided to wait until morning to see if Liam or Denise owned a Shop-Vac. She flipped off the lights and made her way to bed, physically exhausted from the day. Yet, when it was time to close her eyes, her mind had other ideas.

Liz rolled onto her back, stared at the ceiling, and contemplated her next move. What would she tell her parents? Could she stay here? Or should she travel back to Ohio? What if something happened on the flight home? She'd be on the five o'clock news for sure.

Sleep was her enemy. She tossed and turned several times throughout the night. Her throat felt like sandpaper each time she tried to swallow what little saliva she had. She reached for the water bottle next to her bed and shook it, only to hear the scant remnants left at the bottom. There was no doubt in her mind she would need more seawater before she was ever able to sleep.

Deciding she wasn't going to argue with herself, she threw the sheets off her body and put on her still-damp swimsuit. *Just in case*, she told herself.

She tiptoed past Liam, who was still asleep on the couch, and grabbed a flashlight that was resting on the table next to the door. She had learned her lesson the first time and wasn't about to take her phone.

Breathing in the briny sea air, she made her way to the beach. She bent down to fill her water bottle. Normally, the water would feel cooler this early, but to her, it was pleasant. She let the waves wash over her hand for a moment before returning to the shoreline.

Sitting down, she drank from the bottle and leaned back on her elbows to admire the night sky. Tiny pinpricks of white light speckled the black canvas. Gazing to the north, she scanned the starry night for the Big Dipper.

A faint whisper brushed up against the back of her mind, startling her. She sat up bolt straight and listened intently, but as soon as it came, it was gone.

Frustrated by the whispers, she cried out in her mind, *What do you want?* The lull of the waves was the only reply she heard.

"I'm losing my mind," she muttered to herself.

Sighing, she stared out at the inky darkness of the sea. Her legs began to twitch, ready to take her to the last place she wanted to go. Hesitating for a moment, she shoved her water bottle into the sand and stood, letting the sea wash over her feet. Her heart pounded anxiously in her chest.

I must be crazy, she thought, walking into the surf.

The waves gently crashed against her, and a smile crept upon her face. With a deep breath, she dove under, disappearing into the void. Her eyes burned when she opened them. She snatched the flashlight from her waistband, hoping it was waterproof. Thankfully, it was, at least at this depth. Her vision may have been blurry, but the light helped guide her.

For only having a few swimming lessons when she was little, Liz maneuvered through the water like a natural. She could remember going to a pool party at a friend's house and being too scared to go anywhere near the deep end. That fear was now gone.

The area behind and below her earlobes burned slightly. She lifted her hand to feel her neck. The gills had reappeared, yet they were closed. Wondering if Liam was right, she opened her mouth slightly, letting the water flow in, but when she tried to breathe out, the gills remained closed.

Shit, shit! She coughed and gasped for air as she breached the surface. She bobbed up and down with the waves and composed herself. A soft hue of pink glowed behind the silhouettes of restaurants and other buildings as the sun was beginning its daily journey across the sky.

"So no breathing underwater," she noted out loud before diving back under.

Liz was startled when a small group of fish fluttered by her head, causing her to drop the flashlight. She grimaced and dove deeper toward the beacon of light that was slowly sinking beyond her reach. The flashlight flickered a few times before the sea went completely black.

Dammit! Where was it? She fumbled around the sandy bottom until luckily, her fingers grazed the plastic cylinder. She grasped it and slid the power switch back and forth with no luck. Tucking it back into her waistband, she examined her surroundings. The once-clear beautiful aqua waters were now something from her nightmares. A black void of nothing enveloped her. Something brushed against her leg, making her uneasy. Seagrass, perhaps. Or worse, a shark!

She furiously kicked her legs but wasn't sure if she was making her way toward the surface or farther out to sea. Panic filled her as she fumbled with the flashlight yet again, hitting it, praying it would work.

Realizing it was useless, she did her best to calm herself. She squeezed her eyes shut, and tiny pinpricks stabbed at her corneas until sudden pain seared across her forehead. When the pain finally subsided, she opened her eyes a sliver. If she wasn't holding her breath, she would have gasped at the sight before her. It was as if the whole ocean was lit with a million tiny light bulbs, no longer the inky void that once enveloped her. She continued to swim through the waters, twirling about.

This is amazing! she thought, seeing all the plant life and sea creatures clear as day.

"Keep looking!" a deep voice ordered in the distance, stopping Liz in her tracks. This wasn't like the whispers she had heard before. This voice was clear, almost as if someone was shouting. Unless her hearing had greatly improved, but that was impossible. She was deep underwater. And who would be out this early in the morning?

Shadows panned her periphery, and panic set in once more. If anyone saw her, they might question why she was out so far or, worse, they might capture her.

Scanning her surroundings, she spotted a large cluster of rocks. She tried to swim toward them but was denied. Something was holding her back. She turned to see an old fishing net was wrapped around her right ankle. Reaching down, she pulled at the snare and unknowingly let out a soft grunt of effort.

"Shhh. I think I heard something. Ready your weapons," the voice called.

Her eyes widened in alarm. Weapons? Yanking as hard as she could, the line snapped around her ankle, freeing her to hide. Her hands clutched the rough surface of the boulder, and she steadied herself to the ground. She automatically grabbed a nearby rock and held it up. What was she doing? She wasn't seriously considering fighting whoever was down here, was she? She released the rock.

Her hair billowed around her as she tried to peer around the side. However, no one was in sight.

"We've looked all around the island, sir. He's not here," said a second male voice. There was a long pause before he spoke again, but this time his voice became nervous. "Sir?"

"Move out to the other islands, but don't linger. The . . ." the first voice began, but a school of fish swirled around Liz, distracting her from the conversation. " . . . will be waking soon."

Liz stayed motionless for what seemed like an eternity. Finally, when she felt it was safe, she pushed off the ground and kicked up to the surface. Her legs and chest tingled and burned. She didn't even have to look to know what was happening.

The scales were spreading.

Breaking the surface, she drew in the breath of fresh air that her lungs had begged for and was surprised to see the sky was no longer dark. The stars were nearly gone, and soft light made the sky a powder blue with a few wisps of clouds and jet contrails. A silhouette of someone walked along the shore. It wouldn't be long before the early birds came out and looked for shells. She needed to get back before anyone saw her, but she was nearly a half a mile from the beach.

Swimming on the surface back to shore wasn't an option because not only would the lone shadow see her but also because her legs ached too much to kick. It wouldn't take much for the waves to pull her farther out to sea. How would she get back? Maybe there was a way . . . If she was able to control the water like before, maybe she could use it to push her back to land. That was, if she could get it to work.

She dove back under and closed her eyes, trying to clear her mind. The last time, she had forced the power, but maybe that was the wrong way to go about it. Her arms lay at her sides, gently swaying with the current. She thought about the water that surrounded her and how it moved. She concentrated on focusing its motion, and then, without warning, she shot up, nearly flying out of the water.

Lifting her hands in front of her, she let out a quick laugh before going under to try again. Throwing her arms behind her, she let the water propel her like a torpedo, picking up speed. The ocean floor soon rose as the sea became shallower. Before she could stop herself, she hurled out of the water and landed face-first into the sand.

She groaned, rolling onto her back to see the shadow of a man standing over her.

His head cocked to the side, and his arms were folded across his chest. "You have a good swim?" Liam's familiar voice asked before he squatted next to her.

Liz sat up and spat out the sand around her lips.

"I woke up and went to check on you, only to find you were gone," Liam said. "I panicked and went looking for you. It wasn't until I spotted the water bottle in the sand that my mind went to the worst-case scenario. I thought I lost you."

Wiping the sand from her face, she replied in a raspy voice,

"You didn't lose me, and I didn't intend for you to worry." She shifted her body, curling her legs under her.

"What happened?" he asked, plopping his rear onto the sand.

"I couldn't sleep, and I needed more to drink. I came out here to refill the bottle but—" She coughed and reached for her water.

"You don't have to explain. I'm in no place to tell you what to do. I get it now. Next time, though, when you feel like exploring the ocean, let me know so I can bring my swimsuit." He smirked.

"I will." She glanced up at the clear blue sky. "How long was I gone?"

"I was searching for nearly twenty minutes for you, and that was only after I discovered you were gone."

"Twenty minutes? That can't be right. I hardly came up for air," she said, completely baffled.

Liam brushed back her drenched hair. "So you can breathe underwater?"

She shook her head. "No. I tried, but it didn't work. I guess I just held my breath for a really long time. But . . . oh my gosh, Liam! My eyes!"

She told him everything that had happened, including seeing the ocean lit up like downtown Cleveland on Christmas. The whole time, she beamed with excitement, while Liam sat in silence, hanging on to every word. She looked back out into the gulf, desperately wanting to return.

"I'm glad you enjoyed yourself, but next time, seriously, give me a warning, ok? I don't want you swimming away without saying goodbye," he said, pushing the sand around with his feet.

Liz's smile faltered as she turned back to him. "I wouldn't do that."

"I know." He gently nudged her.

Liz's brow furrowed and her gaze returned to the crashing waves.

"Did something else happen?"

"I heard voices," she whispered.

"What do you mean, you heard voices? Like from a boat?"

She shook her head. "I was underwater and could hear them as clear as I'm talking to you now. It was at least two men, but there might have been more. They were looking for someone." Her eyes darkened. "They had weapons."

"Weapons? I don't like the sound of that. Did you see them?"

"No, but they might have heard me. I was able to hide. Thankfully, they didn't stick around long. They moved on to search the other islands. Who do you think it could've been?"

"Even if your hearing improved underwater, it's unusual for boaters to be out this early. What if . . . ?" He shook the thought from his head.

"What?"

"What if they were like you?" Liam suggested with a twinge of nervousness. His body tense, no doubt waiting for her to tear into him about his crazy underwater theories.

She remained quiet for a beat and contemplated the notion. While she wouldn't readily admit mermaids were real, there weren't any other explanations for what had happened.

"Whoever they were, they didn't sound friendly," she replied.

CHAPTER 28

Discovered

Liz collapsed on her bed without a care that sand still clung to her skin. The feeling of the granules between her fingers and toes was somehow comforting. Exhaustion caught up to her, and soon enough she was fast asleep.

Where am I? Liz heard through the darkness of her mind. *No . . . don't make me . . . I don't want . . .*

Startled awake, she convinced herself that what she'd heard was from the end of a dream that she could no longer remember. But she couldn't shake the feeling that something didn't feel right.

Light now poured in through the thin blinds, causing her to groan. She pulled the sheet over her head at the sound of her phone vibrating across the nightstand. After ignoring it for a moment, she let out a sigh and reached out from under the sheet, fumbling around until she felt the rectangular device. Two missed calls from her parents and one missed call from her grandmother. She groaned again into her pillow, closing her eyes for a moment as she tried to push away the onslaught of anxiety that was crashing against her.

She had less than twenty-four hours to figure out what she was going to do or say. Maybe if she brought a bottle of seawater on the plane, that would suffice. *And if you start gasping for air in the middle of the aisleway?*

She pushed her head farther into the pillow. The image of Wyatt with his lips all over Jessica tried to push to the forefront of her mind, and a ghost of pain ached in her chest. She couldn't wallow forever, could she? Her stomach rumbled, letting her know that was a definite no.

Throwing the covers off her, she placed her phone back without checking any of the texts or voice messages. She didn't know how she was going to face any of them after this, but that would be something to figure out after breakfast. Or lunch.

Or never.

"Morning," Liam said, leaning against the doorway. He took a sip of what Liz assumed was coffee from a mug with the words "The Cove" written in a fancy font. Unlike Liz, Liam had been wide awake when he found her on the beach and had decided to go for his morning run.

"Please tell me I'm dreaming and it still isn't morning." She shifted and let her legs hang off the edge of the bed.

"Sorry, not a dream. You sound a lot better though," he commented.

Liz rubbed her fingers along her neck, feeling where the gills once had been. Relief was an understatement. If the openings had stayed, a scarf would have likely been added to her attire. "I just need to stay out of the water."

"In your case, I think that's easier said than done, though. Come on, we can talk more over breakfast." He disappeared into the hall.

"I don't think I have generic Lucky Charms," she quipped.

"Damn!" his voice echoed from the kitchen.

Liz forced herself out of bed, slid her feet into a pair of slippers, and walked to the kitchen island. Hoisting herself onto the stool, she watched him pour the cereal and milk into his bowl.

I . . . to get out . . . here! the distorted whisper from yesterday cried out softly in her mind. She jolted in surprise.

Liam peeked up mid-pour, and worry lines appeared across his forehead. "Are you ok?"

Liz cleared her throat. "Yeah, my phone buzzed," she lied, pretending to look at her phone. Telling Liam she was now hearing voices would only give him more concern. They had already established there was nothing they could really do. Finding her biological parents had been on the top of her list, but if he was right, there would be no way to find them.

He handed her a bowl, the box of cereal, and the container of milk.

"Thanks." She placed her phone on the counter.

He motioned to it. "Your parents?"

"Yeah. They called a few times, but it's been on vibrate." She poured her cereal and drowned it in milk.

Liam gave her a look as if he was holding back a lecture on why she shouldn't ignore them.

"I know what you're going to say." She pointed her spoon at him.

"I wasn't going to say anything."

"I know. But I also know that I need to answer them. I just don't know how to deal with this." She gestured to herself. "I can't tell them what's happening over the phone. They'll think I'm nuts."

"So you're leaving then?"

She tilted her head back. "I dunno. I don't really want to think about it right now."

"I hate to break it to you, but your time is running out."

She wasn't sure if he was talking about her time in Florida or the ticking clock that was spreading throughout her body.

"I wish I could give you some advice." Liam glanced at the round clock on the wall. "Damn, I have to get ready for work!" He shoved a few more spoonfuls of cereal into his mouth and quickly placed the dish in the sink. "Thanks for breakfast. I'll talk to Wyatt for you during my lunch break." He rushed out the door before Liz could tell him not to bother.

Liz finished her breakfast and made her way to the bathroom, forgetting the mess she had yet to clean up. Heavy soaked towels sat in the corner, and the tile floor was still slick but not as bad. She went to grab another towel from the linen closet only to find she had used the last one.

"Great."

Staring at the room for longer than she wanted, she tried to think of a way to dry the bathroom. A Shop Vac? A mop? A fan? She looked down at her hands and chewed her bottom lip. She'd done it just a few hours ago in the water. Maybe it would work this time.

Taking a deep breath, she cleared her mind of all worries, pretending she was back in the ocean. She willed the water to move. Slowly but surely, it gathered around her feet. Her hands rose, bringing veins of water up from the floor. They swirled around her as she beamed at her accomplishment. *I wish Liam was still here to see this!*

She pulled the water from the towels and began experimenting. A few times she lost control and the water fell to the ground, but after several more tries, she became a natural, shifting the tendrils into orbs the size of baseballs while they hung in the air. One by one, she threw them at the shower, and they splashed against the tile.

With the last of the water removed from the floor, she gathered the now-dry, dirty towels and placed them in a pile, then changed into her teal ankle-length surfer leggings and paired it with a matching bathing suit top and a muscle tank T-shirt. Resigned to the fact this was most likely her last day on the island, she decided to tidy up and gather the trash in the apartment.

After slipping her shoes on, she walked across the parking lot to The Cove with bags in tow. Liam was clearing off a patio table as she passed by. She smiled, gave him a slight wave to let him know there wasn't anything to worry about, and continued to the far side of the restaurant where the dumpster was located.

"Here, let me help you with that," Liam called out, following behind her. He lifted the lid while she hoisted the bags in.

"Thanks," she said as the lid slammed back down. She stared out at the beach that was now bustling with tourists and other beachgoers trying to enjoy a beautiful day.

Liam leaned against the brick wall of the restaurant. "Have any plans for the rest of the day?" he asked, drawing her attention.

She shrugged defeatedly. "I don't know. I should probably pack." She bit her bottom lip, trying to keep her emotions under control. "I just don't know what to do anymore. I thought coming here would help me figure out who I was. But now . . . ?" She sighed. "I don't even know *what* I am."

Infuriated, she slammed her hand against the dumpster, shifting it a few feet away.

"Whoa, calm down there, She-Hulk!" Liam exclaimed, taken aback by her strength. He tried pulling the dumpster back, but it didn't budge.

She walked to the other side and pushed it back with ease. She shook her head in dismay. "I'm sorry. It's just—" She noticed something on one of the bricks. Her finger traced a heart that had been chiseled into the hardened clay. "What's this?"

"Oh, yeah. I never noticed it before until Wyatt pointed it out the other day when he was throwing out trash. He was going to show it to you after your dinner as the last thing on that list."

Her brows furrowed in confusion. "I don't remember my grandpa writing to look at some brick wall."

"He didn't. The last thing was a heart inside a rectangle. We just figured it was a quirky drawing, but Wyatt saw this and thought it would be funny to say he actually found it." Liam shrugged. "Guess that didn't pan out well, though."

Liz stared at the heart and thought of her grandfather. "Follow your heart," she whispered. Her eyes narrowed in thought.

"Huh?"

She turned to Liam. "Follow your heart! My grandpa used to tell me that all the time."

"Ok . . ."

"He said to follow my *heart* and he told everyone I was found next to a restaurant. This"—she gestured toward The Cove—"restaurant."

"I'm sorry, but I'm still not following," he said with confusion. "How do you know it's this restaurant? Denise said she doesn't remember a baby being found here."

"It was twenty years ago. I doubt she remembers a cop coming in to question her. Heck, she could have been out that day. Who knows?" She traced her fingers along the edge of the brick. Something was different about the hard stone. It seemed out of place. "What if this was meant for me?" she asked in excitement.

"I mean, if it is, it's not much of a clue. It's just a heart. Maybe this was the spot he was going to tell you about your adoption." Liam looked around at the dingy alleyway. "Although, it's not much of a reveal. I don't think I'd want to remember the day I found out I was adopted next to a dumpster." He paused. "Do you think he knew that you were different?"

Liz picked at the mortar between the stones as Liam's question swirled around in her mind. *You're more special than you know.*

"This brick doesn't match the others, and the mortar isn't as discolored." Her fingers gripped the edges of the brick, shifting it slightly. "See, it moved! Go get a screwdriver or something I can use to pry it out."

"Ok, ok! Let me go look. I think there's one in the back," he said before disappearing around the corner.

While Liam sought out the screwdriver, Liz pictured her grandfather walking past the restaurant, hearing her infant cries for the first time. She brushed her fingertips across the heart. Perhaps he too had traced his fingers along the carving while staring out at the gulf just as Liz was doing right then. She pressed her left hand against the brick and placed her right hand over her heart, being overcome with hope.

Without warning, a muffled groan startled her, echoing in her mind. She looked around the empty alleyway, but before she could make heads or tails of what exactly it was, Liam returned with a flat-head screwdriver.

"Do you want me to do it?" he asked.

"No. This is something I need to do on my own," she replied.

He nodded and handed her the tool. She jammed it between the brick and slowly pried it away from the grout. A few minutes and a bent screwdriver later, the brick loosened.

"I got it!" she exclaimed, carefully pulling it out.

Liam sidled up next to her, and they both peered down at the hollowed-out brick. "Oh, wow," he said in a hushed tone.

Inside was an old, plastic Ziploc bag containing a folded-up piece of paper and a piece of material wrapped around something.

"This is it! It has to be." She removed the bag and returned the brick to its original place. Her hand trembled as she opened it. Reaching in, she pulled out the weathered piece of paper and—

Liz lurched forward as an onslaught of emotions crashed over her. Confusion and fear were prominent, but anger was overwhelming. She clenched her free hand into a fist. Her nails dug into her palm as more jumbled words that made no sense swirled inside her mind.

Need . . . stop . . . destroying, the garbled whisper said.

"What's going on?" Liam asked with concern.

"I'm not sure," she admitted with a shaky voice, touching the side of her head. It felt like tiny electrical charges were shocking her brain. She hadn't told Liam about the voices before in fear he'd worry even more. But she couldn't keep ignoring her problems. "Something doesn't seem right. I'm having those weird feelings again."

His brows knit together. "What do you mean?"

"It's like I'm feeling someone else's fear or anger. And there's this voice . . ." she began before faintly hearing it again.

If . . . succeed . . . everyone.

She furiously shook her head. "God, I sound crazy," she blurted out as she began to pace.

"You're not crazy. Let's get back to the apartment and figure this out. We can open the note there," he promised.

"No, I can't let you leave your—" She pinched her eyes shut.

Liam took the bag from her. "Don't worry about me." He guided her around the corner to The Cove's patio and stopped to let his coworker know that he was helping Liz home. "She's not feeling too great. Tell Denise I'll be back soon."

By the time they arrived at her apartment, Liz was trembling. Sweat beaded her face, and she immediately felt the need to lie down.

Liam quickly unlocked her door and helped her to the couch, careful not to touch her skin. He crouched down next to her. "Do you think seawater might help?"

"It might," she replied.

"I'll go fill up the bottle. Just take it easy," he said before running out of the apartment.

Like she was going anywhere. She sighed, then glanced over at the bag he had placed on the coffee table. It sat next to the necklace Wyatt bought her. She pictured him working at The Cove at that very moment without a worry in the world. If he really cared for her or her feelings, he would give her an explanation or at least an apology for being an ass.

I can't believe I thought he liked me, she thought, feeling foolish. She took a deep breath and tried not to think of him or his gentle smile and sky-blue eyes.

"Wyatt," she whispered and closed her eyes, only to be greeted with a startling image.

She was sitting with her back against a gray brick wall in a large, dimly lit building. It looked like some kind of warehouse. The only light was from the sun brightening the space around her, reflecting off the dust particles that floated nearby. A small group of silhouetted people gathered by a table that sat at the far end of the building to her left. The large steel door creaked open, and she heard a soft hum of a nearby boat.

Footsteps moving closer echoed throughout the building. She peered up to see the hazy image of a man. He seemed tall from where she sat. His arms crossed over a black shirt that clung to his broad chest and seemed ripe to burst from his large biceps. She couldn't quite make out his face since he was backlit with sunlight that poured in through the dirty, broken windows that were situated high above.

"Morning, sunshine," the man's deep, gravelly voice snarled. "You gonna cooperate? Or do you need some incentive?" A gurgling sound came from deep in his chest until he hocked a loogie that almost landed on her.

Ugh, so nasty, she thought, trying to keep the bile down.

Liz tried opening her mouth to speak but she couldn't move. In fact, she couldn't control her body at all as it shot up toward the man before being greeted by a fist.

She tumbled off the couch, and her eyes opened. Looking around, she realized she was back in her apartment. "What the hell was that?" she muttered.

Her first inclination would be to say what she'd experienced was a nightmare, but judging by the pain that radiated from the left side of her face, all reasonable explanations were out the window.

Bewildered, Liz pulled herself up and made her way to the bathroom. Sure her face was bloodied and bruised, she checked her reflection in the mirror, yet nothing appeared out of the ordinary. She had never been punched before, but she imagined that was exactly how it felt. She splashed some cold water on her face and grabbed a towel.

As she patted her skin dry, the once-disjointed whisper that tickled the back of her mind yelled out clear as day. *I need to get out of here. I need to warn them!* a male voice exclaimed. *My father was right, I don't belong here. I never should have come. I let everyone down. My family, Liam . . . Liz.*

Slowly, the towel dropped from Liz's face, revealing the reflection of her wide glowing aqua eyes. She gasped in disbelief. "Wyatt?"

Desperation washed over her. Before she could put all the pieces of the puzzle together, she cried out from what felt like a blow to her ribs and doubled over. Her hands gripped the side of the sink to steady herself. Her scalp began to ache.

Closing her eyes, she tried to breathe through it, only to see the assailant's dark eyes staring right back at her. His hand was clutching the hair on the top of her head, holding her up. One thing was certain: this wasn't a dream anymore. It was a real-life nightmare.

"You come at me again and you're dead," the burly man whispered into her ear. He wiped the blood from the corner of his mouth with the back of his hand. "I don't care what I've been told."

He tossed her to the ground, and that was when she realized she was seeing through someone else's eyes. It wasn't her arm that extended from her body on the floor but a man's. His bloodied knuckles were balled into a fist and were turning white from anger. Around his wrist was not only a shackle connected to a chain but also a bracelet, the same leather bracelet Liz had gifted Wyatt yesterday. The realization hit her like a tidal wave.

Wyatt, she gasped in her mind.

Hello? Wyatt replied, causing Liz's eyes to snap open for a moment, returning her to the bathroom.

"He can hear me?" she questioned, then shut her eyes once more, just in time to see a boot coming at her stomach.

Crying out in pain, she squeezed her eyes tight, forcing them to stay with Wyatt. She had to find out what was going on and why this man was torturing him.

"Start talking!" the man barked.

"Go to hell!" Wyatt's voice retorted out loud.

"You're going to talk one way or another. If I have to beat the living shit out of you, then I will." The man cracked his knuckles one by one. He knelt and grabbed the hair on the back of Wyatt's head, forcing them to look up at him. There was something sinister in him when he spoke. "I'm just supposed to keep you alive. I was never told *how* alive you needed to be."

"I'll never tell you anything," Wyatt spat out.

"Have it your way." He sneered, shoved Wyatt to the ground, and resumed his onslaught.

Oh god! Wyatt! No, no, no! Liz cried out. Pain rippled through her body from the man kicking Wyatt repeatedly. Her knees screamed in agony, and she wasn't sure if it was from the man or if her own body had hit the tile floor. No matter, her eyes remained closed, and she stayed with Wyatt, bearing his pain.

Hands gripped around her middle, and she heard a faint voice next to her.

Liz . . . ahhh! Wyatt cried out until the images unfolding through Liz's mind went black.

Wyatt? Wyatt? Answer me! Please! Please answer me! she screamed through her mind, but there was no reply. The connection had been severed.

Tears streamed down her face, and she sobbed in the dark recesses of her mind. She didn't want to open her eyes in case he regained consciousness, but she knew what had happened. The bastard beat him until he blacked out. All the pain that was inflicted on him began to fade away.

"Liz! Liz, open your eyes! Come on, Liz. Stay strong," Liam's voice became clearer.

Her eyes snapped open to see his worried expression hovering over her. Sometime during the punching and kicking, she had collapsed to the floor. Her eyes darted around for a moment until she realized what she had to do. Without hesitation, she scrambled to her feet and rushed out of the bathroom and toward the front door.

"Liz!" Liam called out, running behind her. "What's going on? Where are you going?"

She froze with her hand outstretched, her fingertips mere

inches from the doorknob. Where was she going? She didn't even know where Wyatt was being kept.

She turned to face him. "It's Wyatt. He's in trouble."

"How do you know?"

She shook her head. "There's no time to explain. We need to find him!"

"What about the letter?" he asked, motioning to the coffee table.

"There's no time. Trust me, we need to figure out where he is before it's too late," she replied with urgency.

"Too late? What kind of trouble is he in?"

The dark haze began to clear as Wyatt opened his eyes to find himself prone on the hard, cold floor. Light shone from the dirty windows above, indicating it was at least midday. His body ached from the beating he took earlier. The last thing he remembered was hearing Liz's voice. If only it was real.

Heavy footsteps approached and a deep voice echoed near him. "I think he's waking up," the male voice called out to someone farther away. There was a reply, but Wyatt couldn't make out what was said. "You want me to knock him out again? It'll be quicker." There was a long pause, and an echo replied. "I understand." He turned to Wyatt. "Lucky you, she's not done with the other guy yet."

The man knelt next to Wyatt, and a large hand forced his head up. Dirty fingers maneuvered around his lips until they forced them open. A small round object was placed on his tongue. Water was poured down his throat, nearly causing him to choke. The man wrapped his arm under Wyatt's chin, forcing his mouth closed.

Poseidon, not this again! Wyatt thought angrily as he pinned the pill to the roof of his mouth with his tongue. *There's no way I'm swallowing whatever that blowhole is giving me again.*

Wyatt was released to the floor with a thud, hurting his already ailing ribs. The man stalked off to the other side of the building.

Wyatt groaned in his mind. He twisted his tongue around until the pill fell out of his mouth. He didn't dare lift his head or make a noise. His eyes darted around to take in his surroundings. It seemed to be an old, cavernous structure. The floors were filthy, and the smell of rotting fish filled the air. He shifted slightly and the man who had beaten him, accompanied by another man, dragged a limp body toward him. Wyatt quickly narrowed his eyes to slits and watched as they chained the bloodied, beaten man.

While he remained still on the ground, Wyatt closed his eyes, and a tear trickled down his cheek. His whole species was endangered because of him. He was smarter than this. To be lured into the arms of a woman he barely knew. How could he be so stupid? How could he let Jessica tempt him? The clues had been right in front of him, even when he first got to know her. She'd talked about how her parents were killed, her mother taken by the sea and her father died from a fishing accident.

Did you know that sailors of the past mistook manatees for mermaids? Am I more beautiful than a mermaid?

Wyatt winced at his arrogance. She had tried to coerce him into the water more than once. And then there was the time during their double date when she'd pulled out the article from Liz's purse about a fisherman who had died. There was rage in Jessica's eyes he had never seen before. Was that article about her father?

He died when I was three. Fishing accident. That was twenty years ago, so I don't remember him too much.

Twenty years ago. His eyes widened. His mother died about twenty years ago because of a fisherman.

Father, what did you do?

CHAPTER 29
Captive

Liam tapped his fingers nervously on the steering wheel as they waited behind another car. Just minutes ago, he had witnessed Liz collapse on her bathroom floor, curled into a ball.

He never would have imagined that she had experienced Wyatt's pain. The scales and gills, he had an idea of what was happening from his research online, but this was something more. He thought back to when he would touch her verses when Wyatt held her hand. There was some kind of bond between them, that was for sure.

Once he had calmed a frantic Liz, they went over what she had seen and heard, ruling out all but two buildings on the island. Unfortunately, they both came up empty-handed.

The car vibrated as he slowly pulled into a parking lot and shifted it into park. If Wyatt wasn't on the island, he could be anywhere by now, but Liam didn't want to tell Liz that.

Pulling out his phone, he scanned the map, trying to figure out where else they could search.

"Maybe we should call the police," she suggested.

His gaze ticked over to her. "And when they ask how we know he was captured?" She didn't answer. He turned back to the screen. "I'll keep looking."

"If he's not in the next one, we get other people involved. I don't care what happens to me." She stared out the window. "As long as he's safe, I don't care."

"Let's try here," he said, pointing to an area on the map just off the island. It looked like an old marina. It wasn't far, and it was secluded enough that it would be the perfect spot to hide someone. He said a silent prayer that Wyatt would turn up, put the car into gear, and drove as fast as possible down the main road.

Liz leaned against the headrest with her eyes closed. She had done this several times during their drive, trying to communicate or see through Wyatt's eyes.

"Anything?" Liam asked, turning the car onto Cortez.

"No."

His hands gripped the leather of the wheel as he slowed the car down behind a line of cars.

Worry lines creased across her forehead, and she moved her head about to see what the holdup was. "What's going on? Why is the traffic stopping?"

"The drawbridge." Liam pointed out ahead. "Don't worry, we'll start moving here soon," he said calmly, even though he was panicking inside. He muttered a few choice words as if the boat would move any faster from his frustration. When it finally passed, and the bridge began to lower, he let out the breath he had unconsciously held.

Traffic crawled forward until they were back to a steady pace, crossing to the mainland. They continued for a few minutes until the GPS told Liam to turn right onto a side street.

"Are you sure this is the place?" Liz asked, looking around at the small residential homes they passed by. "I expected him to be somewhere more deserted."

"Yeah. It's tucked back here," he assured her before pulling off to the side of the road. *Please let this be the place.* A few other cars were parked nearby. He killed the engine and turned to Liz, who seemed puzzled. "If he's in some kind of trouble, we don't want to make our presence known. We'll walk around and scope it out. Once we know he's inside, I'll call the police."

Liz nodded in agreement and got out of the car, careful not to make any noise when shutting the door. Liam walked around to her, and they continued across the street. The gravel and broken shells shifted under their feet as they approached the larger buildings. Liz stopped and closed her eyes once more, only to shake her head in frustration.

"This isn't working!" she growled in a whisper.

"Maybe you're trying too hard," Liam suggested as they crouched down behind an old, rusted boat. "Or it could be like your other powers."

"What do you mean?"

Liam peered around the corner to make sure the coast was clear and turned back to her. "Maybe it's not fully developed yet, and it just worked one time, like your gills. They appeared, but you can't breathe underwater yet. I bet once you become a—"

She scowled at him. "Don't even say it. I'm not a—" She snapped her mouth shut and peered out at an old building at the far end of the marina. "He's in there," she informed Liam. "I can't really explain it, but I think I can feel him."

No one would suspect anyone to be using such a dilapidated place. Nature was reclaiming what once was. Vines twisted along the side of the brick warehouse, climbing up into a hole on the weather-worn roof. The peeling gray paint had seen better days, and the windows were so dirty that Liam would be surprised if any light shined through. The sea air hadn't been kind to the old building either, causing the doors and roof to corrode and rot.

"You might be right. There's no cars over there except one." His jaw tightened as he pointed out at the midnight-blue Jeep. "Jessica's," he growled slightly.

Liz's brows raised. "What are the odds they were both kidnapped?"

"There's only one way to find out," he replied, motioning her to follow him in a crouched stance. The gravel beneath their shoes crunched loudly as they quickly scurried closer.

They ducked behind a tower of pallets just before a metal door creaked open. A large, bearded man peeked out from behind the door. He wore a black T-shirt that was a size too small for his muscular frame and had short jet-black hair. His large arms flexed when he decided it was safe and closed the door.

"I've seen him before," she whispered to Liam.

"Yeah. He's the same guy that Jessica was talking to in front of the Oyster Bar during our double date," Liam said, then remembered Wyatt had seen him at Club 21 as well.

"And he was at the restaurant yesterday after I left Wyatt and Jessica alone to talk. I knew I recognized him." She glanced down. "I never should have left them alone. I could have done something."

"You can't blame yourself. There was no way you could have known this would happen."

"Maybe. Come on, we need to get a better look," she insisted and made her way closer to the building before Liam could protest.

They maneuvered between the wooden crates just outside the warehouse. Most were empty, but a few carried the remains of a fisherman's catch that had never been sold. The putrid smell of rotted fish nearly caused Liam to gag as they tiptoed past. He gestured for Liz to follow until they were crouched under a broken window. Liam rose up slightly to peer through the small opening. Something situated in front of it obscured most of his view, but he could see someone's legs sprawled out on the floor. He looked over at Liz and nodded before switching to let her see. He leaned against the wall, keeping watch.

"Wake up!" a woman yelled from inside, followed by a slap and the sound of metal being dragged against the floor. "Are you going to tell me where it is, or do I have to let my *friend* over here beat it out of you?"

Liam tugged Liz's arm, pulling her back down. "That sounds like Jessica!" he whispered.

Liz nodded with wide eyes.

"She's the one holding him here? I knew she was crazy, but this is taking it to a whole new level."

"They broke up. Why would she do this?"

"She must not have been too happy about it. What if she coerced him to kiss her last night?" Liam wondered. Liz gave him a puzzled expression. "It would make sense. Get him alone and find a way to force herself on him so you wouldn't follow. I mean, it probably made sense in her mind, at least."

Liz returned to the window, and they both continued to listen in.

"Fine, you don't wanna talk. I'll go find your sister and see how she likes being tortured," Jessica threatened.

"Sarah," Liam muttered. It took everything in him not to charge through the door. He had to be smart. For all they knew, the men inside could be armed. "We need to call the police."

They began to turn away from the window when Jessica spoke again. "Or maybe I'll find your little girlfriend," she snapped.

Liz froze.

"If you touch her, I swear to—" Wyatt started

At the sound of his voice, Liz and Liam peered through the cracked pane together, but the only thing visible was steel chains being pulled taut. Liz winced and rubbed her wrists.

"You'll swear to what?" Jessica snapped. "Say it!"

There was a long pause before a punch connected with flesh. Liz dropped down to her knees and gasped for air.

"Liz! Are you ok?" Liam cried in a hushed tone.

She nodded, biting her lip through the pain.

"I think it's time to go. You stay here, I'll make sure the coast is clear," Liam instructed as Liz returned to look through the window. He was about to turn around when something smashed into the back of his head and he was met with darkness.

~

"Liz. Liz, wake up!" a voice murmured in her ear.

Liz groaned at the interruption of her deep slumber. Slowly moving her arms around, she expected to feel the downy sheets of her bed, but instead, she lay sprawled on a hard, gritty surface. There was a weight around each of her wrists, and the sound of a chain rattled from her movement. The nightmare she thought she had awoken from was just beginning.

The sudden realization hit her along with the tremendous pain from the blow to the back of her head. They had been captured.

"Liz, you gotta wake up!" Liam whisper-shouted.

She forced her eyes open and blinked as her vision cleared.

The sound of heels clicking on the ground echoed through the building as someone approached. It was quickly followed by a sickening *thwack*.

"Shut up!" Jessica's voice boomed.

Liz shook the fog from her brain and pushed herself up. Still a bit disoriented, she leaned against the concrete wall. Her head lulled to the left where Liam was situated. He was also bound in chains. He stood silent and rigid in front of Jessica. Liz's eyes closed while her head swayed the other way to find yet another person chained up. They were facedown and beaten unconscious, but thankfully they were still breathing. Their chains were barely attached to the cement wall. Whoever this person was had seemed to put up one hell of a fight.

She turned her head to look straight ahead, and it was as if someone threw ice water on her. She suddenly became wide awake at the sight in front of her. There, bloody and broken, lay Wyatt.

Without thinking, she sprang to her feet and ran toward him, only to be restricted by the chains attached to the wall behind her. "Wyatt!" she cried out, but he remained still.

"Ah, you're awake," Jessica's syrupy voice said as she strolled in front of Liz.

"What did you do to him?" Liz growled.

"Oh, *I* didn't do anything." A smug look appeared on Jessica's face before she turned on her heels. Her leather boots echoed through the barren warehouse as she approached Wyatt and kicked him in the chest. "Wake up!"

Liz tried to grit through the pain of the boots hitting his ribs. If Jessica knew what she was, there was no telling what would happen.

"Liz, I'm so sorry! By the time I realized—" Liam began.

"It's not your fault." She scanned him over, noticing a cut along the corner of his mouth. "You're bleeding."

Using the back of his hand, he wiped the blood away. "It's nothing. Not like . . ." He glanced at his beaten friend.

"Do you still have your phone?" Liz whispered.

He searched each pocket and scowled. "Dammit, she must've taken it."

A soft groan escaped Wyatt. His eyes opened, and peered up at Jessica. Without a word, he turned his head away.

"Get up," Jessica ordered, about to lift her leg for another blow.

"Leave him alone!" Liz screamed.

Wyatt's head whipped around, and he scrambled to his feet before Jessica could inflict any more pain. He stared at Liz and furrowed his brow. "Liz?" He blinked several times. "Liz! Are you ok? Did they hurt you?" His voice echoed through the hollow building.

"I'm ok," Liz replied, looking him up and down. "But you . . ."

"Don't worry about me," he rasped.

"I'm good too, by the way," Liam called out, getting Wyatt's attention.

"Liam? Oh, Poseidon," Wyatt whispered.

Jessica clapped her hands several times to bring the focus back to her. "Maybe now we can get somewhere," she announced loudly.

Wyatt lunged forward, but the chains stopped him just short of grabbing her by the throat. "Let them go! They have nothing to do with this!"

"Oh, they came here all on their own," Jessica explained, folding her arms across her chest. "Turns out, that kiss didn't work as intended. They came here looking for you."

"So this whole time you were playing all of us?" Liam asked. Jessica shrugged with a smirk. He shook his head in disbelief. "This was all planned? Even your little one-night stand?"

Liz's attention quickly went from Liam to Wyatt, who was staring daggers at Jessica. She looked between them, waiting for an answer.

Jessica's laugh echoed through the warehouse. "Please! I'd rather jump into shark-infested waters." She held out her hand, examining her nails. "He disgusts me," she stated simply, then peered up. "I would never debase myself with such an insipid, vile being."

Liam rolled his eyes. "If the thought of dating him revolted you so much, why do it? Why lock lips with a man you despise?"

"A man?" Jessica laughed. "I'd hardly say he's a man."

Wyatt jerked at the chains once more with a growl. Jessica walked over and stopped just inches from Liam. Her lips curled as she grabbed the back of his head and thrust her knee into his groin.

"I did what I had to do to get my way."

Liam dropped to his knees with a groan and barely managed to mutter, "You're sick."

"Why?" Liz chimed in. "Why put up this whole charade? What did you possibly have to gain from going out with him?"

"He had something I needed," Jessica replied. "He was wrapped like a string around my pinky, but then you had to come along. My *charm* wasn't quite as effective as I had intended," she said, rubbing her hand along where her necklace used to be. "As for the . . . sex, my bartender unfortunately spiked his drink a little too much. I didn't need him to become suspicious, so I played the part of—"

"A slut," Liz blurted. "You didn't need to play that up."

Liam squeaked out a slight chuckle.

Jessica glowered at Liz before continuing. "I couldn't get everything from him before he passed out. Nonetheless, I think he'll tell me what I need to know now." She lightly smacked Liz's cheek.

Liz stared defiantly at her. "What do you want from us?"

"It's not what I want from you. It's what I want from *him*." Jessica motioned toward Wyatt, who continued to pull on the restraints, the veins in his arms bulging. "Tell me where it is!" she barked at him.

"I'm not telling you anything," Wyatt growled.

Jessica motioned toward a large man. The same one Liz had seen through Wyatt's eyes, except now a fresh cut appeared on his right cheek. His heavy boots trudged up to Wyatt. With a sneer, he punched him with such force, Wyatt fell to the ground.

"Stop!" Liz cried, dropping to her knees in agony.

"If you don't want to tell me where it is, I'm going to start torturing them!" Jessica knelt next to Liz and grabbed her by the jowls with her nails digging into her flesh. "We wouldn't want to mess up this pretty little face, now would we?"

Wyatt was on all fours, his head hung low. Blood trickled from his mouth, dripping to the ground. He stayed silent. Whatever she wanted to know, he wasn't going to talk.

"Fine," Jessica stated, letting go of Liz. She approached her thug and whispered something into his ear. He nodded his approval. Jessica walked to the far wall, picked up a metal rod with stubby tabs at one end, and handed it to the man.

"What is that?" Liz stammered. She watched anxiously as the large man flipped a switch, causing a bright streak of blue electricity to arc between the tabs. She turned to Liam, who had a look of terror plastered on his face. "Is that a c-cattle p-prod?"

"I find electricity to be quite effective," Jessica informed.

The man's expression was dark as he dragged the prod along the ground, causing sparks to fly.

"Please," Liz begged, taking a few steps back until she was up against the concrete block wall. "You don't have to do this."

"Oh, he doesn't have to, but you'd be surprised what people are willing to do for the right price." Jessica walked back to Wyatt. "Last chance."

"Wyatt, just tell her whatever she wants to know," Liam pleaded as Liz clung to the wall.

Wyatt stared at the floor in silence. *I can't,* his voice whispered in Liz's mind.

"Fine!" Jessica hissed. With a nod, she turned around and walked back to the lone piece of furniture in the building, a table at the far end where a few more of her men lingered.

"Please," Liz begged once more.

The man's muscles bulged as his grip tightened on the torture device. His face was expressionless at first, but Liz caught a glimpse of something dark, the desire to hurt her for no apparent reason. He extended his arm, lunging the prod into Liz's stomach. She screamed out wildly. The electricity pulsed through her until she crumpled to the ground. He pulled the rod away just long enough for her to get her bearings. She gazed over at Liam just as the prod struck her again.

"Stop!" Liam shouted and pulled on the chains. But there was no use.

As the man lunged the cattle prod into Liz again and again, Wyatt flailed around simultaneously. She could barely hear his low groans over her screams.

"You're going to kill her!" Liam shouted at the top of his lungs, causing the man to cease.

Liz let out a quiet sob. She wouldn't let her assailant think he had broken her. Pushing up on all fours, she tried to catch her breath and regain her strength. A glance up showed that the man holding her life in his hands was smirking. The sick bastard was enjoying this.

Without even lifting her head, Jessica waved her hand in the air and called out, "Continue."

"No!" Liam screamed.

No . . . No more, Wyatt's voice was faint in her mind. *Liz . . .*

Wiping the sweat from his brow, the man turned the cattle prod back on and jabbed it into Liz's side before she could even think about moving. Squeezing her eyes tight, she suddenly saw through Wyatt's eyes yet again. She could see her tormented body on the ground, rattling back and forth. With each thrust of the rod, her screams reverberated in her ears like feedback from a microphone. Wyatt's distress added to the chaos in her head, leading to blinding pain. She couldn't bear the sight of being tortured through Wyatt's eyes. She forced hers open, doing her best to endure the voltage ravaging her body.

"Stop!" Jessica announced loudly. She turned and walked with purpose until she was standing in front of Liz. Crouching down, she grabbed Liz's hair and pulled her head back off the ground.

"Please," Liz faintly implored.

Not caring in the least, Jessica took out a red handkerchief, shoved it into Liz's mouth, and tightly tied it behind her head. The man repositioned Liz's restraints so that her hands were bound behind her back.

"I swear, your screams were about to make my ears bleed." She grimaced. "Besides, I can't take any chances of anyone hearing you." Jessica searched her eyes for a moment, and her lips puckered to the side in thought. "I never realized how pretty your face is. I'll fix that, though." She pulled her arm back and punched Liz in the face. "That's for ruining my plans." She sauntered back toward the table.

"What the hell is wrong with you?" Liam cried out. His wrists were nearly raw underneath the restraints. "Answer me!" he roared so loudly that the men gathered around the table turned in astonishment.

Jessica stopped mid-stride. "I don't owe you an explanation," she replied without even looking back.

"I'm pretty sure you do!" He folded his arms across his chest. "You're beating the living shit out of him"—he gestured to Wyatt—"you're torturing Liz, and you're keeping us captive! If you're going to kill us, I'd at least like to know why!"

Jessica spun on her heels and marched over to where Liam was shackled. "They killed my family!" she blurted out loudly, pointing at Wyatt with a shaky hand. Gritting her teeth in anger, she punched Liam. He stumbled and held his cheek. "Don't test me," she hissed, "or your death will be the longest of them all." She turned back around, throwing her hand up in the air. "Continue!"

Liz scowled at the man and channeled all her anger to survive. She felt a familiar spark fly from her fingertips before the prod lunged back into her side once more. White-hot pain seared through her. With her cries muffled, she could hear Wyatt groaning in agony. She kept her eyes focused on him and watched him suffer the same pain she was enduring, but no one was torturing him. Was he channeling her like she was channeling him?

Her vision became blurry from the tears that filled her eyes.

Wyatt, please, she whispered in his mind. *Wyatt . . . please . . . make it stop.*

Wyatt pushed his head up with as much strength as he could muster, which wasn't much, and gazed into her eyes. "Stop," he said weakly.

"What was that?" Jessica inquired, then motioned for the man to keep the prod lodged into Liz longer.

"He said stop! Have you lost your damn mind?" Liam yelled hoarsely.

Jessica raised her arm once more and signaled for the man to halt, leaving Liz in a heap on the ground.

"It's going to be ok, Liz," Liam said, but it was hard to believe his words.

Jessica walked up to Wyatt with a rolled-up paper in her right hand. She unraveled it and held it in front of his face. "Where. Is. It?" she asked through gritted teeth.

Breathing heavily, Wyatt pushed himself up and lifted his trembling finger, pointing to a spot on the paper.

"Now, was that so hard?" Jessica returned to the group of men. "Chart a course to these coordinates," she said, handing the paper to an older bearded man.

She shoved the rest of the papers on the desk into a messenger bag and slung it over her shoulder. She motioned to the man who had been at the restaurant with her and gave him quiet instructions. Nodding, he walked over to Wyatt, unlocked the shackles, and placed his wrists into thick metal cuffs.

"Move!" the man growled, pulling Wyatt to his feet. The man shoved him toward the exit of the warehouse.

"I told you what you wanted," Wyatt said weakly to his captor. "Now let them go."

"Oh"—Jessica placed her hand on her chest—"you thought I was going to let them go?" Her sinister laugh rang through the building. "I never said such a thing. If you're lying, then they'll die one by one." She pointed to everyone, including the unconscious person to Liz's right.

Wyatt sneered. "I'm not lying!"

"We'll see." She started to exit, but she stopped and peered over at the man holding Wyatt. "Keep him down below." Her body shifted to the other hired muscle still holding the prod. "Stay here with them in case plans change." Her lips curled as she glared at Liam and Liz. "And please, feel free to torture them."

"No!" Wyatt shouted. "Kill me, but spare them."

Ignoring his final plea, Jessica opened the door to the outside, letting the wind whip her auburn hair about, and disappeared.

With Jessica's thug no longer beside her, Liz used all her strength to push herself off the ground and stand.

"Move it!" the man ordered, pushing Wyatt forward.

Now knowing the truth and that her fate was unclear, if this was the last time Liz was going to see Wyatt, she was damn well going to fight for him. She tried calling out his name, but it came out muffled from the cloth Jessica had stuffed into her mouth.

Another shove and Wyatt tumbled to the floor. He stared into Liz's eyes one last time.

I hope you can forgive me, Liz. I didn't mean for this to happen. I'm so sorry, his despondent voice echoed in her mind.

Her eyes widened, and her heart raced like a galloping horse. The words were so clear. *Wyatt!* she pushed her thoughts toward him. *I forgive you.* She watched his brows knit in confusion for a moment as the words hopefully registered in his mind. *I forgive you!* she called out to him again.

Liz? You . . . you can hear me? he asked through her mind.

She rushed as far as her restraints would allow. *Yes! Yes, I can hear you!*

The man bent down and grabbed the back of Wyatt's shirt collar. "Get up, you worthless piece of—"

Wyatt threw his elbow into the man's jaw and sent him to the ground. Instead of running out the door to escape, he went straight to Liz and pulled the handkerchief from her mouth, wincing slightly at the state of her face.

If it wasn't for those damn chains, her arms would have been around him in an instant.

"Liz, you have to find a way out of here. She's not going to let you go. I can't lose you," he croaked, his eyes becoming glossy.

"You won't lose me." Tears fell down her cheek as her forehead touched his. "Don't stop fighting."

He cupped her face in his hands. *I'll always fight for you*, his promise echoed in her mind. He tilted his head and slowly moved in. Their lips were about to touch when two pairs of hands gripped his arms and pulled him away from her.

"Nooo!" she screamed. Yanking at her chains, she cried out for Wyatt over and over as the men struggled to drag him outside.

CHAPTER 30

A Storm Approaches

Liz could only watch as Wyatt fought against the two men with what seemed like the last of his strength. However, they overpowered him, and a third man with dark curly hair trudged up and subdued him with a sucker punch. Wyatt's head fell to the side, and blood dripped from his mouth.

She felt the blow whip across her face, but she pushed past the pain. "Let him go, you bastards!" she screamed, pulling on her restraints with everything she had. This couldn't be it. They couldn't take him away from her now.

The man ordered to guard them punched her in the gut. "Shut up!"

The breath whooshed out of her, and she struggled to breathe.

"Hey! Hasn't she gone through enough?" Liam yelled.

"What's going on?" Jessica's voice rang from outside the door.

"Nothing, miss. Everything is under control," one of the men replied as he helped drag Wyatt outside. The metal door slammed shut, echoing through the hollow building.

Liz's tormentor tromped past the heap of a man who let out a low groan. "You're lucky she wants you alive or I'd kill you first," the guard muttered. Making himself comfortable, he took a seat at the table and kicked his feet up on top of it, crossing them at the ankles.

Liz crumpled to the floor. The only thing she could hear was her shallow and raspy breath.

"Liz," Liam whispered. The sound of chains scraped as he shifted closer until his restraints were taut.

"She's going to kill him," she murmured to herself as she stared at the empty chains that had held Wyatt. She then turned to Liam. "She's . . . she's going to kill us. Oh god, my parents! I'll never have the chance to apologize to them." Her voice cracked. She lifted her knees to her chest with her arms still bound behind her and rocked back and forth, letting the tears stain her face and clothes.

"Liz, look at me," he instructed.

All she wanted to do was cower and be left alone. That was her go-to, wasn't it? Cower or run away? Her eyes pinched shut. She was so tired of running from her problems.

A teardrop rolled down her cheek and landed on her lips. Her tongue darted out. She couldn't remember the last time she had a drink of salt water. Her tears weren't going to cut it.

"Dammit, Liz! You need to listen to me!" Liam said.

She lifted her head but still kept her gaze fixated on the ground.

"You're the strongest person I know."

She shook her head, remaining silent except for the quick gasps between sobs.

"Yes, you are!" he argued.

She reluctantly turned to look at him through the strands of hair that clung to her face.

"Not just mentally but physically. Look." He pointed above her head. She peered behind her shoulder, following his line of sight to find one of the bolts halfway out of the wall. The other was just starting to loosen. "You did that. You can get us out of here. I know you can. I'm not strong enough, but you are."

With the guard seemingly more occupied with his phone than

what they were doing, Liz staggered to her feet and wrapped the chain around her hands. Using as much strength as she could muster, which wasn't much, she pulled the chains tight.

The world spun around her, and she fell back to the ground with a groan. "I don't think I can do this. I feel so weak and thirsty," she rasped. It felt like she was swallowing sand. Any longer without water and she was afraid it would be hard for her to even breathe.

"Hey!" Liam's voice reverberated in the empty building. The guard's eyes peeked up for a moment before returning to his phone. Liam jumped to his feet. "Are you deaf?"

That got the man's attention. He lowered his feet to the ground and slammed his hand on the desk. "What?" he barked.

"She needs water," Liam stated, motioning to Liz.

The man narrowed his eyes at them. "Like I care."

"You might not, but your boss will. I mean, what good is it to keep beating us if we pass out from dehydration?"

Growling, the man pushed himself out of the metal chair, almost toppling it over, and stalked up to Liz. He loomed over her. "You want water, huh? Fine, I'll give you some water."

Taking the key from his front pocket, the man unlocked the shackles around her wrists and grabbed her hair, pulling her to her feet. Liz wailed hoarsely, unable to do much more.

"Whoa! What are you doing?" Liam asked, panicky.

The guard's lips twisted up. "She wants water, I'll give her water," he replied, motioning to a lone barrel across from Liam's invisible prison cell.

Liz had been able to hold her breath underwater for a long time before, but in her weakened state, she wasn't so sure. No, in fact, she was positive she would drown first. Panic set in, and she kicked and clawed at the man who was hauling her across the floor. He pushed her against the container and clutched the back of her head. Her eyes darted down. She was relieved to see it was water and not chum. Not only that, but the sweet smell of salt greeted her nose. If she could just get a taste, then maybe . . .

"Let's see how loud you scream underwater." He forced her under before she had a chance to hold her breath.

Seconds turned into minutes, and minutes turned into what seemed like an eternity. She thrashed about. Her neck burned as the gills took shape on the sides of her neck. Her lungs screamed for oxygen until she finally opened her mouth. Water flowed in, but she still couldn't breathe underwater.

Just as she thought she was going to die, her head was raised up just long enough for her to swallow the water and catch her breath before being pushed back under. The man did this several times, each causing her body to grow stronger.

By the fourth dunk, she gripped the rim of the barrel in anger. The metal buckled under the pressure. A strange feeling flowed down the length of her arms, as if a bolt of lightning was racing through her veins. It felt exhilarating. She couldn't see it, but she felt a quick jolt between her fingertips.

"Hey, asshole!" Liam's muffled voice hollered.

The man released his hold on Liz for a moment. The brief pause allowed her to stare at her reflection in the water. Any wounds she had suffered were now miraculously healed.

"Here we go," she heard Liam whisper to himself. "Yeah, you! Why does she get to have all of the fun, huh?"

"What did you say?" the guard asked.

"You heard me!" Liam taunted. "I hardly have a scratch on me, but maybe you can't bear to hurt me. I mean, I'm flattered, but you're not really my type."

"Liam, what are you—" Liz was shoved back under one last time before the guard dragged her back to the holding area. Her hair clung to the side of her neck, hiding her gills. Not that the guard would have noticed anyway. He was so concentrated on giving Liam a beating that he didn't bother to bind her wrists behind her and instead gave her a reprieve, affixing each shackle to her wrist without joining them together.

"You're gonna regret saying that," the guard growled.

"Liam, what are you doing?" she whispered in a raspy voice, trying to catch her breath.

Liam stood tall and rigid, waiting. He peered down at Liz. "Buying you some time."

The guard walked to the table, and Liz doubted he was going for his phone. Instead, he snatched the cattle prod.

"God, I hope this works."

Liz scrambled to her feet. "No, no, no! Liam, you can't! He'll kill you!"

Liam's mouth thinned, and he stared into the dark, cold eyes of his tormentor who was approaching him. "Remember what I said. You can do this," he encouraged. His chest rose up and down with each quickening breath he took. "I believe in you, Liz."

The guard paused, looking Liam up and down as if trying to decide if he was worth the effort.

Liam lunged forward, the restricting shackles stopping him just short of the man's nose. He puffed out his chest. "Come on, you worthless piece of—"

The guard swiftly punched him in the face, knocking him to the ground. Pushing up on his hands and knees, Liam spat blood onto the floor. Before he could retaliate, the prod was shoved into this side, electrifying every inch of him.

Liz watched in horror as Liam's body convulsed. The torture device was applied to him longer than Liz had endured. His painful screams echoed throughout the building.

"Stop! You're killing him!" she cried.

The bastard of a man stopped for a moment and retorted, "Good!" He slammed the heel of his boot into Liam's back several times before resuming the torture.

Liz hugged her arms around her body tightly. The words of Liam, Wyatt, and her grandfather reverberated in her head, one after another.

I believe in you, Liz.

I can't lose you.

You're more special than you know.

She took a deep breath in, allowing her arms to fall to her sides. Filled with determination, she stood and licked the salt from her lips. She wrapped her hands around the chains with a tight grip and pulled as hard as she could. One by one, the bolts ripped out of the wall.

As the final bolt flew across the room and ricocheted against the barrel with a loud clang, Liz fell to the ground. The man whipped his head around, and his eyes widened in surprise. He kicked Liam aside.

The guard pointed the prod at her while marching over. "You trying to escape, little girl?"

Liz rose to her feet and glared at the man who had tortured the people she cared deeply about. With her fingers splayed, she concentrated on controlling the water. Tendrils snaked behind the guard, but she was too slow. The guard lunged the prod into her right shoulder. Her knees crashed to the ground, and she lost focus. The coils of water rained back down to the ground around them. The man pulled back the prod and looked around in confusion before resuming his torture.

"Get up, Liz! You can do this!" Liam encouraged between coughs.

The pain swelled through her, but she used it to feed her anger. The same anger that she had tamped down so many times. Somehow she knew she could use that to her advantage. Something awakened deep inside of her. Warm currents of energy flowed through her body and down to her fingertips, and she welcomed it with open arms. The man pushed the tip deeper into her shoulder, seemingly irate that she had no reaction to his torture.

"What the hell are you?" he asked with a shaky voice.

Liz's chest heaved as she glared at him. She pushed the rod away from her shoulder. When he tried to drive it back into her, she reached out and covered the end of the prod with her hands. The current coursed into her and up her arms. The bright blue voltage ran through her veins, lighting her up and giving her an eerie, otherworldly glow. Liz absorbed all the electricity the device contained, and the arc between the tabs extinguished.

The man stared at his weapon in disbelief. "What the—"

Liz yanked the prod from his hand and swiftly blasted him with an electrified palm strike to his chest. His body flew nearly twenty feet across the room and made a sickening crack as it hit the wall.

Standing, Liz panted heavily, reeling from what had just happened. Her heart pounded so hard that she was afraid it would burst from her chest at any moment.

A deafening silence hung in the air until it was broken by Liam's exclamation. "Holy shit!" he shouted, staring at the seemingly unconscious guard. Liam turned back to Liz with his mouth agape. "Wow. You look . . ."

She brought her shaky hands up to her face and jumped back at the sight of electricity crackling between her fingers.

"Are you ok?" Liam asked with a slight cough as he tried to stand up on shaky legs.

A string of incoherent words erupted from her. "I just . . . I didn't mean . . . I . . . Oh god."

She took a step toward Liam but stopped when she caught sight of a blurred image in a puddle of water. The reflection before her was unrecognizable. She studied the woman who stared back at her. Turquoise highlights streaked down dirty blonde hair, and glowing aqua eyes blinked several times. There was a fierceness behind them, as if the girl staring back at her could take on anything.

"Breathe, ok? You need to breathe and focus," Liam said. "We need to get out of here."

Liz's breath became more shallow as anxiety set in. What had just happened? Had she killed a man?

"Think of Wyatt," he said in a final attempt to calm her.

Wyatt. He was in trouble and needed their help. She took a deep breath, causing the electricity to fizzle out. She glanced down at her reflection to see her hair and eyes return to normal.

"Better?" Liam asked.

Liz stared at the broken body across the building. "I didn't mean to—" Her voice cracked.

"Look at me. You saved us. That's what you did. Now, can you please help me out of these chains?" He raised his shackled hands. "I think the key is in one of his pockets."

Forcing her legs to move, she rushed up to the guard. Smoke billowed from the charred portion of his shirt by his sternum. His chest was still rising and falling. He was alive. At least her conscience would be clear of that. Although, she wasn't sure if she should be glad or worried. Nevertheless, she quickly patted him down until she discovered the key in his front pants pocket and raced back to Liam.

"Here, let me," he said, taking the key and unlocking her shackles. The cold steel fell to the ground with a clang. "How are you holding up?"

"I—I'm not really sure. I just electrocuted a guy with my bare hands." She worked on freeing Liam.

"Is he . . . ?"

She shook her head. "He's still alive." Her eyes darted to him. "For now."

She unlocked his restraints and placed them next to hers. He rubbed the raw skin around his wrists.

"Liz, he was going to kill us. That bastard deserved it. You were unbelievable. You know that, right?" He gave her a slight smile. "I knew you could do it, but damn, that was incredible!"

"I don't know what happened. I just felt something take over, like an instinct."

"Remind me never to cross you," he said, causing Liz to chuckle. "Come on, let's go save Wyatt."

"What about him?" Liz inquired, pointing back at the guard.

Liam lifted the shackles and grinned. "Leave that to me."

"While you do that, I'll tend to whoever that is," she said, motioning to the heap on the ground.

She rushed over and knelt next to the unconscious prisoner.

She carefully rolled them onto their back to reveal a man. The black tattered shorts seemed to be a size too small for him, and his dingy green T-shirt was tight against his broad chest. His long brown hair was sticking to the front of his face due to the many open wounds. She combed his hair back as best she could, revealing a beard crusted with blood, as well as a swollen left eye.

"He's not going anywhere," Liam said, referring to the guard. He hobbled past Liz to the desk and searched the drawers.

She looked Liam up and down for a moment. "You're hurt."

He winced. "It's nothing, probably a broken rib and a couple of bruises, but I'll manage. What about you?"

"I'll be all right," she said, unlocking the third captive's shackles. The truth of the matter was, it had felt like she had been hit by a bus, but since being nearly drowned in the seawater, she felt immensely better. It was almost as if the water healed her.

"Found them!" he exclaimed, holding up his car keys. "Who knows what happened to my phone."

"What are we going to do with him?" Liz gestured to their unknown companion. "We can't just leave him here."

Liam thought for a second. "I'll bring the car around and I'll help you put him in the back seat."

Cautiously, he opened the door and poked his head out to make sure the coast was clear, then disappeared.

A few agonizing moments later, the sound of the car rolling along on the gravel alerted Liz that Liam was outside. The warehouse door opened, and Liam stood with wide eyes. Liz stood side by side with the unconscious man. His arm hung across her shoulder as she held him up with ease.

"How on earth did you lift him?" Liam asked in amazement. "He's gotta weigh like two-fifty, maybe more with all that muscle."

She shrugged like it wasn't a big deal. "Let's get out of here before the other guy wakes up."

As they exited the warehouse, they were greeted with dark ominous clouds in the distance and gusting winds. They hoisted the man into the back seat of the car. He groaned and muttered something she couldn't quite understand. Liz buckled the man's seat belt, and his hazel eyes fluttered open for a moment, staring at her before closing.

She rushed to the front passenger seat and buckled up. "How are we going to find Wyatt?"

"Jessica said to keep him down below," Liam began, putting the car in drive, "and I noticed the big fishing boat that was docked when we pulled in isn't there now." He pointed to a slip just in front of them. "I bet that's what they're on. The question is whether they're heading north or south. If we hurry, we might be able to see them." He turned the car quickly and headed down the road, only pausing briefly at the stop sign before driving to the main road.

"Then what do we do?" Liz asked.

"I thought maybe we could take Denise's boat and . . . Shit, I don't know." He waved his hand in the air. "I'll tell Denise what happened, and we'll figure something out. Can you . . . you know?" He pointed to his head.

Liz concentrated. *Wyatt . . . Wyatt? Can you hear me?* There was no response. She closed her eyes and tried to see what he saw but it was only black.

She shook her head in disappointment. "I think he's still unconscious."

"He's going to be ok." He sped down the main road, but traffic had stopped on the bridge. "Dammit!" he shouted as the gate lowered down a few cars in front of them. A bell rang in the distance, signaling the approaching boat. He pounded his hand on the steering wheel.

Liz frantically searched the bay. "Look out your window. See if you can spot her boat."

"Right there! That's the boat!" He pointed to the crimson fishing trawler in the distance to their left.

"It's heading south," Liz said, then spotted the small sailboat with a large mast approaching the bridge at a leisurely pace. *At this rate, we'll never be able to save him*, she thought, becoming increasingly impatient.

"I'll call the Coast Guard," Liam said.

"There's no time." Liz unbuckled her seat belt and reached for the door handle.

"What are you doing?"

"By the time we get to Denise, they'll be long gone." A rumble of thunder erupted from the sky, and fat raindrops began to hit the windshield. "I have to save him, Liam." She opened the passenger door and swung her legs out.

Liam tried reaching for her arm. "Liz, you can't run to the island. The bridge is up."

"I'm not going to run, and I'm not going to the island." She stepped out of the car and leaned down to face him, blinking back tears. "You're a great friend, Liam."

If she stayed any longer, she would lose sight of the boat.

She slammed the door shut just as Liam cried out, "Liz, wait!"

She ran full speed around his car and under the downed gates.

No turning back now. Taking a deep breath, she placed her feet on the top of the railing. *I'm coming, Wyatt.*

CHAPTER 31

Rescue

Liz plummeted nearly twenty feet off the bridge. The dark, choppy waters stung her skin when she made contact. It only hurt for a moment until the warm embrace of the sea wrapped around her. She opened her eyes to the glowing underwater world and floated for a moment in awe. Her hair billowed around her. To her relief, it remained its natural color. This wasn't the time to explain to Wyatt that she was turning into some kind of undersea creature. That would have to wait until later.

Wincing from the burning sensation along her neck, she raised her fingertips and felt a second gill beginning to form just underneath the first.

Pushing the worry from her mind, she kicked back up to the surface and scanned for the boat. A loud holler caught her attention, and she turned around to find Liam standing by the railing, waving his arms about. She forced a smile and waved before diving back under. Concentrating on controlling the water, she pushed it past her and jetted forward at top speed, only to surface to course correct. She had to save Wyatt.

Liz breached the surface under Longboat Pass. The churning wake of the crimson trawler was just beyond the bridge and headed toward a heavy curtain of rain. Weakened from chasing the vessel, she struggled to stay afloat. The shifting seawater was becoming more violent as it splashed against her face. She dipped her head and took a gulp of it to replenish the energy she had lost. She peered over her shoulder in hopes that Liam had taken Denise's boat. Only a few fishing boats were in the harbor, and they were headed back to the marina. She was on her own.

Lightning streaked the distant sky, followed by a low rumble of thunder. The large boat began to sway. One of Jessica's men was pacing at the stern. She scowled. As if this wasn't hard enough. Taking a deep breath, she disappeared back under.

Just a little farther.

Pushing the water past her, she dove deeper and shifted her body to the right, passing the underbelly of Wyatt's floating prison. The dark shadow of the hull loomed over her. She cautiously surfaced along the boat's starboard side.

Licking the salt from her lips, she pondered how on earth she would board the large ship. A strong wind whipped around her as she searched for anything along the vessel she could grab on to but nothing seemed to be within arm's reach. She thought for a moment and remembered how she'd flown out of the water when she first tried controlling it. She wasn't sure if it would work, but it was her only shot to climb aboard.

She dove back under and swam to the sandy bottom. *Here goes nothing.*

With everything she had, she propelled herself upward and shot straight out of the water. Her arms and legs flailed in midair as she dropped back down. She extended her arms, catching the edge of the deck. Clinging for dear life, she pulled herself up enough to see the deck floor. A flash of forked lightning illuminated the dark clouds, followed by a crack of thunder. She was about to board the vessel when someone spoke.

"Hey, Ronnie!" a male voice shouted over the gale. A scrawny-looking man with a thick beard and tattoos up his arms suddenly appeared, causing Liz to duck her head down. "Do you know where we're going or even what the hell we're supposed to do once we get there?"

Another man, who Liz presumed was Ronnie, walked over. He was the same man she had seen in the restaurant and the warehouse. "No clue, man. She never told me nothing."

"You're not even curious? I've already been to prison once. I'm not about to go back there."

"I couldn't care less. As long as I get the rest of my money," Ronnie replied.

A droplet of water hit her shoulder. Then another and another as the rain picked up.

"I just . . ." The scrawny man paused for a moment. "I'm fine with beating the shit out of guys, no questions asked, but explosives? I dunno."

Liz nearly lost her grip. *Explosives? What is she planning?*

"Then you should have stayed on land," Ronnie said with disdain.

"With Trent? No way. That guy is unhinged. He had way too much fun torturing that girl."

"I thought you didn't care about beating people up?" Ronnie questioned.

"I ain't about to beat up a defenseless girl."

Defenseless? Tell that to Trent. Liz snorted to herself.

Just then, a woman's voice boomed through the air. Between the wind gusting around Liz's ears and the rain that was now a steady downpour, it was hard to hear. However, Liz knew exactly whose voice it was.

Jessica.

Liz's jaw clenched. Just hearing her voice sent a small spark from her fingertip.

"Guess the boss wants us," the scrawny guy announced.

The two men walked off, giving Liz ample time to hoist herself up and hide behind a nearby crate. She crouched down, hissing at the burning sensation under her clothes. When she rolled up her right pant leg, the aqua pattern had spread even farther down.

With a heavy heart, she rolled it back down, pushing the pain aside. She peered around the crate and spotted another man coming toward her. How many men were on this boat? Turning, she pressed her back against the large box as her heart pounded wildly.

Once he moved past her to the bow of the boat, she crouch-walked to a nearby door. She gripped the handle with her left hand, making a fist with her right, preparing for whatever may be on the other side. Upon slowly opening it, she was grateful to find an empty kitchen. She hastily closed the door behind her, doing her best not to make a sound.

Wringing out her hair, she nearly toppled to the side. The boat swayed back and forth, tempting Liz to empty the contents of her stomach. With a hard swallow, she looked around the room and found a large piece of paper secured with paper-weights on a dingy, food-encrusted table in front of a cushioned bench. Still squatting so no one could see her through the large window, she approached it. It was a map of the Gulf of Mexico. She took a quick look at it to see an X in the middle of the waters.

What is she planning?

A blurry image of a man walked past the window, and Liz ducked underneath the table. Seconds later, the rain-soaked man entered. His heavy boots squished against the thin, green carpet and stopped mere inches from Liz. He rolled up the map and exited, allowing her to release the breath she didn't know she was holding.

Continuing her search, she left the kitchen and went down a corridor lined with doors. A sign indicating stairs at the far end of the passage caught her eye. Through the door, the roar of the engine was loud enough to mask her descent.

Wyatt? she called out in her mind over and over as she searched below. *Dammit! Come on, Wyatt, wake up!*

A few moments passed until a faint whisper echoed through her mind. *Liz,* Wyatt's groggy voice spoke, startling her.

Wyatt!

Liz? Are you ok?

I'm fine. I'm in the engine room, she informed him, causing panic to wash over her. His panic.

The engine room? You're here? I thought Jessica left you behind with Liam.

I can't lose you, Liz replied. She was about to ask where he was being held, but she knew he was close. She wasn't sure how, but she could feel his presence now that he was awake, as if a rope of energy tied her to him. She followed it and peered around the corner, spotting the cargo bay access hatch.

You need to get out of— Wyatt began before Liz shushed him.

The room spun for a moment. She took a deep breath and held onto the cool metal door. The air felt thin. She touched the sides of her neck to find the second slits were nearly formed like the ones above it. Time was running out.

She fixed her hair to hide the gills, straightened, and yanked the latch on the door down using all her strength. The locking mechanism broke.

She opened the door and could have sworn she saw Wyatt's blue eyes pierce through the darkness. Light flooded the dark room to reveal his battered body. His wrists were bound behind his back, and his bloodstained shirt was ripped in several places. A bruise was forming around his left eye, and dried blood surrounded the corner of his mouth. He looked like hell for the most part, but his spirit lit up when she entered.

"Liz," he rasped with relief.

There were so many things she wanted to say, but instead, she rushed over and wrapped her arms around him. She never wanted to let him go.

When she pulled away from him, he asked question after question about how she had escaped and come to be on the ship. Unfortunately, there wasn't enough time to explain herself.

"It's not important right now." She maneuvered around to his back. "What's important," she said through gritted teeth as she worked to free him from his shackles, "is getting off this boat. I don't know what her plans are, but they involve explosives."

Wyatt's head tilted back, and his warm breath tickled her cheek. "Explosives?" His eyes dipped down in thought for a moment, then returned to Liz. "I have to stop her."

"Wyatt, no. She'll kill you. Plus, there are at least a half dozen men up top," she stated with concern as the shackles snapped under her strength.

Wyatt pulled his wrists in front of him and rubbed them. "How did you—"

"I found a key in the desk." She threw the mangled restraints into a dark corner. "Are you ok?"

"Yeah." Wyatt stood and extended his hand out. He pulled her up just inches away from his face. "I am now." His lips kissed her forehead and lingered for a moment. "Thank you for rescuing me, but I can't put you at risk anymore. Stay here. I'm going to stop Jessica."

Liz grabbed his arm, halting him. "You're already hurt. Our best bet is to escape."

Wyatt opened his mouth to argue when a muffled voice sounded outside. He motioned for her to be quiet and rushed out of the room.

"What the—" a male voice cried out but was cut off by a loud thud.

Wyatt came back in, placed his hands on her shoulders, and stared deeply into her eyes. "Please. This is all my fault, and she's going to hurt a lot of people if I don't stop her. I have to do this. I have to fix my mistake."

After a beat, Liz replied, "Ok. On one condition."

"Anything."

"We do it together."

His mouth thinned, and his eyes darted away for a moment in

thought before he nodded. "Together," he agreed, squeezing her hand.

With her breathing becoming more difficult, Liz followed Wyatt to the stairwell. Her hands gripped the railing as she tried to steady herself from the rocking boat. She fumbled over a step, and Wyatt caught her before she fell.

"Are you all right?"

"I'm fine. Keep going," she huffed, gripping the railing tightly. Not wanting to waste any more time, she bounded past him but not before he took her arm. Invisible threads of energy laced between them, radiating throughout their bodies.

"Liz, I, um . . ." he stumbled over his words as if he wanted to tell her something important.

"We have to go," she whispered urgently.

His hand slid into hers, and they continued their journey until they arrived in front of the door leading outside. Wyatt cracked the door open, and water from the deck washed across her shoes. The sea beckoned to her, and it took everything in her not to bolt out of the door and dive in. She kept reminding herself that soon enough she would feel the warm sea embracing her again, but right now, helping Wyatt was her priority.

With the heavy rainfall, it was difficult to make out how far the island was behind them. However, it wasn't hard to find one of the men at the back of the boat holding onto the railing. The sound of thunder rumbled in the distance.

Liz, Wyatt's call punctured her roaming thoughts.

She turned her attention to him and gave a slight smile. She didn't know how this was happening, but hearing his voice in her mind felt comforting.

You ready? he asked.

Yeah.

Stay behind me, he instructed.

Liz placed her hand on his shoulder, stopping him. *Wait. We can't go in guns blazing. What's the plan?*

I don't really have one, he confessed.

Liz thought for a moment. *Ok. We just need to stop her from using the explosives, right? We have to find where they are and dump them into the gulf. If possible, disable the boat's steering so she can't go anywhere. Leave that part to me. I'll go first, just follow my lead.*

I'll follow you anywhere, his voice whispered.

She wasn't sure if he intentionally meant for her to hear that, but it made her breath catch. Opening the door farther, Liz crept out into the downpour with Wyatt one step behind her. Making their way out of the cabin area, they moved with stealth toward the ship's starboard side.

"Where do you think you two are going?" a voice growled from behind them before they rounded the corner.

"Find the explosives. I'll distract the big guy," Wyatt instructed.

"I'm not going to leave you," she replied, taking his hand.

"I'll be ok. I promise." His eyes darkened, and he pulled away from her. "Go!"

She nodded and turned, but not without stopping to peer over her shoulder. *Wyatt?* There were so many answers she needed, yet the only thing she could bring herself to say was, *Be careful.*

You, too, he replied before rushing full speed at the guard.

A loud crack sounded as Wyatt thrust his shoulder into the guard's jaw and sent the man falling to the ground. The sudden commotion attracted the attention of two more guards.

Liz knew what she had to do. Disappearing around the corner, she sprinted down the right-hand side of the boat. Stopping midway, she peered up at a long metal arm. It extended out over the churning waters, and the crates labeled 'Explosives' swayed back and forth. Now she needed to find a way to release the cargo in the net.

She spun around by the ladder of the wheelhouse and smacked into the broad chest of a man twice the size of the one Wyatt had knocked down.

"Guess I'm taking care of the big guy," Liz muttered.

A sudden, terrifying scream drew the attention of both Liz and the man. Liz took advantage of the distraction, kneeing the man squarely in his crotch. She turned back in the direction of the scream. A massive wave had hit the back of the boat and pulled a blonde-haired man overboard. She relaxed her shoulders a bit, relieved it wasn't Wyatt.

"What the hell is going on down there?" Jessica yelled from above through the cracked window of the wheelhouse.

Liz's fists clenched. The explosives were no longer on the top of her list to stop. Gripping the sides of the ladder, she hastily climbed it. She was nearing the top when a strong, thick hand wrapped around her ankle and yanked her to the deck floor.

Her assailant threw back his soaked jet-black hair and sneered. "Nothing we can't handle, miss." He narrowed his eyes on Liz and flashed a smile of crooked, yellow teeth. A shudder trailed down her spine.

Liz jumped to her feet. Pulling her arm back, she readied a punch but not before her legs faltered beneath her. She fell to the ground with a grimace. The pain radiated through her feet like fire. Her toes were spreading outward, pushing against the insides of her shoes.

Before she could discern what was happening, a strong arm snaked around her waist and pulled her to the railing. The thug leaned her body over the water that was luring her in. *Not yet*, she told herself.

She gripped the handrail, trying to resist. As the boat hit a swell, a wave crashed over them, sparking something inside of her. Adrenaline overwhelmed her, and the steel of the railing crushed under her hands. She threw her right elbow back into the man's temple, staggering him. She focused on the sea below and drew it toward her. A tendril of water rose beside her, like a kraken from the deep. The man's eyes went wide with terror. Liz thrust her arms out and launched the water into him. The man was thrown back against the bulkhead with such force it knocked him unconscious.

Liz? Wyatt's voice called to her. *Are you ok?*

Yeah, I'm still trying to find the controls, but I'm by the ladder to the steering, she replied, not about to admit that their enemy was at the top. Jessica was on her turf now. Liz could take her.

Go, then. Disable it and I'll meet up with you after I— There was a pause before Wyatt continued. *I'll be there soon.*

Her feet were in agony from her too-small shoes as she ascended the ladder. She was halfway up when something flew past her, causing a sudden, sharp pain in her upper arm. She glanced down, surprised to see blood oozing from a small cut. A flash of lightning streaked across the sky.

"I don't know how the hell you got here," Jessica snarled from below, holding a speargun, "but you're going to regret boarding my boat!" Her eyes filled with rage and vengeance as thunder cracked.

Liz was about to climb up the rest of the way when the boat lurched to the side, causing her foot to slip. Clutching the railings, she regained her footing and scrambled up the rest of the way. She peered down, but Jessica was nowhere to be seen.

She opened the heavy metal door and entered the wheelhouse. An elderly man stood stock still with his back to her. His long narrow fingers wrapped around the worn steering wheel.

"Did you take care of—" he began before turning to see Liz standing in the doorway.

"Turn the boat around," she demanded, stepping closer to the grizzled captain.

"Sorry, miss. I only take orders from her," he said, pointing his wrinkled finger past Liz's shoulder.

Liz spun on her heels to find the she-devil standing in the doorway.

"You can't stop me." Jessica leveled the gun at Liz with narrowed eyes.

Liz's heart pounded against her chest as she stared at the silver tip that was aimed at her heart.

What's going on? Wyatt's panicked voice asked in her mind.

Jessica. Her heart ticked up a beat as Wyatt's fear took hold.

Liz, you need to get out of there!

There wasn't any time. Liz had one chance to stop her. She slowly raised her hands in surrender, all the while controlling the rainwater to snake behind Jessica. The tendril slithered around her feet, slowly winding about her ankles. With a flick of the wrist, Liz manipulated the water to tighten its hold and pull Jessica's feet out from under her. Jessica went face-first to the floor, setting off the gun.

Liz rushed out of the wheelhouse, unfortunately without doing any damage to the steering. Instead, she slammed the door shut and broke the handle with her strength, trapping Jessica inside. A deep howl rang out.

Liz peered through the glass window to see a spear lodged into the old man's leg. A hand slammed against the glass, startling Liz. Jessica's face appeared with gritted teeth as she tried the door handle. Unable to open it, she pounded her fists in anger, screaming obscenities.

"Liz!" Wyatt huffed as he neared the top of the ladder. He frowned at the sight of blood trickling down her arm. "You're hurt."

"I'll be fine," she replied, checking for any more guards.

"Where's Jessica?" The banging on the glass caught his attention. "Never mind."

"I'm not sure how long that'll hold her." Liz glanced over her shoulder to find Jessica turning the wheel violently. "It may not have been my best idea."

The boat veered sharply. Wyatt and Liz lost their balance and fell to the deck below. Breaking Liz's fall, Wyatt groaned underneath her. Her head rested on his chest for a moment before she pushed herself up and helped him up. As he stood, the sound of shattered glass pierced the air.

"We don't have much time," she rasped. She wasn't just talking about Jessica. She looked away, grimacing in pain.

"Dammit." Wyatt looked over at the arm that extended above them. "We need to figure out how to release those crates."

Following the rope that held the explosives up, they arrived at a crank at the rear of the boat.

"There!" Liz pointed.

Running up to the device, Wyatt grabbed the lever and pulled it, releasing the net into the water.

A sinister laugh cut through the sound of waves crashing against the boat. Jessica stood above them and flung her wet auburn hair away from her face. She pulled out a small black toggle from her pocket.

"No!" Liz gasped. Wyatt turned to her in confusion. "Run! She's going to blow it right now!"

She took his hand and fled along the port side to the front of the boat. A low rumble vibrated beneath them, shaking the boat. Water erupted into the air, rocking the side of the vessel. Liz lurched forward onto the slick deck, and all the air seemed to escape her. It felt like someone had shoved a bunch of cotton balls down her throat. The slits on either side of her neck were now fluttering to breathe.

The clock was speeding up. It wouldn't be long now.

As she pushed herself up, everything seemed to happen in slow motion. Liz turned to find Jessica looming above on the side of the wheelhouse. The waves jostled the boat, pitching the bow upward. Jessica lifted the speargun, and as the vessel traversed the wave, she pulled the trigger.

Without any time to stop her, all Liz could do was close her eyes and accept her fate. Within seconds, a white-hot flash of pain forced her to her knees. She opened her eyes, expecting to see the spear protruding from her chest, but instead, nothing was there. There wasn't even a scratch, yet the pain was unbearable.

Wyatt was crumpled to the ground a few feet in front of her with the spear lodged in his shoulder.

"Nooo!" Liz scrambled to her feet and rushed to him. She placed her hands on his chest, feeling his shallow breath. Hot, thick blood seeped through his tattered shirt and onto her hands. "No, no, no! It should have been me!"

"I had to protect you. I'll always protect you." His voice was weak. Fumbling with his wrist, he took off the braided leather bracelet. "Take this." He slipped it around Liz's wrist as she shook her head several times. "And remember me."

Uncontrollable tears streamed down her face. "No, I can't lose you now! Stay with me, Wyatt!" she pleaded, touching her forehead to his.

Lifting his head slightly, he gently placed his hand along her cheek and tilted his head to kiss her. Before their lips could touch, he was jerked away from her by two men.

"You'll suffer the same fate as my father!" Jessica's voice roared as she sauntered along the main deck. "I *will* have my revenge! You think those were the only explosives on this ship? You can't stop me!" She signaled to the men and walked past Wyatt and Liz. "Dispose of him. Then kill her."

"No!" Liz howled, reaching out for him. Her fingers curled around his in a futile attempt to hold on as the men dragged him away.

I love you, Elizabeth Brander, Wyatt's voice echoed through her mind. *Forever.*

The men hefted him over the port side, letting his body drop to the depths below.

Liz's screams pierced the thick air around her. She stretched out her hand, trying to control the water to catch him, but nothing happened. She was too weak.

Holding herself on all fours, she struggled to breathe. If her time was truly up, then she had to finish what Wyatt had started. She wasn't going to run away this time. Anger overtook her whole body just like it had back at the warehouse.

"For Wyatt," she whispered to herself as she staggered to her feet.

An electrifying heat flowed down her arms, igniting her veins into a bright blue glow. Two men who were about to grab her jumped back at the bizarre sight. She stared daggers at Jessica, who was clutching her weapon with shaky hands.

"You're wrong. I will stop you!" Liz exclaimed.

Extending her arm, Liz aimed the electric current at the deceptive woman. With a scream, she channeled all of her anger and let it pour out of her. It hit Jessica with a blow to her chest, hurling her through the air before she could pull the trigger. Uncontrolled bolts of electricity flew from Liz's fingertips into everyone and everything around her. The nearby men were flung against the guardrails and sent overboard, and the errant blast sparked several small fires across the boat.

Liz collapsed to the floor, exhausted. The deafening screams of the remaining crew who struggled to find safety were muffled as she gasped for air. It wouldn't be long before the fire reached the remaining explosives. Her gaze dipped to see the bracelet adorning her wrist.

I love you, Elizabeth Brander. The memory of Wyatt's voice whispered in her mind and gave her the strength to move.

Choked by the dark smoke billowing from behind her, Liz slowly crawled toward the port side railing. The struggle to breathe was agonizing as she fought her way to safety. A small explosion went off and shook the rain-soaked deck beneath her.

Time's up.

CHAPTER 32

The Path Forward

The last thing Wyatt saw before he sank into the depths of the sea were the dark clouds above him.

The comforting warmth of the water surrounded him, yet he remained still, his body numb. He watched a trail of blood seep from his wound. This should have been the part where he transformed. It was the only way he would be able to survive, but instead, he just stared up at the blurry image of the dark vessel. Maybe this was how he was supposed to go. This was his purpose in life, to protect his family and his people.

He wondered if anyone would mourn him. How would his father take the news? He had already lost his wife and now his youngest son. All those times his father warned him, he had never listened. Yet if he had never come to the surface, he wouldn't have met Liz. He didn't belong in the sea or on land. He belonged with her. She was his home.

His heart ached at the thought of leaving her. It was his fault she had gotten mixed up in all of this. He just hoped she would find happiness again with someone else.

A burst of light flashed above as the remaining explosives ignited. Debris littered the water, plummeting around him. His vision began to veil as his oxygen ran out. This was it. He was ready to see his mother again. He could almost see her swimming toward him as the light faded. Her hair billowed around her and she wrapped her arms around his middle just as everything went black.

A beautiful bright white light blinded Wyatt as a voice urgently called out, "Fight."

I'm so tired, he thought as he tried to let go.

Ultimately, he had no choice. The feeling of water expelling from his lungs snapped him back to life. Coughing and sputtering the rest of the water up, he attempted to lift his head before the darkness took hold of him again.

A muffled voice cried out, causing Wyatt to stir. He heard it again, but this time clearer.

"There!" a man cried out. "I see him!"

The low hum of a motor rang through Wyatt's ears before he heard a loud splash, followed by the sound of arms slicing through the waves. He forced his tired eyes open. He was alive, barely. His gaze darted down to find that he was sprawled out on what looked to be a piece of wooden debris from the trawler.

"Oh my god!" Liam bobbed next to him. "HE'S ALIVE!" he shouted to the boat in the distance before frantically scanning the area. "Hold on. You're going to be ok," he assured, helping Wyatt onto a life preserver buoy. Wyatt held on as Liam pulled him to Denise's boat that was just beyond the wreckage.

Multiple hands pulled Wyatt on board and gently placed him on the soft leather cushions. His head was swimming, and a cluster of voices all spoke at once.

"Is he ok?"

"How hurt is he?"

"We need to get him to a hospital."

"We need to get out of here," Denise spoke up.

Wyatt's eyelids felt heavy, and he was about to let sleep consume him when Liam asked, "What about Liz?"

"Liz . . ." Wyatt muttered before a sudden burst of energy made him sit straight up. She was still on the trawler. "No . . ."

He gasped at the sight of fire engulfing half of the vessel as it slowly sank. The other half was scattered around the gulf. Wyatt gripped the railing and pulled himself to stand.

"Whoa, you need to sit down," a voice said from behind him.

"Liz!" Wyatt shouted hoarsely. His eyes darted around.

Liz! Liz, where are you? he cried out in his mind. When there was no response, he slammed his palm against the steel railing, bending it slightly.

He turned to see Denise and Sarah by the wheel. "We have to go back! We have to find her!"

"We've been searching, Wyatt," Sarah informed him softly. "We almost lost hope in finding you. Especially after that last explosion. It tore the boat in half."

"We have to get out of here before the Coast Guard comes," Denise insisted.

Liz, please! I know you escaped. Please tell me you escaped! he pleaded. Again, there was nothing but silence.

"No. No! She's out there! I know she's out there! I have to find her! LIZ!" he screamed at the top of his lungs. He hoisted his body up, ready to dive back into the water, but several hands wrapped around his biceps, holding him back.

Denise's soft hand touched his shoulder, but he shrugged her off. "Wyatt. You need to calm down. You're making your wound worse." She motioned for everyone to let go of him. "Liam, start the engine and take us back."

"You don't understand," Wyatt growled.

"I do, Wyatt. I, more than anyone on this boat, understand what it's like to lose someone you love and not be able to do a damn thing. I feel your pain." She leaned closer and whispered, "But I also know that Liz unknowingly risked her life to save your people. Jumping in the water right now and exposing who you are would undo everything she did."

Wyatt knew she was right, but he didn't want to believe it. He shook his head furiously with tears streaming down his cheeks. "I just found her. I-I can't lose her now. She can't be gone," he said, letting his body go limp into the bench.

"I know, honey. I know," she replied, rubbing his back.

Exhaustion suddenly took hold of him, and he lay across the bench with his back to everyone.

"Liam, we need to go before anyone sees us. We don't need anyone asking questions," Denise stated.

Wyatt felt nothing. He let the hum of the engine bring him the sleep he desperately needed.

Wyatt stirred, hoping he was waking up from a terrible nightmare. His eyelids fluttered open, and the fog began to lift. The pain radiating from his chest brought him crashing back to the reality of what had happened. His heart felt heavy. Too heavy. He wanted to scream, cry, punch something, but he felt completely numb. Perhaps he was still in shock.

Clutching the soft material under him, he realized he was back on land in an unfamiliar bed. The blinds did their best to limit the sunlight trying to stream into the dark room. There was a small dimly lit lamp on the dresser.

He carefully sat up and draped his legs over the edge of the bed with a groan. Staring at his reflection in the dresser mirror, he examined his body to find soaked pieces of cloth clinging to his bare chest. He peeled them away to reveal the nearly healed cuts and bruises that he had suffered at the hands of Jessica and her men.

He pushed himself up on wobbly legs and stepped a few feet to the dresser. Rubbing his hand along the scruff of his face, he wondered how long he had slept. A large piece of gauze was wrapped around his shoulder. He unraveled it and grimaced at the packed hole where the spear had been lodged. Gripping the wooden dresser, he squeezed his eyes shut, thinking back to the moment he dove in front of Liz. He hadn't cared what happened to him, as long as she was safe.

The edge of the furniture cracked under his strength just before muffled voices came from outside the door.

"Is he going to be ok?" Denise asked.

"Yes, just give him some time," a male voice replied. "The wound is deep. It will take some time to heal. He's fortunate to be alive."

The voices grew faint for a moment before the floor creaked. Hearing the doorknob turn, his focus shifted to see Denise standing in the doorway with a small box under her left arm and a bowl of water in her right hand.

"Wyatt," she greeted with a soft smile before she noticed his hands tightly gripping her furniture. "That dresser is older than me. So I'd appreciate it if you loosened your grip a bit," she said.

Wyatt released his hold and slumped back onto the bed. He hung his head, studying the grains of the floorboards. Denise shut the door slightly and placed the items next to him.

"Do you remember what happened?" she asked, bringing a trash can over. She gathered all the cloth he had left on the dresser and threw them away.

"I—" his voice rasped. It felt like he had swallowed a handful of sand, finding it difficult to speak.

"Here." She handed him a glass of water from the nightstand and watched him drain it in a matter of seconds. "Better?"

He cleared his throat a few times. "Yes, thank you." He handed the empty glass back, and she returned it to the nightstand. "It's starting to come back to me. It feels like a nightmare." He took her hand as she was about to undress his bandages. "Denise, please tell me it was a nightmare."

Her eyes softened and she frowned, giving him a sorrowful expression that told him everything he needed to know. "I wish I could, dear."

She carefully pulled at the long piece of gauze that was packed inside his wound. It seemed to go on forever. Wyatt tried not to watch as he hissed in pain.

"How did this happen?" she asked, motioning to his injury.

He looked at her in confusion. "A spear. It was Jessica."

Denise paused in the middle of pulling out the packing. "She tried to kill you?"

"She aimed it at Liz." He swallowed hard. "I jumped in front of her. Then Jessica's men threw me overboard." His jaw clenched when Denise pulled the end of the bloody gauze out and tossed it in the trash.

"You're lucky to be alive. A few more inches to the left and you wouldn't be here," she said. "Not to mention if you hadn't removed the spear, you wouldn't have started to heal while in the water."

"You didn't take it out?" he asked.

Denise shook her head. She placed a towel in the bowl of salt water and wrung it out. "You were like this when we found you."

"I don't under—" Wyatt started before the door swung open.

"You're awake!" Sarah exclaimed, rushing into the room. She ran to the other side of Denise and wrapped her arms around him. Wyatt groaned. "Sorry," she apologized, pulling back. "We've all been worried sick, especially Liam."

His shoulders slouched. "How is he?" he asked Denise.

"Why don't you ask your sister?" Denise replied with a grin.

His eyes darted to Sarah, whose cheeks were flushed.

"She's been tending to him," Denise said as she cleaned his wound.

"It's nothing," Sarah interjected with a shrug. "The hospital wanted to keep him for a few days, and he doesn't have any family close by. So, I figured I'd stay with him and keep him from doing something stupid again."

"He's doing as good as expected, though," Denise explained, placing the wet, bloodied rag down. "A cracked rib and some mild burns. He said one of Jessica's men used a cattle prod?"

Wyatt nodded as he rubbed his side. He shuddered at the memory of the electricity jolting through his body, as well as Liz's.

"She could have killed you, Wyatt," Sarah said.

He frowned. "She almost did."

I wish she had.

"What do you mean?" his sister asked as Denise began packing the wound in Wyatt's upper shoulder.

Denise spared Wyatt from repeating the details and reiterated it back to Sarah.

"It's still a bit fuzzy, though," Wyatt added.

Sarah's hands clutched over her chest. "You risked your life for Liz?"

"I know what you're going to say, but—"

"No, you don't," she stopped him. "Yes, it was idiotic, but that was the most selfless thing you've ever done. Then for her to . . ." She paused and turned away for a moment, trying to compose herself. "I'm sorry, Wyatt. I know you cared for her."

"Thanks." He looked down at his bare wrist.

Liz, he softly called out in his mind. His heart grew heavy at the deafening silence.

"I'm just relieved you're alive," Sarah stated.

"We all are," a deep voice spoke up from beyond the doorway.

A man entered the room. His long brown hair was tied back, with a few loose wisps dangling by his beard. He wore brown cargo shorts and a lime-green T-shirt from The Cove. There were a few faint bruises scattered around his body, as well as a gash on his left forearm that was nearly healed.

Wyatt's eyes widened. "Varian? You're here." He slowly stood and approached his big brother.

"I am," Varian replied with a weary smile and brought his arms around Wyatt for an unexpected hug. He pulled away, frowning at his brother's nasty injury.

"He was in the warehouse with you. Liam saved him," Sarah explained.

"Wait. What?" Wyatt asked in disbelief. The pieces began to

fall in place. The other person Jessica's men beat unconscious had been his brother that whole time.

"I had a feeling Sarah knew where you were hiding," Varian explained. "I followed her until she arrived at the shore of an island. Imagine my surprise when she transformed and walked right out of the water. After I found out she had one of mom's necklaces, I felt a little foolish wading in the shallows, trying to will my tail into legs for hours on end."

A smile tried to form on Wyatt's lips at the image. It was amusing to say the least.

"I finally gave up and resorted to the old method," Varian continued. "I never felt so much pain in my life. After I transformed, I found some clothes drying outside a nearby house and took them. I don't know if I was at the wrong spot at the wrong time, but a bunch of men grabbed me before I even had time to fight back. Being a soldier, I should have known better," he scolded himself. "I'm used to threats underwater, not on land in the black of night."

Varian rubbed the scruff of his beard and sighed. "The next thing I knew, I was being chained in an empty building and that eel of a woman demanded to know where our kingdom was." He massaged the remnants of his left forearm injury. "When I didn't cooperate, she had her men torture me. She underestimated my resolve to protect our people."

"Varian, I'm sorry." Wyatt frowned. "This is all my fault."

Varian guided him back to the bed. "It wasn't your fault, Wyatt."

"Liam told me everything," Sarah said. "We understand."

"Father won't see it that way," Wyatt muttered.

"Screw what he thinks," Varian said, catching everyone off-guard. He looked around. "Did I not speak it correctly?"

A slight chuckle escaped Wyatt. "No, you did."

Denise continued to wrap a wide piece of gauze over Wyatt's wound and around his body, tying the end snuggly in place.

"If it wasn't for you," Varian continued, "we would've never known about this threat. The anger she held for us"—he folded his arms across his broad chest—"she was . . . determined. She would have found Aquana one way or another."

"I suppose you're right," Wyatt said.

"At least she's gone," Sarah said, trying to be optimistic.

"No one has confirmed it yet," Denise pointed out. "There's still a lot of wreckage they're going through."

Wyatt was afraid to ask, but he needed to know. "What about . . . ?"

Denise shook her head in dismay. "I'm sorry. Every confirmed victim has been male. It's going to take a while to identify all the remains that were found."

Wyatt squeezed his eyes tight. *Liz, please answer me*, he continued to call, only to be met with a heavy sadness.

"Dammit," Wyatt muttered. He let out a deep sigh.

"You've been through a lot," Denise said. "You should get some sleep."

"Thanks, but I feel pretty rested. How long was I out?"

"We brought you back two days ago," Sarah explained.

Wyatt's stomach rumbled loudly.

"You must be starving," Denise said. "What would you like?"

"I could go for some shrimp."

Denise gave a nod and gathered her things.

"Oh, and um . . . maybe some dessert?" Wyatt asked with a somber smile.

"You don't even have to ask. I already have some ready to go," Denise replied, then turned toward Varian with an accusing expression. "Although, I hope *someone* didn't eat them all."

A guilty Varian licked a spot of glaze on his thumb as she walked out of the room.

Silence hung in the air as Sarah looked between her two brothers. "I'm, um, sure Denise could use some help. I'll let you two talk." She gave Wyatt one last hug before leaving them alone.

Varian pulled the vanity stool over and sat across from Wyatt.

He nervously fumbled with the familiar ring pendant necklace their mother had saved for them.

"Legs look good on you," Wyatt started, breaking the awkward silence.

"Yeah, I guess they're not half bad." Varian wiggled his toes. "And the food here . . ." His eyes lit with excitement.

"I know, right?" Wyatt exclaimed. "You've already had Denise's cinnamon rolls?" He smirked.

"One of the first things she made me eat." He chuckled. "I have to admit, I was apprehensive about talking to a land-dweller at first. But she's pretty cool."

"Cool?" Wyatt couldn't help but grin. "You've been hanging out with Liam, haven't you?"

"I visited him yesterday with Sarah," Varian replied. "I introduced myself and thanked him for helping me. I wanted to hear everything from his point of view as well." He shuffled his feet around as if his next words were hard to swallow. "He's pretty *cool*, too. I guess some land-dwellers aren't all that bad."

"Humans," Wyatt corrected. "And it makes me happy to hear those words coming out of your mouth."

Varian crossed his arms over his broad chest. "I'm surprised he doesn't know about you, though. The way he was so concerned was almost brotherly. You two are pretty close, huh?"

"He's pretty much been there for me from the start," Wyatt replied with a smile, remembering their first encounter. "I'm pretty good at keeping it a secret. He doesn't know anything."

Varian pursed his lips in thought before relaxing his body. "Sarah and Denise told me how happy you are here. But it doesn't take a manta to see that." When Wyatt laughed, Varian gave him a puzzled look. "Did I not refer to the proper fish?"

He shook his head. "No, you did. Mantas are smart. It's just . . ." His spirits lifted a bit at the memory of him and Liz walking along Bridge Street. Her infectious laughter made him feel whole. The corners of his mouth ticked up. "I would constantly make fish references around Liz, and she would laugh. Now I know why. It sounds a bit ridiculous."

Varian chuckled. "Poseidon, you've been dragged through the trenches, yet you still manage to smile."

He shrugged. "I smiled in Aquana."

"Not like this." Varian shifted in his seat. "Father was wrong. No," he corrected, "*we* were wrong to keep you in the kingdom. You deserve to be happy, and if staying here makes you happy, then I support you."

"Thank you, Varian, that means a lot. And I was happy. I mean, I am happy but . . ." He hung his head.

"I know," Varian solemnly replied. He leaned forward and placed his hand on Wyatt's shoulder. "I'm truly sorry, Wyatt. If anything ever happened to Lyra, I . . . I don't know what I'd do." After a beat, he pulled back and straightened in the chair. Clearing his throat, his voice turned more serious. "I know this isn't what you want to hear right now, but I need you to come back to Aquana."

Wyatt's head shot back up. "What the hell? You can't be serious. You just said I deserve to stay here!"

"And I still firmly believe that, but I need support."

"Support? For what?"

"I need to explain to Father what happened and how close our people were to being attacked," Varian replied. "What if there's more humans like Jessica? Our kingdom needs to bring mers to the surface to monitor for threats."

Wyatt scoffed. "He'll never go for that."

"I've heard talk of other kingdoms sending out sentries to live along the shores and report any suspicious activity. We can't shelter ourselves in our protective bubble forever." Varian gave a deep sigh. "Aquana deserves better."

Wyatt looked at him, surprised. He hadn't expected his brother to say that.

"As hard as it is to say, this experience has been eye-opening. I'm not saying I want to stay on land by any means, but we can't risk something like this happening again. Times are changing, and we've been stuck in the past for far too long."

"Wow," Wyatt said as he stood and walked over to the window, opening the blinds. Sunlight cascaded in, brightening the room.

"What?" Varian shifted in his seat.

Wyatt turned back with a smirk. "You already sound like a king."

"I don't want to be like Father. I want to be a different king, one who understands that, despite our differences, we are far more similar to humans than we care to admit. They share many of the same great qualities that mers possess."

Wyatt gazed back out at the shimmering blue waters before turning around and leaning against the windowsill. "You don't know how happy it makes me to hear you say that." He paused, and his lips thinned. "And I appreciate that you want things to change, I really do. Showing mers that humans aren't as dangerous as we thought is a step in the right direction, but, Varian . . . I can't go. I can only imagine the repercussions when Father finds out I've been living on land."

"Please, Wyatt," Varian pleaded. His eyes darted to the ground as if he were ashamed of his own words. "I'm tired of being kept in the confines of the kingdom as well. I always have, but being the next-in-line, I accepted my duty and what Father expected of me. I . . ." He stopped short, then stood.

So many times Wyatt had wished to hear those words from his brother or sister. All this time he had felt he was the only one who felt trapped, but hearing his brother's admission provided a sense of relief. "Why are you telling me this now?"

He took a step closer to Wyatt. "I'm planning on proposing to Lyra, and I certainly don't want our honeymoon to be at the palace. I want to have the chance to travel the ocean and take her somewhere special."

Wyatt broke into a huge smile, pushing away from the sill. "Varian, that's wonderful news! She's very lucky to have you!"

"I'm the lucky one, and I have you to thank," he confessed. "I'm afraid Father's expectations have blinded me from seeing what's truly important to being a good king. I'm truly fortunate she's been so patient with me. You helped me see there's more in life than obligations. Thank you." He wrapped his arms around Wyatt.

"Wow, two hugs!" Wyatt said in surprise when they separated.

Varian pointed his finger at his brother's chest. "Don't tell Father I've gone soft on you." He smiled before getting back on topic. "So, will you come back with me? I promise it won't be for long."

Wyatt crossed his arms with a wince and thought for a few long moments. "You're not trying to trick me into coming back?" he asked with narrowed eyes.

"No trick. I just need support. I never had your back, and for that, I'm sorry."

"You have to give me your word that I'll return within a week's time," Wyatt stated.

"I promise, I'll bring you back home."

Wyatt furrowed his brows.

"Your home, here on land," Varian reiterated. "Even if Father locks you up and I have to commit treason to help you escape, I will do so." He placed his fist to his chest and bowed his head.

"Poseidon, help me," Wyatt muttered. "Ok, I'll go."

There was a quiet knock at the door, and a second later it opened. Sarah's head peered in.

Varian smiled proudly. "Wyatt agreed to talk with Father."

"Oh, good!" Sarah said happily.

"Oh no, *you're* talking to Father," Wyatt said to Varian. "I'm just coming for moral support. Maybe with all three of us there—"

"Well," Sarah interjected, "I won't be joining you."

"What?" Varian and Wyatt asked in unison.

"I need to stay here for a bit. Liam is coming home soon, and he's still distraught about everything," Sarah explained. "He's been through a lot, and I just want to be there for him."

"I knew you liked him," Wyatt teased.

Sarah blushed but didn't deny it. "So, when are you leaving?"

"As soon as possible," Varian replied, then turned to Wyatt. "Being in the water will help us heal as well."

"Then we should go tonight before I change my mind," Wyatt said. "I should visit Liam and tell him I'm leaving, though."

"Leave that to me," Sarah suggested. She looked him up and down. "You healed way too quick, and he might become suspicious. I'll tell him you're staying with Varian."

"And I'll cover your shift until you come back," Denise added as she entered the room.

"All right." Wyatt sighed. "I guess I'm going back to Aquana."

Wyatt walked down the beach, admiring the pink, deep red, purple, and orange colors painted across the sky by the setting sun. He stood at the shore's edge and let the waves wash over his feet, causing them to sink into the soft sand. With his eyes closed, he breathed in the salty air, feeling the warm water swirl around his ankles. He pictured Liz's smiling face in front of him.

I miss you, he pushed his thoughts out, even though she would never hear him again. His heart ached.

A splash startled him, and he opened his eyes to catch a glimpse of a tail diving back underwater. A fluke? It wasn't Sarah since she was with Liam, and Varian had assured him that no guards swam this far out or that close to land.

He shook his head. *My mind must be playing tricks on me. It was probably just a dolphin.* Perhaps leaving the island for a few days would do him good.

Something in the water brushed up against his leg, and he peered down to see a small ringed object in the water. He grabbed it before the sea could pull it away from him.

"Liz," he whispered, staring at the braided leather bracelet he had taken off and given to her before being tossed overboard. A sharp laugh bubbled from his chest.

"What's so funny?" Varian's deep voice asked from behind Wyatt.

Wyatt turned around, holding up the band.

Varian stared at it curiously. "What's that?"

"A cruel joke from Poseidon," Wyatt stated.

Varian's forehead creased in confusion as he approached his brother.

"Liz gave this to me at the end of our date," Wyatt explained, running his fingers along the braid. Memories flashed in his mind from their date. "She bought it for me when I wasn't looking. Did you know it's the first genuine gift I've ever received? No other female has ever cared enough. They only cared about me being a prince."

Wyatt glanced up at his brother, who was listening intently. "I was going to tell her everything, Varian," he admitted before returning his gaze to the band. "I know what you're thinking, but I knew I could trust her. There was something . . . different about her." He paused for a beat and scowled. "Then Jessica showed up and everything went to the trenches. After I jumped in front of Liz to save her, I gave her this." He held out the bracelet nestled in his palm. "I told her to remember me." His fingers curled around it tightly. "Now in a cruel twist of fate, it washes ashore as a reminder that she's gone."

He turned, cocking his left arm back to throw it back into the gulf.

"Don't," Varian protested, grabbing his brother's wrist.

Wyatt searched his brother's eyes.

"Don't," Varian calmly repeated.

Wyatt dropped to his knees and fell forward with his head resting along his forearms. He shook as he silently sobbed, letting the tears fall. "It was supposed to be me. It . . . it was supposed to be me, n-not her."

Varian crouched next to Wyatt and wrapped his arm around

him. "I'm so sorry." After a few moments, he pulled Wyatt's clenched hand open and took the bracelet, fastening it around Wyatt's left wrist. "Perhaps there was a reason Poseidon returned it to you."

"What's that?" Wyatt sniffled, sitting back up.

"As a reminder."

"For what? That I couldn't save her?"

Varian shook his head and placed his hand on Wyatt's shoulder. "As a reminder of who you really are. And to always remember Liz. Even though she wasn't a mer"—he looked out into the gulf with a half-smile—"I believe she's a part of the ocean now. Maybe this was her way of telling you to continue living and be happy."

Composing himself, Wyatt wiped the tears with the back of his hand, cleared his throat, and stood up. The heaviness in his heart slowly lifted. He stared out at the colorful hues of the setting sun reflecting off the glistening waters. Taking a deep breath, he ran his fingers across the leather braid.

He turned his head to Varian. "Thank you."

Varian tipped his head in response and looked out at the picturesque scene in front of them. "I never imagined the surface world could be so beautiful."

"I don't think I'll ever get tired of this."

"Are you ready?" Varian turned around and picked up Wyatt's waterproof sling bag that carried extra clothes and a few other necessities. He slung it over his shoulder and across his chest.

"Not really," Wyatt confessed. "But I know this is what I have to do. I'm glad you'll be by my side."

Epilogue

Sparks of light. That was all she saw as her body flew through the air.

It seemed like everything passed by in slow motion, as if the impending death wouldn't come fast enough. When she finally landed, all that could be heard was the sound of a sickening crack before the veil of darkness fell.

Was this it? Was she dead? It was impossible to tell if a moment had gone by or an eternity when muffled screams resonated through her ears. She groaned as she struggled to open her eyes to the all-encompassing chaos.

"Abandon ship!" a man shouted over a distinct crackling sound.

Her eyes shot open. Abandon ship? What was he talking about?

She forced herself up and pushed back the wet tendrils of hair from her face. The rain was still constant but not as heavy. She scanned the area. Crates, netting, and ropes surrounded her on the deck of the boat. A gray haze billowed around her, and a fiery inferno blazed twenty feet away.

Her gaze darted back to the larger crates farther away. The explosives! One had already gone off. Or was it two? Were there any below? She couldn't be sure. Either way, she realized what would happen without an escape from the tinderbox of a boat.

She attempted to scramble to her feet to run to the railing and hoist herself overboard. However, her legs remained a heavy mound of flesh, holding her back from escaping what could soon be imminent death.

Shifting slightly, she examined her nonresponsive legs and tried moving them again, but still, they didn't budge. Her eyes darted back to the fire to see that it had jumped closer to a nearby wooden crate.

"Come on. Come on!" she cried out. "Move, dammit!"

She grabbed anything that could help her to her feet. With all the strength she could muster, she pulled herself up, only to crumple when her hand slipped. The now-raging fire was bearing down on her.

A loud explosion shook the boat, and a wooden crate shot into the air like a mortar. She ducked and covered her head. Splinters of hot charred wood rained down on her back and arms. Tiny cuts on her forearms and legs bled

An eerie silence filled the air except for a high-pitched tone and the pounding of her heart. Thick gray smoke engulfed her, but muffled cries penetrated the acrid haze. What few men survived were fleeing for their lives.

The fire was drawing closer, and she was running out of time.

A faint voice echoed through her ears. A man's face appeared through the smog as if he were a ghost. He was unrecognizable with the deep gash from his left temple to his right cheek, but she could tell he was trying to tell her something through the ringing in her ears.

"... going to blow! We have to jump! Give me your hand!" he ordered, extending his arm out.

Not wasting any time, she placed her hand in his. He began to pull her up, but her legs refused to cooperate.

"Get up!" His gruff voice became louder as the ringing in her ears halted.

"My legs. They won't work," she explained.

With this revelation, he threw her to the ground. "You're dead weight to me."

"No! Please!" she pleaded, grasping the bottom of his pant leg. He shoved his boot into her sternum and ran off. "No!" A lump in her throat formed. She quickly pushed it down and shook her head. She refused to die this way. *Get up!* she coaxed herself. *You can't let them win! You have to fight.*

Determined to keep living, she crawled toward the edge of the vessel. The railing was nearly within arm's reach. Sweat dripped from her brow. When she made it to the edge of the boat, she fell flat for a moment to catch her breath.

Pulling with all her might, she lifted herself with a scream that pierced the air. After what seemed like an eternity, she managed to lift her body and lean over the railing. Panting, she peered down at the dark waters crashing against the burning boat, then looked down at her useless legs. How would she survive once she was in the water? Her eyes darted to the fire that was licking at her feet. She couldn't afford to argue with herself.

As she swallowed her fear and hoisted herself over, an explosion from below blasted the vessel, sending her flying overboard. A feeling of a thousand needles pierced her upper body as she smacked the surface of the water. She fell under for a few moments until she came to her senses. She flailed her arms wildly and pulled her head above water with a loud gasp.

She scanned the area to find not only debris all around her but also death. A contorted, disfigured body floated a few feet in front of her. It was the same man who had left her to die. Three more men floated face-down before the waves ravaged their bodies. Her eyes darted up and widened at the massive fire sending black smoke into the heavens.

A large wave crashed from behind her, forcing her under. She pushed back up and coughed up seawater. Never in her life had she been this fearful, but there wasn't any time to dwell on her emotions.

Forcing herself to continue, she swam away from the boat, jutting her arms out as far as they could go. Every time she swam one stroke forward, the waves seemed to send her two strokes back as if Poseidon was sealing her demise. She didn't dare stop.

"Keep going," she asserted before another wave washed over her, trying to pull her back into the inky abyss.

A dark figure floated past her. She prayed it was a piece of debris and not a shark. Gasping for breath, she pushed her wet hair from her vision and looked toward the small island that seemed miles away.

I need to get to land, she thought. Her heart pounded against her chest. Drowning from exhaustion might have been the least of her worries with whatever was swimming below her.

Suddenly, a faint voice yelled in the distance from the other side of the boat.

Without hesitation, she cried out, "Help!" She waited for a response, but none came. "HELP!" she screamed as loudly as she could but her voice was lost in the crackling of the burning boat between them. A sob escaped her along with a solemn tear.

The once serene waters of the gulf now seemed like a nightmare. A dark tail fin appeared out of the water and began to circle her. Grabbing a piece of debris next to her, she threw it toward the black demon, hoping to scare it off.

Before she could call out for help once more, a large swell came out of nowhere and sent her tumbling underwater. Her arms burned as she tried to swim back to the surface. She managed to surface for one quick breath before another wave crashed over her. It felt as if the sea was swallowing her whole, spiraling her down.

Disoriented, she thrashed about, trying to get her bearings. However, no matter how hard she tried to swim, she couldn't find the strength to go on. She let her fatigued arms relax and watched the fiery glow from the boat grow fainter. It was only a matter of time until she would need oxygen. She pondered on letting the water pour into her mouth and ending it right then.

This is my fault. I did this. I deserve to die, she declared to herself.

She peered into the darkness. It was eerie, yet peaceful. Seagrass swayed, tickling her sides as her body softly hit the sandy bottom.

The pressure was nearly unbearable, and without any sunlight from above, it was hard to tell what surrounded her. However, she could feel something, a presence looming over her.

Just open your mouth and end it! You don't want to be eaten by a shark, she thought, angry at her hesitation. Yet intrigue got the better of her from a faint light gleaming in the distance. As soon as she blinked, it disappeared.

What the hell?

She lifted herself and looked around, waiting for whatever it was to come. Ruby eyes glowed faintly through the darkness, startling her. The silhouette of a tail kicked from the ground, floating closer. Her heart pounded out of her chest. Either she was going to be mauled to death or drowned. Panicking, she pushed away until her back hit solid stone.

Just open your mouth and die already before you get eaten!

Fear like nothing she had ever felt washed over her. She knew she deserved to die, but there was so much she wanted to do in life. Now she was going to perish in the depths of the sea with whatever the hell this thing was in front of her. If only she could get a good look at what was about to devour her.

When it drew closer, the sea suddenly lit up from what looked like tiny bioluminescent plankton. She jumped, and when she saw that the owners of the glowing ruby eyes weren't a shark but in fact a mermaid, she pushed farther into the wall. The mermaid stared into her soul.

Marveling at what she saw, she felt relief that at least she wouldn't be pulled apart and eaten after her untimely death. At least, she didn't think the mermaid would eat her. Still, this was far from how she thought she would go.

Her lungs screamed for air. Her time was up.

Not wasting another second, she closed her eyes and unclenched her jaw. Her eyes shot wide open as she gasped and her body lurched, begging to be saved. This was it. She was going to die. She accepted her fate. If only she didn't have an audience.

The mermaid watched her suffocate, emotionless about what was happening. In a blink of an eye, the creature thrust her face into the ground and held her there.

She's going to kill me! she cried in her mind as her throat constricted, fighting the water that tried to fill her.

Something hard punched her back, and it wasn't until reality set in that a burning sensation took over. If she wasn't drowning, she would have thrown up for sure. The cold steel of the blade was pulled out and tossed to the side. Her body continued to flail under the mermaid's hold. She turned her head to see the mermaid's glowing eyes narrow in satisfaction.

Is she enjoying my suffering? she wondered, wishing death would come quickly.

She forced herself to breathe in the water to speed up the process. Soon, she stopped convulsing, and her vision began to fade. It would be over soon.

As she felt her life slip away, the mermaid leaned in close. "You're safe now, Jessica," she whispered.

~

Our story will continue in book 2 of Intertwined Souls . . .

Acknowledgments

Never in a million years would I have ever thought I would be writing acknowledgements for a book I wrote and published. Saying that I have been writing since a child would be a lie. In fact, I didn't start writing until a few years ago. However, the story of Lost has been evolving in my mind since I was a teenager.

I have many people to thank, but this book wouldn't be possible without the encouragement of my supportive husband. I cannot express my gratitude enough. If it wasn't for you this little story would still be on my computer. You spent nearly every evening for months helping me edit my rough draft into something that wasn't a complete hot mess. (To be fair, you were also trapped with me during the pandemic, so you might not have had much of a choice haha!) You were a shoulder for me to cry on when I didn't believe in myself, but you kept pushing me and helping me brainstorm ideas to get it done. You are and will always be my *soul mate*.

To my son, who's given me input and even ideas. You are an inspiration, and I hope your imagination leads you to do great things!

To my family, thank you for believing in me during this crazy journey. Especially my grandma, who was my first reader. You said it was a great story even though it was a very (and I mean VERY) rough draft. I wish Grandpa was here to read it too, but I know he was with me in spirit.

To my girl, Marci, for telling me 'You got this' many times in texts, memes, and our video chats. You kept me grounded.

Amanda M., you went above and beyond being a beta reader, and I appreciate every note and word change you gave me! You're a great friend, and I apologize for constantly venting about my writing haha! I can't wait to give you my draft of book two once I'm finished. I hope my writing has greatly improved by then.

Nicole, you are an amazing friend and "sister." I love you! I'm so glad you were my beta reader and gave me your honest opinions. I look forward to our next breakfast date!

Aimee, thank you for giving me your own author advice to this newbie and being my beta reader! I can't wait to read your next book.

To my friends that have supported and cheered me on in-person and on social media—you don't know how much I needed to hear your kind words.

To my editor, Sara from Telltail Editing, who encouraged me, helped me figure out how to develop a story, and also schooled me on how to properly use commas. You have helped me become a better writer, and I appreciate all of your advice! (Did I use the comma in the right place? Haha!)

My absolutely amazing cover designer, Rena from Covers by Violet—you took something I created on a scrap piece of paper and turned it into something from my dreams. It is absolutely gorgeous, and I cannot wait to see what you do with the rest of the books!

To anyone that reads this book, you make it all worth it. I hope you join me through my writing journey!

And last but certainly not least, thank you to the *mermazing* Mer community! When I began to dive into my story, you gave me so much inspiration from your social media pages. I had no clue there were so many of you and how truly wonderful you all are!

About the Author

M.E. Greenfield is a stay-at-home mom who lives in Ohio with her wonderful husband, imaginative son, and two rescue rabbits. When she's not fantasizing about relaxing on a hammock on the beaches of Anna Maria Island, Florida, she's either writing her next book, reading, or binge watching television while crafting.

You can find her on social media or her website:
https://www.authormegreenfield.com/

facebook.com/AuthorMEGreenfield
instagram.com/megreenfield_author